ONLY ANARCHISTS ARE PRETTY

A NOVEL

by

Mick O'Shea

First edition published in 2004 by Helter Skelter Publishing
South Bank House, Black Prince Road, London SE1 7SJ
Copyright © 2004 Mick O'Shea

Cover design by Dan Angel
Typesetting by Caroline Walker
Printed in Great Britain by The Bath Press, Trowbridge

A CIP record for this book is available from the British Library

ISBN 1-900924-93-5

ONLY ANARCHISTS ARE PRETTY

A NOVEL

by

Mick O'Shea

Helter Skelter Publishing

In Remembrance

Sid Vicious (b John Simon Ritchie, 1957 - 1979)

Joe Strummer (b John Graham Mellor, 1952 -2002)

Joey Ramone (b Jeffrey Hyman, 1951 - 2001)

Dee Dee Ramone (b Douglas Colvin, 1952 - 2002)

Nils Stevenson (1953 - 2002)

Johnny Thunders (b John Anthony Genzale Jr., 1952 - 1991)

Sadly gone, but not forgotten..."hey-ho, let's go..."

Introduction

I guess in a lot of ways this book begins with another Sex Pistols publication, because you could argue that without *Satellite* Mick O'Shea and I might never have spoken about this or any other book. On the other hand you could put the blame squarely onto the doorstep of *The Filth And The Fury* (both fanzine and movie) because they both started up many a conversation between the pair of us, that usually ended in a curry, somewhere cold, very late at night, and we are both responsible for each other taking the next day off work at least once in our lives...

The book you're now reading could also have been linked without question to the reunion of a punk band, who don't even get a mention in the text, yet without knowing it (or each other for that matter!) both myself and Mick spent time during the punk years hanging out with The Stiffs. But that's another story, for another place, and knowing Mick he's probably already written the first six chapters of it. No doubt all will be revealed over another curry one night. The first mention of "Only Anarchists Are Pretty" took place in a pub in Blackburn town centre, although to be fair it didn't have a title at that point but was already a good idea looking for somewhere to happen. Mick asked me, in my position of published writer, what I thought of his idea regarding a written history of the Sex Pistols with a new twist. I'm not sure how much encouragement he was looking for, but I'm sure I said something like; "Well don't just talk about it – do it!", because that's what mates are for, right? And blow me down if he didn't just go away and do it. Personally I blame the lager, but that, once again is another story...

So the book is a history of the Sex Pistols up to and including 1st December, 1976, because after that everyone on planet Earth that wasn't hiding in a rabbit hole knows what happened anyway. In brief they left EMI, sacked the bass player – or he walked, depending on who you choose to believe – hired the Icon, spent 7 days with A&M, had a mad Jubilee, signed with Virgin, and split up in front of their biggest crowd ever, 3,500 miles away from where they began, and then their Icon died age 21 suspected of his girlfriend's murder. In 1996 they reformed because the money was finally right and since then it's been pretty much business as usual.

This version of their story is based on 100% fact regarding days, dates and places. The other 100% of its story comes from the mind of Mick O'Shea, based on what he knows about the band members and their personalities, plus

---

a few ideas about the times thrown in either for good measure, or for those who didn't live through them. You will find it interesting, funny, and down right off the rails, but it could all so easily be true. For instance one summer evening in Maida Vale, after a quick meeting with another publisher, myself and Mick were planning to nip into my local and have a couple of pints before heading into the West End for a curry. As we were about to leave the pub in walked Glen Matlock, so we finished up at my place 20 minutes after last orders and still without the nearest sniff of a curry; now how many times has that happened to you? Exactly, so read on...

Alan Parker
(Some kind a Gimmick in W9)

Only Anarchists Are Pretty

The idea for this book came about over a pint one cold Thursday evening in Blackburn in November, 1999, with fellow author and Sex Pistols aficionado Alan Parker. Yes, there have already been plenty of books written about the Sex Pistols – I should know, as I've bought most of them. My idea, however, was to try and tell their story from a different perspective by using my own experiences as an aspiring guitarist to recreate the situations that the group – and any other would-be musicians – would face when not just first trying to put a group together, but the trials and tribulations thereafter.

From a historical viewpoint, all the factual information within these pages is, to the best of my knowledge, correct: people, dates, places, etc. As for the rest, it's a story – and hopefully one that you'll enjoy. For a purely factual account of the Sex Pistols career, and the Punk Rock movement as a whole, then I thoroughly recommend the book *England's Dreaming* by Jon Savage (Faber & Faber), accompanied by *Satellite* by Alan Parker and Paul Burgess (Abstract Sounds) for a pictorial history of the Sex Pistols.

I was only fifteen years-old when the Sex Pistols played at the Winterland Ballroom in San Francisco, on 14 January, 1978, and as the group split-up shortly thereafter, I didn't actually witness them performing live on stage until they played Finsbury Park on 23 June, 1996, on their Filthy Lucre reunion tour. The "Filth & Fury" banner headlines of December 1976, which resulted from the group's infamous appearance on *The Today Show* completely passed me by, and I only became aware of the Sex Pistols during the national furore over the release of their second single "God Save The Queen" in May, 1977. Those three minutes and 17 seconds of guitar-fuelled angst and mayhem changed my life forever and I was consumed with an insatiable desire to learn everything I could about Johnny Rotten, Sid Vicious *et al*. I can still remember the mischievous thrill that surged through my body upon purchasing a copy of "Never Mind The Bollocks" upon its release in October, 1977, much to the utter dismay and horror of my parents, who even now, some twenty-seven years later still refer to my dalliance with punk rock as "That Time!" Well mum, all I can say in my defence is that it was "Time" well spent.

It is true to say that the publication of this book would not have been possible without the continued faith – and hard work – of Alan Parker, who, if it was possible, was even more determined than I to see the story reach the nation's bookshelves. For this, and being a good mate – thank you. Special thanks also to Sean Body at Helter Skelter Publishing for stepping where others feared to tread, Dan Angel for providing the artwork, Edward Christie for giving me my first break, Paul Young (not the singer) for being a constant source of amusement and inspiration, Steve Diggle, Brian Jackson (the Sixth Pistol), Tommy (Vomit) Crookston, Tom Griffin, Elizabeth Ashworth, who after being called upon to edit the finished manuscript, surprised herself – and me – by enjoying the task (Elizabeth.Ashworth@btinternet.com). And last, but by no means least, I would like to thank John Lydon, Steve Jones, Glen Matlock, and Paul Cook for giving the British music scene the kick up the arse it so desperately needed... Are you sitting comfortably, children?

Mick O'Shea
15 June, 2004

I would like to dedicate this book to my wife Jakki for her understanding and patience while I hammered away on my word processor, oblivious to anything and everything else around me.

Most of what follows is true

CHAPTER ONE

It wasn't until Paul happened to glance sideways and catch his reflection in a shop window that he realised he'd been talking to himself.

"Where the fuck...?" he muttered to himself as he searched through the Saturday afternoon shoppers. "There he is!" Paul shook his head and started to walk back down the King's Road in Chelsea. "Come on Steve, for fuck's sake," he yelled just as his best mate looked over to him and signalled that he was coming. Steve was in conversation with some girl and although Paul could only see her from behind he could tell that she was a real piece of work. Paul Cook was eighteen years old, almost a year younger than Steve was, and they had been friends since they had both attended the Christopher Wren School on the Wormholt Estate in Shepherd's Bush. Paul had been a bright pupil and all his teachers thought he would do well. However, from the age of fourteen his report cards started to show a steady decline and teachers began to notice that Paul was easily distracted; even Paul had to admit that this was one of his worst faults and with Steve being his best mate, enough said.

"Hold up, I'm coming," shouted Steve as he dragged on a cigarette. "Did you see that bird? Fuckin' gorgeous. She was wearing one of them T-shirts with the smiley face. I'd make her fuckin' smile!" As he said this he looked over his shoulder trying to catch a glimpse of the girl in question.

"Yeah," replied Paul, nodding his head, following Steve's gaze. "What did you say to her?"

"Well," said Steve, exhaling a plume of cigarette smoke into Paul's face. "When I clocked her, I saw that she was about to light her fag so I just asked her if she had a spare one and then I started chattin' her up like."

"Get anywhere?" asked Paul.

"Nah," replied Steve, shaking his head, "could have done though."

"Oh, yeah!" said Paul, smirking.

"Yeah!" replied Steve. "She was one of them foreign birds an' they're just dyin' for it!" He placed his arm around Paul's shoulders. "But we've gotta get to the shop, right!"

"Fuck off," replied Paul, grinning. "Come on."

▭ ▭ ▭ ▭

Saturday afternoons were always busy on the King's Road, especially if Chelsea FC were playing at home. Paul and Steve made their way past the 'Man in the Moon', one of the pubs they often frequented as they spent most Saturdays at the 'World's End', the Bohemian centre of London, where the weird and wonderful paraded themselves to "see" and be "seen". Paul and Steve loved it here and felt right at home. The King's Road and especially the 'Worlds End' was famous for the clothes shops like 'Alkasura' and 'Granny Takes A Trip', but even by the summer of 1975 the "hippie" culture from the 1960s was still dictating London's fashion. Flares were still the order of the day, flowered prints on shirts, blouses and long flowing dresses, people wore coloured beads and platform shoes and almost everybody had long hair, the longer the better. The older generations struggled to tell the difference between the two sexes, wondering what the world was coming to. Paul and Steve stood out from the crowd because of the fact they both had short hair. Paul's was blond and slightly feathered on top while Steve's was a tightly curled dirty brown colour. Both boys were wearing 'Straight Leg' trousers and 'Brothel Creepers'; the shoes were favoured by the 'Teddy Boy Culture' from the 1950s and had made a comeback in the early 70s. Paul and Steve were heading for the only shop in London, if not the whole of England where this kind of exciting clothing could be found. An entrepreneur called Malcolm McLaren and his girlfriend Vivienne Westwood owned No. 430 King's Road. The couple had been running a shop there for about five years.

When the shop first opened, they had called it 'Let It Rock' and had sold original clothing and records from the 1950s. In 1973 they changed the name of the shop to 'Too Fast To Live Too Young To Die' in honour of the American actor James Dean, who had been killed in a car crash in 1955. The shop also began to sell leather motorcycle gear to its assorted clientele. By the summer of 1974 the shop's owners had become bored with this and after a complete redesign of the shop's interior Malcolm and Vivienne started to sell leather and rubber fetish wear. They also changed the name of the shop yet again, now it was simply called "SEX".

As Steve headed for the front door of the shop he glanced upwards to the large pink padded PVC letters denoting the name of the shop. Behind the letters Malcolm had spray painted the motto "Craft must have clothes but the truth loves to go naked". He'd told the boys that it was from someone called Rousseau. Steve didn't know who this Rousseau guy was but he was sure it would be one of them "posh gits" that Malcolm claimed to have "hung out" with when he lived in Paris. Steve had pestered Vivienne to arrange a meeting with Malcolm in the hope of getting him interested in managing their group. Steve and Paul along with their friends Wally and Glen, who would also be at the meeting, had been playing together for about two years now and had started to take it more seriously. Malcolm had recently returned from New York where he had spent the last six months managing The New York Dolls, a trash-glam outfit given to wearing make-up and female clothing as part of their stage act.

Steve had never been one to stop and analyse situations but it never ceased to amaze him that he was the singer in a pop group. He'd always been interested in music and always went to watch the hottest groups with his mates although he'd never thought of learning to play a musical instrument. Despite the difference in age there was a definite bond between Malcolm and Steve and they could always have a laugh together. Before Malcolm went to America he used to take Steve to a club called the "Speakeasy", a favourite haunt for "Rock" musicians and the young impressionable Steve had loved every minute of it and had begun to steal musical instruments as a way to feel involved.

His mother and stepfather had brought up Steve in Shepherd's Bush. His real father, an amateur boxer called Don Jarvis left the family home while Steve was still very young. As he grew older, there were problems between himself and his stepfather. By the time Steve was fifteen years old, he had left home and lived for a short time with one of his friends from school, Stephen Hayes, who had been involved in the formation of Steve's group but had little incentive to learn to play an instrument. Steve later moved in with Paul's family in Hammersmith taking over the room vacated by his sister when she left to get married. Paul's brother-in-law, Del, had also been involved in the group as the bass player but once Paul's sister had given birth to their first child he'd only turned up occasionally for rehearsals before giving up coming altogether.

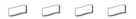

Steve and Paul liked to spend their Saturdays in "SEX" because they could spend the whole day in the shop and wouldn't be hassled by the assistants. In most of the shops on the King's Road people, asking if you needed help, would instantly surround you. The interior of "SEX" was like no other shop in London. The walls were covered with spongy black foam with layers of pink surgical rubber draped over them. These sheets had been sprayed with quotations from the likes of Valerie Solanas, the American Author of the SCUM (Society for Cutting Up Men) manifesto who had gained notoriety for shooting the artist Andy Warhol in 1968 and the Scottish Beat writer Alexander Trucchi, author of *School For Wives* and *Thongs*.

It was impossible for passers-by to see inside the shop because of the heavy drapes that hung down in front of the door and windows for this very purpose. "SEX" was most definitely not a shop for the average person. The shop's windows were crammed with the headless torsos of mannequins wearing leather straps and studded thongs. The shop even boasted a surgical bed from some long forgotten hospital ward that lay hidden behind a curtain of pink and black rubber. In the corner of the shop stood an original 1950s jukebox, which played all of Malcolm's favourite Rock 'n' Roll records from artists like Marty Wilde, Jerry Lee Lewis and Billy Fury. There was also a selection of modern day artists like The Stooges, The Flamin' Groovies and Alice Cooper.

Apart from the leather and rubber fetish clothing the shop still sold original 1950s clothing left over from the 'Let It Rock' days such as brothel creepers and zoot suits. Malcolm and Vivienne had also started to create their own T-shirts. These had originally been printed on Vivienne's kitchen table using stencils cut out from potatoes and a child's printing set, but were now being screen-printed by a friend of Malcolm's called Bernie Rhodes. Their early designs included prints of a prepubescent boy casually smoking on a cigarette, a black man with a large erect penis and others of an equally disturbing sexual nature. The latest design the couple had been working on was from an idea that Malcolm had come up with which comprised two lists printed down either side of the front of a shirt; on one side a list of "Loves" and on the other a list of "Hates". Emblazoned across the top of the shirt was the slogan: "You're gonna wake up one morning and know which side of the bed you've been sleeping on". The hates included the names of the Rolling Stones' Mick Jagger, Elton John and the television presenter Melvyn Bragg. On the loves list were the names of Rock 'n' Roll legends Eddie Cochrane and Gene Vincent, the Great Train Robber Ronnie Biggs, and it also contained the name Malcolm had suggested for Steve's group: "Kutie Jones and his Sex Pistols". Malcolm had probably included the name more out of his friendship with Steve than from any desire to promote the group, but not surprisingly this just happened to be Steve's favourite item of clothing and he was wearing the T-shirt that afternoon.

Malcolm McLaren had met Vivienne in 1965 through her brother Gordon Swire. By this time she had already been married three years to her husband Derek Westwood. Vivienne was originally from somewhere in Cheshire but had moved to London with her parents in 1957. This was at the time that Malcolm was still using his real name of Edwards. Later that year Vivienne left Derek for Malcolm taking their two-year-old son, Ben, with her and moved in with her parents. On 30 November 1965 Vivienne gave birth to Malcolm's son who they named Joseph. Malcolm was now attending Croydon College of Art & Design. In 1968, Malcolm went to live in Paris and would later claim to have taken part in the student riots, although these had taken place some three months before his arrival in the French capital.

By October of 1968, Malcolm was enrolled at the Goldsmiths College of Art in South London studying Film & Photography. It was here that he began an affair with a wealthy South African called Helen Minnenberg, though whether Malcolm was attracted to her wealth or the fact that she was a dwarf, nobody was quite sure. While he was at Goldsmiths College Malcolm began working on a project titled "Oxford Street". A fanciful tale giving the history of the famous London thoroughfare, full of Dickensian intrigue and murder, he would leave the college, graduating in the Summer of 1971, without finishing the project. In October of the same year Malcolm had a chance encounter with a guy called

Bradley Mendelson, the Brooklyn-born owner of a fashion boutique at 430 King's Road. The American remarked on the trousers Malcolm was wearing and the two men struck up a conversation on fashion. In November, Malcolm and Vivienne moved into Mendelson's shop and began trading as 'Let It Rock'.

Steve and Paul entered the shop and walked over to sit by the window. The other two members of their group, Glen and Wally, were already there, sitting talking to the shop's two assistants, Michael Collins who was acting as shop manager and a very striking girl who was calling herself 'Jordon'. Jordon's real name was Pamela Rook; she came from the seaside town of Seaford in Essex. Although small in height she used every inch of her size to maximum effect. As a child she had begun to study ballet and had carried on until the age of eighteen. She believed her body to be a work of art and would spend at least two hours every morning "creating" herself. Jordon was laughing at something Glen was telling her. She reached down by her side for a carrier bag while serving a customer. As she did this everyone close by was treated to a generous view of her cleavage as her breasts threatened to spill out of the leopard-skin print basque that she was wearing. Wally had had a huge "crush" on her ever since first seeing her in the shop and spent much of his spare time and cash there.

"...think of the rehearsals last night?"

"Ugh, what?" mumbled Wally, still mesmerised by the sight of Jordon's tits.

"I said, what did you think of the rehearsals last night!" Paul repeated, shaking his head at his friend. "Anyone would think you hadn't seen a pair before."

"Oh, it went all right, I suppose," replied Wally, finally turning to face Paul.

Warwick "Wally" Nightingale was the guitarist in the group; it had been his idea to form a group when he, Paul and Steve had bunked off school spending their days at his parents' house on Hemlock Road in East Acton. Wally had received a Gibson Les Paul Copy electric guitar and a small amplifier suitable for home use as birthday presents and he'd started practising regularly. Steve had "acquired" a set of drums but hadn't shown either the interest or the talent required for learning the instrument and had given the drum kit to Paul. Paul had shown even less interest, preferring to spend his time sunbathing in Wally's back garden, drinking Wally's father's beer.

Steve had finally pestered Paul into at least learning the basics on the drums whilst nominating himself as singer, as it hadn't gone unnoticed by Steve that it was mainly the singers of pop groups that the girls fancied. Wally was desperate for the group to succeed, at any level. He felt it gave him some sort of credibility because most of his school friends had looked upon him as a "geek" or a "nerd". This was mainly down to his appearance; he was forced to wear thick "jam-jar" spectacles to help his poor eyesight and he also had thick wiry hair. If Wally hadn't been so desperate to be in the group he might have

----

told Paul a few home truths about the previous evening's rehearsals.

To Wally, Steve's singing was hopeless and Paul was out of time more often than not. The group might never have got to the stage they were at had it not been for Steve approaching Malcolm and telling him about their group. Although Malcolm himself was far too busy with the day-to-day running of the shop to take much of an interest in them, he did mention that the lad who worked in the shop on Saturdays was learning to play the bass guitar. Malcolm, Steve, Paul and Wally took the opportunity to approach Glen when they were all attending a Thin Lizzy gig at the Marquee on Wardour Street in Soho; a second meeting was arranged with Glen for him to come to Wally's house on Hemlock Road for an audition.

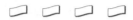

Glen Matlock was also eighteen years old; he had worked Saturdays at SEX a couple of years back but was now attending St. Martin's College of Art on Charing Cross Road. Malcolm still managed to make use of his former employee by getting Glen to screen-print T-shirts for his shop using the College's equipment. Glen had shied away from doing this because of the strong sexual content and more importantly he didn't want to be thrown out of the College if he got caught. Glen had known Paul, albeit vaguely, from when they had played for rival football teams as kids, but had got to know him and Steve through seeing them both hanging around in Malcolm's shop. He remembered Malcolm telling him to keep an eye on them as they were always trying to nick stuff. On the day of the arranged rehearsal, Glen's dad dropped him off at the corner of Yew Tree Road. After collecting his bass guitar from the back seat of the car he set off along Hemlock Road checking off the numbers of the houses until he arrived at Wally's parents' house.

Wally answered the door himself and showed Glen up to his bedroom. Paul and Steve were already waiting for him. They were both sitting on Wally's bed flicking through some battered editions of the football comic *Shoot*. Glen glanced at the two-page colour picture of the England 1970 World Cup squad on the bedroom wall held in place by a couple of rusted drawing pins. He shook his head at the painful memories of how that team, smiling happily for the camera, threw away a two-goal lead against the old enemy, West Germany, in the quarter final to lose 3-2. But if people thought that was bad enough, then the shock of failing to qualify for the 1974 Finals in West Germany was unbelievable. What was it that Brian Clough had called the Polish goalkeeper who had ended England's dreams at Wembley? A "clown"! Well he certainly had the last laugh on England. Steve, tossing down the comic he'd been reading, brought him out of his reverie, purposely making eye contact with Glen as he slowly reached down for another one.

Glen, being naturally shy, hated awkward moments like this, meeting people with a view to something more. It was like being the new kid at the school where everyone else knows each other. Although he'd seen these three hanging around Malcolm's shop he hadn't really spoken to them until now. Glen mumbled an all right and nodded his head at Steve and Paul then crouched down to open his guitar case. He carefully removed the bass from its protective cushion and rested it across his knee. He hadn't brought his amplifier along to the audition because they were fucking heavy things to hump around. Wally had said it would be okay for Glen to use his guitar amplifier just as long as they kept the volume down so as to avoid the risk of blowing the speaker.

By the time Glen was ready Steve and Paul had put down the comics and were eyeing him up. It seemed to Glen almost as if they were trying to unnerve him. Steve hadn't been all that keen to try Glen out for the group in the first place; there was something about Glen that he didn't like. Glen had attended St. Clement Danes Grammar School so he wasn't one of the lads. He was a "snob" and a "mummy's boy'. Paul looked at Glen for a few moments before turning to Steve to give him a "he looks all right" look. After all, he did have the same "look" as them. His dark hair was cut short, he was wearing "straight-leg" trousers and striped shirt and his favourite black Harrington jacket and he obviously shared their passion for brothel creepers. Steve pulled a face and shrugged his shoulders slightly, refusing to give Glen the benefit of the doubt.

Wally checked that everything was plugged in and switched on and asked Glen to play something while he made the necessary adjustments to his amplifier. He stood up and signalled that Glen could start whenever he was ready, then nudged Paul's feet to make room for him. Paul begrudgingly shifted his legs to allow Wally to sit down on the bed. Strangely enough it was Steve who broke the uncomfortable silence by asking Glen which groups he liked. Glen looked down at the fretboard of his guitar giving himself time to think; musical taste is such a personal thing but at times like this you really want to be hip to the coolest groups while knowledgeable at the same time.

"I like all sorts really," he said, looking from one expectant face to another. "I like the Doors and the Kinks are pretty good." He paused for a moment. "Who else," he said, thoughtfully. "The Stones and I really like the Faces." He stopped and looked at them, feeling that he'd given them enough to be going on with. "What do you want me to play then?"

"I dunno," said Steve, matter-of-factly, "just play somethin' that we all know."

Glen had seen the looks of approval on their faces when he'd name-checked the group The Small Faces and decided to play them a few bars from a song of theirs called "Three Button Hand Me Down" that had a tricky bass part. Glen, comfortable in his own ability, quickly lost himself in the tune. When he had finished he glanced at the three open mouths on the bed and knew that he'd passed the audition.

Glen moved over to join the others when Jordon stood up to answer the telephone. When she had first started working in the shop she would always answer the phone by saying: "Hello, SEX. Can I help you?" But she had quickly tired of hearing giggling or "yes please darlin'" from the other end of the line. Now she would simply say "430 King's Road". Jordon listened to whoever was speaking while glancing over towards Steve and the others. "Yes, I'll tell them. No... everything's fine...bye." She replaced the receiver on its cradle and strolled over to rejoin the boys.

"Who was that?" Steve asked. He was curious to know who or what had caused Jordon to look in their direction.

"That was Malcolm," replied Jordon, placing her hand on her hip. "He told me to tell you that he's running a bit late but you should wait here because he won't be too long." She glanced round at Michael Collins as he placed his hands on her shoulders while he asked if anyone wanted anything from the shop around the corner. Steve leaned forward and said he could use some fags, hoping to get a response from Collins but it was obvious he'd already heard that one before.

"You got any money on you?" asked Paul, turning to his friend. Steve shook his head, ruefully indicating that he was skint again. He smiled hopefully at Paul.

"Don't look at me!" said Paul, shaking his head. Although he was the only one of the four members of the group with a full time job, his wages as an apprentice electrician didn't go far. "I've got enough to get us home on the bus." He patted the pockets of his trousers to emphasise the point. Steve, never one to be easily dissuaded looked eagerly at Wally.

"Come on Wally, mate," he said, smirking, "you've always got plenty o' dough on you."

"No, I haven't," said Wally, squirming in his seat. "I'm broke, honest!" Steve got up out of his chair and stretched casually before moving across to where Wally was sitting.

"So," said Steve, grinning at the others, "I can search you then." He reached out towards Wally's pockets. Wally placed his own hands over the pockets of his trousers in a vain attempt to fend off Steve, but Steve wasn't having any of it. "Grab his arms, Paul," he yelled while grabbing a nearby stool and sitting himself in front of the helpless Wally.

"Fuck off, Paul!" cried Wally, weakly struggling against Steve's grip. He looked towards Glen for help but Glen was clearly enjoying watching someone else suffering at the hands of Steve and Paul. Paul had managed to pin Wally's wrists down by the sides of his chair. Steve pressed one hand down on Wally's thigh while his other was poised inches above one of his trouser pockets.

"Right, then," said Steve, "I can keep any dough that I find in 'ere." He began to dig his hand into Wally's pocket while Wally wriggled in protest. He struggled so much that his spectacles worked themselves loose and clattered to the floor, but if he thought that this would release him from his torment then he was sadly mistaken. Steve and Paul were both laughing and showing little sign of giving up.

"All right, all right!" he yelled. "I give in, just get off me." He leapt up out of his chair now that Paul had released his grip on his arms, bent down to retrieve his glasses and gave them a cursory wipe on his shirt while he scowled at his two assailants.

"Come on, Wal," said Steve, trying not to laugh, "we're your mates."

"Yeah," agreed Paul, "we're in a group."

"Some fuckin' mates you are!" said Wally, still rubbing his wrists from where Paul had been holding him. "How much do you need?" he asked Steve. He'd learned long ago that there was no point asking Steve how much he'd like to borrow because Steve would only need to borrow more money from you to pay you back.

"How much you got?" asked Steve, still smirking at Wally.

"You can have a quid," said Wally, reaching into his pocket, "an' that's all!" He pulled out a crumpled note and handed it over.

"Fuckin' hell, you miserable git!" said Steve, holding up the note for the others to see. "You're fuckin' loaded an' you don't want to buy me some fags?" He looked away shaking his head. "And I thought you were a mate."

"Yeah," said Paul, quietly dropping his eyes to the floor.

"But I need it!" protested Wally. "I..." He realised that he'd been set up again when Steve and the others burst out laughing.

"Oh you really are easy, aren't you?" said Jordon, grinning at Wally, which made him feel even worse.

"Anyone got a jacket that I can borrow?" asked Steve, thrusting the crumpled pound note into his pocket.

"What do you need a jacket for?" asked Glen, frowning. "It ain't raining, is it?"

"No," said Jordon, pulling back the heavy drapes and glancing outside. "It's still lovely out."

"I don't need a jacket because o' the fuckin' weather," said Steve, looking at the sea of puzzled faces in front of him. "I need somethin' with pockets in." He winked across at Paul, who'd been the only one to realise what Steve had in mind.

"Yeah, right," he said, smirking. "Steve needs a jacket, preferably one that's long and with loads of inside pockets." Michael Collins came over and handed Steve a three-quarter-length sheepskin jacket that had been lying around in the back of the shop for as long as anyone could remember.

"Here you go," he said, smiling, although he still had no idea why Steve needed the jacket as he'd missed the wink between the two friends. He even held the jacket up while Steve slid his arms in.

"Perfect," said Steve, examining the inside pockets. "Do you want anythin'?" he asked Paul, as he and Collins headed towards the front door.

"Yeah," replied Paul, nodding, "get us a can of Coke."

"An' I'll have a Mars Bar," said Wally.

"Got any money?" asked Steve, looking seriously at Wally for a moment, but he couldn't keep his face straight.

"What about you Glen?" asked Collins, looking over at Glen. "Can I tempt you with anything?" He gave a suggestive smile and winked at him. Glen looked over at Collins knowing full well where this was heading.

"No thanks, Michael," he replied, smiling, "I wouldn't want to get it stuck between my teeth now, would I?"

"Oh, how cruel," said Collins, feigning a look of indignation, "you wouldn't want it stuck in your ear as a wart." And with this he strutted out of the shop closely followed by Steve.

Paul nudged Glen in the ribs with his elbow, a serious look on his face. "What would you do," said Paul, leaning closer to Glen, "if Collins jumped on your back?"

"What would I do?" asked Glen, looking puzzled.

"Would you let him shag you or would you toss him off?"

"What do you think I'd do?" said Glen, indignantly, "I'd toss him..." He realised what he was saying and since everyone else had been listening to the conversation he could feel himself blushing. "Leave it out, Paul," he said, shaking his head. "It's gettin' a bit boring now."

Glen stood up and walked over to a clothes rail and pretended to examine a pair of trousers. He was angry with himself more than anything for falling for Paul's joke. He was still considered an outsider by the other three although they'd been playing together for almost two years and he'd been working in the shop before any of them had even heard of it. He glanced at his watch. It was going on for half past four. Collins would want to close the shop soon and Malcolm still hadn't turned up. He glanced over his shoulder towards Paul and Wally to see if he was still the subject of their amusement. He saw that Jordon had rejoined them, she was winding down for the day. Wally looked to be delighted yet terrified at the same time. He felt he was safe to go over and sit with them while they waited for Malcolm.

"So, how's this group of yours doing?" Jordon asked Paul.

"Oh, all right, I s'pose," replied Paul, smiling faintly.

"Is that why you're all here?" she asked, "to see if Malcolm is interested in being your manager?"

"Well, yeah," replied Paul. "Steve had a word with him before he fucked off to America. I didn't think anythin' would happen but he did get us a place where we could have a proper rehearsal."

"Where's that, then?"

"In Covent Garden," said Glen, nodding his approval, "and he asked his mate Bernie to help us out."

"Do you mean Bernie Rhodes?" asked Jordon, looking at Glen.

"Yeah, that's him," replied Glen. "How well do you know him?"

"Oh not that well, really," replied Jordon, shaking her head. "He comes in here to talk with Vivienne. Have you noticed how serious he always seems to be?"

"Yeah, you're right there," said Paul, nodding his agreement. "I think he's got some sort of political agenda or somethin'."

"Yeah," said Glen, smirking, "he's always goin' on about 'right wing' this and 'left wing' that. He gets really intense and it's so funny when he tries to give Steve these lectures on politics and Steve doesn't have a clue what Bernie's on about."

"Steve don't even know who the Prime Minister is," said Paul, grinning.

Jordon leaned forward and placed her hand on Wally's knee while she fiddled around with one of the straps on her leather boots. Wally had tensed up and was staring at Jordon's hand. Glen and Paul weren't sure whether she knew about Wally's crush on her or not as she didn't seem aware that he existed most of the time, but they were enjoying his reaction all the same.

"So has this group of yours played anywhere?" she asked Wally, as she sat back in her chair. Wally was still staring at the place on his thigh where she had rested her hand. "Hello, you can speak can't you?" she asked, frowning at Wally.

"We played at a café just down the road," said Paul, deciding to help Wally out.

"Really," said Jordon, turning away from Wally, "which one?"

"You know 'Tom Salters'?" Paul asked her.

"Yeah, I know where it is," replied Jordon. "I've been in a couple of times for lunch."

"Well, someone we knew was having a party in the room upstairs and we got to play some songs," explained Paul.

"It's hardly the Rainbow, is it," said Jordon, sarcastically, referring to the famous music venue in Finsbury Park.

"No, it ain't," said Paul, defensively, "but we'll get there, you wait an' see." He sounded less than convincing, but there's something about being in a group which makes its members very protective about it. Jordon seemed to have lost interest in talk of the group and had gone back to altering her bootstraps. Paul and the others were quite happy to let her as they watched her tits being forced up and down with every movement; they were sure that they were going to pop out. If they had to admit it even Paul, Glen and Steve were a bit intimidated by Jordon, she was around the same age as them but she seemed so sure of herself. Then again, working in a place like SEX she needed to be.

The door opened suddenly, breaking the silence that had filled the shop. Steve and Michael Collins came in looking quite shocked at something; they heard him telling Steve that he'd never been so embarrassed in his life.

"Fuckin' doubt it," said Steve, inbetween mouthfuls of food. Jordon stood up and went to join Collins to see what he'd brought back with him.

"You should have seen him!" said Collins, pointing at Steve, who had now rejoined his friends and was handing out various goodies.

"How did you get all this with a quid?" asked Glen, cupping his hands together to catch a Kit-Kat.

"Easy!" said Steve, popping the last bit of a sandwich into his mouth.

"We went to the little shop around the corner," said Collins, carrying on with his story, "you know, the one where Katie works," he said, for Jordon's benefit. "She's such a dear, well, I went over to the counter to see what sandwiches she had on offer today and he comes over," he jerked a thumb at Steve, "and he tells me to keep her busy, before disappearing." Collins paused for breath before continuing. "So, I'm stood there at the counter trying to think of something to say to her but I could tell she knew something was going on because the poor girl kept looking over my shoulder to see what "Raffles" here was up to!"

"I paid for the fags, didn't I?" said Steve, looking up as though this somehow excused his antics.

"Paid for the fag's what?" said Jordon, trying to keep a straight face then covering her mouth with her hand and looking over at Collins. "Sorry, Michael, you know I'm only joking."

"You didn't have much choice, did you Steve," replied Collins, feigning a hurtful look for Jordon's benefit, "they keep them behind the counter!"

Steve opened the said packet of cigarettes and after removing one offered the packet towards Collins.

"So where's my change?" asked Wally, reaching across to accept one of the cigarettes.

"Fuck off!" said Steve, shrugging himself out of the sheepskin coat. "You can get some more off mummy when you get home."

"Fuckin' hell," moaned Wally, shaking his head, "it's like being in a group with Dick Turpin!"

"Yeah," said Glen, nodding in agreement, "but at least he had the decency to wear a mask!"

Steve handed the sheepskin back to Collins then stood up and brushed crumbs from his trousers. "What have we missed?" he asked.

"Nothing much," said Jordon, throwing her empty sandwich wrappings into the bin.

"We were tellin' you about our group!" said Paul.

"Like I said," replied Jordon, smirking, "nothing much."

"Oh, how exciting," said Collins, clapping his hands together, "I'd love to 'come' and see you play." He looked over at Glen, grinning at this blatant innuendo. "And I'll bring all my friends."

"Well, we're still busy sortin' out the songs, an that," said Steve.

"Are you still in Covent Garden?" asked Jordon.

"No, we've got somewhere better than that," said Glen, proudly. "You know the old BBC Studios on Crisp Road in Hammersmith?"

"Yes," said Collins, glancing across at Jordon.

"You've got that place, how?"

"Well," said Steve, pointing at Wally, "his dad's got a contract to fix the place up, so we got ourselves a set of keys cut and it's ours for now."

"That's right," said Glen, nodding seriously, "the room we're set up in has the best acoustics around." The conversation suddenly halted as everyone turned around at the sound of the door opening.

CHAPTER TWO

"**What's going on here**, then?" asked Malcolm, furtively. Judging by the expression on his face anyone would have thought he'd just uncovered the Watergate burglary. He closed the door behind him and walked into the middle of the shop, his eyes never leaving the group of people gathered by the window. Malcolm had been back in England for about a week. For the last six months he'd been in America trying to manage the New York Dolls. Unfortunately for Malcolm, he arrived on the scene just as the Dolls were beginning to fall apart.

Malcolm, ever full of radical ideas, persuaded the group to adopt patent red leather stage outfits and play in front of a backdrop made out of a large Russian flag complete with hammer and sickle. This wasn't what mid-seventies America was ready for especially as the situation in Vietnam was reaching its sorry climax. The Dolls quickly fell apart due to alcohol and drug abuse amongst its members. Before returning to England, Malcolm witnessed what was happening on the music scene in New York City at clubs such as Max's Kansas City and CBGB's down on the Bowery where groups with little or no talent were playing in front of ecstatic audiences. These raw energetic young groups reminded him of Steve Jones' group back in London.

Malcolm was dressed as immaculately as ever in leather trousers, Cuban-heeled boots and a very expensive looking jacket that he'd bought in New York. "So, Jordon my girl, how's business been while I've been away?" he asked her. "London's still full of perverted souls, I hope."

"Oh, yes," replied Jordon, smiling at the slight American twang in Malcolm's accent. She glanced over at Collins who was standing near the shop's cash register. "They just can't seem to keep away, can they, Michael?"

"No," replied Collins, smiling. "How was America, Malcolm? Full of rugged handsome cowboys?"

"Yes, you should get out there, Michael," said Malcolm, returning the smile. He turned to face Steve and the others. "Steve, my boy, how have you been getting on?"

"All right," said Steve, nodding thoughtfully.

"Love the T-shirt," said Malcolm, pointing at the "what side of the bed" shirt Steve was wearing and wondering if he'd paid for it. "Has Bernie been looking after your little group?"

"Yeah," replied Steve, getting up out of his chair and stretching his arms above his head, "but it's you that we want to talk to."

"Well, why don't we shut up shop and go down to The Roebuck for a drink?" said Malcolm, beaming. "I've got lots of stories to tell you about America. You boys would love it over there."

"What were the Dolls like, Malcolm?" asked Glen, eager for information.

"All in good time boys, all in good time," replied Malcolm, as he surveyed the youths gathered before him. The smile faded when his eyes fell upon the bespectacled Wally. He had seen for himself what was happening down in the Bowery on New York's Lower East Side. The American kids were flocking to a club called CBGB's to see new exciting groups with names like Television, The Ramones and Talking Heads. Malcolm knew that he could easily mould Steve's group into something very similar but his plans certainly didn't include Wally Nightingale. For that matter, Paul and Glen were also expendable, it was Steve that Malcolm was interested in.

"I spoke to Bernie last night and he's been telling me good things about you lot," he said, striding over to a clothes rail and giving one of the shirts a cursory inspection. "Can this be right?"

"Too fuckin' right it is," replied Steve, walking over to join Malcolm, "we're gettin' songs together an' that."

"So," said Malcolm, casually rubbing his chin, "maybe I should come down and see for myself what you've got to offer."

"Would you?" gasped Steve, becoming very animated. "When?"

"Let me see what I can arrange," said Malcolm, getting hold of the sleeve of a purple velvet shirt and brushing his hand against the nap of the velvet. He knew that he had their full attention by the way they were hanging onto every word and he was thoroughly enjoying himself. "Of course," he said, turning back to face Steve and the others, "I can't promise anything, you know, what with the running of this place." Malcolm threw up his arm and waved it around for emphasis. There was no point in seeming too interested at this stage because that would never do. "Now then," he said, smiling broadly, "who's coming for that drink I mentioned earlier?" Collins thanked Malcolm for the offer but declined the invitation as he'd already made plans for the evening. Jordan on the other hand wanted to go with them. She wanted to hear Malcolm's stories about his time in America but sensed that this was going to be a "lads" thing so instead, she said she would help Collins close up the shop then head off to her friend's house in West Kensington.

Steve could hardly contain himself now, as far as he was concerned what Malcolm had just told them about coming down to see them was the best news he'd had in ages.

"Yeah, come on you cunts," he said, urging Paul and the others out of their chairs, "that's where the action is." As he said this Paul and Glen looked at each other and groaned. This was Steve's current saying when he was excited about something; they had heard it so often and were by now sick of hearing it. Earlier that week, during a rehearsal Bernie had told Paul that if he heard Steve say "where's the action" one more time he wouldn't be held responsible for his own actions.

"So, how much money have you got, then Steve?" Paul asked his friend.

"I've got the money Wally gave me," replied Steve, pulling a face at Paul.

"I don't remember giving you anything!" moaned Wally, scowling at Steve.

"You'll want a drink though, won't you?" said Steve, fishing the loose change from out of his pocket.

"We won't get pissed off that though, will we," said Paul, leaning forward to check the amount of money in Steve's hand.

"Come on, Wal", said Steve, grinning sheepishly. He shoved the money back in his pocket and walked over to Wally. "It's gonna be great." He threw an arm around Wally's shoulder and leaned closer to him. "It'll be a right laugh and I'll blag Malcolm for a couple of beers when he's pissed." Steve whispered this last bit while glancing over his shoulder to see if Malcolm was listening.

"Yeah, but it's always me, innit?" Wally grumbled. He wanted to hear Malcolm's stories about America and the New York Dolls but he didn't see why he should be the one to pay for everyone else's pleasure as well.

"Boys, boys," said Malcolm, clapping his hands to get everyone's attention. "It was my invitation, so I'll pay for the drinks, OK." This certainly got their attention. Anyone who knew Malcolm, knew that he was as tight as two coats of paint.

"Right, you're on," said Glen, not waiting to be asked twice. He headed for the door closely followed by the others. Malcolm paused for a moment then headed towards Collins, who was standing at the cash register ready to sort out the day's takings. He leaned across Collins and pressed the button that released the cash drawer and helped himself to a ten-pound note. He checked Collins' face for any reaction then slid out another note. "Not a word to Vivienne!" he said, smiling as he left the shop.

Once they were all settled around a table near to the jukebox in The Roebuck Inn on the King's Road, Malcolm asked Steve about the T-shirt he was wearing. "Is that new, boy?"

"Nah," replied Steve, swallowing his first mouthful of beer, "I've 'ad it a while now."

"Did you pay for it?" asked Malcolm, tapping the table edge with his finger.

"No, he fuckin' didn't!" exclaimed Paul, staring at the T-shirt in question. "I did, and I've only worn it once myself."

"That's my boy," said Malcolm, a mischievous glint in his eye.

That evening Malcolm held court in the Roebuck, Steve and the others held onto every word as he regaled them with stories from his six months' stay in America. He would often get carried away; his arms gesticulating wildly and he would put on exaggerated American accents where he deemed them necessary.

"Let me tell you boys," he yelled, jabbing a finger into the air for emphasis. "The New York Dolls could have been massive!" He paused to take a sip from his glass then looked around the table at each young face before continuing.

"But it was the drugs that finished that band off!"

"Bad, was it?" asked Glen.

"Bad!" Malcolm gasped, shaking his head. "Bad is not the word. Old Thunders didn't know if it was New York or New Bloody Year and as for Jerry Nolan, he was even worse!" He picked his glass up from the table almost spilling its contents on Steve's leg.

"Stay away from drugs boys, nothing but trouble will come of it." Malcolm grew quiet; his mind seemed to drift off as if he was reminiscing about his time in America.

"So what happened?" asked Glen, bringing him back from his reverie.

"Ah, what did you say, boy? What was that?" asked Malcolm, looking in the direction from where the voice had come.

"What happened next?" asked Steve, butting in. He wanted Malcolm to get on with the story. He loved to hear Rock 'n' Roll stories, especially when they involved his heroes like Johnny Thunders.

"Where was I? Oh, yes, that's right," said Malcolm, smiling. "Well, I arranged a few concerts for them down in Florida – no drugs down there." He waved his hand in dismissal. "It's all 'Rednecks' and Disneyland but as soon as we arrived there things just went from bad to worse!"

"How?" asked Paul.

"Well, the band had written some new songs that I personally felt they should play at a slower pace than anything they'd done previously." Malcolm paused again to take another drink. "Of course, Thunders and Nolan didn't want to know. They just wanted to play every damn song as fast-as-the-last and twice as loud!" He paused yet again, to wipe his mouth with his handkerchief. "Johansen and Sylvain were always more open to ideas and willing to try a different approach. But we had more problems with Walter Kane. It was almost impossible to communicate with him as he was always pissed! Speaking of which!"

He hadn't failed to notice that his audience had long since finished their drinks and he reached into his pocket to produce more of the money he'd taken from the shop. "I'll have the same again boy." Malcolm pushed the money across the table towards Glen. Glen looked surprised at being given orders and thought about telling Malcolm that he didn't work for him anymore, but then again, free beer was free beer.

"Go on, Malcolm," said Steve, urging him to carry on. "What happened?"

"Like I was saying, we were in Florida staying at Jerry's mother's house down in Tampa," continued Malcolm, staring into space. "Thunders announced that he'd had enough by then, he couldn't function without his supply of heroin so, he and Jerry quit the group and headed back to New York." Glen arrived back at their table carrying the drinks on a tray. Nobody spoke while the empty glasses were removed and replaced with the full ones.

"What have I missed?" he asked them, while he handed Malcolm his change.

"Nothin'," said Steve, dismissing Glen. "Go on Malcolm, carry on."

"Thunders and Nolan had announced that they were quitting the group!" repeated Malcolm, for Glen's benefit.

"So, what did you do?" asked Wally, reaching for his drink.

"Well, as far as I was concerned we still had commitments to fulfil. Those American kids had paid good money to see the New York Dolls and I wasn't going to disappoint them!" Malcolm drained the remnants from his first drink. "We quickly hired a drummer and finished the tour. You must always finish what you start or you're the one who's finished." He eyed each of them to see if they were paying attention. "Anyway, with the tour finished, Johansen and Kane cleared off leaving me and Sylvain stranded in Florida with a battered Stationwagon, a few hundred dollars and not much else, so we thought we might as well try our luck in New Orleans."

"I'd fuckin' love to go there," said Paul.

"Yes," said Malcolm, nodding at Paul, "I'd always fancied the idea myself."

Everyone used the pause in the conversation to take a drink. Steve had been so engrossed in Malcolm's tale that he missed his mouth and spilt beer down his chin.

"You sloppy cunt!" said Paul, grinning.

"Fuck off!" yelled Steve, pulling his T-shirt from out of his trousers and wiping it across his face.

"That's my fuckin' shirt you're usin' there!" said Paul, shaking his head, "you can't take him anywhere twice."

"Well, you can," said Glen, smirking, "only the second time's to apologise."

"Okay, settle down," said Malcolm, smiling at Steve's antics. "Like I said, we had the idea to go down to New Orleans. That's in Louisiana." Malcolm pointed a finger in the air to emphasise this fact. Glen smiled to himself. You had to hand it to Malcolm. He loved to feel like he was teaching you something. Glen had always thought he'd picked the habit up from Vivienne, who had once been a schoolteacher.

"We wanted to see what would happen," said Malcolm, wagging his finger at them again. "Or see what we could make happen!" He paused to see if anyone had a question before continuing. "There was just one small problem."

"What was that?" asked Paul, who began tapping his fingers against an empty glass in time with the drum beat from Roxy Music's "Virginia Plain," which was blaring out from the pub's juke box.

"Well, boy," replied Malcolm, looking over at Paul, "neither Jerry nor myself could drive the damn car, well, not legally anyway."

"Umm," said Glen, nodding in agreement. He was learning to drive himself so he could empathise with Malcolm. "So, what did you do?"

"Luckily for us, we met two college girls who were hitch-hiking across America during their summer vacation and just happened to be on their way down to New Orleans," said Malcolm, smiling. "So we offered them the chance of a lift, just so long as they did the driving."

"Did you shag 'em?" asked Steve, leering at Malcolm.

"Now, now Stephen," said Malcolm, holding up his hands in mock protest.

"Decorum dictates a gentleman should keep certain things private."

"Bollocks," said Steve, shaking his head, "you must have shagged 'em."

"Yeah," said Wally, wiping his spectacles on his shirt. "Shag or walk bitch!" He jerked his thumb up and down in the hitchhiking manner, grinning at Steve.

"How?" exclaimed Malcolm, as if he was talking to a moron. "We needed the bitches, as you so eloquently put it, to drive the bloody car!"

"So, you shagged 'em when you got there, right?" said Steve, butting in. He was determined to find out if Malcolm had done anything with these two girls.

"Is... is that all you can think about?" Malcolm gasped, reaching for his drink. "Let me tell you something. There is nothing romantic about travelling all the way across America in a 'fucked-up' station wagon. It's all flies, dust and intolerable heat! The next time I go to America, I'll do all my travelling by plane."

Malcolm had excused himself while he went to the gents' toilets. The four lads sat around in silence, each lost in their own thoughts on what Malcolm had told them about managing a pop group. If his experiences with the New York Dolls were anything to go by he might not be in too much of a hurry to take on another group. Glen watched Malcolm as he made his way back to the table. He seemed oblivious to the stares he was getting from some of the punters at the bar; not everybody shared their passion for fashion.

"So, what was New Orleans like?" asked Glen, once Malcolm had sat down. He was hoping to change the subject on to music.

"Ah, yes," replied Malcolm, dreamily, "a beautiful place. I fell in love with the ambience and..."

"And one of them college bitches," said Wally, looning at Steve.

"For God's sake, grow up!" snapped Malcolm, angrily. "I've got better things to do than sit here with you lot, you know!"

"Yeah, shut up Wally!" said Glen, annoyed at having the conversation interrupted. "You were saying, Malcolm?"

"It's, oh I don't know," said Malcolm, seemingly lost for words adequate enough to describe how he'd felt when he'd first wandered the streets of New Orleans. "It has a certain *je ne sais quoi*. We went cruising through the French Quarter of the city. That's where Elvis made *King Creole* you know, absolutely magnificent."

"I read somewhere, that there are loads of 'Blues' musicians playing for small change right there on the street," said Glen, "an' they're supposed to be 'shit-hot' as well."

"Yes you're right there, Glen," said Malcolm, shaking his head slowly. "It's a sad sight really, because those guys can play like the Devil!"

"What, as good as Jeff Beck?" asked Wally, as if this bordered on the sacrilegious.

"They probably make Jeff Beck sound like you!" said Paul, laughing while he gave Wally a dig in the ribs.

"They get by playing to the tourists," said Malcolm, staring into space. "It just goes to show that so-called musical ability counts for nothing. It's the attitude that counts and a good image naturally." He stood up and straightened the crease of his trousers. "You boys want another?"

"Does a fish piss in the sea?" said Steve, grinning. "We'll pay you back when we're rich and famous."

"I may just hold you to that," said Malcolm, placing some money on the table.

"Who's goin' to the bar?" asked Glen, leaning back on his stool. "I ain't going. I went last time." He slid the money across the table in front of Wally.

"Why me?" moaned Wally, sulking.

"For fuck's sake, you're a real 'whine' merchant," said Paul, giggling at his own joke. Wally pulled a face but he scooped up the money and trudged off to the bar. "He really gets on my tits sometimes." He and the others looked over at Wally as he stood at the bar waiting to be served.

"Nah, he's all right," said Steve, a wistful smile on his face.

They continued chatting about Malcolm's time in America and the music scene in general but Malcolm didn't mention the exciting new groups that were playing in New York at Max's Kansas City and CBGB's.

"Has that cunt not been served yet?" said Steve, glancing towards the bar.

"No!" replied Glen, looking over at the forlorn figure of Wally, who was still trying to get served. He must have sensed that they were talking about him because he turned round to look at his friends and offered them a shrug as if to say he didn't know why it was taking so long.

"Come on, boy!" yelled Malcolm, beginning to lose patience. "Get a move on!"

"Yeah, come on!" shouted Steve. "I'm as dry as a nun's cunt!"

"How very eloquently put, Stephen," said Malcolm, shaking his head. "What a lovely analogy."

"Thanks," replied Steve, beaming with pride.

"Hurrah! At last!" said Paul, offering mock applause for Wally as he returned with the round of drinks.

"Weren't my fault," muttered Wally, placing the drinks on the table. "That bitch is useless!" He jerked his thumb over his shoulder towards the barmaid in question.

Malcolm was about to ask Wally about his change when he saw Paul nudging Steve while muttering something that he didn't quite catch, but he could tell it was something to do with him because they both stopped when he looked at them.

"Go on Steve," he said, slowly, "spit it out boy."

"Are you still interested in being our manager?"

"Well, like I said earlier, Steve," Malcolm looked round the table at the four anxious faces waiting with bated breath for his reply, "I'll come down and see for myself. When does this group of yours rehearse?"

"Every night," said Glen, throwing down the beer mat that he'd been toying with. "Even if it's just for half an hour!"

"Well. All right then," said Malcolm, stroking his chin. "What about next

Wednesday evening?"

"No problem," said Paul. "We're usually down there from about seven o'clock."

"Good," said Malcolm, nodding thoughtfully. "I'll be there about eightish. That should give you boys a chance to warm up."

"Fuckin' great!" said Steve, clearly more relaxed now that Malcolm had agreed to a definite meeting.

"You are going to tell me where I have to be for this pleasurable experience," said Malcolm, after a couple of minute's silence.

"Oh, yeah," said Glen, grinning, "sorry."

Malcolm sat listening to them talking excitedly about which songs they were going to play for him. He smiled when one of them looked in his direction but other than that he'd mentally switched off. He really should be going back to the flat to see Vivienne and the boys. He wasn't interested in the slightest which songs they were going to play. If what he had witnessed in New York was anything to go by, then it was attitude that counted and Steve had plenty of that. As for the image, well that should be easy enough; he would supply the clothes at a reduced price, which would also be free publicity for the shop. He could leave the mundane day-to-day running of Steve's group to Bernie, leaving himself to collect the money. There was no reason to tell them his plans at this stage. There would have to be changes but he would tread carefully until the time was right. He knew from past experience that timing was everything.

CHAPTER
THREE

Glen arrived at their rehearsal place at the old BBC studios on Crisp Road on Wednesday evening at just after seven-thirty. He'd had to fare-dodge on the tube again. He'd swapped trains twice and then doubled back on himself to avoid capture when an inspector had boarded the train he was on. Still, he mused as he made his way along the corridor, it added to the adventure. He called out a greeting as he opened the door to the room where they had their gear set up. He could see the others gathered in the makeshift bar. Because Paul worked at Watneys Brewery, he had "borrowed" a few barrels of ale plus all the gear necessary to set up a small bar complete with pumps. Steve, Paul and Wally were sitting on top of spare amplifiers, each of them with a drink of Watneys Red in their hand.

"Evenin' all," he said, in his best Jack Warner's *Dixon of Dock Green* voice, "What's goin' on here, then?"

"All right, Glen," said Steve, failing to be impressed with Glen's threat to Mike Yarwood's career. "I see you got my message, then." Steve wanted everything to be perfect for when Malcolm turned up because they might not get another chance. He had told the others to wear their best "street gear" to look the part and all four members of the group were wearing items from Malcolm's shop.

"Have we decided which song we're going to play first?" asked Glen, removing his jacket and tossing it onto a nearby table. "We don't want him to scarper before we start, do we!"

"We should definitely do 'Scarface', said Wally, picking up his guitar and slipping the strap over his head.

"Just because it's your song!" snapped Steve, glaring at Wally. Christ, he really is a geek, he thought to himself. Even wearing the best gear he still looked awful. Steve knew that Paul was getting fed-up with the group. If he jacked it in, that would leave him with Glen the mummy's boy and Wally the...wally! It really didn't bear thinking about.

"No," said Wally, defiantly. "I just think we should play one of our own songs for Malcolm, that's all."

"It's our only fuckin' song, innit," said Paul, laughing from behind his drum kit.

"We could jam some stuff for him," said Glen, running his fingers up and down the fretboard of his bass guitar. "You know, twelve-bar-blues stuff. Malcolm loves that shit."

"Whatever," said Steve, fiddling with his microphone. "Let's just get fuckin' started!"

▱ ▱ ▱ ▱

Malcolm arrived at the studios in Hammersmith by taxi; he paid the driver and surveyed the outside of the building while the driver sorted out his change. Steve and the boys had done well to land themselves such splendid rehearsal facilities but if things worked out the way he planned he didn't think they'd be there much longer. He went through the front doors and stumbled his way along the corridor towards the room that Glen had told him they would be in. He'd declined the offer of a diagram, as he was sure he'd find them easily enough by following the racket they were sure to be making, though he hadn't said that out loud.

Malcolm arrived at the door, which was slightly ajar, allowing just enough light to filter through for him to find his footing. He waited just on the other side of the door and listened to them playing while they were still unaware of his presence.

He winced at Steve's voice as he struggled to hit the right notes to the song they were playing. Malcolm shook his head in dismay. It was pitiful. Steve calling himself a singer was surely breaching the Trades Descriptions Act. He waited for a lull in the proceedings then called out to announce his arrival. He could hear Steve saying something and then the sound of footsteps approaching as he opened the door.

"What do you think?" Steve asked, as he ushered Malcolm into the room.

"Where on earth did you get all this?" Malcolm gasped, as his unbelieving eyes took in the Aladdin's Cave full of expensive-looking equipment. There was enough gear here to stage the Isle of Wight Festival. He was, momentarily, lost for words. Then he caught the sparkle in Steve's eye and he knew where it had come from. It was stolen! "This is your doing, isn't it?"

"Well we can't fuckin' afford to pay for it!" said Steve, by way of explanation. "So, we nick it!"

Malcolm's face broke into a malicious grin. This was pure mischief. He could see it all now. He felt like the character Fagin from Charles Dickens' novel *Oliver Twist* and Steve was his Artful Dodger. "Where did it come from?" he asked, running his hand across the controls of an amplifier. "You've got an entire P.A. system here, boy! There's thousands and thousands of pounds worth of equipment!"

"Oh, we borrowed that off David Bowie, didn't we Steve," said Wally, grinning.

"Yeah," said Steve, casually, "must be a couple of years ago now."

"Do you want a beer, Malcolm?" Paul asked him from their homemade bar.

"What?" asked Malcolm, still in shock at what he was seeing. He thought he'd heard Paul wrong but almost choked when he saw the bar. "What do you mean, you borrowed it?"

"When Bowie was doin' his farewell tour for Ziggy Stardust at the Hammersmith Odeon a couple of years back, Wally and me sneaked in through the back door and waited 'til all the roadies and that had fucked off. Then we helped ourselves," said Steve, matter-of-factly.

"But how on earth did you get it all out of there?" asked Malcolm, as he waved his arms around pointing at various pieces of equipment.

"Steve nicked a mini-van the day before," said Wally, grinning at Steve.

"We've even got Neumann Microphones," said Glen, holding up one of the said microphones, "and they cost a packet!"

"Bloody amazing!" said Malcolm, sitting himself down on one of the spare amplifiers and taking a sip from the drink Paul had given him.

Malcolm sat listening as the boys played various cover versions of songs like "It's All Over Now" by the Rolling Stones and "Build Me Up Buttercup". He thought that the song was originally performed by The Foundations but he wasn't really sure.

"This one's called 'Scarface'," snarled Steve, in an attempt to make the song's title more menacing.

"It's one of ours," added Wally, grinning proudly.

"Now there was a boy with a real clean face, plenty of birds all over the place," yelled Steve, into his microphone. To Malcolm's mind, there was nothing special about the tune and as for the lyrics, well, the less said the better, but there was the street element that Malcolm had been looking for.

"What do you think?" Steve shouted over when they had finished playing the song.

"Not bad," replied Malcolm, noncommittally.

"We've got another one," said Wally, hopefully. "It's not quite finished yet though."

"Really," replied Malcolm, shifting in his seat.

"Yeah, it's called 'Did You No Wrong'," said Wally, as he began playing the opening chords of the song.

Malcolm sat listening while he drank his second beer. It was all very Small Faces he thought, but he supposed every group should have some sort of reference point. He glanced at his watch again then waved his arm up and down signalling for them to stop playing before tapping his watch to indicate he would have to leave soon. "Steve, could I have a quick word before I go?" he said, placing his unfinished drink on the floor.

Steve replaced his microphone in its cradle and walked over to join Malcolm while the others put down their instruments and went towards the bar area. Wally had propped his guitar against his amplifier without switching the amplifier off and it started droning with feedback. Malcolm clasped his hands over his ears grimacing with pain as the droning got louder and louder.

"Turn that fucker off!" Steve yelled over to the others. He was pretty sure that Malcolm hadn't been too impressed by their performance. He'd been watching the shop owner for any encouraging signs but the only impression he got was that Malcolm had been bored shitless.

"Could you come by the shop tomorrow?" asked Malcolm, once he'd removed his hands from his ears. "I'd like a word with you."

"Sure," replied Steve, nodding. "What time?"

"Oh, anytime after lunch will be fine," said Malcolm, pulling on his jacket.

"Right, I'll be there," said Steve, opening the door for Malcolm.

"You get back to the others, I'll see myself out," said Malcolm, smiling as he watched Glen and the others refilling their glasses. "Oh, and make sure you come alone tomorrow." He nodded his head towards the bar. "There are things we need to discuss."

With that, Malcolm turned away and walked down the corridor leaving Steve feeling slightly confused as he went to get himself a drink.

Steve arrived at SEX at around two o' clock the following afternoon for the arranged meeting with Malcolm. He'd spent the night at Paul's house in Mrs Cook's spare room and this had proved very convenient because there was a bus service, which took him all the way to the shop. When he entered the shop Jordon greeted him. She was alone, idly flicking through the pages of a lingerie magazine. Weekday afternoons were always quiet, the punters would be in there at lunch times and then things would get busy again towards the end of the day when people called in after work.

"Has Malcolm been in yet?" Steve asked her, glancing over her shoulder at the magazine. "Look at the corrie on that!"

"No, he hasn't," replied Jordon, shaking her head at Steve's comment, but she was smiling as well. "Vivienne has though and she was in a real strop over something or other." She closed the magazine and replaced it under the counter. "I think they've been arguing again."

"Who?" asked Steve, holding up a suede boot to examine the heel. "Her an' Malcolm?"

"Yeah," replied Jordon. "I can always tell when they've been at it."

"Ughh!" said Steve, pulling a face.

"I didn't mean like that," Jordon said, laughing.

"Do you reckon they do It, though?" asked Steve, looking thoughtfully at Jordon.

"Fuckin' hell, Steve, leave it out!" said Jordon, wincing, "I've just had my lunch! Still, I suppose they must have. At least once anyway."

"Yeah," agreed Steve, nodding. "Young Joe must have come from somewhere."

He placed the suede boot back on the shelf before wandering over towards the clothes rails. It was mostly leather and rubber gear but some of the T-shirts were great. He occasionally pulled something from the rail to have a closer look at, but at the prices Malcolm charged, looking was as close as Steve got to the clothes, unless he nicked them.

"What the fuck is this?" he asked, holding up what looked like a deflated rubber ball with eye sockets and a plastic cap-seal like the beach balls the kiddies might play with on the sands at Margate.

"Oh, that," said Jordon, walking over towards Steve. "It's a rubber mask that you put over your head and then you inflate it with a bicycle pump through here." She indicated the plastic seal with her finger.

"You're fuckin' havin' a laugh, right?" said Steve.

"No, honest!" replied Jordon, taking the mask off Steve. "You'd be amazed at who buys this sort of thing. There's this one bloke..." She was distracted when the front door opened; it was Malcolm, carrying what looked to Steve like a flight case for a guitar. Malcolm ignored them both, seemingly preoccupied with something. He paused by the counter and bent down as if searching for a particular item.

"Have you seen the shit under here, Jords!" Malcolm got back to his feet holding up a shower attachment. "What on earth is this thing doing under here?" He examined the object in his hand for a few moments then shaking his head he tossed it back under the counter. He muttered to himself for a moment then looked towards Steve, as if finally noticing that he was in the room. "Ahh Steve, my boy, glad you're here." He motioned for Steve to come and join him as he sat down on one of the chairs near the window.

Steve was still eyeing the flight case that was lying on the floor as he sat down beside Malcolm. It couldn't be a guitar, could it? Maybe the case was for carrying a machine gun just like Al Capone and all them other gangsters used in the films he'd watched on the telly when he was a nipper. Then again, it would have to be an extremely big machine gun. Jordon had retaken her seat near the counter and resumed reading the lingerie magazine.

"This," said Malcolm, bending down to release the chrome coloured clasps positioned round the case's lid, "belonged to Sylvain Sylvain from the New York Dolls." He lifted the lid to reveal a Gibson Les Paul guitar; the guitar was an off-white colour with a black trim.

"It's fuckin' beautiful," said Steve, admiringly. He watched Malcolm gently lift the guitar from its cushioned compartment and hand it to him. Steve looked at the guitar then at Malcolm. He wasn't too sure what was happening. Malcolm must want him to shift it for him; he surely couldn't be giving it to him. Malcolm wouldn't give you the fucking time never mind a Gibson Les Paul guitar.

"You want me to sell it for you?" asked Steve, glancing down to the guitar. He dragged his thumb against the six strings listening to the sound of each one as he plucked them. "I might know someone down Camden who'll take it off us."

"I don't want you to sell it, boy!" said Malcolm, shaking his head.

"What then?"

"I want you to take it away and learn to play the damn thing!" said Malcolm, stabbing a finger at the guitar.

"Me!" said Steve, frowning, "but I'm the singer, remember?" He turned the guitar over in his hands. "Wally'll show me, I s'pose."

"Ahh," said Malcolm, pursing his lips, "that's what I wanted to talk to you about."

"What do you mean?" asked Steve, looking Malcolm in the eye.

"He's not right for the group!" said Malcolm. "You only have to look at the guy to see that."

"But he can play all right!" protested Steve. "an' he's my mate!"

"A tough decision, I know," replied Malcolm, pausing to allow Steve the chance to say something else. Steve had looked away from Malcolm and was toying with the pictures of two cowgirls Sylvain, or somebody else, had stuck onto the body of the guitar. One of the smiling cowgirls was playing a small acoustic guitar while the other was seated on a shiny black vinyl disc. When Steve didn't reply Malcolm continued. "Look, Stephen, what I'm saying here is, I am prepared to help you with this group of yours but not until you get rid of Wally." Malcolm could tell that Steve was running the idea through his head and decided to quit while he was ahead. "Talk to Paul and Glen and see what they have to say about it." Malcolm stood up and waited for Steve to look at him. "Let me know what you decide."

"All right, I'll talk to 'em," Steve mumbled, picking at the edge of one of the cowgirls with his thumbnail.

"Look Steve, I really don't see you as a singer." He raised his hands to cut off Steve's protests. "Let me finish!" He walked off a few feet towards the middle of the shop before continuing. "In my opinion, you don't look comfortable in front of a microphone like say, Marty Wilde or Billy Fury. You're not doing anything to capture anyone's attention." He pointed to the guitar lying in Steve's lap. "You could use that as a prop or...maybe even look for a new singer."

Steve nodded thoughtfully then replaced the guitar back inside the flight case before standing up. Malcolm stooped down and picked the flight case up by the handle and handed it to Steve. He placed his hand on Steve's arm and gently guided him towards the shop door.

"I expect, I'll be hearing from you soon," said Malcolm, smiling as he closed the door on Steve.

Steve walked off down the King's Road, a whole multitude of scenarios running through his mind. What if he couldn't play the guitar? Would the others then decide to keep Wally and chuck him out? How long did it take to learn to play the guitar anyway? Steve shook his head in dismissal. He was pretty sure what Malcolm had in mind but would speak to Paul when he got home from the brewery. He ended up down by the Victoria Embankment wandering along aimlessly. He stopped to light a cigarette, cupping his hand to protect the flame from his match against the wind blowing up from the river, then leaned on the wall to watch a large dredger as it made its way up the Thames.

He arrived at Paul's house about five-thirty and rang the doorbell. Paul's younger sister Margaret showed him through to the kitchen where Paul was sitting at the table having a cup of tea, his empty dinner plate still in front of him. Paul's Mum handed Steve a cup of tea and a jam sandwich before Paul escorted him up to his bedroom.

"Are you fuckin' mad!" said Paul, once he'd closed the bedroom door, "bringing that here!" He jerked his finger at the guitar case now lying on his bed.

"What're you goin' on about?" asked Steve, before taking a large bite from the sandwich.

"That's what I'm goin' on about!" yelled Paul. "Where did you nick it?"

"I didn't fuckin' nick it!" said Steve, defiantly. "Malcolm gave it to me today."

"Sure he did, now pull the other one," replied Paul, shaking his head.

"Fuckin' ask him if you don't believe me!" snapped Steve, turning away from Paul and looking out of the window. Paul looked at Steve for a few moments realising his friend was telling the truth and felt a twinge of guilt for having assumed Steve had stolen the guitar. But having known Steve since childhood he couldn't really help jumping to conclusions. He already had a criminal record for petty theft and stealing cars. He'd even served a custodial sentence at Ashford Remand Centre.

"So, why has Malcolm given you a guitar?" he asked, sitting down on his bed beside the flight case. He listened quietly while Steve told him everything about his meeting with Malcolm at the shop.

"So what do you think?" Steve asked his friend.

"Fuck's sake, I don't know!" exclaimed Paul, shaking his head. He looked from Steve down to the flight case. "Wally can play the guitar like, an' you can't."

"I know," said Steve, sullenly. "Malcolm said that I should switch to playing guitar and look for another singer."

Paul sat quietly for a few moments absent-mindedly drumming his fingers on the flight case. "You gonna show me this guitar then or what?" he said at last, his face breaking out into a grin. Steve grinned back as he snapped the clasps and lifted the lid.

"Malcolm said it belonged to Sylvain Sylvain from the Dolls, an' anyway, it can't be that fuckin' hard learnin' to play guitar if Wally can do it."

Steve and Paul met up with Glen in order to discuss what Malcolm had proposed to Steve. They met at their rehearsal room in Hammersmith after Glen had rung Wally to inform him that there wouldn't be any rehearsal that evening because Paul had to work late at the brewery. They had had a scare when Wally asked if Glen still wanted to meet up and practise, but Glen's quick thinking saved the day when he announced he would be spending the evening working on a project from college. Once the three of them were settled around a table with a drink in front of them, Steve told Glen all about his meeting with Malcolm.

As Paul was already aware of Malcolm's intentions he decided to use his time productively by giving his drum kit a good cleaning as he couldn't remember the last time, if at all, that he had last done so. Paul would glance over occasionally to try and gauge Glen's reactions. To be honest, he really didn't give a flying fuck if Wally stayed in the group or was given his marching orders, as he didn't see much of a future for the group anyway. And being a "sparky" for a brewery wasn't too bad a way to earn a living.

Glen sat listening to what Steve had to say without interrupting him. He wasn't all that surprised by what Malcolm was planning, after all, he'd worked for the guy for long enough. He was surprised, however, to find he was being asked for his opinion as he'd always thought that he would be the one getting slung out.

"Who does Malcolm have in mind for a singer?" asked Glen, once Steve had finished.

"Fuck knows," replied Steve, shrugging his shoulders. "Malcolm knows loads o' people, doesn't he! He might get someone from America, I dunno."

"No, you don't and neither do I," said Glen, seriously. "That's the point! We haven't got a clue what Malcolm's up to. We've been together, what…two years? And just when things are starting to gel, this happens!" He looked over at Paul who was busy wiping a cymbal with the rag he'd brought from home. He could tell by the way that Paul was keeping quiet that the decision had already been made. "I'll feel like some sort of traitor though," he said, at last.

"Don't know why," said Paul, pausing from his cleaning. "It's not that long ago Wally was saying we should get rid of you!"

"What!" Glen gasped. "Well fuck him!"

"Right," said Steve, looking relieved, "so we're agreed then." He stood up and reached into his pocket for a cigarette. "Don't say nothin' yet. I've got to learn to play this fuckin' thing first!" He pointed to the Gibson lying in its case with the lid open. "Can you show me anythin'?"

"Yeah," replied Glen, reaching over and lifting the guitar out of the case. "Heavy things, these Gibsons." Glen played a familiar bass riff on the guitar. "I know a few guitar chords and I can show you the basics."

"Sorted," said Steve, nodding.

"I'll write out the notes for each string, if you like," said Glen, handing the guitar back to Steve.

"Whatever," replied Steve, "but I don't want nothin' flash."

During the next few weeks the group carried on rehearsing as normal and still spent time together but it was becoming more and more difficult for Steve, Paul and Glen to act as if nothing was wrong. They were all feeling guilty about Wally, especially when Wally would talk about his ideas for the group's image and songs. The situation was beginning to get out of control. Malcolm had told Vivienne of his plans to get involved with Steve and his group. She in turn had told Bernie Rhodes, who was now asking anyone that came into the shop if they knew anyone who might be interested in singing with the group. If Wally had any idea what was being planned he didn't show it. He turned up early for every rehearsal and didn't seem to notice that Steve spent the entire evening watching where he placed his fingers on his guitar during the songs.

Steve was busy practising every day with help from Glen and even Paul had to admit he was improving rapidly. The main problem was thinking of different excuses to tell Wally why Malcolm hadn't come to a decision on becoming their manager. Malcolm hadn't been in contact with them since the initial meeting with Steve and wouldn't be doing so until Wally had been sacked although he had expressed his interest in disposing of some of the group's masses of equipment on his and Bernie's business trips.

Glen didn't care what went on just as long as he wasn't involved because sometime the year before he had been duped into trying to sell a Fender bass guitar that Steve had stolen from a shop in Shaftsbury Avenue to impress a current girlfriend. Glen had been totally unaware of the guitar's history and had unwittingly taken it to another hock shop, which was situated close to St. Martin's College on Charing Cross Road. The shop's owner, having grown suspicious as to the instrument's true ownership, had called the police and Glen could still remember the looks on the faces of his fellow students as he'd been led away in handcuffs and placed in the panda car by the arresting officer. Glen had been very fortunate and received nothing more than a caution. A grinning Steve had later told Glen that he had done it to test Glen's bottle.

Malcolm hadn't been ignoring Steve and the others intentionally. He'd made his offer and until Steve got back to him the matter was closed. Malcolm's preoccupations were more to do with the fact that the shop was doing really well. He'd noticed the steady stream of kids that were coming into his shop to buy the T-shirts that he and Vivienne had made. Their latest design featured a print of the hood worn by the Cambridge Rapist; this was the name given by the press to the man who had been terrorising the university town. Underneath the picture of the hood, they had written the title to the Beatles' song "A Hard Day's Night" – a reference to the Fab Four's manager, Brian Epstein, who had died in 1967 as a result, it was alleged, of sadomasochistic sexual practices. Another favourite design of Malcolm's was a T-shirt depicting two cowboy dudes dressed in full Hollywood cowboy regalia of stetsons, neckerchiefs, waistcoats, gun belts and cowboy boots. The two cowboys were, however, minus their trousers. Their exaggerated flaccid penises were almost touching each other.

Vivienne was becoming worried that selling clothes with such an explicit sexual content would land the shop in trouble with the Authorities. It was one thing to sell leather and rubber fetish gear, which could be obtained in any red-light district in any city around the world, but selling obscene T-shirts was another matter entirely. She began to create designs of a more political nature in the hope of steering Malcolm away from his obsession with sex, which strangely seemed at odds with everything that they were trying to do with the shop. Bernie sided with Vivienne but still carried on screen-printing Malcolm's T-shirts for him.

On 20 July, Steve, Glen and Wally helped Paul celebrate his nineteenth birthday in a public house close to their rehearsal place. As luck would have it Wally announced that he would have to leave early and nobody raised any objections. Once he'd left the pub, Steve, Paul and Glen remained behind to decide the best way of telling Wally that he was surplus to requirements. Steve was dying to try out his blossoming guitar skills in their rehearsal place with all the right equipment and the backing of Glen and Paul. Although the two still had reservations about Steve's competency on the guitar they wanted to get the matter resolved as soon as possible and if Steve couldn't cut it then they could always rely on Malcolm to find them somebody else. At rehearsals the following evening Steve brought along his Gibson guitar and calmly set about tuning the instrument. Glen watched in silence for a few moments, wondering what was happening.

"Hang on a minute!" he said, looking from Steve to Paul. "You'd better get that out of sight before he gets here!"

"I thought we were tellin' him," said Steve, scowling at Glen.

"I know, I know, but who said anything about tellin' him tonight?"

"Me an' Paul decided on the way 'ere," said Steve, matter-of-factly.

"OK," nodded Glen, "which one of you is gonna do the honours?"

"Uhh, we think it's best if you tell him," replied Steve, glancing towards Paul.

"Why me!" Glen gasped, "he's your mate. You've known him longer than I have."

"We know," said Paul, sheepishly. "That's why it's best if it comes from you."

Glen was about to protest but before he could continue he heard Wally coming through the door behind him. Steve and Paul both looked away, pretending to be occupied with something.

"All right," said Wally, brushing past Glen and heading towards his amplifier. He nodded at Paul, who was sitting behind his drums, then noticed the Gibson resting on a stand next to Steve. "Wow, a fuckin' Les Paul. Who've we nicked it off?" He crouched down in front of the guitar, gently stroking the strings.

"We haven't nicked it," said Steve, avoiding eye contact with Wally. "Malcolm gave it me."

"But you don't play guitar!" said Wally, frowning. He looked at Paul and Glen, a smile frozen on his face, waiting for someone to let him in on the joke. The looks on his friends' faces told him that something was wrong. "What's goin' on?" he asked, sitting down on his amplifier. Glen was the first to react; he placed his bass guitar on its stand and turned to face Wally.

"There's no easy way to say this, Wally but...you're out of the group."

"What!" Wally gasped, pushing his glasses further up his nose. "You're kiddin', right?"

"It'll probably be me next week," said Glen, trying to make light of the situation, but Wally didn't seem to be listening to him.

"It's nothin' personal," said Steve, finally looking at Wally. "Malcolm thinks..."

"Oh right, now I get it," said Wally, standing up. "That's why he hasn't been around here! He'll be your manager just so long as you get shut of me!" He walked past Steve without looking at him, picked up his guitar case and headed towards the door. His eyes were beginning to fill up and he didn't want them to see him cry.

He was still standing outside watching the traffic making its way along Crisp Road when Steve and Paul came out to see him. "I'll get my Dad to give me a lift moving my stuff out." He especially made sure that they heard his emphasis on the word "Dad" because if he wasn't in the group, then they weren't going to be practising there either.

"No rush," said Steve. "Why don't you come for a drink with us. We're still mates right?"

"All right," whispered Wally, brushing his hands against his eyes when the other two had stepped back inside the studios to tell Glen and to put away the guitars.

They called in at the same pub that they had frequented the previous evening for Paul's birthday. Steve was buying the ale seeing as he was flush with cash from Malcolm having sold some of the surplus musical equipment on one of his business trips. Once Steve had bought the drinks they sat down at a table near to the jukebox although none of them bothered to put any records on. Paul and Glen vainly tried to keep the conversation going, but it was clearly not working. Steve was staring into space, absentmindedly tearing small strips from a beer mat and Wally sat silently staring at the floor, his mind obviously elsewhere. He was picturing the scene when he told his Mum and Dad that he'd been sacked from the group that had been his idea to form in the first place. What were they going to say? What could they say! The only friends he had were sitting here at this table and they were the ones who were sacking him. The group had been the only good thing in his life. Hell, it was his life! He'd never had any luck with the girls, but thought he'd stood more of a chance by being in a group. He glanced up at Steve, who was still purposely avoiding having to look at him and felt his eyes starting to well up again. He grabbed up his guitar case and rushed out of the pub without bothering to look back at his so-called mates. He stood looking at the pavement for a few moments, not knowing what the fuck he was doing or where he was going, then trudged up Crisp Road in search of a taxi.

◻ ◻ ◻ ◻

"Phew!" said Steve, looking greatly relieved. "Thank fuck that's over."

"Yeah," said Paul, nodding his agreement, "he'll be all right. He's good enough to join another group."

"Maybe," said Glen, staring at the stool vacated by Wally.

"Pass me his pint," said Steve, nodding towards the untouched pint on the table. He picked it up and filled his own glass then passed it to Paul.

"When are you going to give Malcolm the good news?" asked Glen, accepting

Wally's drink from Paul and emptying the remnants into his own glass.

"I'll ring him tomorrow," said Steve, his freshly filled drink poised in front of his mouth. "Now we've done what he wanted he'd better come up with somethin' fuckin' good!"

Malcolm was as good as his word and didn't waste any time bringing in a replacement for Wally. Nick Kent was a journalist working with the weekly music paper the *New Musical Express*, more commonly referred to by its readers as the *NME*. Kent was also a regular visitor to 430 King's Road through his relationship with an American girl called Chrissie Hynde, who had been working for Malcolm and Vivienne on and off for a few months. Malcolm knew Kent played the guitar, having been taught by Hynde. She had played in a number of groups herself and had only recently returned from a sojourn in Paris where she had been playing in a group.

Kent readily agreed to meet Steve and the others and although he considered his guitar playing to be rudimentary at best, he felt himself to be competent enough to play with the group. Rehearsals had been pretty sporadic since losing the BBC Studios which Malcolm knew would be the price for Wally's departure, but he had also realised the possibilities open to him with a respected music journalist in the camp.

Kent had been playing with the group for about a month when he called in unexpectedly at the shop to see Malcolm.

"Nick, my boy," he said, smiling at the journalist, "come in. How are things?"

"Good," replied Kent, returning Malcolm's smile.

"I don't know where Steve and the boys are, I'm afraid," said Malcolm, gesturing around the empty shop with his hands.

"That's why I've come to see you, Malcolm," replied Kent.

"Really!" said Malcolm, feigning concern. He set aside a swatch of materials he'd been examining and motioned for Kent to take a seat near the window.

"I think it's time we got something sorted out," said Kent.

"And how can I help?" asked Malcolm. The smile was still fixed on his face but he'd been expecting something like this as Steve and the others had expressed the problems they'd been having with Kent trying to take control of the group. To Malcolm's mind Kent would have been a useful connection to the musical papers, nothing more, and certainly not a permanent member of the group.

"There's nothing happening, Malcolm!" said Kent, sitting there dressed like his hero, the Rolling Stones' guitarist, Keith Richards. "They're happy jamming the same old shit they've been doing since they started. I think it's time someone took control and gave it some direction."

"You mean yourself, don't you, Nick?" said Malcolm, eyeing the journalist sitting before him. He stood up and pulled back the drapes with his hand to check on the weather. "What did you have in mind, Nick?"

"Well," replied Kent, "Chrissie reckons..."

"Sorry, Nick, who did you say?" asked Malcolm, frowning.

"Chrissie, Chrissie Hynde, my girlfriend," replied Kent, scratching the side of his face. "Chrissie reckons she could help out with..."

"Oh you mean the American girl who works here, occasionally?" said Malcolm, nodding. "What's she got to do with anything?"

"Well, she's had lots of experience playing in groups," said Kent, nervously shifting position. "I think she could be a great help."

"Leave it with me, Nick," said Malcolm, standing up again, indicating that the discussion was over. "I'll sort it out."

Kent stood up looking pleased with himself. He was about to leave when he turned back to Malcolm.

"Did you want something else, Nick?"

"I was wondering," said Kent, approaching Malcolm, "do you have those in a size eight?" He pointed towards an elegant ankle boot made from black Italian suede.

"Oh, yes, I'm sure we have," said Malcolm, beaming. "A lovely choice, Nick."

Steve, Paul and Glen were gathered in the shop listening to Malcolm as he told them about the surprise visit from Nick Kent and the journalist's plans for the group. He was only half way through his story when Steve leapt up from his chair.

"Bollocks!" yelled Steve, angrily, "That cunt's not even in the fuckin' group as far as I'm concerned. He's too old. Tell him to fuck off!" He looked at Paul and Glen who both nodded their agreement with Steve's sentiments. "I'd rather have fuckin' Wally back before that cunt!"

"Steady on," said Paul, grinning at Steve.

"I never thought of him being a permanent member of your group, Stephen," said Malcolm, placating Steve. "Kent could have been useful to us, that's all."

"I know where he lives," said Glen, looking at Malcolm. He had recently passed his driving test and didn't need much of an excuse to get behind the wheel of his Dad's car. "I could go round there an' tell him not to bother coming back."

"Very well, as long as we're all agreed," said Malcolm, crossing his legs and resting his hands on his knees. "I'll see what I can do about finding a suitable replacement."

"Steve can play as good as Kent anyway," said Glen, casually.

"Fuckin' better," said Steve, leaping up and windmilling his arm in an imitation of Pete Townshend, the guitarist from The Who.

"Yeah, fuckin' miles better," said Paul, laughing at Steve.

Malcolm sat looking totally bemused by their antics. He glanced towards Glen seeking confirmation of Steve's boast and seemed satisfied with Glen's nod of the head.

"See," said Steve, grinning, "there's fuck all to it!"

Malcolm's attentions to the group were temporarily side-lined when Alan Jones, one of his assistants from the shop, was arrested in Piccadilly Circus for wearing one of Malcolm's cowboy T-shirts. There was no need for Jones to tell the arresting police officer where he'd purchased the offending T-shirt as Malcolm and Vivienne had the name and address of their shop on the labels sewn into each item of clothing they sold. Malcolm was beside himself with anger as he paced up and down inside the shop, arms gesticulating wildly while ranting about his democratic rights and how England was still stuck in the nineteenth century. He was also doing his best to avoid Vivienne's "I told you so" look.

"Don't you worry, Alan my boy!" said Malcolm, walking over towards Jones. "We'll get you a good lawyer. One who really knows his stuff!"

"Thanks, Malcolm," said Jones, smiling weakly.

"They can't do this sort of thing and get away with it. It's...it's victimisation, that's what this is. Bloody victimisation!"

To make matters worse for Malcolm and Vivienne, the arrest of Alan Jones made the front page of the 2 August edition of *The Guardian* newspaper in connection with a television documentary called *Johnny Go Home*, focusing on teenage boys living as prostitutes in London. Malcolm failed to deliver the legal backing he'd promised Jones and in court Jones pleaded guilty and was fined thirty pounds, which the unfortunate youth had to pay out of his own pocket. A few days later, the police paid a visit to 430 King's Road, seizing various items of clothing, including all of the offending cowboy T-shirts, and on 7 August, Malcolm and Vivienne were themselves arrested and charged with "exposing to public view an indecent exhibition".

Malcolm, having decided that any publicity is good publicity, was now revelling in all the attention the shop was receiving. Both he and Vivienne had noticed an increase in clientele and therefore an increase in sales, and, once more, he was free to turn his full attention to Steve's group. Everyone was told to keep an eye out for anyone deemed interesting enough to be approached for an audition as the group's new singer. And after several meetings between Malcolm, Bernie Rhodes and the three members of the group, a name for the group was decided upon. Malcolm had shortened the name which had appeared on his "You're gonna wake up" T-shirt by removing the Kutie Jones from the title. From now on, the group would be known as the Sex Pistols.

CHAPTER FOUR

It was a glorious sunny Saturday afternoon; Malcolm was strolling along the King's Road heading towards the shop. He stood at the kerb, waiting for a Ford Cortina to turn down into Langton Street.

"Jesus!" he exclaimed, quickly raising his hand to shield his eyes from the glare of the sun that was reflecting off the car's windscreen and almost blinding him. As it was a Saturday, the King's Road was its usual bustling self and Malcolm smiled to himself at the prospect of another good day's trading. As far as he was concerned, it didn't matter what the weather was like as SEX catered for any situation. In the summer months he would sell his T-shirts and when it was raining, which was normally the case, he could sell his rubber wear.

Malcolm had overslept that morning and Vivienne had already left the flat by the time he'd risen. He'd been up most of the previous night making transatlantic calls to New York, but the time, not to mention the money, had been wasted. Sylvain Sylvain, the guitarist from the now defunct New York Dolls had changed his mind since their last meeting and wouldn't be coming over to London to form part of Malcolm's new group. The American had however, been very interested to know when Malcolm was going to send him the money from the sale of his Gibson Les Paul guitar which Steve was now using. At that point in the conversation Malcolm had pretended that there must be a problem with the line connection and terminated the call.

The guy Malcolm had really wanted to bring over to London, Richard Hell, the frontman from the New York group Television, had also refused to leave his home town. He'd now developed a drug habit and Malcolm had been adamant that Hell would have to clean up his act before coming to England.

He reached the front door of the shop, pausing outside to allow two teenage girls to pass him as they left clutching their new purchases in their hands. They seemed titillated that they had dared to buy something from a shop called SEX. He was almost tempted to ask the girls what they had bought, but thought better of it and gave them a smile instead as he closed the door after them.

Malcolm waved casually at Michael Collins who was assisting a customer near the jukebox, which was blaring out the song "Three Steps to Heaven" by Eddie Cochrane. This was the young up and coming Rock 'n' Roll singer who had died tragically in March 1960 as a result of his injuries when the taxi taking Eddie, his girlfriend Sharon Sheeley, and fellow Rock 'n' Roller Gene Vincent crashed into a roadside lamppost on the A4 near Bath, as they were on their way to Heathrow Airport at the end of Eddie's first British tour.

"Where are you when I need you, Eddie!" Malcolm muttered to himself thinking about the as yet unfilled position of lead singer in Steve's group. He smiled at Jordon as she approached the counter with another satisfied customer. She was looking her normal striking self, if "normal" was a word to describe Jordon. She was wearing a black vinyl leotard, a pair of ripped fishnet stockings and suspender belt and black ankle boots. She had painted a zigzag stripe across her face and her blonde hair was immaculate as ever, styled into a "Beehive".

"Has the football season started yet?" Malcolm asked her.

"I've no idea," replied Jordon.

"It starts today," said the guy Jordon was serving.

"Are Chelsea at home?"

"Yes," replied the guy, nodding. "I've put them down for a score draw on the coupon."

"Thanks," said Malcolm, dismissing the guy. "Listen girl, any sign of those fucking hooligans and you lock the door and call the police!" He started to walk past her. "On second thoughts, don't call the police."

"Don't worry, I know the score," said Jordon, laughing at her unintended pun.

"Where's Vivienne?" asked Malcolm, moving aside to allow the customer to leave.

"She's upstairs," said Jordon, pointing towards the ceiling.

Malcolm made his way up the narrow flight of stairs to the storeroom. He could hear muffled voices and when he reached the door, which was slightly ajar, he saw Vivienne and Bernie standing close together in front of a table. The pair were too engrossed in their conversation to notice anyone approaching.

"Good afternoon, Bernie," he said, striding into the room. He smiled weakly at Vivienne, but offered no greeting.

"Oh, hello, Malcolm," replied Bernie, moving to one side to allow Malcolm to see what he and Vivienne had been discussing. There was a batch of T-shirts that Rhodes had screen-printed for the shop. Malcolm picked one up and held it up to the sunlight flooding in through the small window.

"Yes," said Malcolm, looking pleased with the results, the T-shirts were made from two square pieces of cloth, sewn together up each side, leaving holes for the arms and a similar one for the head. The shirts would be worn inside out with the seams showing. The slogan printed on the front of the shirts was taken from Alexander Trocchis' *School for Wives*; the opening lines were "I groaned with pain as he eased the pressure in removing the thing, which had split me". Malcolm smiled as he read the words aloud.

"I especially like this idea," he said, toying with the two small zips that had been sewn into the shirts to allow the wearer to expose the nipples.

▢   ▢   ▢   ▢

"Is there any news from America?" Bernie asked Malcolm.

"Unfortunately, yes," replied Malcolm, replacing the T-shirt back on the pile. He gave Bernie and Vivienne a brief outline of his conversations with Sylvain and Richard Hell.

"And we all know who'll be paying the bill," said Vivienne, speaking for the first time since Malcolm had arrived.

"What would you rather I do?" asked Malcolm, sarcastically, "fly out there and have lunch with these people!"

"I'd rather have you get your priorities right and realise that we have a business to run!" yelled Vivienne, before storming past Malcolm and out of the room.

"So what do we do now?" asked Bernie, almost as if Vivienne's outburst hadn't happened.

"Now?" said Malcolm, absent-mindedly staring at the doorway. "Oh, you mean with the group?"

"Yes," replied Bernie, nodding, "have you any ideas?"

"I must admit I'm at a loss," said Malcolm, wistfully. He started for the doorway followed by Bernie. "You know, it's a pity Jordon is a girl. She would have made a great Sex Pistol!"

"Yes, but would Steve and the others play with a girl?"

"Oh, I'm sure that Steve would love to play with Jordon!" replied Malcolm, smiling at Bernie's poor choice of words. "If the randy bugger hasn't done so already!"

"You know what I mean!" said Bernie, feeling slightly embarrassed at his slip of the tongue.

"Yes, I knew what you meant," replied Malcolm, pausing on the stairs. "But I don't want a girl in this group, too many complications!"

"I may have found someone," said Bernie, casually. He'd wanted to tell Malcolm his news ever since Malcolm had first arrived, but he'd also wanted to savour the moment.

"Go on!" said Malcolm, wearily. "Who?"

"I've seen this young kid on the King's Road who might just be what we're looking for," said Bernie, as he and Malcolm entered the downstairs shop. "He's got green hair sticking up at all angles, but the thing that struck me most was the T-shirt this kid was wearing."

"Really," said Malcolm, smiling to himself. He was expecting to hear Bernie tell him it was one of his own designs.

"It was a Pink Floyd T-shirt!" said Bernie, causing Malcolm's smile to fade instantly. "But, this kid had written 'I hate' across the top of the shirt and he'd burnt out the eyes from the group's picture underneath. Malcolm was intrigued by Bernie's description of the, as yet unknown, youth, when Bernie interrupted his train of thought by pointing at Glen who was busy searching through the pairs of trousers on one of the clothes rails. It was his birthday at the end of the month and he was deciding how to spend the money he'd receive from his parents. "Glen's seen him as well."

"Glen, my boy," said Malcolm, heading towards him. Glen had seen Malcolm and Bernie come into the shop from the stairway and had also noticed Bernie pointing at him although he'd been unable to hear what they were saying about him. He really hoped it wouldn't be anything to do with screen-printing T-shirts for Malcolm and he was trying to think of an excuse when Malcolm called his name.

"What is it you're looking for?" Malcolm asked Glen. Business always came first with Malcolm.

"Umm, I'm looking for a pair of black straight-leg trousers," replied Glen, indicating the rack of trousers in front of him. "Now that you're our manager, do we get a discount?"

"You don't miss a trick, do you?" said Malcolm, a wry smile on his face.

"Well, if you don't ask..." replied Glen, hopefully.

"Listen, Glen," said Malcolm, lowering his voice, "Bernie tells me that you've seen this kid with the green hair. Do you think he's worth approaching?"

"For the group?" asked Glen, relieved that this had nothing to do with T-shirts.

"Yes! Of course for the group," replied Malcolm, exasperatingly. "What else?"

"Possibly," said Glen, nodding slowly. "He's been in here a couple of times."

"Well, why didn't you speak to him, boy?" asked Malcolm, glancing at Bernie.

"He's always got his mates with him," said Glen, defensively, "and they're always pissing about!"

"Okay," said Malcolm, placing his hand on Glen's shoulder. Talk about having to do things yourself. "But the next time you see this kid, arrange a meeting, anything, then let me know!"

"Right," said Glen, nodding seriously. "What about the discount?" Malcolm looked as if he was going to shout at Glen but he stopped himself.

"Ten per cent!" he nodded at Jordon standing a few feet away, then left the shop with Bernie.

It was later that afternoon and Glen was heading back up the King's Road towards SEX. He'd tried his luck in some of the other shops to see if he could find a pair of trousers similar to the ones Malcolm sold. Even with the ten-percent discount, they were still pretty expensive. Glen hadn't found anything even remotely like the trousers in SEX, which probably accounted for the exorbitant prices Malcolm and Vivienne charged. He entered the shop, heading straight for the rail containing the trousers he'd seen earlier, hoping that they were still there. The pair of trousers he'd seen were black straight-legged with see-through plastic rear pockets, which was okay just as long as he remembered not to keep anything valuable in them. He quickly found the trousers and turned towards Jordon standing at the counter, ready to remind her about Malcolm's promise of a discount when he spotted the kid with the green hair coming into the shop and his three friends were with him yet again.

"Doesn't he ever go anywhere alone!" thought Glen, as he watched the four lads walk past him towards the jukebox in the corner. The wild-looking one with the blond hair was entertaining the others with some story or other. Glen handed his money and the trousers to Jordon while observing the kid with the green hair as he looked through a pile of T-shirts. He remembered Malcolm's instructions to see if green hair would be interested in joining the group and strolled over towards him, casually picking up one of the T-shirts and pretending to examine it. When green hair moved away towards another rail, Glen followed.

"Can I have a word?" he asked, when green hair glanced in his direction.

"You just had five," replied green hair, smirking at his mates.

"Listen," continued Glen, ignoring the sarcasm, "me and a couple of mates have got a group together and we're looking for a singer."

"What's that to me?"

"Would you be interested in coming to an audition?" asked Glen, tiring of green hair's responses.

"God!" exclaimed green hair, "Me sing! I dunno. I've never thought of doin' anything like that." He turned to look at his friends who had gathered around when Glen had started the conversation. "Yeah why not? When?"

"What about meeting the others tonight?" asked Glen, trying not to sound too keen. "At the Roebuck, about seven?"

"I'll be there."

"Great, I'll see you then," replied Glen, smiling. He turned to leave when he realised he hadn't asked green hair his name. "What's your name?"

"I'm John!"

"Glen!"

"No, John!" said green hair, smirking again.

John was nineteen years old. The eldest son of Jim and Eileen Lydon, he had been born in London and after a few years living in different places the family returned to London to live in a council flat in Pooles Park in Finsbury Park. As a child, John had contracted the disease meningitis, which had left him with a slight stoop and bad eyesight. He had attended William of York Catholic Comprehensive School in Pentonville, and in 1973 he attended Hackney Technical College to study his "O" levels. By the summer of 1975 John had been thrown out of the family home for his outlandish behaviour such as dyeing his hair green. He was now living in a squat with a friend of his called Sid.

Glen returned to the counter to collect his new trousers and his change from Jordon. She had already placed the trousers in a carrier bag for him and had been eagerly watching Glen's encounter with the lad with green hair.

"Is Vivienne still here?" he asked Jordon, pocketing his change.

"No," replied Jordon, shaking her head, "she's gone home for the day."

"What about Malcolm and Bernie?"

"I haven't seen those two since they were in here earlier," said Jordon, "when you were talking to them."

"Would you try ringing the flat for me?" asked Glen, as he watched John and his friends leave the shop. "The Roebuck at seven, yeah, John."

"I'll be there," said John, without turning round, as his friend with the blond hair closed the door.

"I'll try," said Jordon, reaching for the phone. "Is it to do with that lad with the green hair?"

"Yeah!" said Glen. "He's agreed to come and meet Steve and Paul at the Roebuck tonight. All I need to do now is get hold of everybody and tell them!"

Jordon dialled the number of Malcolm and Vivienne's flat on Nightingale Lane but there didn't seem to be anyone home. She held the receiver towards Glen as the phone at the other end droned away in the empty flat. She was about to terminate the call when somebody at the flat answered.

"Just a minute, Malcolm!" said Jordon, handing the phone to Glen.

"Hi, Malcolm, it's me, Glen...listen, I've just seen the guy with the green hair...what...yeah, he's called John...tonight, at the Roebuck...seven o'clock...yes, they're always in there at opening time on Saturdays...right, see you then, bye."

Malcolm had wanted to know if Glen had seen Steve or Paul as it would be best if everyone was there for the meeting, if John bothered to turn up. Glen would be meeting Malcolm and Bernie at quarter to seven outside the shop and they would then go to the Roebuck together.

Glen didn't have to wait long before a black taxicab pulled to the kerb outside SEX.

"Jump in, boy!" yelled Malcolm, winding down the window in the back of the taxi. "Have you heard from Steve and Paul?"

"Yeah!" replied Glen, pulling down one of the spring loaded seats after he had closed the taxi's door. "I rang Paul's house when I got home and explained everything."

"Marvellous!" said Malcolm, a satisfied grin on his face. "The Roebuck, driver!" Malcolm sprang out of the taxi as soon as it stopped outside the public house on the King's Road closely followed by Glen, who had no intentions of being landed with the fare. The three of them entered the Roebuck and went over to join Steve and Paul who were sitting together at one of the tables near the pool table.

"No sign of this 'John' character, yet then?" said Malcolm, pulling out a stool from underneath the table and giving it a cursory wipe with his hand before sitting down.

"Are you gettin' 'em in, Bernie?" asked Steve.

"No, I'm not!" replied Bernie, shaking his head. He only had intentions of getting his own drink, having already been stung for the taxi fare.

"Excellent idea, Steve," said Malcolm, nodding at Bernie. "I'll have a gin and tonic."

"He's here!" said Paul, tugging Malcolm's sleeve.

"Who's here?" asked Malcolm, turning towards the door. "Oh, right, go on, Glen." Glen stood up and went to the door where John was standing with one of the lads Glen had seen him with earlier.

"Hi, John!" said Glen. "Come on over and I'll introduce you to everyone." Malcolm felt slightly unnerved by John's gaze as they were introduced. It reminded him of how a rat might look when it's cornered. He was, however, suitably impressed by John's image. He took in the green hair, hacked off at different lengths. The "I hate" scrawled across the top of the T-shirt just as Bernie had described and the pink school blazer, ripped at one shoulder and held together with a couple of safety pins. John's hands were buried deep inside the pockets of his baggy striped trousers, which tapered off at the ankle; he was also wearing a pair of plastic toeless sandals.

"I like your style, John," said Malcolm, on seeing that John had been watching him while he examined his clothes. "Would you and your friend..."

"Gray," said John's companion.

"Would you and ah 'Gray' like a drink?"

"Two pints of Guinness," said John, nodding.

"Same for me," said Gray, smirking at Malcolm.

"Two pints of Guinness, Bernie!" said Malcolm, giving John and his friend a wry smile. He didn't even bother to look at Bernie, who had only just sat down after buying the round of drinks. "Glen has filled me in about your meeting this afternoon. Would you be interested in joining the group?"

"That's why I'm here!" replied John, flatly. He was still eyeing the people sitting around the table with suspicion.

Christ, what a stroppy little bugger! thought Malcolm. "Can you sing?" he asked John.

"Never tried!" replied John, his face devoid of expression, "so I wouldn't know."

"Well, do you know what you want to do?" asked Malcolm, becoming annoyed with John's attitude.

"I want to play the violin!" replied John, chewing on one of his cuticles.

"Can you play the violin?" asked Malcolm, clearly puzzled by John's reply. He wasn't sure where this was heading.

"Only out of tune," replied John, who hadn't relaxed his stare during the entire conversation. Malcolm glanced at Glen and the others, at a loss for words.

"He's takin' the fuckin' piss!" yelled Steve, jumping up from his stool. Malcolm leaned back to get out of the way, thinking that Steve was about to attack John.

"Steady on, Steve!" said Glen, trying to calm things down. "If you're not interested, John, then why are you here?"

"Didn't say I wasn't interested, did I!" sneered John, quietly watching Steve who was standing a few feet away. "Or I wouldn't be here!"

"What about coming down for an audition, then?" Glen asked John, who glanced at his friend Gray, then shrugged his shoulders noncommittally.

"What are we doin' with this cunt?" snarled Steve, almost knocking the two pints of Guinness from Bernie's hands as he returned from the bar.

"Leave this to me!" said Malcolm, standing up. "I've got an idea!" He waited until he had everyone's attention. "Why don't we go back to the shop now, and have the audition there?"

"But we ain't got any of our gear there!" said Paul, speaking for the first time since Glen had brought John over to their table.

"No matter," replied Malcolm, smiling at John, "you can sing something from the jukebox. What do you say?"

"All right," said John, thoughtfully. "I'll finish my drink first, though!"

After the drinks were finished, everyone made their way back along the King's Road to number 430. Malcolm, Bernie and Glen led the way closely followed by John and his friend Gray with Steve and Paul bringing up the rear. Glen could hear Steve moaning about John, who must also have been able to hear Steve but he didn't show it.

"It's a fuckin' waste of drinking time, this is!" hissed Steve, pointing at John. "He's a right cunt!"

"Well, we'll soon find out, won't we!" replied Paul. Malcolm unlocked the door and switched on the lights and waited for the others to enter before closing the door behind him, giving instructions to Bernie to plug in the jukebox in the corner while he and Glen brought the chairs over from in front of the window.

Gray sat down on the surgical bed casually running his fingers along the soft pink rubber sheets. John was standing a few feet away near to the jukebox, which was now illuminating the corner where they were all gathered. The bravado John had been displaying in the Roebuck seemed to have deserted him momentarily. He was looking decidedly nervous as Malcolm approached him.

"Right, John," said Malcolm, sounding more confident now that he was back on his own territory. He placed a hand on John's shoulder and guided him towards the jukebox. "What do you want to sing for us?"

"I dunno!" replied John, staring at the jukebox. Malcolm ran his finger down the glass panel covering the numbers required for each of the selections, looking for something suitable.

"Yes," he said at last, "this'll do nicely!" He glanced around at John. "Do you know this one? It's called 'Eighteen', by Alice Cooper."

"Yeah!" replied John, nodding, "I've heard it before." He watched Malcolm press the buttons required to activate the jukebox's mechanism.

John watched in silence as the mechanical arm swung down and selected one of the shiny seven-inch discs from the rack and placed it on the revolving turntable. The arm containing the record needle swung across, descended slowly onto the disc and the shop filled with crackling sounds as the needle settled into the groove. Then the tune started. It seemed strangely louder than normal but this was probably due to the fact that the section of the King's Road that ran past the shop was relatively quiet during the evening. John stood in front of the jukebox glancing at each of the faces watching him with interest. He could see that the one called Steve was glowering at him as the voice of Alice Cooper, the flamboyant American singer noted for his painted face and wild stage antics, which often included the use of swords and live snakes, filled the room. John was still standing there, motionless.

"Hold on, boy!" yelled Malcolm, above the music as he dashed across the shop towards the counter. He ducked down for a few seconds and then came back holding up the plastic shower attachment that he'd come across the other day. "Here, use this!" he said, handing it to John. "Pretend it's a microphone!"

John stood expressionless for a moment, realising it was time to shit or get off the pot, then suddenly he sprang into action, twisting and contorting his body as if he was racked by spasms, screeching into the shower attachment poised in front of his mouth. "I'm eighteen. I can do what I want! I'm eighteen, sex in the grass!" He leapt around in front of the jukebox, hunching his back like a modern day Quasimodo. It wasn't until he opened his eyes and faced his audience that he realised everyone was creased up laughing at him, including his friend Gray. John's face broke into a grin and he tossed the shower attachment onto the surgical bed feeling slightly embarrassed.

"He's fuckin' worse than me!" said Steve, when the song had finished.

"No, he ain't!" said Paul, laughing at Steve's crestfallen expression. Malcolm waited for everyone to quieten down before asking John if he was willing to come for a rehearsal with the group at their latest place, in a room above a public house in Rotherhithe called The Crunchie Frog. John was guarded but agreed to come along. He slipped the piece of paper containing the shop's and Glen's telephone numbers that Malcolm had given him into his pocket before he and Gray headed towards the front door.

"You can slag me off now," said John, turning to face Malcolm and the others before leaving.

"We're not havin' that cunt, are we?" asked Steve, turning to face Malcolm once John had left.

"We probably won't see him again, anyway!" said Glen, quietly. "Not with the way you were acting!"

"You're not fuckin' serious!" said Steve, angrily.

"Well, there isn't anyone else, is there?" said Paul, looking at Steve.

"Let's give him a try!" said Malcolm, holding out his hands in a gesture of appeasement. "Like Paul says," he pointed at Paul who was sat twiddling the shower attachment in his hands, "there isn't anyone else!"

Malcolm could understand Steve's reluctance to give John another chance, but there was something about the green haired youth that appealed to his sense of mischief. He could see a lot of himself in John but he was too afraid to put himself in the spotlight, preferring to operate in the background.

"All right," said Steve, glancing at Malcolm thoughtfully, "we'll give it a go but if he fucks me about, I'll give him a good kickin'!"

"Are you gonna show at this place in Rotherhithe?" Gray asked John, as they were walking back down the King's Road towards a bus stop.

"Might as well," replied John. "Can't be any worse than standing in front of a jukebox with a piece of fuckin' plastic in your hand miming to Alice Cooper, can it!" The two of them burst out laughing, drawing funny looks from the young couple already standing at the bus stop. "It could even be amusing."

"The one with the dark curly hair looks a mean fucker," said Gray, referring to Steve.

"Umm, I don't think he likes me," replied John, accepting a cigarette from his friend. "Oh dear, too bad." He had every intention of showing up for the rehearsal. This was an opportunity for him to rant about the things that mattered to him and he might even end up getting paid for it.

"So what if I can't sing!" he said, watching the bus coming towards them, "I bet they can't play a fucking note!"

CHAPTER FIVE

The following Monday night, John, again accompanied by his friend Gray made the journey all the way across London down to Rotherhithe. After stopping several passers-by, they finally managed to get someone who wasn't wary of John's appearance to give them directions to The Crunchie Frog. Although late themselves there was no sign of Glen, Steve or Paul.

"Did you phone Glen?" asked Gray, as they waited on the street corner outside the pub.

"No," replied John, flatly, "they're the ones who fuckin' asked me to come here, remember?"

"I know. I was there!" retorted Gray. "I'm just saying it might have made more sense if you'd arranged to meet them somewhere else, that's all."

"Well, we're here now," sighed John, glancing up and down the street, "so we might as well wait. Have you got any money on you?"

"Yeah," replied Gray, "we'll have a drink, an' if they haven't shown by the time we've finished, we'll fuck off."

"They'd better fuckin' show!" snarled John, as they entered the public house.

The downstairs saloon was quiet, which was typical for a Monday night. The two of them walked up to the bar. There were perhaps five or six other people in the room and all eyes were on John.

"What'll it be, lads?" asked the landlord, openly staring at John's green hair.

"Two pints of Guinness, please," said Gray, digging into his pocket for his money. He glanced around the room, smirking at the stunned expressions. Still, it wasn't every day they saw someone like John. Two elderly blokes were sitting at a table at the end of the bar playing dominoes, the game temporarily halted by the Martian invasion. One of them turned casually to the other and nodded his head towards the bar.

"If that lad starts drinking with his finger, I'm off."

John and Gray waited inside the saloon bar for almost an hour. By now, it was obvious that the others weren't going to show; they drained their glasses, left the pub and walked back to the tube station. John was furious at the no-show and was busy plotting his revenge. They decided to make something of the evening by paying a visit to the squat where their friend Sid was living. John occasionally shared squats with Sid but was temporarily back living with his parents in Finsbury Park. Another friend of theirs, the blond haired Wobble, was also there drinking himself into a stupor. John told them about the failed rehearsal, while helping himself to one of Wobble's cans of cheap lager.

"What!" shouted Wobble, staggering to his feet and spilling beer down the front of his shirt.

"Why would they ask you to go all the fuckin' way down to Rotherhithe and not show up themselves?" asked Sid, reaching out to steady Wobble, who was swaying precariously.

"Let's go give 'em a good kickin'!" slurred Wobble, collapsing on the sofa.

"Fuckin' right!" agreed Sid, grinning. "Wankers!"

A couple of days later, Bernie paid Malcolm a visit at the flat on Nightingale Lane in Clapham. He was there principally to discuss ideas for a new range of T-shirts but he was also curious to find out how the rehearsal with John had worked out. He said a quick hello to Vivienne, who was in the living room playing with her two boys Ben and Joe, then followed Malcolm through to the kitchen.

"Any news on the group?" he asked after a couple of minutes, sensing Malcolm's mind was elsewhere.

"You mean the rehearsal with John?"

"Yes!" replied Bernie. "How did it go?"

"It didn't go," said Malcolm, glancing up from the designs spread out on the table. "Apparently Steve and the others didn't bother to turn up!"

"But why?" gasped Bernie, removing his spectacles to give the lenses a quick wipe with a tissue.

"I think Steve is responsible for that," said Malcolm, shaking his head. "You know what he's like."

"I think they're making a big mistake."

"I agree," replied Malcolm, sighing, "but what can I do? Paul will always side with Steve."

"What about Glen?"

"I'm not sure," replied Malcolm, glancing towards the stove as the kettle reached boiling point. "Coffee?"

"Do you want me to have a word with Steve, see if I can persuade him?" asked Bernie, accepting a mug of steaming coffee from Malcolm.

"Yes," said Malcolm, nodding his agreement. "You talk to Steve and I'll have a word with Glen to see if he can get hold of John!" He handed Bernie one of the sheets of paper he'd roughly sketched his designs on. "What do you think about this one?" he asked, changing the subject.

Bernie eventually managed to bring Steve around to the idea of giving John a proper rehearsal with the group; it hadn't been easy as Steve was convinced that it would be a waste of time. The ace up Bernie's sleeve had been Malcolm's promise to find them a new rehearsal room more central to where they all lived. All that was required now was for Glen to contact John to see if he would even be willing to listen to him.

▢ ▢ ▢ ▢

"I'll fuckin' kill you!" John screamed down the telephone. "I will, I'll fuckin' kill you!"

"Listen, John," said Glen, replacing the receiver to his ear after John's sudden outburst. "We're sorry about the other night, honest! Will you come along to another rehearsal?"

"Where?" asked John, after a few moments silence, "cos, I ain't fuckin' goin' down to Rotherhithe again!"

"You don't have to," replied Glen, sensing John's change of mood. "Malcolm's got us a place in Wandsworth, at a pub called The Rose And Crown."

"Are you cunts gonna show?" John growled down the phone.

"Yes, definitely, I promise!" said Glen. "So, you'll come down, then?"

"I s'pose so," replied John. "When?"

"How about Monday night, about seven o'clock?" Glen smiled to himself when John agreed to the time. "And come down on your own John. It's better when it's just the people in the group!" He replaced the receiver before John had a chance to speak.

▢ ▢ ▢ ▢

When Glen, Steve and Paul arrived at their new rehearsal room the following Monday night, John was already there waiting for them. His eyes narrowed as they approached him, as if he almost expected them to attack him now that he was on his own. Glen and Paul both said hello, which seemed to diffuse the situation, but Steve clearly hadn't given up on his objections despite the carrot, in the shape of the new rehearsal room, dangled by Malcolm. Once they had all bought a drink they made their way up the stairs to view their new place. Unfortunately it was no different from the room in Rotherhithe, not so much a rehearsal room, more like the landlord trying to earn a few quid leasing out the empty rooms above his pub.

"Fuckin' typical!" moaned Steve, looking around the room. "It ain't even sound-proofed!"

"Well, we'll just have to keep the volume down then, won't we?" said Paul, who was happy enough now that they wouldn't need to travel across London to rehearse anymore.

"Let's just get all the gear up here and then we'll worry about it!" said Glen, shrugging his shoulders.

It took the four of them less than half an hour to unload their gear from the back of the transit van, which Malcolm had borrowed for the evening. The room was little more than a cubicle really. The landlord had had a larger room partitioned off into several smaller spaces, allowing for greater profits. John had been eager enough to help carry the equipment but hadn't realised just how much of it they had between them. Once Paul had set up the drums on a piece of old carpet to stop them sliding around when playing the songs, the amplifiers were plugged in and the guitars tuned they were ready to begin.

"These are all the lyrics that you'll need," said Glen, handing a notebook to John. "All the songs that we do are in there."

"Have you got any of your own songs?" asked John, flicking through the pages of the notebook.

"Oh, yeah," replied Glen, nodding. "They're in there somewhere."

"All two of 'em," said Paul, grinning from behind his drum kit.

"Yeah," said Glen, shrugging. "I don't think Lennon and McCartney have anything to be worried about at the moment."

"Oh, you'll have to watch Glen," said Paul, turning towards John, "closet Beatles fan."

"No, I'm not!" protested Glen. "I'm just saying...oh, never mind, shall we get started?"

"What're we doin' first?" asked Steve.

"I don't know," replied Glen, leaning over John's shoulder. "What about 'Substitute'?"

"All right," said John, turning the pages until he found the song originally performed by The Who. Paul counted time by clicking his drumsticks together, then Steve played a chord in "E" as he and Glen launched into the song. John stood in the centre of the room in front of the microphone waiting for his cue from Glen. Paul thrashed out a drum roll to bring in the first verse and Glen nodded at John.

"You think that we look pretty good togeth-er!" screamed John, leaping into spasms just like he had in the shop. "And you think my shoes are made of leath-er."

He was totally absorbed in what he was doing, occasionally losing his place and ad-libbing with various noises when he forgot to read his lyrics.

"That wasn't too bad, was it?" said Glen, smiling at John once they had finished the song. "You wanna try it again?"

"OK," said John, feeling better now that they'd actually played something. He pulled out a handkerchief from the pocket of the striped baggy trousers he'd been wearing when they first met him. He was also wearing a tatty red pullover that was at least two sizes too small for him and had clearly seen better days and a pair of purple brothel creepers.

"We'll keep at it until you get used to the song," said Glen, wiping the fretboard of his guitar with a beer towel he'd spotted when they had first arrived.

They had been rehearsing for about an hour when Paul called a halt to the proceedings because he needed to piss, emerging from behind the drums, careful not to trip over the guitar leads snaking across the floor.

"Where are the bogs?" he asked, grimacing.

"Downstairs, I s'pose," replied Glen, smirking at Paul's discomfort. He removed his guitar and placed it on a stand. "So what sort of music do you like?" he asked John, remembering the afternoon of his audition at Wally's house.

"I like all kinds," replied John, lighting a cigarette. "I love reggae."

"Reggae," said Steve, speaking to John for the first time that evening. "What else?"

"All sorts," said John, turning to face Steve. "Have you heard of Captain Beefheart?"

"I've heard of Captain Pugwash!" grinned Steve.

"Aye, aye, you'll always find Seaman Stains with Master Bates," said Glen, laughing. "Captain Beefheart, eh, John?"

"Yeah, cos he's really different," said John, still laughing at Glen's joke. The conversation halted when Paul returned carrying a fresh pint.

"Where's mine?" Steve asked him, hopefully.

"This is research," said Paul, taking a drink, "checking out the opposition!"

"Paul works for Watneys," said Glen, explaining to John.

"Lucky bastard," said John, seemingly impressed. "Is there a better way to earn a living?"

"What about a 'Johnny' tester for Durex?" said Steve, smirking.

They played "Substitute" several times until they were playing it through to the end without John losing his place. He seemed confident enough to sing the song without the use of the hand-written lyrics.

"Can we play somethin' else?" moaned Steve. "I'm fuckin' fed up with playin' that one!"

"I didn't know you were a fan of Eddie Cochrane," said Glen, grinning at Steve's blank expression.

"What the fuck are you on about?" asked Steve, clearly baffled at Glen's comment.

"'Somethin' Else'! It's a classic by Eddie Cochrane...Oh, never mind! You knew what I meant, didn't you, John?"

"Yeah," replied John, nodding. "Now, c'mon everybody, let's do another one." Steve stood looking from one to the other as John and Glen chuckled away. He was sure they were laughing at him but couldn't prove it.

"What about one of our songs?" said Paul.

"OK," replied Glen, picking the notebook up off the floor. "What about 'Did You No Wrong'?"

"Yeah, all right," said Steve, reaching out for Paul's drink. "Give us a drink of that first, though."

"Paul wrote these," said Glen, finding the lyrics for John. "Didn't you?"

"I like the first verse," said John, looking up from the notebook.

"It's just an idea, I had," replied Paul, looking pleased with himself.

"What John means is," said Steve, smirking, "is that the rest of it's shit!"

"Yeah," agreed John, nodding at Steve. Then they both burst out laughing at Paul's hurt expression.

"You can change it if you want," said Paul, quietly, which had Steve and John howling. Even Glen was grinning.

"We did agree that the singer could change any lyrics that we came up with," said Glen, when the laughter had died down.

"I'll use these for now," said John, wiping his eyes, "but I'll take them home tonight and see what I can do with them."

"When can you come down again, John?" asked Glen, lifting his guitar strap over his head.

"Whenever you want," replied John. "I ain't got fuck all else to do!"

"Malcolm's paid for a full week," said Glen, "so we might as well make use of it."

"What's the story with you lot and this Malcolm?" asked John, pulling out his cigarettes, this time offering one to Steve.

They took a break while they told him all about Malcolm's involvement with The New York Dolls and how they had pestered him into managing them.

"And where does Bernie Rhodes fit in?" asked John.

"Bernie's like Malcolm's partner, I s'pose," replied Paul.

"When it suits Malcolm!" said Steve.

"He's a partner in the shop, then?" said John.

"No!" said Steve, shaking his head. "He just runs Malcolm's errands for him."

"He has a lot of good ideas though," said Glen.

"Oh, yeah," agreed Steve, nodding his agreement. "He's helped us out."

They stayed for another half an hour, playing the tune for "Did You No Wrong" while John sat listening. Before they finished they ran through "Substitute" just to make sure John would remember it.

"Our gear'll be all right here, won't it?" asked Steve. "It won't get nicked?" John stood looking baffled as Glen and Paul fell about laughing at what seemed to him to be a perfectly reasonable question.

"It's a long story, John," said Glen, by way of explanation. "We've got our own keys for the room," he said, jangling the keys in front of Steve's face. "And the landlord will be here every night."

"That's what worries me!" replied Steve, scowling. "I'm takin' my guitar home!"

"Good idea," said Glen thoughtfully, before going back to retrieve his bass guitar from where he'd left it. "Do you want a lift anywhere, John?"

"Which way are you headin'?" asked John.

"Well, I'm dropping these two off in Shepherd's Bush, if that's any good to you?"

"Great," said John. "I've got some mates who have a squat in Hampstead."

As they had arranged to rehearse the following night, Glen offered to give John a lift to Wandsworth, as John had told him he'd probably be staying at the squat anyway. He arrived at the address John had given him in his father's Austin Cambridge. He pressed the car's horn a couple of times and peered through the windscreen for any sign of John.

"Christ, what a shit-hole!" Glen muttered to himself. The Victorian houses were in a state of decline; the doors and windows were all boarded up with sheets of corrugated iron but one or two of the sheets had been prized open to allow entry by people claiming squatters' rights. These were students and immigrants mostly, desperate for somewhere to stay. Glen was about to press the horn again when he saw John coming out of one of the houses opposite. He reached over and released the lock on the passenger door and restarted the engine as a tall, thin lad approached from the other direction, staring into the car to see who was inside.

Who's this, thought Glen, trying to act casually as the lad reached the car at the same time as John. He said something to John, which made him laugh then crossed the road heading towards the house that John had just come out of.

"Friend of yours?" asked Glen, as John climbed in.

"Yeah," replied John, nodding as he pulled the safety belt over his shoulder. "That's my mate, Sid."

"Strange name," said Glen, pushing the car into second gear.

"Strange boy," laughed John. "Nah, he's all right when you get to know him. You can have a laugh with Sid."

"Wouldn't want to bump into him on a dark night," said Glen, indicating as he approached the turning onto the main road. "What did he say to you?"

"He asked me if I still wanted him to give you a good kickin'!"

"What!" gasped Glen, almost stalling the car. "Why? What've I done?"

"I'm only jokin!" said John, grinning. "He got excited when I told you lot didn't turn up the other night."

"Speaking of which," said Glen, "there's been a change of plan for tonight."

"Really," said John, suspiciously. "We're still rehearsin', right?"

"Oh, yeah," replied Glen, glancing at John, "only, it's Steve's birthday today, so we're gonna run through a couple of songs then we'll have a few beers afterwards."

"He never said anythin' last night," said John.

"No," replied Glen, pulling the car to a halt at a red light. "He was hoping that we'd forgotten."

"Why?"

"He's twenty today, no more being a teenager," replied Glen, grinning. "We're gonna give him some right grief."

By the time Glen and John arrived at the Rose and Crown in Wandsworth, Steve and Paul were already waiting in their room with a drink each.

"Happy fuckin' birthday, granddad!" said Glen, smirking.

"Yeah, yeah," said Steve, scowling. "I've 'ad enough shit off this cunt!"

"No, you fuckin' ain't," said Paul, grinning. "Here's us trying to be the new kids on the block and you're ready for your bus pass!"

"Maybe you should audition for the Groaning Bones," said John.

"Who?" asked Steve, frowning.

"The Groaning Bones," repeated John, waiting for Steve to catch on. "You must be the same fuckin' age as Mick Jagger."

"Are we gonna rehearse, or not?" asked Steve, standing up and reaching for his guitar.

"Careful!" said Paul. "You might hurt yourself." Steve ignored the laughter and strummed a few chords to warm up.

"When you're ready," he said, looking up from his guitar.

"Oh, we're ready when you are granddad," John muttered under his breath. He glanced at Glen to see if anyone had heard him and judging from the smirk on Glen's face it was obvious they had. Steve looked over at John and mouthed the word cunt, his face breaking into a grin.

"It's gonna be all right!" Glen thought to himself, watching the banter between Steve and John. "This is it. We're a group!"

Later on that evening, after the rehearsal, the four of them went down to the bar in the Rose and Crown. They talked about music in general and the groups that they'd seen, before moving onto the topic of football. Paul admitted to having a soft spot for Queen's Park Rangers.

"The only soft spot I've got for 'em is Romney Marsh!" howled John, chanting songs about his beloved Arsenal.

"He plays for QPR, don't he?" said Steve.

"I said Romney Marsh not fuckin' Rodney Marsh!" said John, shaking his head.

"Are we staying here or moving somewhere else?" asked Glen, placing his empty glass on the table.

"Might as well stop here," said Paul, still chuckling over Romney Marsh playing for QPR.

"Yeah, I'll have another," said Steve, draining his glass and belching loudly.

"Did Malcolm get hold of you?" Glen asked Steve. "I forgot to mention it to you earlier."

"He certainly did," beamed Steve, pulling out a wad of cash. "He's shifted a bit of gear for us lately."

"Umm, same again for me please," said John, his eyes lighting up at the sight of the money.

"No problem," replied Steve, sliding out one of the notes and passing it to Glen.

"It's like a wrestler's neck!" said Glen, watching Steve slip the wad of notes back into his pocket.

"You robbed a bank or somethin'?" asked John, narrowing his eyes at Steve.

"No, not quite," replied Steve. "We, uh, sold some equipment that we didn't need."

"Ahh I see," said John, putting two and two together. "I've been wondering where you'd got all that gear from." He jerked his thumb up towards the ceiling.

"What do you mean?" asked Steve, smirking.

"It's stolen!" said John, in a hushed voice. "That's what I mean!"

"Well, let's just say the people that we borrowed it from didn't exactly give us permission," said Paul, grinning.

"That's right," said Glen, standing up to go to the bar. "The next time you see Mr. Bowie, don't forget to thank him for the use of his microphone. Not that I had anything to do with it," he added hastily, before leaving to get the drinks.

"Ain't got the fuckin' 'bottle'!" sneered Steve, watching him go, but if Glen heard him he didn't respond.

"Malcolm thought it would be too risky playing around London with all that hooky gear," said Paul.

"That's right," agreed Steve. "We'd soon have the Old Bill breathin' down our necks."

"Yeah," said Paul, nodding. "The only gigs we'd be doin' would be at the local nick!"

Glen returned with a tray of drinks, placed them down on the table, collected the empty glasses and took them back to the bar.

"You can tell he's been trained, can't you," said Steve, shaking his head as Glen returned.

"Either that or he fancies his chances with Dolly," said Paul, smirking. "Have you seen the size of them tits?"

"You can see 'em before you get through the fuckin' door!" said Steve, swiftly necking the whisky chaser Glen had bought him.

"Yeah," said John, leering over at the barmaid, "you don't get many of those to the pound!" He stood up and looked around the room. "Where are the toilets, Paul?"

"Over there, near the pool table."

"Have you noticed how intensely he stares at you when he's talking?" said Glen, watching John make his way across the room, oblivious to the stares from the two guys playing pool.

"Yeah," replied Paul, nodding.

"He reminds me of that actor I saw in a film on telly last week," said Glen. "Oh, what's his name?"

"Fuck knows!" said Steve.

"Robert Newton!" cried Glen, excitedly. "He played Long John Silver in Treasure Island."

"Long John fuckin' Steptoe, more like," said Steve, taking a drink from his glass.

"What?" asked Glen, looking puzzled.

"His fuckin' gear!" said Steve, tugging his own shirt for emphasis. "He looks like that old git off Steptoe and Son."

"Ha-ha-ha, Long John Steptoe," said Glen, nodding. "What is his surname, anyway?"

"Dunno," replied Paul, quietly, before nodding to indicate that John was coming up behind him.

"We were just wondering, John," said Glen, as John sat down next to him, "what's your surname?"

"Why?" asked John, eyeing Glen with suspicion.

"No reason," replied Glen, shaking his head. "Just asking."

"It's not important," said John, lifting his glass to his mouth. "John will do very nicely, thank you!"

CHAPTER SIX

By mid-September, the group had moved to a new rehearsal place close to the Roundhouse on Chalk Farm Road in Camden Town. The sound-proofing was just as bad as the other places they'd used but it would have to suffice until Malcolm made good his promise to find them somewhere permanent. Glen had called in on Malcolm at the shop to see if he would be interested in an advertisement he'd spotted in the property section of that week's edition of *Melody Maker*, one of the weekly music papers he read avidly.

```
TIN PAN ALLEY: MUST BE USEFUL FOR
  SOME MUSICIANS, AGENTS OR SUCH.
TO TAKE OVER SMALL LOCK UP PREMISES.
    Store gear, meet, rehearse.
 Hire it out etc. sacrifice — 455-7487
```

Glen showed it to Malcolm half-heartedly hoping it just might spur him into making the agent an offer. Malcolm scanned the page until he found the advert circled in biro. "OK," he said, after he'd read the advertisement. "Give them a call and offer them one thousand pounds blind."

Glen didn't wait to be asked twice, he reached for the telephone on the counter and dialled the number on the advert. The phone at the other end of the line buzzed a couple of times before being answered.

"Hello," he said, resting his elbow on the counter, "I'm calling about your advertisement in this week's *Melody Maker*...Yes...that's the one...listen, I reckon my mate's mad, but he's told me to offer you one thousand pounds without even seeing the place!" He placed a hand over the mouthpiece and turned towards Malcolm. "He wants to know when he'll get his money."

"Arrange a time to meet him, then!" replied Malcolm.

"Hello...what time can we meet you?" He was waiting for the guy at the other end of the phone to give him the details of where they could meet when Malcolm seemed to lose patience and grabbed the telephone out of Glen's hand.

"What's his name?" he asked Glen.

"Collins," said Glen, hoping Malcolm hadn't suddenly lost interest, "Bill Collins."

"Hello, Mr. Collins," said Malcolm, smoothly, "or may I call you

65

Bill?...Splendid...It's Malcolm McLaren here...yes...yes, that could be arranged...great...well, I'll see you tomorrow then...goodbye." He handed the receiver back to Glen.

"Have we got it? asked Glen, barely able to contain his excitement.

"Yes, boy, we got it!"

Glen had notified the others to be at SEX the following day, so that they could all go together to see their new rehearsal place. John surprised everybody when he arrived. He'd dyed his hair again and now it was an orange-ginger colour, which, set against his pale skin, resulted in a striking effect. Glen had borrowed his father's Austin Cambridge for the occasion, although it would be a bit of a tight squeeze fitting five people in the car. For Malcolm, there was now the added romance of having the group's new home in Tin Pan Alley, the area that had been famous throughout the world as the heart of British music in the 1950s and 60s.

"I can't find Tin Pan Alley on this map you've given me!" said Steve, tossing the scrap of paper into the front of the car.

"That's because it's proper title is Denmark Street, Stephen!" said Malcolm, retrieving the map from where it had landed in his lap, "but we'll need this to find the place, because it's in between numbers six and eight. You find it by going through an archway, which leads through to a small courtyard."

"Well, we're about to find out," said Glen, slowing the car down and flicking the indicator switch, "cos this is it. This is Denmark Street."

"Pull over here, boy!" said Malcolm, pointing out of the window. "It's next to the Tin Pan Alley Club. Well, that's the club, right there!" He stabbed a finger towards the small archway opposite. "There it is!"

Glen had to wait for a delivery van to pull out from the kerb before he could park up the car.

"Well, here we are boys," said Malcolm, after getting out from the car. He stood in the middle of the street gazing around him, taking in the atmosphere, as if he could feel the presence of his hero Larry Parnes, who had run his stable of British singers here such as Marty Wilde, Billy Fury and Vince Storm. The five of them crossed the street and walked through the alleyway, which brought them into the small courtyard at the rear. It was a grim looking building from the outside, the windows in the ground floor room had been bricked-up by the previous tenants to improve the soundproofing. Malcolm unlocked the door with the set of keys he'd collected from Collins earlier that day and waved the others through.

"Well, it's not as bad as I expected," he said, flicking on the light switch.

"Just needs a bit of cleaning," said Glen, nodding in agreement.

"A bit of cleaning!" exclaimed Paul, surveying the litter-strewed floor.

"Fumigating, more like," said John, sniggering.

"Let's take a look upstairs," said Malcolm, purposely ignoring John's comment.

The five of them climbed the narrow stairwell that led up to the entrance on the first floor. It stank of stale piss; either that or something had crawled in there to die.

"God, what a shit-hole!" said John, grimacing. His feet were sticking to the filthy sodden carpet.

"What's that smell?" gasped Paul, wrinkling his nose. He walked towards the other end of the dingy room. "Aghh, fuckin' hell!" He retreated away from the small toilet situated in the corner. "It's fuckin' disgustin'!"

"Take a look over 'ere!" said Steve, pointing up to the broken skylight.

"No wonder it's so fuckin' damp in here!" said Glen, shaking his head with dismay.

"We can live 'ere, as well as rehearse!" said Steve, spreading his arms out as if he was some half-assed estate agent trying to impress a pair of newlyweds about the potential of the two rooms.

"You can live here, if you want!" said Paul, laughing.

"I've seen better squats than this," said John, dismally.

"Steve's right," said Malcolm, stepping into the middle of the room, "slap a bit of paint on the walls, get some decent carpet down on the floor, then it won't be so bad."

"I'll do that," said Steve, nodding in agreement with Malcolm.

"And get the skylight fixed!" added Glen, glancing up to the ceiling.

"A few pieces of furniture and Stephen here," said Malcolm, putting his hand on Steve's shoulder, "will have his very own W1 address!"

"There's room for two in here," said Glen, frowning when everybody stared at him. "What? I've been thinking of leaving home for ages now!"

Finally, everything seemed to be fitting smoothly into place. The group's line-up was complete; they had their own permanent rehearsal room where they could settle down to write their own songs. Two of the group members, Steve and Glen, were actually living in the upstairs room, which would also double up as a place for group meetings. Malcolm could now concentrate on giving Vivienne all the help she needed to run SEX, as well as helping out more with the two children, Ben and Joe. So, it came as a total surprise to Malcolm when Paul called round at the shop to tell him that he was leaving the group.

"Why?" he asked, beginning to wonder if he hadn't been a bit hasty fronting the one thousand pounds for the place on Denmark Street.

"It's not going to work," replied Paul, fidgeting with the zipper on his jacket. "I don't think Steve's got what it takes to be a guitarist, and I really don't want to play in a group with anyone else."

"So, why don't we just get another guitarist to help you out?" asked Malcolm, slowly. "I've no objections to this group of yours being a four, five or even a six-piece, just so long as it gets somewhere!"

"I don't know," replied Paul, frowning. "We tried havin' two guitarists with Nick Kent, remember?"

"I know," said Malcolm, sensing that Paul was weakening, "but you all said that Kent was no bloody good!"

"So, what're you sayin'?"

"Why don't we place an advertisement in the *Melody* whatcha-macallit?"

"*Melody Maker.*"

"In the *Melody Maker.*" He smiled gratefully at Paul. "And then you can have your pick from a hundred guitarists!"

"Well, all right," said Paul, nodding reluctantly.

Malcolm didn't waste any time in contacting the music paper to place the advert and placed the following notice in the Musicians Wanted section which appeared in the 27 September issue:

```
               WHIZ KID GUITARIST.
               NOT OLDER THAN 20.
    NOT WORSE LOOKING THAN JOHNNY THUNDERS.
          AUDITIONING TIN PAN ALLEY.
           RING 351 0764 673 8055.
```

In the meantime Malcolm gave instructions that Steve should be practising every day and that since Glen was living with Steve, he should help him. Unfortunately for Malcolm, out of all the people who turned up for the auditions the only guitarist worth considering was a fifteen-year-old kid called Steve New. But, after careful deliberations, it was decided that although the advertisement in the Melody Maker had stressed that the applicants should not be older than twenty they all felt that fifteen was too young.

It was around this time that Bernie Rhodes became involved with a group of musicians who were rehearsing in the basement of a café on Praed Street in Paddington. Malcolm was keen to nurture a stable of up and coming groups just like his hero, Larry Parnes. He instructed Bernie to bring these young kids round to Denmark Street to meet up with Steve and the boys. When they arrived, Bernie introduced them to Steve, Paul and Glen but the mysterious John wasn't present – he'd gone down to Highbury with his friend, Gray, to watch Arsenal playing in the League Cup. Bernie and the four newcomers followed Steve and the others down into their rehearsal room, so as to get an idea of what sort of music they were playing. Steve couldn't look at either Paul or Glen without smirking at the four long-hairs that Bernie had brought with him. Glen couldn't believe that Bernie could even think that these four guys with their hair half way down to their arses would have any similarity to what they were doing.

Malcolm had arrived during the impromptu rehearsal, seemingly disgruntled that John was absent. Steve took this as his cue to stop playing and removed his guitar, placing it on a stand next to his amplifier. The boys had been busy cleaning the downstairs room since first taking over the place but the pervading smell of stale piss hadn't quite yet disappeared. Glen and Paul followed suit and came over to see what Malcolm was saying to their four guests. It seemed he was busy regaling them with tales of how he had spent six months in America managing The New York Dolls and that the time was right for new groups such as themselves to get their chance to succeed in the music industry.

Glen, having heard the party line several times before, decided he'd make better use of his time cleaning his bass guitar, though he occasionally glanced over towards the others, wondering if Malcolm had ever thought of going into politics as he never seemed to be at a loss for words. One of the four guys with Bernie would occasionally look round to see what Glen was doing, giving him an expression of "when's this guy ever going to shut up" or more likely "does this guy ever shut up!" When it was time for Malcolm, Bernie and his long-hairs to leave, the one who'd been watching Glen decided to stay behind for a jam with Steve, Paul and Glen, impressing them with his abilities to create simple and catchy riffs on the guitar.

The next afternoon, Glen called round at the shop on the King's Road. He'd borrowed his father's car as it was quite a journey across London from his new home on Denmark Street, especially when money was a problem, and just lately it was definitely a problem. He was there to give Malcolm his report on Steve's progress on the guitar and, more importantly, to find out what Malcolm and Bernie had in mind for the guys from Paddington.

"It was just an idea I've had," said Malcolm, when Glen quizzed him about the previous evening. "There's no harm in pooling your resources and they aren't hippies!"

"No, I suppose not," replied Glen, "no harm pooling resources, I mean."

"How is Steve getting on, anyway?" asked Malcolm, looking directly at Glen.

"Oh, he's coming on great," said Glen, hoping to sound convincing, "but I've had an idea, as well."

"Really! What about?"

"Well," said Glen, pausing while he chose his words carefully. "You remember last night, the guys Bernie brought round with him?"

"How could I forget!"

"Well, one of them stayed behind to have a jam with us," continued Glen. "He's called Mick and he can play pretty good!"

"But wasn't he one of those *hippies*?" said Malcolm, accenting the last word and grinning at Glen.

"I know, I know," said Glen, grinning back at Malcolm, "but I reckon we could work well with Mick, and I'm sure that Steve would really learn stuff from him as well!"

"What's his name?"

"Mick Jones."

"And where does this Mick Jones live?"

"I'm not sure," said Glen, frowning. "He mentioned something about squatting in a house somewhere on London Street in Paddington."

"Well, that's a start, I suppose," said Malcolm, thoughtfully. "What about his hair?"

"We can cut his hair!" said Glen, laughing. "And give him a change of clothes. Did you see those leopard-skin flares?"

"How could I miss them?" replied Malcolm, grinning. "Can you borrow your father's car?"

"Oh yeah," said Glen, nodding, "I've got it now for the whole day!"

That evening, Glen and Malcolm drove over to Paddington to see if they could locate the house where Mick Jones was staying. After knocking on several doors and being told to "Fuck off" in no uncertain terms, Malcolm was ready for giving up and going home, but Glen wasn't about to be dissuaded so easily.

"Let's try another one," he said, knowing that Malcolm didn't really have much of a choice in the matter seeing as he was the one driving. Glen hammered on the door a couple of times to no avail. "I can't believe Bernie doesn't have his address!"

"Well, that's irrelevant right now, isn't it?" said Malcolm. "Jesus, boy! They all probably think we're the police, with you trying to batter their front doors down!"

What, with you dressed like that? thought Glen, glancing round at Malcolm, standing there in his leather trousers, laced shirt and three quarter length coat.

"We've gotta make sure they can hear us!" he said instead. Glen looked up at the boarded up windows. There was no sign of anyone living there, but that was the whole idea of squatting.

"Go away!" said a foreign-sounding voice from the other side of the door.

"We're looking for a Mick Jones!" said Glen, crouching down and peering through the letterbox. "Do you know anyone of that name?"

"Why should I tell you?" asked the unseen voice from behind the door. "What's in it for me?"

"For fuck's sake!" said Glen, becoming frustrated. "Just tell us where he lives!"

"I never said I knew him!" replied the voice, sounding disgruntled.

"Well, do you?" asked Glen.

"Like I said, what's in it for me?"

"Listen here, you scrounger!" yelled Malcolm, losing patience with the tiresome charade, "if you don't help us, I'll report you to the bloody police myself!"

"Oh, well done, Malcolm!" said Glen, standing there bewildered. "That's really helped!"

"Is he still there?" asked Malcolm.

"I can't see anyone," replied Glen, crouching down in front of the letterbox again.

"Oh, I can't be bothered with this!" snapped Malcolm. "Let's get out of here!"

"Where are we going now?" asked Glen, turning away from the doorway.

"Firstly, you can take me back to the flat before I freeze to death!" replied

Malcolm. "And then you can go and see if you can convince Paul to stay in the group!"

Glen drove Malcolm to the flat in Clapham in silence, although Malcolm did mutter a good night as he closed the car door. Then he drove over to Paul's parents' house in Hammersmith, pondering how best to handle the situation. It would have been so much easier if they'd managed to find Mick Jones. He turned onto Paul's street, relieved to see a chink of light shining through the curtains in the front room. He really didn't fancy having to shout through another letterbox this evening. He was just about to knock for a second time when Paul's younger sister Margaret opened the door.

"What's up?" asked Paul, following Margaret into the hall from the living room. "Come on, we'll go up to my room."

Once they were settled on Paul's bed, Glen told Paul about the evening's fruitless search for the guitarist.

"Pity," said Paul, grinning at the thought of Malcolm wandering the streets of Paddington and shouting through letterboxes, even if it had been Glen that had been doing the actual shouting. "He's not bad, that Mick, is he?"

"No," replied Glen, shaking his head, "but we don't even know if he lived at that place, anyway!"

"So now what?" asked Paul.

"Well, we could wait until Malcolm sees Bernie again," said Glen, "but I reckon Bernie will want to keep Mick with his guys from Paddington."

"Umm," said Paul, nodding thoughtfully, "knowing our luck."

"Steve really is improving every day," said Glen, seriously. "You should have heard him this morning."

"Yeah, I know," replied Paul, wistfully, "it's just that I've got my apprenticeship at the brewery to think about, an' I could be putting in some overtime instead of fuckin' about down Denmark Street!"

"I know," said Glen, sullenly, "but I've got college, remember?"

"Look, I want this group to work as much as any of you!" said Paul. "I'm just being realistic, that's all!"

"Well, give it a few more weeks then," said Glen, sensing Paul was beginning to weaken. "We haven't even played a gig, yet!"

"Don't remind me," said Paul, pulling a face. "That's all I get off my mates at work!"

"So, what do you say?"

"I'll give it 'til Christmas," replied Paul, sighing.

"Great!" said Glen, nodding cheerfully. "There is just one more thing."

"What now?"

"How come I've got a mate who works in a brewery," said Glen, "and I'm still sat here without a drink!"

The lads spent the next few weeks rehearsing solidly and improving their headquarters upstairs, although the skylight was still in need of urgent repair, especially now that winter was on its way with a vengeance. They had also performed wonders with the downstairs rehearsal room; it was looking very professional now that they had all the sound-proofing on the walls. The four members of the group were sitting upstairs trying to decide on which songs they could incorporate into a set for when they were ready for their first gig. John, poised with his pen, read out each song title from the list. Each of them was entitled to an opinion, either for or against, then John would place a small tick next to the song or scrub it out altogether. So far, they had voted in favour of the cover versions of "Substitute" by The Who, the very first song John learned upon joining the group; "No Lip" by the sixties' crooner, Dave Berry; "Whatcha Gonna Do About It?" and "Understanding", both by The Small Faces.

These were all songs that they felt they could relate to, especially John, who seemed to have developed a real talent for twisting the lyrics of the songs to give them a totally different meaning. To his mind the opening line to the song: "Whatcha Gonna Do About It?" was far more potent by simply changing it to: "I want you to know that I hate you, baby", because now you were saying something.

"What about 'Thru My Eyes'?" asked John, reading the next song title on the list.

"Well it's all right, I suppose," said Paul, stretching out his arms to relieve a cramp in his shoulder, "but it ain't anythin' special."

"Is that a yes or a no?" asked John, glancing at the other two, pen ready to strike it from the list.

"It's a fuckin' no!" said Steve, reaching for his cigarettes. "Next?"

"What about the new stuff?" asked Glen, referring to their own material.

"Well," said John, holding up the pad containing all of his lyrics, "there's 'Only Seventeen'..."

"We have been busy," said Paul, grinning at John.

"That's the title of a song, dear boy," replied John. "It's pretty much finished. Now, as for the rest, they're still nothin' more than ideas."

"Have you come up with any new lyrics for 'I Did You No Wrong'?" asked Paul.

"Yes," replied John, rolling his eyes at Paul, "so it's a far better song now."

"So we've got two songs then," said Steve, lighting two cigarettes together and passing one over to John. "Show 'em the one we've been workin' on," he said to Glen.

"It's just something that me an' Steve have been messing about with," said Glen, handing John a folded piece of paper.

"What do you think?" asked Steve, sitting forward.

"Rubbish!" said John, turning his head to one side and blowing a lump of snot onto the floor.

"Fuckin' hell!" yelled Steve, looking with disgust towards John. "You're always doin' that, you dirty cunt!" He stood up and crossed the room. "You're fuckin' rotten, you are, like your fuckin' dog-end teeth!"

"Yeah," said Paul, grinning at Steve's outburst, as he was hardly the cleanest person around. "Johnny Rotten, that's you!"

"Johnny fuckin' Rotten!" said Steve, walking back towards the others, "that's your fuckin' name from now on!" For the rest of the evening, every time John asked them a question they answered him by calling him his new nickname, much to his annoyance.

It was during their time rehearsing on Chalk Farm Road that Malcolm had approached John and Glen with an idea for them to write a song about sexual submission, which would help promote the S&M clothing that he and Vivienne were selling in the shop. John, being left to his own devices, had written an amusing tongue-in-cheek lyric in which the submission was all about a submarine mission and full of innuendoes. Once he'd finished the set of lyrics he showed them to Glen, who quickly came up with a bass line. They both felt that the song should have a slower tempo than anything they'd done so far, yet still have the power which was becoming their stock-in-trade. Glen borrowed the riff from one of his favourite songs, "All Of The Day And All Of The Night" by The Kinks; he just changed the key from a G to a C, playing it slower than the original and, hey presto, a new tune. When he played the bass line to Steve and Paul they worked out a pattern for the song. This was how they seemed to work best. One of them would come to a rehearsal with an idea and they would jam the basic structure until they had a finished song, which they could then add to their repertoire.

Glen was returning to his new home in Denmark Street after a visit to his parents in Greenford. Although he no longer lived there, it was nice to surround himself with all the comforts his parents' home offered, while getting his washing done at the same time. His mother would always insist on feeding him enough food to last him a week because she fretted that he was wasting away. She had joked with him, as he was leaving, that she would get him a magic basket, just like the one she had in her bathroom, into which he could throw all his dirty clothes only to find them washed, ironed and hanging in his wardrobe the next time he needed them. "Yes!" he thought, climbing the stairwell of his new abode. "We could certainly use a magic basket here!"

He wrinkled his nose in disgust as the smell hit him full in the face. It was definitely getting worse. He'd also begun to notice tiny pieces of the cork material that the previous occupants had used to help sound-proof the walls, lying on the floor and small holes had suddenly appeared in the corners. So either Steve wasn't too fussy what he ate or they had houseguests – or maybe that should be mouseguests.

Steve was sprawled on his bed, idly flicking through his collection of porn magazines; his Gibson guitar was lying on the floor beside the bed within easy reach.

"I've been down to my parents' house to get the washing done," said Glen, sitting on the corner of Steve's mattress and placing a carrier bag full of clothes next to the guitar. "And, funnily enough, some of your dirty gear was in my bag!"

"Yeah," said Steve, obviously distracted by what he was looking at, "funny that, innit!"

"Nice tits," said Glen, glancing at Steve's magazine.

"An' look at the corrie on it!" said Steve, turning the magazine round for Glen. Glen knew that Steve had little use for the lewd story lines, as he'd left school with difficulties in both reading and writing, but boy did he like to look at the pictures.

"Have you been out shopping?" asked Glen, pointing to a loaf of bread lying on the floor on the opposite side of the bed.

"What?" asked Steve, still engrossed in the vital statistics of Debbie, who judging from the pictures in the magazine, must have been a semi-professional contortionist. "Oh, that! Do you want some?" Glen failed to notice the grin spreading across Steve's face as he watched him examining the loaf.

"What's inside it?" asked Glen, holding the loaf up for closer inspection.

"Liver," replied Steve, propping himself up on one elbow.

"Liver," said Glen, frowning, "but it's not cooked!"

"Course not!" said Steve.

"You a closet cannibal?" asked Glen, gingerly prizing the slices of bread apart to inspect the contents. "How can you eat raw liver?"

"Who said anythin' about eatin' it?"

"Well, what do you do with it?"

"I shag it!" said Steve, howling with delight as Glen hurled the loaf across the room, wiping his hands on his jeans as if he'd been contaminated. "It's fuckin' great! It's just like the real thing!" He stood up and went over to retrieve the loaf from where it had landed near the window.

"Don't bring it near me!" yelled Glen, backing away from Steve.

"What you do is, you cut the bread in half..."

"I don't want to know!" protested Glen.

"Then rip out the middle," continued Steve, ignoring Glen's protests, "then you add the liver and pour hot water on it."

"What!" gasped Glen, shaking his head in disbelief.

"Not too fuckin hot, mind," said Steve, smiling, "you don't want to burn your knob!"

"You're fuckin' depraved, Jonesy!" said Glen, crossing the room to his own bed.

"Well, it's better than a posh wank, innit?" said Steve, innocently.

▭   ▭   ▭   ▭

It was now the end of October and the boys were beginning to suffer from cabin fever. It was time to get out there gigging. They had enough songs ready to play a thirty to forty-five minute set, which would be ample for a support slot.

"Look," said John, during one of their regular in-house meetings, "if we fuck-up, who's gonna know?"

"He's got a point," agreed Glen.

"Let's just get out there an' fuckin' play!" continued John. "I don't give a fuck if we make a million mistakes!"

"What about seeing if you can get a gig at that college of yours?" said Malcolm, looking over at Glen.

"Shouldn't be a problem," replied Glen, nodding thoughtfully. "I can sort that out. I know the guy that does all that."

"What name are you gonna give 'em?" asked Steve.

"What do you mean?" asked Malcolm, frowning. "I thought we'd sorted all that out!"

"What, you mean Sex Pistols?" said Glen.

"Yes, boy!" replied Malcolm. "What's wrong with that?"

"Well, it's all right," replied Glen, noncommittally.

"Why not just call ourselves Sex?" offered John.

"Sex!" gasped Malcolm, stepping into the middle of the room. "What's Sex?" He was growing red in the face. "You're not saying anything, boy!" He stopped himself, realising he had almost fallen into John's trap, after all SEX was the name of his shop.

"All right," he said, slowly. "Sex is provocative but Sex Pistols are sexy young assassins. You're active, immediately!" He glanced over at Steve and Paul, expecting the block vote as usual.

"Me?" asked Steve, realising that Malcolm was expecting an answer from him. "I'm just fuckin' glad it ain't Kutie Jones and his Sex Pistols!" He winked at John as he said this.

"Right," agreed Paul, nodding at Steve, "I just thought we might have come up with somethin' a bit more normal, that's all!"

"Normal!" yelled Malcolm, hardly believing his ears. "Who the fucking hell wants normal?" Paul shrugged his shoulders and looked away.

"Well, it's better than anything we've come up with!" said Glen, looking at Malcolm.

"Yeah," said Steve, wincing. "Kid Gladlove. Can you imagine playin' somewhere with a name like that?"

"I quite liked The Damned!" said Glen, referring to another one of Malcolm's ideas for a group name.

"So, are we finally agreed then?" asked Malcolm, looking at each of them in turn. "Then Sex Pistols it is!"

CHAPTER SEVEN

Paul was heading back towards the rehearsal place on Denmark Street after telephoning Malcolm from the telephone box just around the corner, in front of St. Giles' Church. Malcolm had failed to show up that afternoon after promising that he'd be over to tell them what his plans for the group were. Normally, his presence or the lack of it wouldn't be of any particular concern but today was different. Glen had arrived earlier with the news that he'd got them their first gig, at his art school, St. Martin's on Charing Cross Road. They would be the supporting act for a group called Bazooka Joe, on Thursday 6 November. Paul was sure he'd never heard of them before, though Glen had mentioned something about them being a Rock 'n' Roll revival group. But Paul didn't care. To him the first gig was the first step to stardom and he didn't give a flying fuck who they supported.

He was walking through the archway leading to the courtyard at the back when he felt another rush of excitement and the accompanying strange butterfly sensation in his stomach. He had to admit that things were definitely starting to happen, one way or another.

If Steve and John had been surprised at Glen's news, then wait 'til he told them what he'd just heard, he thought.

"Malcolm's left Vivienne!" he yelled, as soon as he entered the upstairs room. Everybody stopped what they were doing and stared at Paul, waiting for him to continue.

"What the fuck are you on about?" said Steve, draining the last mouthful from his can of lager and tossing the empty can at Glen.

"Straight up!" replied Paul, brushing some of Steve's clothes from the bed and sitting down. "I've just been on the phone to the shop, haven't I?" He reached across and helped himself to one of Steve's remaining cans. He pulled the metal ring and took a mouthful.

"Go on, Paul," said Bernie, exchanging glances with John. They'd been discussing the kidnapping of Dr. Tiede Herrema by the IRA. The industrialist had been held captive for over a month now, without any sign from the British government that they were closer to bringing about his release. The Irish police had besieged a house in County Kildare for the last seventeen days, but had made no attempt to free Dr. Herrema since he'd last appeared in the doorway. One of his captors had been holding a gun to his head as the industrialist had pleaded with the police not to storm the house.

"Well, it was Jordon that answered," said Paul, pausing for another swig from his can. "So I says, can I speak to Malcolm, and she says, 'he's gone!'"

"Gone where?" asked Glen, the gig at St. Martin's temporarily forgotten.

"Well, that's what I asked her!" replied Paul, continuing with his tale, "and she says, he's gone, he's left Vivienne!"

"Fuck off, she's havin' you on," said Steve, giving his can of lager a quick shake before he pulled the ring, spraying Paul with lager.

"Honest!" said Paul, spurting Steve with lager from his mouth.

"Come on, boys!" said Bernie, trying to restore order. "What else did Jordon tell you?"

"She said he's moved out of the flat in Clapham and gone livin' on Bell Street."

"That's just off Edgware Road, isn't it?" asked Glen.

"Think so," replied Paul, nodding.

"So who's livin' there then?" asked Steve.

"He's moved in with some dwarf!" said Paul, beaming. He'd been saving this piece of information until last.

"A fuckin' dwarf!" gasped Steve, who'd almost choked on his lager.

"She's called Helen!" said Bernie, quietly.

"Helen?" said Steve, frowning. "Who the fuck is Helen?" He seemed quite shocked that Malcolm had been keeping secrets from him.

"He met Helen when they were at Goldsmith College together," said Bernie, not sure how much he should tell them. He removed his spectacles and wiped them on his shirt before continuing. "She's from South Africa..."

"An' is she a fuckin' dwarf?" said Steve, grinning at Bernie; he was trying to imagine Malcolm with a dwarf, and grinned even more.

"Yes Steve, Helen is a dwarf!" replied Bernie, giving Steve a scathing look. "She's a lovely girl...and she's also very wealthy!"

"You've got to hand it to the cunt, haven't you?" said Steve, shaking his head.

"And what does madam Vivienne have to say about all of this?" asked John, speaking for the first time since Paul dropped his bombshell.

"Jordon says she don't seem too bothered," said Paul, shrugging. "She reckons he'll be back, because he hasn't taken all his gear with him."

"Life's never dull with Malcolm around, is it?" said John, resuming his reading of the kidnapping story in the newspaper.

When Malcolm did put in an appearance at Denmark Street the following afternoon, he carried on as if nothing was out of the ordinary. It seemed as if he was trying to play down any adverse effect his change of address might have on his involvement with the group. He was even managing to ignore Steve's constant jibes and snide remarks about the group having Snow White as a manager. John, ever keen to fuel the fires of mischief, had surprised everybody by coming to Malcolm's aid by chastising Steve for his insensitivity. Then, in his inimitable deadpan droll and his face devoid of expression, he had told Malcolm that hopefully, size and lack thereof, would not be a problem. Malcolm's relief was short-lived however. He soon learned that John's charitable act had been nothing more than an opportunity to deliver the knockout verbal punch when, with an obvious glance towards Malcolm's nether regions, John added, "For both of you!"

Malcolm smiled wistfully. Boys will be boys, he thought as he glanced round the room, his eyes resting briefly on each of the young faces before him. "Nothing has changed as far as I'm concerned," he announced. "There is no reason," he stopped briefly to clear his throat, "why everything should not continue as normal, both with the running of the group and the shop." This last comment raised a smile from Paul as he remembered Jordon telling him that Vivienne was refusing to hand over Malcolm's share of the profits.

"The main benefit of me staying with Helen," he continued, "will be that I shall use it as my office." He then handed out slips of paper containing the address and telephone number of the flat on Bell Street. He waited for anyone to speak and when they didn't, he turned his attentions to the impending gig.

"So, tell me all about the show," he said, glancing over at Glen. Glen quickly gave Malcolm the details of how he'd secured them their first gig. It hadn't been all that difficult for him really; he'd been involved with the booking of groups to play at St. Martin's during his foundation year at the college. A couple of days later Glen obtained a second gig for the group for Friday 7 November, which should certainly liven that weekend up for them. This gig was at the Central School of Art, in Holborn. Glen was especially pleased to have landed this gig because they would be the support act for a group called Roogalator, who were already quite well known on the London college circuit. Maybe, just maybe, this might be the break they were looking for. If they played well, maybe Roogalator would let them act as their support group in the future.

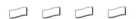

"So where are we playin'?" asked Steve, when Glen told him about the second booking.

"The Central School of Art," replied Glen, throwing himself on top of his bed. "It's in Holborn."

"How'd you get it?" Steve was really excited at the prospect of playing two gigs in two days.

"I spoke to some guy called Sebastian," replied Glen, "who just happened to be the social secretary there. "At least, I think that's what he said!"

"What do you mean?"

"The poor sod's got an awful lisp! I've invited him and his friend to come and see us play at St. Martin's."

"Oh well," said Steve, grinning, "if that don't put 'em off, nothing will!"

"Shall we go over to the shop and tell Malcolm the good news?" asked Glen, a mischievous glint in his eye. "We can see how he's dealing with Vivienne."

"You're on!" replied Steve, jumping up off his bed and reaching for his shoes.

"Maybe we can scrounge some money off him for some grub as well!"

"Great idea," replied Glen, nodding his agreement. "I'm starving!"

"We can tell Rotten and Cookie about the new gig when they get 'ere tonight," said Steve.

"He's stuck with that name, isn't he?" said Glen grinning, as they descended the stairwell leading to the courtyard.

"What, Cookie?" asked Steve. "Yeah, the poor cunt was born with it!"

"I meant John!" said Glen, shoving Steve down the last couple of steps. They walked out onto Denmark Street, crossing over at the junction leading onto Charing Cross Road.

"It's gonna be a famous landmark one day," said Steve, pointing over towards St. Martin's Art College.

"Course it will!" replied Glen, zipping up his Harrington jacket. "People will come from all over the world to gaze at the place where the world famous artist, Sir Glen Matlock, once studied."

"Sir Glen Matlock the piss artist, more like!" said Steve, grinning.

"Yeah, probably," sighed Glen.

It was almost four o'clock when they reached SEX. Steve went straight over to see what Malcolm had to offer in the way of T-shirt designs; he would pull one out and then shout across the shop at Malcolm to see how much he could have it for. Glen stopped to chat with Alan Jones for a couple of minutes, then went over towards Malcolm, who was standing near the jukebox talking with Michael Collins. He nodded at Collins and was about to say something to Malcolm, when their attentions were distracted by the sight of Jordon trying to help a middle-aged man squeeze himself into a rubber T-shirt, which was obviously a couple of sizes too small for him. The customer became even more agitated when Steve came over and started giggling. Malcolm decided it was time to intervene. He handed the swatch of cloth samples to Collins and gently guided Steve away from the customer.

"Steve, my boy," he said smiling, "what brings you all the way over here?"

"We've got another gig!" replied Steve, pulling away from Malcolm to get another look at the poor sod standing with his arms up in the air while Jordon struggled to lift the rubber T-shirt over the man's head. But the more he struggled, the more he perspired, and now the rubber was sticking to him.

"That's very interesting," said Malcolm, blocking Steve's view again. "Why don't we go and grab a coffee? Then you can tell me all about it." He glanced over his shoulder to see how Jordon was coping. Michael Collins was helping her now, by holding the customer around the waist while Jordon continued pulling the garment over his head.

"It looks like your fuckin' him, Mikey boy!" yelled Steve, as Malcolm began shoving him out of the front door. Suddenly, there was a loud commotion as the rubber T-shirt finally released its hold on the customer's sweat-covered skin, forcing Jordon to tumble backwards, while Collins and the customer fell in the opposite direction, crashing into one of the clothes rails. Steve darted past Malcolm and stood howling as the red-faced customer grabbed his own clothes and ran out of the shop.

"May I suggest a larger size next time, sir!" said Malcolm, still holding the shop door open. "Clean up in there, would you Michael?" he called out over his shoulder as he left with Steve and Glen.

The three of them settled at a table in a nearby café on the King's Road. Glen started to tell Malcolm all about how he had landed the group their second gig, but as soon as he mentioned Sebastian Conran's name, Malcolm seemed far more interested in him than the proposed gig.

"Is he related to Terence Conran by any chance?" Malcolm asked Glen, taking a sip of his coffee.

"I don't know!" said Glen, feeling slightly annoyed.

"Who's he anyway?" asked Steve, his mouth crammed with half of the ham and cheese sandwich that Malcolm had bought each of them.

"Who's he, boy?" gasped Malcolm, staring at Steve like he was from another planet. "Terence Conran is the owner of Habitat! Don't you read the newspapers?"

"No!" replied Steve, casually, before shoving the rest of his sandwich into his mouth.

"He got very excited when I told him the name of our group," said Glen, wanting to get Malcolm's attentions back onto the group.

"Really?" said Malcolm, his eyes lighting up. "What did he say?"

"Well, he said something like, 'With a name like the Thex Pithtols, we mutht definitely have you here.'"

Malcolm narrowed his eyes towards Glen who was giggling with Steve. "Are you feeling all right, boy?"

"He's got a lithp!" said Steve, as he and Glen began howling.

"You're going to need transport for the seventh, then!" said Malcolm, after waiting patiently until Glen and Steve had calmed down.

"What about the gig at St. Martin's?" asked Steve, frowning.

"You can walk!" snapped Malcolm. "Jesus Steve, it's only across the bloody road!"

"What about all the gear?" protested Steve. He had imagined himself travelling in style to gigs, not having to hump everything around like some packhorse.

"I hardly think it necessary to stretch my limited finances on the cost of hiring a van to travel, what...?" He stopped to drink his coffee before continuing. "What is it? A hundred metres from your place?"

"But..." Steve managed to blurt out before Malcolm cut him off.

"Like I said, I'll arrange for a van for the Friday night but as for Thursday...?"

Malcolm paused while he drained the rest of his coffee, "you'll have to manage without!" He saw the look that passed between Glen and Steve but neither of them said anything more about it.

"Anyway," he said grinning, "tell me more about Johnny Rotten. How on earth did that all come about?"

Glen sat back while Steve told Malcolm about how John had been christened with his new nickname.

"And does John mind being called Rotten?"

"Don't fuckin' care!" replied Steve.

"We don't call him that all the time," said Glen.

"I fuckin do!" said Steve, smirking at Malcolm.

"Yeah, you do!" grinned Glen, "but when we're rehearsing, me an' Paul still call him John."

"Ahh, but!" said Malcolm pondering briefly before pointing a finger towards Glen. "Ahh but," he said, wagging the finger, "think of the publicity we'll get with a group calling themselves the Sex Pistols, whose singer's called Johnny Rotten!" Glen smiled at Malcolm's use of the word "we", whenever there was the chance of some publicity for his shop.

"It's all right for you," moaned Steve, "you don't have to watch the dirty cunt snottin' all over the place!"

"It all reminds me of the late 1950s and early 60s when there were a whole host of British pop stars with exciting names like Vince Storm, Marty Wilde, and of course the wonderful Billy Fury." Malcolm seemed lost in time as his mind drifted back to the time when London was at the forefront of Rock 'n' Roll. What better reason could there be for renting a place in Tin Pan Alley? He'd wondered since if he would have been quite so keen to part with a thousand pounds if the studio had been somewhere like Peckham.

"An' Gary Glitter," said Steve.

"What?" gasped Malcolm, snapping out of his reverie. "Oh well, yes, I suppose one could include young Gary's name on the list." He glanced at his watch; he really needed to be getting back to the shop just in case Vivienne decided to have the locks changed or something. "So, everything's sorted for Thursday night then?" he asked, getting up from his chair.

"Yeah," replied Glen. He'd been as disappointed as Steve that there wouldn't be any transport provided for their debut gig at St. Martin's as he'd been hoping to impress his fellow students. "We've to be there at seven-thirty and we'll probably be going on stage about nine o'clock."

"Splendid!" said Malcolm, "and I'll see who I can round up to come and witness the birth of the Sex Pistols! Have you got any posters put up yet, at that college of yours?" he asked Glen.

"Course I have!" replied Glen. "I'm not that stupid!"

"Let me have a couple, will you?" said Malcolm, thoughtfully. "I'll get Michael to put them up in the shop."

"Are you goin'?" asked Steve, glancing up at Malcolm.

"Yes, while I still have a shop to run! I can't sit around all day dreaming of becoming a rock star!" Malcolm paused for a few moments, waiting to see if Steve and Glen were going to follow him. "Are you two staying in here?"

"Too right!" said Steve, nodding towards the front door. "It's fuckin' freezin' out there!"

"Only trouble is, it's warmer out there than it is in our place!" said Glen, referring to the lack of heating in their home on Denmark Street. Malcolm had thoughtfully provided a one bar electric fire, which struggled to provide enough heat for them to make toast, never mind heat up the room.

"I still can't see him with a dwarf," said Steve, as they watched Malcolm heading out of the door.

By the Thursday afternoon – the day of their first gig – Steve was shitting himself. The anticipation that had been growing with each passing day was becoming almost unbearable and he was increasingly worried that by the time of the gig the slight trembling sensation in his fingers would have become so uncontrollable that he'd be unable to play the songs. He and Glen had practised a few tunes earlier and Steve, failing to banish the bum note demons from his mind, had grown more and more frustrated as he kept hitting the wrong string or playing the wrong note. Glen had tried to calm him down by telling him that he would be all right when it mattered, but Steve wasn't so sure. John arrived around five o'clock, the notebook containing all his lyrics tucked under one arm. He seemed quite calm considering that he wouldn't even have the luxury of having his instrument to hide behind on stage.

While they waited for Paul to arrive, they checked one last time to make sure that they had packed everything they'd need for the gig. John tried to lighten the mood by announcing that he'd gladly run back over the road should they discover that something was missing during their performance, but the brittle nervous laughter was short lived.

Glen wandered over to John, who was wrapping the guitar leads before placing them into a carrier bag next to him. "Are we gonna play 'Go Now' tonight, or not?"

"Well, I ain't fuckin' singin' it, if that's any help to you!" said John, glancing up at Glen, a contemptuous sneer tugging at the corner of his mouth.

"Why not?" shouted Glen, angrily.

"Cos it's fuckin' awful, that's why," replied John, angrily. He picked up another guitar lead and proceeded to wrap it round his elbow.

"But I like it!" said Glen, glancing at Steve who had wandered over to see what all the fuss was about. The last thing he needed was to have these two at each other's throats.

"You would!" yelled John. "You fuckin' wrote it!"

"Well, I'll fuckin' sing it then!" yelled Glen. "It's another song, isn't it?"

"Well, I don't mind playin' it," said Steve, noncommittally. "That's if I can remember how it goes."

"Fine!" said John, tossing the guitar lead he'd finished wrapping into the carrier bag. "You can sing it, and I'll go and stand at the bar!" With that, he walked out of the room and went upstairs.

"It's fuckin' freezin' out there!" said Paul, coming through the door. He'd managed to get a lift off Del, his brother-in-law, who'd been the original bass player when they'd first started the group. Paul had detected a whiff of jealousy from his in-law now that they had reached the stage of gigging, and although Del had wished them good luck, he'd come up with some pitiful excuse as to why he couldn't come to watch them.

"Where's John?" asked Paul, pausing beside his partially dismantled drum kit.

"He's sulkin' upstairs," said Steve, glancing up at the ceiling. "Give him a shout. It's time we got this lot over there anyway!"

If Paul was curious as to why John was sulking he didn't bother asking either of them. He simply disappeared out of the room to tell John it was time to go. When John finally reappeared downstairs he seemed to have calmed down, but avoided making eye contact with Glen. The plan was to get all of their gear out onto the pavement on Denmark Street; Paul would then stand guard while Steve, Glen and John carried it over the road to the College.

"Hold up!" yelled Steve, as Glen was about to lock the door. He bounded up the stone stairs two at a time before heading towards the top drawer of the battered cabinet next to his bed. He yanked the drawer open and rummaged around until he finally found what he was looking for – a bottle of mandrax capsules. "These had better fuckin work!" he said to himself, popping one into his mouth.

Paul stood on the pavement outside Zeno's bookstore. None of the passers-by seemed to be particularly interested in the collection of musical instruments gathered on the street. Steve and Glen had already made one journey across Charing Cross Road and were now heading back to collect some more. John was leaning against one of the amplifiers, his head purposely turned away from the others whilst absent-mindedly studying his fingernails.

"Are you gonna help, or not?" asked Glen, scowling at John.

"Rod Stewart wouldn't have to do this!" said John, not bothering to look at him.

"He would if he were in this fuckin' group!" yelled Steve, angrily. John pulled a face and muttered something under his breath, but he grabbed hold of Paul's hi-hats and set off towards St. Martin's.

It took them less than half an hour to carry everything over to the college. They would be playing in one of the upstairs rooms, but fortunately there was plenty of room on the stairway to manoeuvre the heavy amplifiers. Once they had their gear inside the actual room of the gig, they set it up against the back wall, close to the electrical sockets.

They were totally oblivious to the small number of people already gathered inside the venue, who were all either members or friends of the main act, Bazooka Joe. All eyes seemed to be on John as he strolled around the room. His crudely cut Vaselined ginger hair was sticking out at all angles, and he was wearing a natty red pullover, which was ripped completely up the right-hand side. This, he'd informed them, had nothing to do with making a fashion statement, but rather the fact that the garment, in its previous state, had been at least two sizes too small.

There was a definite feeling of safety in numbers when Malcolm arrived with various friends and employees from the shop, although Jordon seemed to be causing as much of a stir as John. Steve was slightly disappointed that Malcolm hadn't brought the dwarf along though by this time the mandrax was beginning to kick-in and he didn't really care.

Malcolm stood close to where they had set up the equipment and seemed very pleased to see that Glen, Paul and Steve were all wearing clothing from SEX. Glen was wearing a pink jacket, which really went well with his black straight-leg trousers that he'd customised by splattering white paint on them – very Jackson Pollock. Paul was wearing one of Malcolm's Cambridge Rapist T-shirts, although it would be obscured from view by his drum kit during the performance and Steve was wearing Paul's "You're gonna wake up" T-shirt.

The one disappointment, as far as Malcolm was concerned, was that John, the group's frontman, wasn't wearing anything from the shop. This didn't really surprise him as they had argued over it several times since John had joined the group. John openly admitted how much he liked the clothing Malcolm and Vivienne sold in SEX, but he was adamant about his right to wear what he wanted, whether Malcolm liked it or not, and judging from the reaction of the students and the small crowd there for Bazooka Joe, John was certainly the focus of attention.

"We're on, now!" said Glen, rejoining the others sitting at the table nearest to their equipment. "It's nine o'clock!" He could feel his heart pounding in his chest and his mouth had suddenly gone dry. He reached over and helped himself to a drink from Paul's glass. "That's better," he added, nervously.

The four of them casually made their way over to the stage area and made some last minute adjustments. Malcolm and their other friends came closer to get a better view. Paul beat out a monotonous rhythm on his bass drum while he waited for Glen and Steve to check the tuning on their guitars. Steve had to move around in front of his amplifier to reduce the amount of feedback, although there wasn't all that much room for him to move around in. John stood with one hand casually resting on his microphone stand, smirking at some of his mates standing over at the bar.

"Are we ready yet?" he turned around and asked Glen.

"As I'll ever be!" replied Glen, wiping his hands on a beer towel.

"Fuck 'em!" said John cocking his head towards the members of Bazooka Joe and their small entourage. "Too bad if they don't fuckin' like us, we'll just treat it like any other rehearsal!"

"Come on freak, get on with it!" an unseen voice heckled from the crowded bar.

"Does your mummy know you're out past your bedtime?" replied John, drolly, glancing in the heckler's general direction.

Paul clicked his drumsticks together and Steve and Glen launched into "Did You No Wrong". This was the culmination of everything they'd worked for; the countless hours spent rehearsing the same songs over and over again, ever striving towards the all-important milestone of being capable of playing a half-hour set. This was the moment they had once hardly dared dream of. Yet here they were, playing the music they wanted to listen to. We are the Sex Pistols and you will like us on our terms. The word compromise is not in our vocabulary. As the song finished in a crescendo of wailing feedback from Steve's guitar, they could hear Malcolm, Jordon and some of the others clapping wildly and offering shouts of encouragement. There was nothing but total silence from the crowd gathered at the other side of the room.

During their second number, "Substitute", the feedback from Steve's guitar was threatening to drown out the rest of the group, but if Steve was aware of it he didn't show it. He was at Wembley Stadium, playing to a sell-out crowd that idolised him.

"What the fuck is he on?" yelled John, glancing towards Paul. But Paul was far too busy concentrating on maintaining a steady drum beat to understand what John was trying to tell him.

Steve had somehow decided that he wasn't loud enough and cranked up the volume on his amplifier, which created even more feedback. Glen had been forced to turn up the volume on his amplifier to compete with Steve.

"We're gonna bring the fuckin' ceiling down at this rate!" he muttered to himself. It was chaotic, but exhilarating at the same time. He glanced down at his hand-written set list taped to the floor to check which song they would be playing next; "Only Seventeen", one of their own. He hit the last notes of the song "No Lip", letting the last one ring out to accompany Steve's wailing feedback. In the excitement of it all they were playing far too fast. They'd already played four songs and they hadn't been on stage for more than ten minutes or so.

"We need to slow down a bit!" he shouted in John's ear before glancing across at Steve. Steve, who had no idea that his friends were beginning to worry about him, merely offered a lop-sided grin. By that point he was far away on the good ship mandrax and there was stormy water ahead.

"You try tellin' him!" said John, nodding in Steve's direction as their self-named guitar hero blasted into "Only Seventeen". They were half way through the song when suddenly the power died. Glen stood looking mystified, as did Paul, who had stopped playing. Even Steve had realised something was wrong.

"What the fuck's goin' on?" snarled John, glaring at the fat guy standing in front of him wearing an Elvis T-shirt before hurling his microphone stand down to the floor. It seemed that the show was over.

"What on earth's going on?" asked Malcolm, coming over towards John.

"Looks like they've had enough of us!" snarled John, jerking his thumb towards the crowd with Bazooka Joe. "Thank you very much Bazooka Joe. You bunch of cunts!"

Paul, Steve and Glen moved their gear away from the stage area while Malcolm and John continued their argument with the members of the main act. Glen spotted Sebastian Conran and his friend Al McDowell, who was, for some bizarre reason, dressed like a cheap 1940's British Music Hall act.

"That was um...interesting," said Al McDowell, nodding his head thoughtfully.

"Thanks," replied Glen, feeling strangely subdued now that it was over. "Are we still on for tomorrow night?"

"Thertainly," lisped Sebastian, nodding. Glen could see Malcolm hovering in the background and knew that he was awaiting an introduction.

"These are the guys I was telling you about," he said as a means to make the obligatory invitation and motioned for Malcolm to join them.

"Delighted to meet you," said Al McDowell, stepping forward to grasp Malcolm's hand. "I'm Al McDowell and this is my good friend Sebastian Conran."

"You're not one of the Conrans, are you?" asked Malcolm, dismissing McDowell and grasping Sebastian's hand.

"Why yeth," replied Sebastian, smiling. "Do you know my father?"

"Know him? Yes, of course I know him!" said Malcolm, gently guiding Conran away from his friend Al and Glen. "Well, when I say, I know your father, what I mean is...would you like another drink?"

"Oh-oh," said Glen, watching Malcolm at work. "I think he's a gonner!"

"Yes," replied McDowell, following Glen's gaze. "It's amazing, how often that happens to Sebastian!"

Steve came over to tell Glen that the others wanted to get the gear back over to their place on Denmark Street as they had no intention of staying behind to listen to Bazooka Joe. It took them considerably longer to carry their equipment back to the rehearsal room. The adrenaline and Steve's mandrax had worn off, making the amplifiers seem twice as heavy as before. Once they had finished the task, John went off with his friends. Glen headed back to St. Martin's to meet up with Al McDowell, leaving Steve and Paul to wander off around Piccadilly before crashing out on the two beds upstairs to talk about the evening's events.

CHAPTER
EIGHT

"Morning," said Glen, glancing up from the pages of the *New Musical Express* weekly music paper. Steve mumbled an incoherent response, then rolled over and covered his head with the covers. Glen got out of his chair and put the paper aside before approaching the bed. "How are you feeling?" he asked, grinning at his friend's deathly-white complexion.

"What a fuckin' night," groaned Steve, reaching across the mattress for his cigarettes. "Is Paul still here?"

"No, he wasn't here when I got back."

"What did you think about last night?" asked Steve, coughing out the day's first lungful of cigarette smoke.

"Apart from the fact that you were oblivious to what was happening; not being able to hear myself playing because of the feedback and being chucked off half way through the set?"

"Yeah, apart from that."

"I fuckin' loved it!"

Steve threw back the bed sheets and gingerly lifted his head away from the pillows. He then repeated the process with the rest of his body before retrieving his trousers from the spot where they had landed the previous night.

"What are you reading?"

"The *NME*," said Glen, holding up the music paper to show Steve. "But there ain't much in it this week!"

Steve raised his arms to pull his grubby T-shirt over his head and immediately flopped down on the bed as his throbbing head went into overdrive.

"You had a few last night, didn't you?" said Glen, shaking his head slowly.

"Umm, I need some food cos I'm fuckin' starving!"

"You got any money on you?" asked Glen, hopefully.

"No, have you?"

"Yeah, but not enough to feed us with and my stomach's beginning to think my throat's been slit!"

"Fuckin' marvellous!"

"I've got an idea, though,"

"Go on," said Steve. "I'm listening."

"Why don't we pay Malcolm a visit? See if we can scrounge some breakfast."

"And how do we get from here to Bell Street?"

"Easy, we can fare-dodge on the tube. I'm gettin' quite good at it now."

"Lead the way," said Steve, forcing himself up from his bed and reaching for his woolly jumper.

Steve and Glen strolled down Tottenham Court Road heading towards the tube station. They had already formulated a plan to get to Malcolm's place on Bell Street without either of them having to buy a ticket. They would wait near the entrance until the solitary guard was busy concentrating on the commuters coming out of the lift, then make a run for the stairs. They didn't have to wait long before the metal door to the lift slid open and, as luck would have it, the compartment was full of Japanese tourists, clutching their expensive cameras and guidebooks. The London-hungry tourists swamped the poor guard, requesting that he show them the way to "Buckerham Paris".

Steve and Glen almost felt sorry for the guard as they bounded down the spiral stairway leading to the platforms. They changed trains at Oxford Circus before getting off at Edgware Road. Once again there was a guard on duty at the station's entrance, but he was too busy helping an elderly lady as she struggled with her luggage to notice a pair of freeloaders. They casually strolled past them and headed off down Bell Street in search of number 93.

Glen knocked on the door a couple of times without any response. They were beginning to think that they'd made a wasted journey when there was the sound of movement coming from within the flat. They heard the key turning in the lock and then Steve and Glen found themselves face to face with the mysterious Helen. This was the diminutive female who had lured Malcolm away from Vivienne.

"Umm we're...we're here to see Malcolm," said Glen, suddenly lost for words.

"Come on in," replied Helen, smiling at them. "Go straight through. Would you like a coffee or something?"

"Umm, lovely," replied Glen, wiping his feet on the mat.

The pair entered the small living room and found Malcolm busy on the telephone, which was why he'd been unable to answer the front door, leaving the unfortunate Helen to get out of bed. He waved them over, pointing towards the sofa while he carried on his telephone conversation.

"Yes, that's right...the son of Terence Conran...yes, Habitat...Oh, yes, plenty of opportunities there...yes, I'll be seeing him tonight. The boys are playing at some college in Holborn." He smiled at Steve and Glen. "Yes, yes...I'll see you this afternoon."

Malcolm replaced the receiver but didn't bother to reveal who he'd been speaking to. He declined Helen's offer of coffee as she placed two cups down in front of her guests.

"So how does it feel to finally get the show on the road?" he asked, grinning broadly.

"Feels fuckin' great!" said Steve. "Only trouble is, I can't remember much about it!"

"Yeah," said Glen, grinning at Steve, "he was well out of it!"

"It was marvellous!" exclaimed Malcolm, rising out of his chair. "Those morons didn't have a clue what was happening right before their eyes! How could they go on stage after a performance like that?"

"What did we sound like?" asked Steve, taking a sip of his coffee.

"Sound like?" repeated Malcolm, frowning at Steve as if he was speaking in a foreign language. "Who cares what it sounded like?"

He leapt up out of his chair again. Steve and Glen exchanged bemused glances as they watched their manager and friend pacing up and down in front of them. They had made the journey to Bell Street in order to check out the new chick and get a hearty meal in the process, not to hear their manager belittle their efforts. One out of three was a poor result by anyone's standards and they were beginning to regret their decision. Even Helen seemed to be going dizzy as she tried to keep her eyes on Malcolm.

"It's the attitude!" said Malcolm, gesticulating at them again. "That's what's important! Show the audience that you don't care if they like you or not!"

"Malcolm?" said Steve, interrupting him.

"Yes, boy, what is it?"

"You got any food? We're fuckin' starvin'!"

"I'll get you boys something to eat," said Helen, rising to her feet, glad of the chance to escape the room. "Will ham and cheese toasted sandwiches be all right?" The look on Steve and Glen's faces was all the answer she needed.

Steve and Glen soon relieved the plate of its cache of sandwiches and were munching their way through a packet of chocolate digestives as they listened to Malcolm's plans for that evening's gig at Holborn.

"I've already arranged a van for the equipment," said Malcolm, turning to Glen, who was now fighting Steve for the last biscuit. "Are you listening, boy?" he gasped.

"Yeah!" replied Glen, bitterly as he watched Steve cram the last biscuit into his mouth, "I'm listening."

"You can collect the van at six thirty. I'll give you the telephone number that you'll need. It belongs to an acquaintance of mine that lives on Old Compton Street, so you won't have too far to walk."

Steve let rip with an enormous belch that threatened to shatter the windows. "You are comin' tonight, aren't you?"

"Of course I am!" replied Malcolm.

"What about you, Helen?" asked Glen.

"Well, I'd love to Glen," replied Helen, glancing over at Malcolm. "But unfortunately, I've ahh...already made other plans."

"Never mind," said Steve, "maybe next time."

"We're supporting Roogalator tonight," said Glen.

"Oh that'll be nice," replied Helen, although the blank expression on her face left it obviously clear that she had never heard of the group.

Glen collected the van from the address that Malcolm had given him earlier and left the flat with the owner's warning, that he'd better get his van back in one piece, still ringing in his ears. Steve, Paul and John were waiting for him at the rehearsal room on Denmark Street; the gear was just as they'd left it from the previous evening. Paul was acting as lookout and he disappeared to collect the other two once he saw Glen coming around the corner.

"Where the fuck did Malcolm get that from?" asked Steve, coming through the archway.

"Some miserable git that's got a fruit and veg stall on Berwick Street market!" replied Glen, slamming the van door shut. "It fuckin' stinks of cabbages in the back!"

Together they loaded up the gear and set off towards Holborn. Glen and John sat in the front of the van, with Steve and Paul huddled in the back with the equipment.

"You do know how to get there, right?" shouted Paul, above the grinding noises from the van.

"Course I do!" replied Glen. "No problem."

John had collected a small pile of mouldy brussels sprouts from the back of the van while he'd been helping load the gear. The offending vegetables were now nestled in his lap and he would occasionally hurl one out of the passenger window at some poor unsuspecting pedestrian, cackling wildly to himself whenever he hit the target.

"The entrance should be somewhere down here," said Glen, turning the van onto Procter Street. "Yep, there it is." He pulled up at the kerb in front of the Central School of Art and Design. "Apparently we're playing in the cafeteria on the first floor."

"And just how do we find this cafeteria?" asked John, tossing the few remaining sprouts into the road.

"Al gave me a diagram last night," said Glen, fishing the piece of paper from his back pocket. "He told me they've even built a small stage!"

"Al gave me a diagram last night," mimicked John, in an exaggerated falsetto voice before scraping up the phlegm from the back of his throat and spitting out the offending mucus towards the college's gates.

"Are we leavin' the gear in the van 'til we've found the place?" asked Paul.

"Sounds good to me," said Steve, walking towards the entrance. "Let's go an' check out the crumpet."

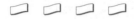

By the time the Sex Pistols were due to go on stage there was quite a large crowd gathered inside the cafeteria. The majority of them were obviously there for the main group, Roogalator, as they'd been playing on the London college circuit for ages now and had built up a good reputation amongst the music loving students. Malcolm arrived with Bernie Rhodes and another business acquaintance of theirs called Andy Czezowski. He was the owner of Acme

Attractions, a fashion boutique which was also located on the King's Road. Malcolm noticed straight away that there was a similar situation to the night before.

"It was like this last night!" he told Czezowski, pointing over towards John and the others, who were sat in isolation at a couple of tables positioned well away from the rest of the crowd. It was as if someone had drawn a line across the centre of the room, which the small throng of students was quite evidently fearful of crossing.

Upon her arrival, Jordon, dressed in full SEX regalia and painted face, had stunned the students into total jaw-dropping silence. She had immediately taken her place beside John as if to complete the image of maniacal bookends. Michael Collins was also sitting with the group in a show of SEX solidarity. Malcolm could also see Sebastian Conran and his friend Al, standing close by.

"It's definitely a them and us situation!" he said.

"Anyone would think they had the plague!" said Bernie, as they watched the four Sex Pistols stroll over to the small stage.

From the opening chords of "Did You No Wrong", through to the final song, their own version of the Small Faces' song, "Understanding", the reactions from the students watching ranged from disbelief to open hostility. They were booed and jeered at the end of each song.

John rose to the occasion magnificently, retaliating with put-downs and insults when anyone tried to have a go at them, and wishing that he'd kept the last of the sprouts for something slightly more painful than his steady supply of verbal ammunition. It was obvious from the start that he was the centre of attention; the eyes of the crowd were still riveted upon him, even when he left the stage and stood with Malcolm and Bernie while Glen sang his own composition "Go Now".

After they'd finished their full set, all four members of the group were pleased with the way they had played; it had been a much better performance than the one at St. Martin's. Paul had given Steve a bollocking for playing the songs at too fast a tempo, and although he knew that it was mainly due to nerves, the mandrax hadn't helped matters.

"There ain't many good looking birds here, is there!" grimaced Steve, glancing round the room. "An' I could do with a shag!"

Paul was only half listening to his friend because he'd noticed that Glen was in some sort of discussion with one of the guys from the main group and he thought there might be trouble. "What did he want?" he asked Glen, once their bassist had rejoined them.

"He was asking me if he could borrow my bass and amplifier for when they go on."

"Cheeky cunt!" said Paul, looking over at the guy in question.

"He's well impressed with my set-up."

"Fuckin' should be!" said Steve, "after all the trouble I had nickin' it!"

"Are we stayin' here to listen to this rubbish?" asked John, looking thoroughly bored with the proceedings.

"I'll have to," replied Glen, pointing over at the stage. "They're gonna use my gear."

"Well I don't!" scowled John, standing up. "What about you two?"

"Might as well stop here," replied Paul, shrugging. "It's Saturday tomorrow, so I get a lie in for a change."

"Yeah!" said Steve, looking up at John, "an' there's fuck all else to do!"

"And it's on until midnight," said Glen, indicating his watch.

"Well, I might turn into a bumpkin if I stay here much longer!" replied John, grabbing his jacket. "I'll see you tomorrow."

"What about the fuckin' gear?" yelled Steve, as John walked towards the exit. But if John heard him he didn't respond.

Now that the group had played their first gigs everyone seemed far more relaxed. There was a confidence now that had been lacking before St. Martin's. They still rehearsed every evening in order to get the songs tighter and Glen and Steve had sorted out the arrangement for the song "Submission", whilst John was currently working on a set of lyrics for a riff that Steve had played to him a few days ago. He was going to call this new song "New York", as a put-down to Malcolm's endless tirade about the exciting music scene that he'd witnessed during his six-month stay in America. They were hoping to have the song finished for their forthcoming gig on 21 November at Westfield College in Frognall.

Steve and Glen were standing in the centre of their rehearsal room trying to work out a basic pattern for "New York". Glen was playing the bass line to see if it fitted in with what Steve would be playing. Paul was waiting patiently behind the drums, twirling a drumstick in his hand; he looked over at John who was crouched in the corner writing out the verses, occasionally glancing up from the pages to see if anyone was watching him.

"Are we ready to try it yet?" asked Paul, stifling a yawn with his hand. "Some of us have got work tomorrow."

Glen looked over and nodded then went back to his own amplifier. John stood up clutching his lyrics and stood by the microphone. "How does it start?" he asked nobody in particular with both hands resting on the microphone stand while he slowly swayed from side to side.

"We start together," replied Glen, indicating himself and Steve. "We said two bars, didn't we?" He glanced over at Steve, who nodded his confirmation. "Yeah, it's two bars, then Paul comes in on the toms and then we'll bring it back in and that's when you come in with the vocal."

"God, you've lost me!" said John, turning to Paul. "Just start the fuckin' thing an' I'll find it."

Paul, as usual, counted them in by tapping his drumsticks together and Steve and Glen began the intro. Steve's eyes didn't leave his guitar while he played his fancy riff then he glanced up at Glen, who nodded back. The three musicians then played the opening two bars again in order to bring John in with his vocal.

"An imitation from New York, you're made in Japan from cheese and chalk." "You're hippie tarts hero cos you put on a bad show, put on a bad show an' don't it show!"

John turned away from the microphone while he coughed up the phlegm from the back of his throat and spat it out across the room, then he held up his hand for the others to stop playing.

"What's up?" asked Glen, once the music had died down.

"Is that where the chorus comes in?" John asked him between glances at his lyrics.

"Yeah."

"The chorus is in 'E', as well, isn't it?" asked Steve, positioning his fingers on the fretboard.

"Yeah, it is," replied Glen, nodding, "only play it lower, with your bottom 'E' string open."

"Are we doin' it again?" asked Paul.

"We'll run through it once more," replied Glen, "to see if we can get the chorus worked out. Then we'll knock it on the head for tonight."

On the Friday that the group was due to play at Westfield College, Malcolm received a telephone call from someone claiming to be on the college's student committee. The person said they were calling to inform him that unfortunately the Sex Pistols wouldn't be able to play that evening because the Student Union at the college had overspent on their budget. At first, Malcolm thought that this was some sort of cop-out by the college, but after offering the group's services free of charge he was told that there would be no objection to letting the group play. All he had to do now was break the bad news to the boys.

When he called round at Denmark Street, he found Steve, Glen and John there waiting for him but Paul was still at work. When he had finished telling them about his conversation with the guy from the student committee at Westfield College he asked them for their views on whether they were willing to play for free. John's view was that there wasn't much point in refusing to play that evening's gig as they hadn't seen a penny from the two gigs they'd played so far. Glen and Steve agreed with him, much to Malcolm's relief. He hadn't relished the thought of having to tell them he'd already agreed to let them play.

"So, I can ring the college and confirm the booking?" he asked, avoiding eye contact with any of them.

"We might as well play," said Glen, handing John a segment of his Kit-Kat chocolate bar.

"Is this all you two cunts eat?" scowled John, accepting the chocolate.

"I mean," continued Glen, ignoring John's comment, "we've been slogging our guts out all week gettin' a set together!"

"I suppose so," shrugged Steve, pulling out his cigarettes. "It's either that or stop in an' wash my hair."

"I agree with Glen," said Malcolm grinning at Steve's comment as he moved into the centre of the room. "You boys have worked really hard for tonight!" He paused while he thought about something. "So I'll need to sort out the arrangements for the van, won't I?" And with that he strolled out of the room.

Malcolm, had arranged for the Sex Pistols to play at the Queen Elizabeth College in Kensington the following Friday, 27 November. The college was holding its annual Christmas Ball and all the students had been asked to wear formal evening dress. Earlier that day John had called in at SEX, out of sheer boredom rather than for any other reason and was listening in while Malcolm told Bernie what few details he had so far.

"And Georgie Fame will be topping the bill!" he said triumphantly, before turning to face John.

"Wow!" replied John, drolly, "can't wait for that!" He spotted the newspaper that Bernie had brought with him, lying on one of the stools near the window and wandered over to see if there was anything inside about Arsenal. He scoured the sports pages at the back of the paper but didn't find anything of interest. He idly flipped the paper over and was drawn to the banner headline on the front page; it was all about the civil war raging in Angola.

"It's terrible, isn't it?" said Bernie, looking over John's shoulder. "That's what civil war does to a country!"

"Yes, it's comforting to know that we've already had ours, three hundred years ago," said Malcolm.

"Little bloody good it did!" John retorted indignantly. "We've still got a bloody useless monarchy!"

"Well, yes," agreed Malcolm, nodding, "but they don't have the powers that they once had."

Bernie jabbed his finger against the type-print. "It says that there's over forty thousand people been killed!"

"Listen to this," said John, holding the newspaper up to continue reading the journalist's gruelling account of the war. "Rival gangs are roaming the bush, raiding villages and farms in a bitterly contested three sided war." He looked at Bernie and Malcolm. "How the fuck does anyone have a three sided war? Are they gonna have some sort of fuckin' half-assed semi-final to see who gets to blow each other's brains out?"

"And who'd be the referee?" said Malcolm, glancing at the pages.

"It says here," said John, resuming reading the article, "there's the MPLA, then there's the FNLA and last, but by no means least, we have the UNITA!"

"That's right," said Bernie, nodding. "Basically the MPLA are communists and the other two factions are anti-communists but they can't stop fighting amongst themselves!" He again stabbed a finger at the paper in John's hands.

"The American CIA is supplying weapons to the FNLA and the UNITA. Then you've got British and South African mercenaries heavily involved! You see, John, this is a perfect example of what I was saying to you before. For every action there has to be a reaction!" He pointed to a grainy black and white photograph which accompanied the article. The photo was of several smiling African soldiers – all heavily armed. "The MPLA has caused this action in the first place, so whatever anybody else does, good or bad, has to be the reaction!" He looked at John again, to see if he understood the analogy he was trying to make.

"So what you're saying," said John, looking at Bernie and Malcolm, "is that what we're tryin' to do with the group is the action, and that what everyone else does…"

"Is the reaction!" interrupted Malcolm, looking really pleased with himself.

"Exactly!" grinned Bernie.

God, these two are priceless! thought John, turning his attentions to the story on the next page about a police raid on a high-class brothel in Knightsbridge.

The build up to Christmas was a busy time for the Sex Pistols. It seemed that every college in London and the surrounding area was booking groups to play for the students, to help get them into the festive mood before they all went home for the holidays. Malcolm seized this opportunity to book as many dates for the group as possible. On Friday 5 December he booked the group to play at the Chelsea School of Art, on Manresa Road and, seeing that Malcolm had his shop on the King's Road, Chelsea was, in his opinion, the place to be and he'd invited everybody that he knew to the gig.

This was the first time that the Sex Pistols would be the only group performing, although there would be a Disco beforehand. The boys arrived at the college feeling very relaxed. This time there would be no disputes about where they could set up their equipment; the stage was theirs and theirs alone. Malcolm had paid for the promotional posters, which were on display all around the college, and as there were no NUS restrictions for the evening, a decent sized crowd had already gathered inside the hall. There was an assortment of students, employees and customers from SEX, and a small coterie of Malcolm and Bernie's friends. There was a gang of Steve and Paul's mates making a lot of noise at the bar, not to mention John's friends. Gray was walking round with a borrowed camera and amusing himself by playing at being David Bailey for the evening.

The Sex Pistols went on stage around 10.30 p.m. John looked particularly menacing in his Cambridge Rapist T-shirt and seemed to be spitting out the lyrics rather than singing them. He was at war with conventionalism and taking no prisoners. Steve was wearing one of the Cowboy Dudes T-shirts that had landed Malcolm and Vivienne in Court that summer. He loved every second of being on stage. It gave him an identity, a newfound status and was better than getting his cock sucked – well almost. He was busy strutting around perfecting his Johnny Thunders' moves, but was careful not to get so carried away that he wouldn't hit the right notes at the right time. Glen and Paul, the group's rhythm section, had developed an understanding that was vital for any group and were keeping the chaos from jumping the rails. Glen was bare-chested beneath his black leather jacket except for the small imitation razor blade medallion fastened around his neck. The group were playing to their peers and although the songs were still disorganised, the sheer energy more than made up for it. There was no jeering or insults from the crowd that night.

CHAPTER NINE

Tuesday nights were tedious in Bromley. Come to think of it every night was tedious. The disillusioned Simon Barker was wandering around the main hall inside Ravensbourne College; the reason for his solitary prowl was his friend Steven's point-black refusal to leave his stool at the student bar. Simon was on the look out for a brunette that he'd spotted earlier that evening when he'd first arrived. He was pretty sure that he didn't know the girl but there had definitely been eye contact between them. He'd spent the last twenty or so minutes looking in all the usual places for the mysterious brunette without success and was ready for giving up and rejoining Steven in the bar when he was distracted by the raucous noise coming from another room at the end of the corridor.

Simon and Steven had seen the posters advertising tonight's group, who were calling themselves Fogg. Apparently the group was from Newcastle and although he had no intention of watching the Geordies' act, the possibility of finding his mystery girl somewhere in the crowd might be worth the effort. He pushed his way through a group of students who were blocking the doorway.

"Fuck me, it's busy tonight!" he thought to himself as he threaded his way through the crowd to get a better view of the group. He'd never heard of Fogg but one thing was for sure, they were making a bloody awful racket. It was at this point that Simon realised something rather strange was happening. He'd always considered it normal practice for the audience to be massed in front of the stage in order to get a better view of the group, not standing at the back of the room as if ready to escape in the event of a fire. In fact, the area in front of the stage was completely deserted. This was contrary to any gig he'd been to before and although the music was a bit shambolic, the group on stage were visually captivating and were like nothing he'd ever seen before.

The Sex Pistols finished the song they'd been playing. They were oblivious to the jeers and heckling, and the fact that their audience had fled to the back of the hall for fear of becoming contaminated. What really caught Simon's attention was when he heard the urchin-like singer shout out: "Why don't you all just fuck off and die?" Simon couldn't believe what he'd just heard and frantically glanced around the room to check the reactions of the people standing near him. He was about to return his gaze towards the stage when he spotted a face he recognised. The elegantly dressed guy with the wiry ginger hair was standing off to one side of the stage and seemed to be gauging the reaction of the crowd just like Simon was.

Where do I know him from, Simon pondered, while trying to put a name to the face. Then it came to him. It was the guy that owned SEX, in the World's End.

"Fuckin' hell!" he shouted out suddenly, not caring who heard him. The reason for his spontaneous outburst was because the group was playing "No Fun" by The Stooges. He almost thought of going off to drag Steven away from the bar to hear the group's rendition, but the performance on stage had rendered him incapable of movement. When the song came to an end Simon leapt up and down and shouted out his appreciation, not caring that he was the only person doing so. He was still clapping wildly well into the group's next number and when Simon turned around he noticed that the guy from SEX was looking directly at him.

With the show over and, with the exception of Simon, no request for an encore the four Sex Pistols were busy dismantling their equipment at the front of the stage. By this time Simon had learned that the group wasn't called Fogg and he was curious to find out more about them. He spotted the guy from SEX making his way towards the stage and without further thought Simon bounded towards the ginger-haired figure whilst trying to remember the guy's name. Malcolm, that's it, he thought. That was his name!

"Are you with the group?" he asked.

"Yes, I suppose you could say that," replied Malcolm, glancing at John and the others. "I'm their manager. What did you think of the show?"

"I thought they were brilliant!" replied Simon, glancing over towards the stage area.

"Really?" said Malcolm, looking bemused at the blond-haired youth standing before him.

"I couldn't believe what I was hearing when they started playing a song by The Stooges!"

"I think the rest of the audience would agree with you there."

"What are they called anyway?" asked Simon.

"Sex Pistols!" replied Malcolm, waiting for Simon's reaction.

"Sex ...oh, right, yes," said Simon, nodding thoughtfully as he made the connection between the name of the group and the shop on King's Road. "What a great name for a band. When are they playing again?"

"I'm not sure," replied Malcolm, rubbing his chin. "Listen, I own a shop in the World's End..."

"I know," said Simon, interrupting him, "I've been in!"

"Oh good. Well, why don't you pop in some time and hopefully I'll have more details for you." Malcolm looked up sharply when Steve called out to him. "Now if you'll excuse me young man," he said, patting Simon on the arm, "it seems that I'm wanted."

"I've just seen this amazing group!" said Simon, excitedly, once he'd returned to his inebriated friend in the bar. "They're into The Stooges, and listen to this...their manager is the owner of SEX!"

"SEX!" slurred Steven, repeating the name several times without making a connection with what his friend was trying to tell him. He'd had a merry old skinful and was having difficulty just trying to focus on Simon, let alone make sense of the commentary.

"You must remember the shop that Sue took us to?" said Simon. "The one in the World's End?"

"I didn't know he was in a group!" mumbled Steven, gently rubbing his closed eyelids with his fingers.

"He's not in the group!" said Simon, shaking his head at his friend's drunken state. "He's their manager."

"And what're they called again?" asked Steven, opening one eye.

"Sex Pistols!" repeated Simon patiently. He waited to see if Steven made the connection between the group's name and the shop but he was definitely pissing upwind on that errand. "Wait 'til we tell Sue and the others!" he said to no-one in particular as he helped himself to Steven's beer.

It was New Year's Eve and the four Sex Pistols were sat in the Cambridge pub close to their place on Denmark Street. They had managed to play a couple more gigs before Christmas but it was becoming increasingly difficult to get bookings; it seemed that the word was out about the Sex Pistols. Malcolm, to his credit, had tried various ploys to obtain gigs for the group. He'd tried telephoning the colleges pretending to be a friend of someone on the student committee or claiming that he was connected with the groups already booked to play. He would then inform the college that he had another group – careful to avoid mentioning them by name – which had been promised a half-hour support slot. Sometimes this ploy worked, but mostly his pleas fell on deaf ears despite offering the group's services for free.

Paul was eyeing the new digital watch on John's wrist. The watch had been a Christmas present from his mum and dad. "What time is it?" he asked.

"Nearly quarter to eleven," replied John. "In fact," he said, studying the dial closely, "it's seventy six minutes to 1976. Fuckin' hell, I'll be twenty next month!"

"That right?" asked Steve, grinning, "then just you wait, you cunt!"

"Umm, he who laughs last an' all that, I s'pose!" said John, looking chagrined.

"Well, I'll be the last one laughing then!" said Glen, cheerfully, "cos I'm not twenty 'til August!"

"It's gone fuckin' quick though. This year, I mean," said Paul, thoughtfully.

"Too right, it has!" replied John, reaching for his drink. "It's like, goin' on four years since I left school!" He hesitated for a second. "No, that's a lie. It's five years. They kicked me out when I was fifteen!"

"What? Really?" gasped Paul. "What the fuck did you do?"

"They said I had a disruptive attitude!"

"Can't think where they got that idea," said Steve, glancing slyly at John to see if he'd heard him.

"No, neither can I!" replied John.

"Which school did you go to, John?" asked Glen.

"William of York, a Catholic School over in Pentonville, and it was probably worse than the fuckin' Prison!"

"Me an' Steve went to Christopher Wren in Shepherd's Bush," said Paul. "What about you Glen?"

"St Clement Danes," replied Glen, knowing full well why Paul had asked him. He'd already been through this when he'd first joined the group. "It's a grammar school," he added, for John's benefit.

"Oh very la-di-dah," said John, sticking his nose in the air.

"Yeah, but it's next door to Wormwood Scrubs!" said Glen, defiantly.

"All fuckin' schools are prisons, when you stop to think about it," said John, reflectively. "You get a five year stretch at both places!"

"At least with school you get to go home every day!" said Glen, cheerfully.

"An' that's a good thing, is it?" scowled Steve, draining his glass. "Who's round is it, anyway?"

"You're the only one with some money!" said John, "thanks to Malcolm and Bernie acting as fences for your dodgy gear!"

Steve ignored John's comment. Instead, he asked what the others thought about Malcolm's trip to France to promote the Sex Pistols in Europe.

"To be honest," said John, tapping his empty glass on the table edge, in the hope of getting Steve to buy him another, "I never expected anything to come out of it. The French are far too busy looking up their own arseholes to give a fuck about what's goin' on in London!"

"We need some proper gigs!" said Glen. "I'm fucking sick of playing to students!" He stopped suddenly, going red in the face as he realised what he was saying. "You know what I mean?"

"Well, I fuckin' refuse to degrade myself by playing in pubs to a bunch of brain-dead pissheads!" said John, angrily.

"Me an' all!" said Steve, nodding in agreement. "I ain't playin' 'Johnny B fuckin' Goode' in some shit-hole where no cunt's even listenin'!"

"Yeah," agreed Paul, "but to play proper venues you've got to have people who are willin' to pay and watch you! And unless you count Malcolm's Chelsea crowd, we ain't got anyone that even likes us!"

"That's true!" said Glen, nodding ruefully. "We'll just have to see what happens next year!"

John sat nodding his head thoughtfully before speaking. "If someone had said to me this time last year that I'd be singing in a group, I'd have laughed at them. Me sing? I can't even be bothered talking!"

"Where did you get that idea?" asked Paul, grinning.

"You know what I mean!" replied John, smirking at Paul's comment. "I mean, I was rubbish when I started."

"You still are!" yelled Steve, howling with delight at John's sullen expression.

"Yes, most amusing, children," said John, chuckling. "Seriously though, I can't believe that you put up with an idiot like me screaming away like some demented cat!"

"We couldn't get rid of Johnny Rotten!" said Steve, grinning at John.

"You're not still goin' on about that, are you?"

"You're jokin' ain't you?" said Paul, grinning at his friend. "Malcolm's tellin' anyone who'll listen that we've got a singer called Johnny Rotten!"

"Looks like you're stuck with it!" said Glen, tapping the rim of his empty glass. "Just like I seem to be stuck with this!"

"All right, for fuck's sake!" said Steve, digging his hand into his pocket. "Here!" He thrust a ten-pound note towards Glen. "I'll have the same again!"

"Nice one, Stevie boy!" said Glen, rising up off his stool. "I'm serious though, about what we were saying earlier. We could always hire somewhere for the night and charge, what, fifty pence to get in?"

"You're not just a pretty face, are you?" said John, warming to Glen's idea.

"We've all got mates that we can get to come along, even if it's just to prop up the bar all night!"

"I reckon I could get some of the lads from the brewery to come," said Paul, watching Glen threading his way through the festive crowd towards the bar. "an' we can put some posters up, like."

"What about your friends, John?" asked Steve. "I still ain't seen the photos your mate Gray took yet!"

"Neither have I!" replied John, shaking his head.

"What did he say about the gig at Chelsea College?" asked Paul.

"He said we were great!" replied John, "but then again, he would do wouldn't he? Then tell everyone else that we were shit just to make me look a cunt!"

"Who looks a cunt?" asked Glen, setting the tray down on a nearby table and handing out the drinks.

"You!" said Steve, curtly, before bringing Glen into the conversation. "I was just sayin' that I ain't seen the photos from the Chelsea gig!"

"I wouldn't mind getting a copy of them myself!" said Glen.

"So you can show mummy and daddy!" said John.

"There's nothing wrong with that!" said Glen, pulling a face at John. "When's your mate Sid gonna come and see us play?"

"Well, Sid does his own thing you know," replied John, taking a drink of Guinness. "I ain't gonna drag him along and force him to watch us! He's into his Roxy Music phase at the moment anyway. A total fashion victim."

"Why the fuck do you call him Sid?" asked Steve, looking puzzled. "Or is that the poor cunt's real name?"

"Ha-ha, I called him Sid after the pet hamster we used to have," replied John, chuckling at the memory. "It had no teeth and all its fur was fucked up! Of course he made the fatal mistake of tellin' me how much he hated the name, so he's been Sid ever since!"

"So what is his real name?" asked Glen, grinning at John's explanation.

"John! There's four of us see, all called John, which tends to get a bit confusing so I gave them all nick-names." He held up his hand and began counting the names off on his fingers.

"There's Sid, Gray, and Wobble – please don't ask!" he said, cutting Steve off as he was about to say something.

"I wasn't going to say anythin' about that!" replied Steve, picking up his glass.

"Well, what then?" asked John, eyeing his friend suspiciously.

"I was about to say happy new fuckin' year, you cunts!" he yelled, as the room suddenly erupted with celebrations.

"I'm fuckin' fed up!" snarled John, standing at the window in the upstairs room on Denmark Street. He was watching the rain hammering down on the roof opposite. The guttering was blocked, which was forcing the overflow of rainwater to run down the walls and form an ever-growing pool in the corner of the courtyard. "An' I'm fuckin' freezin' an' all!"

"Well, what do you want me to do about it?" shouted Glen, looking up from his college coursework. The first few weeks of the New Year had been pretty bleak for the Sex Pistols. There had been no gigs, no money and precious little support from Malcolm; it seemed his priorities lay elsewhere.

They were supposed to be rehearsing but John had been in a foul mood ever since he'd arrived and was now going out of his way to provoke an argument. The latest target for his vitriolic outbursts was the seemingly non-existent managerial support.

"If he's our manager, then how come we never see or hear from him?" he yelled, before sitting down on the floor in front of the electric heater and hogging what little heat it was giving off. "For fuck's sake, a manager is meant to get you gigs!"

"Well, if he can't be bothered," said Glen, fed up with John's ranting, "why don't we do something about it?"

"Like what?"

"Well I don't know, do I?" replied Glen, shrugging his shoulders. "I'm just as frustrated as you are!"

"Can we get back downstairs an' start rehearsin' or somethin'?" said Paul, sighing. "I can think of better ways to spend my weekends!" Begrudgingly, John rose to his feet and headed for the stairwell behind Paul, closely followed by the others.

"You got any ideas?" Steve asked Glen, slipping his guitar strap over his head.

"No," replied Glen, shrugging, "nothing!"

"You must have somethin'!" said Steve, giving Glen a dirty look.

"Yeah!" snapped Glen, turning on Steve. "What about you! You haven't come up with fuck all lately!"

"Yeah!" said John, jumping straight onto Steve's case. "You lazy cunt! You're in here all day!" He jabbed a finger at Steve's guitar. "Some fuckin' guitar hero, you are!" This was a dig at the slogan that Steve had painted on his amplifier.

Paul could see that Steve was close to losing his temper and would soon start lashing out at either John or Glen if they continued. "What about that one you were playin' this morning, when I got here?" he asked, stepping out from behind his drums.

"Which one?" asked Steve, turning away from his antagonisors towards the approaching Paul.

"I don't fuckin' know, do I!" sighed Paul. "You were playin' somethin' when I came in this morning!"

Steve sat silently for a moment, gazing at the fretboard of his guitar as if it might suddenly start magically playing the tune for him. "I think I remember the one you're on about!" he said, strumming various chords. He found a basic pattern by playing the D, C and A chords. He glanced up at Paul, who nodded for him to keep playing as he picked up his drumsticks and climbed back onto his stool. Glen picked up his bass, watching what Steve was playing, then joined in with a bass line that complemented both Paul's steady beat and Steve's guitar.

John was feverishly scribbling away on his pad as the other three worked out a pattern for the tune. He would occasionally gaze into space as if waiting for some unseen inspiration. He had resumed his frenetic scribbling when Glen held up his hand signalling for Steve and Paul to stop playing.

"That sounds really promising," he said, nodding enthusiastically. "Where does it go after that?"

"Fuck knows!" replied Steve, shrugging.

"It's not the tune I was on about," said Paul, shaking his head, "but I like it."

"Yeah," agreed Glen, "it's definitely catchy, but it needs to go somewhere else." He walked over to Steve, careful not to trip on his guitar lead. "Try coming up here," he said, placing his finger on Steve's fretboard, "after you've played the A chord."

"Yeah, all right," said Steve, concentrating as he played the basic pattern then slid his fingers up to play a B chord, followed by a C and a D.

"Now go back to what you played at the beginning," Glen shouted, loud enough to make himself heard above Steve's guitar.

John was still scribbling away while tapping his foot to the beat from Paul's bass drum. After several minutes he stood up and walked over to his microphone, waving his hands in the air until the others had stopped playing.

"Play it again from the beginning, an' I'll come in after that change you've worked out."

"What?" gasped Steve, incredulously. "You've got a lyric down already?"

"Yeah," replied John, holding up a sheet of paper. "It still needs a bit of work but I've got most of it."

"What's it called?" asked Paul.

"'Problems'!"

⬯   ⬯   ⬯   ⬯

Malcolm hadn't been avoiding the group on purpose; he'd simply had higher priorities. On 4 February, he and Vivienne had been invited to give a talk about their ideas and radical designs at the Institute of Contemporary Arts as part of a season called Fashion Forum – New Designers. He saw this as a chance to promote both the shop and the Sex Pistols, who would be sitting in the audience so that the other guests would get the chance to see their clothing at first hand. John, much to Malcolm's chagrin, was spoiling things by refusing to wear anything from SEX. He claimed that he was nobody's clothes horse, although once again his unique style ensured that he was the centre of attention for the entire evening.

Malcolm had been hoping that the evening would be the first of many such events that would give him his "entrée" into the world of fashion design that he so desperately craved. He also realised that he wouldn't be able to give his full attention to the Sex Pistols and run a successful business, so he decided to approach a friend of his to see if he'd be interested in helping him with the day-to-day running of the group.

Nils Stevenson was twenty-twp years old. He'd been brought up in Dalton before moving to London to attend Barnet Art School. He had quit the college in the early seventies and had spent time living in Paris and San Francisco. By 1976 Nils had done various jobs, which included working for Richard Buckle, the ballet critic for the *Observer* newspaper. He was now running a small stall on Beaufort Street market on the King's Road, selling revival clothing from the 1950s and 60s. His friend Alan Jones, who'd taken him to SEX after a drinking session in the Roebuck one Saturday afternoon, had introduced him to Malcolm and Vivienne. The main reason for Malcolm's decision to approach Nils was the fact that he was dating June Child, the ex-girlfriend of the glam rock star Marc Bolan. Child was working for Blackhill Enterprises, the music management company who had represented Bolan and Pink Floyd amongst others.

Malcolm would often meet up with the pair for a drink and interrogate June about the music business, claiming that he was toying with the possibility of opening a club in London. Malcolm and Vivienne would also invite Nils to parties hosted by the sculptor Andrew Logan, at his studio on Butler's Wharf at New Tower Bridge. They would often make up a foursome by bringing along another of their friends and one time SEX employee Chrissie Hynde, who had recently returned from living in Paris.

It was after one of these parties that Malcolm had shown Nils some of the posters that he'd brought back with him from New York. These posters were flyers advertising gigs at CBGB's for the groups Television and The Ramones. He then gave Nils a brief outline of what he was hoping to achieve with the Sex Pistols who, he claimed, would be the new Bay City Rollers. The obvious next step was to introduce Nils to the group, but when he turned up at the Roebuck for the arranged meeting only Steve and Paul were actually present. Although the three of them got on well together Nils didn't really see much point getting involved with the Sex Pistols but did however agree to accompanying Malcolm to watch the group if they ever managed to secure another booking.

In response to Malcolm's lack of involvement with the group, John and Glen decided to go out and see if they could get themselves a gig. Glen had heard that the group Eddie and The Hot Rods were showcasing a gig at the Marquee Club, situated on Wardour Street in Soho. The Hot Rods were from the Isle of Dogs and were openly being touted as the new kings of Street Rock. Glen and John reckoned that this would be an ideal opportunity for the Sex Pistols to get themselves noticed.

They had walked the relatively short distance from their place on Denmark Street to the Marquee – one of the most famous and prestigious music venues in Britain, if not the world. On entering the club they asked to see the manager who, after staring open-mouthed at John for several seconds, finally listened to what the pair of them had to say. To their amazement he agreed to the Sex Pistols supporting the Hot Rods for their showcase gig on 12 February.

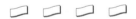

Glen climbed the narrow stairway leading up to the tiny room he shared with Steve. As he reached the top step he could hear strange noises coming from within. He walked in to find Steve going hell for leather on top of some girl who, to Glen's mind, didn't just look like she'd been hit with the ugly stick, there was a very strong case for a GBH assault charge.

"All right, Glen," panted Steve, briefly glancing up at his roommate. He didn't even bother breaking stride.

"Don't mind me!" replied Glen, slowly backing out of the room. He'd had an idea for a new song and had been hoping that Steve would be on hand to add some guitar. He headed downstairs and switched on the light in the rehearsal room. It was absolutely freezing and he was forced to rub his hands together to get some warmth into them before unpacking his bass guitar.

Glen soon lost himself in the pattern for the new tune and when he opened his eyes he was startled to discover Steve and his lady friend standing in the doorway watching him.

"I fuckin' like that!" said Steve eagerly. "Won't be a minute!" He quickly ushered the girl towards the door. Glen could hear her muffled protests at not being allowed to stay the night, as Steve must have promised in order to lure her into bed.

"Nice girl!" he said, as Steve came back into the room.

"Fuck off!" replied Steve, stooping to remove his Gibson Les Paul from its case. "I don't give a fuck what they look like!"

"Obviously," replied Glen, grinning. He ran through the change he'd worked out for the new tune while he waited for Steve to tune his guitar. "It's in the key of A," he said, playing the corresponding note on his top string. "It's the same pattern twice over for the verses, A down to G then up to D then back to A again." He played the relevant notes as he spoke. "Then play an E, but you'll need to play it low with the bottom E string open."

"Don't gimme all that technical bollocks!" shouted Steve, becoming irritated at Glen's musical jargon. "Just play the fuckin' thing!"

They played the pattern a few times to allow Steve to familiarise himself with the new tune.

"I've got some lyrics for it as well," said Glen, holding up a tatty sheet of A4 paper.

"I'll read 'em after," replied Steve, adjusting the tuning on his guitar strings.

"I'll show you the chorus, then," said Glen, "it's D, then down to C and then back to A." He sat watching Steve as he played the corresponding chords.

"Yeah, that's it," he said, nodding, "but stay longer on the D, before sliding down the C. Watch I'll show you." He played the pattern for the verse once, then played the notes for the chorus.

Steve stood watching him for a few seconds then joined in to run through the tune again, adding occasional riffs to help fill out the sound. Glen listened to Steve as he fingerpicked a repetitive, yet catchy, riff over the A chord at the end of each chorus.

"That sounds really good," he said, once they'd finished playing. "Try playing that riff you were doing from the beginning and I'll join in after a couple of bars."

"Yeah, all right," said Steve, feeling pleased with himself. "What's it gonna be called?"

"'Pretty Vacant'," replied Glen. "You remember those posters that Malcolm has in the shop, the ones from New York?"

"Yeah, what about 'em?" asked Steve, wondering what this had to do with anything.

"Well, there was one called 'I belong to the Blank Generation' and I've been thinking about writing something along those lines because we belong to a generation that's got fuck all to look forward to!"

Steve still looked puzzled at Glen's explanation as he began strumming the chords for the tune, but by the end of the next rehearsal they had completed the new tune for "Pretty Vacant" and John had even been happy to use Glen's lyrics, although he had changed a couple of lines in the second verse.

▢ ▢ ▢ ▢

On Thursday 12 February the Sex Pistols supported Eddie and The Hot Rods. There was a decent sized crowd inside The Marquee although the majority of them were there for the main group with only a handful of people, including Nils Stevenson, who were there to see The Pistols. Everything had gone well for them at the soundcheck, though when the time came for them to go on stage John found that the monitors, to help the musicians hear themselves while performing on stage, suddenly weren't working.

During their half hour set they played the new songs "New York" and "Pretty Vacant", which meant that their set now comprised as much original material as it did cover versions.

John was in a particularly wild mood that night. He began throwing a few plastic chairs around the stage and smashing the non-functioning monitors, which belonged to the Hot Rods. The Sex Pistols even came back on stage for an unscheduled and mostly unrequested encore, which was strictly against the Marquee's policy. Some heckler standing close to the stage had tried goading the members of the group by shouting out that they couldn't play, to which Glen had responded blandly, "So what?"

After the performance the four Sex Pistols headed backstage to find Malcolm busy trying to placate the Hot Rods' management by claiming that the destruction of the monitors had been an accident. He seemed oblivious to the fact that the entire audience had casually watched John while he smashed them. Steve and Paul were far more interested in adding their names to the hundreds of scribbles and slogans, which adorned the dressing room walls. They were interrupted from their task by the quiet voice coming from behind them.

"Hi, I'm Neil Spencer. I'm with the *NME*," the guy informed them. "Could I have a word?"

"Hello, I'm Malcolm McLaren. The sole management of the Sex Pistols!" said Malcolm, rushing over from where he'd been arguing with the manager of the Hot Rods. He signalled for Steve and Paul to continue with their handiwork whilst guiding Spencer towards the centre of the room so that he could supply him with a few choice quotes from his manifesto for the Sex Pistols.

"What was it that they were trying to do with the, er...music?" asked Spencer.

"Actually," said Steve, interrupting before Malcolm could offer a response, "we're not into music."

"What then?" asked Spencer, a bemused look on his face.

"We're into chaos!"

Two days later on Saturday 14 February, the Sex Pistols played at the St. Valentine's Day Ball at Andrew Logan's studio on Butler's Wharf. Malcolm had arranged for the group to play during one of his previous visits, assuring Logan that everything would be all right. He then set about inviting anyone that he could think of. A small stage had been erected especially for the occasion, using an assortment of materials from the children's department of the recently closed Biba superstore and scenery from Derek Jarman's film *Sebastiane*. Jarman was also there filming the evening's events on his hand-held Super Eight Camera.

Most of Logan's celebrity friends were there and were also the clientele of SEX but Malcolm and Vivienne secretly despised them. Malcolm had brought Helen with him to the party and this was the first time that she and Vivienne had been in the same room together and everybody expected that there would be trouble, but Vivienne seemed to be taking it in her stride. He had also invited Simon Barker, the blond haired youth he'd met when the Sex Pistols had played at Ravensbourne College the previous December. He in turn had brought several of his colourful friends along with him who were all into what the Sex Pistols were doing after witnessing various live performances by the group.

Steve, Paul and Glen were already playing on the small stage but there was no sign of John. This was actually part of Malcolm's plan, as he knew that the mysterious singer Johnny Rotten fascinated his friends and they were all dying to meet him. In fact, Malcolm hadn't even bothered to tell John about the party until earlier that evening and then when John did arrive he tried to arrange it so that he wouldn't be allowed in.

John was not one to be easily dissuaded.

"Where's the fuckin' drink?" he yelled, barging past Vivienne and almost knocking her to the floor. He was off his head with the effects of a combination of sulphate and acid that he'd taken earlier. Unfortunately for John, the limited amount of alcohol provided by Logan had long since been consumed by the masses of people that Malcolm had invited.

As John lurched up to the makeshift stage the clearly unhappy Logan protested to Malcolm that these awful people were damaging his precious sculptures. The sculptor squealed aloud at the sight of John swinging the microphone stand above his head and condemning another of Logan's prized possessions to the dustbin.

Malcolm smiled apologetically but, after spotting Neil Spencer standing in the doorway, quickly turned his back on the whimpering Logan. "Jords, come here girl!" he yelled, whilst waving an arm to catch her attention. "The *NME* are here. Get up there girl, and take your clothes off!"

"I'm not doing that!" exclaimed Jordon, horrified by Malcolm's suggestion.

"Just do it girl! We haven't got much time!" Malcolm yelled while pushing her towards the stage.

"I'll do it if John agrees to it," said Jordon, in an attempt to deter Malcolm.

"Whatever!" replied Malcolm, with one last shove. He watched John kicking things around the stage floor chanting the words "No Fun" over and over, oblivious to what song the others were playing.

Eventually Jordon reached the stage and nervously began gyrating to the music.

"Come on boy, do something!" Malcolm muttered to himself, keeping one eye on the stage while keeping the journalist under observation. John turned around as if suddenly aware that Jordon was on stage. He grabbed her by the wrist and pulled her towards him and proceeded to rip the top that she was wearing much to the delight of Steve, who was treated to a clear view of her large pendulous tits.

Neil Spencer pushed his way through the crowd of onlookers and began clicking away with his camera. Perfect! thought Malcolm, smiling to himself. One of these photos would surely be in the next issue of the music paper and all four Sex Pistols were wearing T-shirts from his shop.

"Somehow I don't think we'll be invited back!" he said to Helen as they both watched their host crawling around on his knees searching for the missing head of the marble figurine that he was clutching in one hand.

Glen took a sip of coffee as he eagerly flicked through the pages of that week's *NME*. He was hoping that there just might be a mention of The Marquee gig from the previous week – though even if there was, it would be about Hot Rods, as it was their gig after all. He paused briefly at the centre pages, dedicated to Genesis, the Prog-Rock group, whom the music press was currently championing. There was a large feature on Patti Smith, the New York Punk Poet; her picture was adorning the front cover. Eventually he found the section he'd been looking for – the live reviews section. The main reviews were of American rocker Alice Cooper and country & western singer Emmylou Harris. He smiled to himself as he looked at the photo of Alice, resplendent in his full stage make-up, remembering John's audition at the shop when he'd sung Cooper's "Eighteen" in front of the shop's jukebox.

Glen was still slightly angry with John, whose antics at the Marquee gig had resulted in the group being banned from ever playing the club again.

"Well, at least I got to play there once!" he thought ruefully, as he turned the page.

His mouth went dry and he felt his stomach lurch, filling him with a lovely butterflies sensation, as he stared open-mouthed at the photograph of John and Steve.

"Fuck!" he gasped, quickly glancing up to see if anyone had heard him. He grinned at the banner headline. "Don't look over your shoulder but the Sex Pistols are coming!" The article didn't even mention the headline act, Eddie And The Hot Rods. He studied the photo of John and Steve, which had obviously been supplied to the *NME* by Malcolm. The photo hadn't been snapped by Spencer at the Marquee, but was one of the photos taken by John's friend Gray at the Chelsea College gig the previous December.

He was slightly peeved that he'd been cut from the photo as he'd seen the original print one evening at Denmark Street and thought it to be one of the better ones, particularly as he'd looked pretty sharp in the shot. He soon cheered up though as he read the accompanying article, which even name-checked one of his songs: "'I'm Pretty Vacant' – a meandering power chord job that produced the chair throwing incident." The article also went on to mention his encounter with the heckler although it didn't actually mention him by name. The best however had been saved until last. At the end of the article, Spencer had related his encounter with Steve, who'd told him that the group "wasn't into music – they were into chaos." Glen wasn't too sure if he was going to be able to stand up properly as the sensations in his stomach had now spread to his legs, and the hairs of the back of his neck were tingling.

When Glen arrived back at Denmark Street he found Malcolm, Paul and John were all there with Steve and were all as equally excited as he was. Paul had even finished work early because he'd been unable to concentrate on anything else since reading the article that morning. Malcolm was ecstatic; the fact that the article had included the photograph that he himself had sent to the paper's offices was very good news. It would give a much wider audience their first visual experience of the Sex Pistols and the fact that both John and Steve were wearing SEX T-shirts meant something far more important to Malcolm; it meant money.

But there was no time to sit back and bask in the limelight because another gig had been lined up for the following evening at the St. Alban's College of Art & Design. Nils, upon accepting Malcolm's offer to co-manage the Sex Pistols, had offered to drive the group to the college. He'd been absolutely mind-blown by the gig at the Marquee and been greatly relieved that they were nothing like The Bay City Rollers. He had also told his brother all about the evening at the Marquee.

Ray Stevenson, a rock photographer since 1965, had photographed David Bowie and Marc Bolan when they were both relatively unknown performers but had grown disillusioned when they both abandoned him once they had achieved stardom. Nil's description of the Sex Pistols had roused his brother's curiosity enough for him to accept an offer to accompany him to the proposed gig and agree to take some photographs of the group.

The St. Alban's gig was reasonably well attended. Simon Barker and the rest of the Bromley Contingent, as Vivienne referred to him and his friends, were there dressed to impress and Ray used up a couple of rolls of film on them alone. Intent on learning more about the group he found himself offering his services for the following two evenings when the Sex Pistols would play at a St. Valentine's dance at Buck's College of Higher Education in High Wycombe and then on to Welwyn Garden City the day after.

On the afternoon of the High Wycombe gig, three young men approached Malcolm in his shop on King's Road. Two of them had apparently travelled all the way from Manchester after reading Neil Spencer's article in the *NME*. The two guys, Howard Trafford and Peter McNeish, had telephoned the *NME* offices and had learned that the Sex Pistols' manager owned a fashion boutique on the King's Road. They then contacted another friend of theirs who invited them to stay with him at his home in Reading. Their visit to SEX paid unexpected dividends when they learned about the two proposed gigs in High Wycombe and Welwyn Garden City.

For Friday's gig at High Wycombe, the Sex Pistols would be supporting Screaming Lord Sutch and had been given permission to use some of Sutch's equipment. During their performance the microphone that John was using suddenly packed up and, upon realising he couldn't be heard above the music, he dropped to his knees and proceeded to smash the defective, yet still rather expensive, microphone against the stage floor. The security people acting on behalf of Lord Sutch were quickly called upon to intervene, only to be met by a group of Steve and Paul's mates at the front of the stage. A small fight ensued, but the Sex Pistols seemed unconcerned and continued playing.

"Weren't me!" scowled John, staring at Lord Sutch as he and one of his friends cornered the singer in order to question him about the broken microphone.

"But we saw you do it!" replied Sutch, frowning. "Everybody here saw you do it!"

"No, weren't me!" repeated John, defiantly. Sutch and his friend looked at John for a few moments longer before bursting into fits of laughter.

"Who's your manager?" asked Sutch's friend, wiping his eyes.

"You won't get fuck all out of him!" sneered John. "We don't!"

"I just want to talk to him," he replied, looking over at the ginger-haired guy that John was pointing to. "What's his name?"

"Malcolm, but you're wastin' your time!" John shouted as he wandered over towards Malcolm.

John nodded briefly towards Lord Sutch, as if indicating that the inquest about the broken microphone was over, before heading towards Steve and the others. He still kept one eye on Sutch's friend who was standing talking to Malcolm, as he wanted to be sure that they weren't talking about him.

"These lads have come from fuckin' Manchester just to see us!" said Steve, bringing John's attentions back into focus.

"They've what?" gasped John, thinking he'd misheard Steve.

"Manchester!" said Glen, nodding his appreciation of the efforts made by the two Mancunians.

"Fuck me!" said John, shaking his head in disbelief. "You came all the way down here just to see us?"

"Too right we did!" replied the smallest of the three lads. "We read about you in the *NME* and thought bloody hell, who are these crazy people? So we came down to stay with Richard – he pointed towards one of his two friends – so we could come to London and see if we could find out where you were playing next. Didn't we, Howard?"

"That's right," said Howard, the tallest of the three.

"What's your name?" asked John, glancing back to the one standing in front of him.

"I'm Pete."

"My name's John."

"Yeah, we know," said Howard, grinning at John.

"Are you coming to see us tomorrow?" he asked, feeling slightly embarrassed that people in Manchester knew who he was. He knew that the article in the *NME* would have been seen and read by thousands of people around the country, but he still felt unnerved by the sudden attention.

"Oh yes, definitely!"

"Wouldn't dream of missing it!" added Howard. He could see that John was checking out the flared cord trousers he was wearing.

"They're tremendous those, aren't they John?" said Pete, grinning as he pointed at his and his two friends' clothing. "We're well known for our sartorial elegance up north!"

"Oh, I know," replied John, a look of mock sincerity on his face. "I know".

At last, things seemed to be gathering momentum for the Sex Pistols. They had played at a prestigious London venue and received their first review in the music press. They had also acquired a colourful and dedicated, if somewhat small, following in the Bromley Contingent. There was also the possibility of the group being invited to travel up to Bolton in Lancashire to play at the college attended by Howard Trafford and Peter McNeish.

Malcolm had more exciting news for the boys when he arrived for one of their impromptu group meetings at Denmark Street. He had just returned from a meeting with Ron Watts, the friend of Screaming Lord Sutch who had attended the High Wycombe gig. Watts was the promoter for a small jazz club on Oxford Street called the 100 Club. He had approached Malcolm after the show at High Wycombe with a proposal for the Sex Pistols to play a gig at the basement venue, with a view to offering them a Tuesday night residency.

Malcolm chose this meeting to inform them about Nils's acceptance of his offer to help him with the day to day running of the group. For some reason Bernie Rhodes, who had been instrumental in helping with the early development of the Sex Pistols, had suddenly defected in order to take on the role as manager of another group. The nucleus of this new group apparently consisted of the group of longhaired musicians that were jamming together in the basement of the cafe on Praed Street in Paddington.

The guitarist in Bernie's new group was Mick Jones, the guy that Glen and Malcolm had tried to contact with a view to him joining the Sex Pistols. Glen and Mick had since become quite good friends and Mick had told Glen the reason behind Bernie's defection. It seemed that Bernie had been reluctant to hand over the budding guitarist to Malcolm, and was using him as the ace up his sleeve to force Malcolm into offering him an equal partnership in view of all the hard work he'd put into the Sex Pistols. In the end, he got what Malcolm felt he deserved, which was nothing.

CHAPTER TEN

Steve was sitting at the end of his bed concentrating on working out a tune for the set of lyrics that John had given him earlier in the week. The new song was to be called "Satellite". John had written the song based on the group's experiences while gigging around the suburbs of outer London – the satellite towns as John liked to call them, hence the title of the song. Steve had soon put together a chord sequence for the verses but was struggling to find a way of introducing the chorus into the pattern.

"All right!" said Glen, cheerfully as he bounded into the room grinning like the proverbial cat from Cheshire.

"What're you looking so pleased about?" asked Steve, watching Glen as he crossed the room towards his own bed.

"I've got a date!" said Glen, removing his shirt and tossing it onto the mattress.

"Yeah! Do I know him?"

"Very funny, Steve," replied Glen, pulling on his freshly ironed blue shirt, courtesy of his mother. "You can't say anything, not after what you brought home the other week!"

"What was wrong with her?" Steve immediately wished that he hadn't asked, as he wasn't sure that he wanted to hear Glen's opinion.

"What was right with her!" gasped Glen, smirking as he combed his hair. "She looked like a bulldog chewing a thistle!" He stopped to look at Steve, pointing the plastic comb at him. "I'd rather have a J. Arthur Rank than fuck that!" He resumed combing his hair. "You'd be better off sticking with your liver sandwich!"

"So what's she called?"

"Celia," said Glen. "And no, you don't know her!"

"Where did you meet her?"

Glen sat down on the corner of the bed while he changed his socks. "It was at Chiswick Poly last week," he said eventually. "I went there with Mick Jones to watch some of his mates. They're in a group as well!"

"Who fuckin' isn't these days?" said Steve, lighting his last cigarette and hurling the empty packet at Glen.

"Celia was with some guy that Mick knows. He's called Larry, no it's Barry," said Glen, batting the missile away with his hand.

"You've nicked someone's bird?" This newsflash almost had Steve choking on his cigarette smoke.

"Well, yeah, sort of," replied Glen. "Nothing happened though."

"Not yet!"

"I just sort of asked her for her phone number, you know?" said Glen, standing up and smoothing the creases of his trousers. "And I left it at that."

"You sly fucker!" said Steve, reluctant to admit to himself that Glen had just risen in his estimation.

"Then Mick tells me she's given this Barry the push!" said Glen, a smug self-congratulary grin spreading across his face. "So, I gave her a call."

"Bet that's not all you've given her!"

"She's not like that!"

"Fuck off," said Steve, shaking his head. "They're all like that!" He paused to exhale another cloud of cigarette smoke. "Well, the ones I know are."

"Umm," said Glen, grinning, "exactly!"

"Just remember to show her your Sex Pistol!"

"What?"

"Your Sex Pistol!" repeated Steve, thrusting his pelvis up and down. "Sex Pistol! Do you get it?"

"Yes, Steve," replied Glen, "I get it!" He scooped up the cash from the cabinet at the side of his bed. "Don't wait up!" he called out as he left the room.

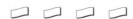

The Sex Pistols were definitely on a roll but they refused to get carried away by the recent events and kept themselves busy by constantly rehearsing their set, which was gradually being filled with their own material. No sooner had the song "Satellite" been completed and slotted into the set list than John presented his fellow band members with another set of lyrics for them to work on.

"I've called this one 'No Feelings'!" he announced, showing the lyrics to the others.

"I don't know where you get 'em from," said Paul, handing the sheet of paper to Glen.

"Well I can only write about the way I feel about somethin'," replied John, tapping a finger against his forehead. "There ain't no love songs in here!"

"I reckon the tune that me and Steve have been mucking about with should fit this," said Glen, studying the words to the new song.

"How the fuck do you know that?" asked John. "You've only just seen 'em!"

"Genius, I guess!" replied Glen, smirking.

"Well let's try it," said Steve, slipping his guitar strap over his head.

The three musicians played the basic tune several times while John sat leaning against the wall holding his hands in front of the electric fire.

"When you get to the end of the chorus, you play an F7!" Glen told Steve, once they had stopped playing.

"I fuckin' did!" yelled Steve, angrily.

"Show me what you're playing!" retorted Glen, moving closer to Steve.

"That's right, innit?" asked Steve, showing Glen where he had positioned his fingers.

"No! That's an F5!"

"Bollocks!" shouted Steve. "It fits, don't it?"

"Sounded all right to me," said Paul, from behind the drums.

"Me an' all," said John, enjoying putting Glen on the defensive.

"But an F7 will allow me to come back in with an F!" protested Glen.

"Forget all that technical shit!" shouted John, lifting himself up off the floor and coming towards Glen. "It sounded fuckin' fine to me."

"All right, all right!" shouted Glen, realising that he was outnumbered. "I'll see what I can do!" He moved back over to his own amplifier.

"Whatever," said John, switching on the microphone. "Can we try the fuckin' song now, please?"

On 30 March the Sex Pistols played their first gig at the 100 Club on Oxford Street. Ron Watts had booked them to play as part of a new groups night; if everything went well, they would be offered a Tuesday night residency.

"It isn't very big, is it?" said John, sourly, as he surveyed the tiny basement venue.

"It don't need to be big, does it!" shouted Paul, from where he was standing on the club's small stage. "Not with the crowds we get!"

John ignored Paul's comment and walked over to where Steve was sitting on one of the tables.

"Don't we get some free drinks?" moaned Steve, as John slumped down next to him. They watched in silence while Glen helped Paul assemble his drum kit in front of the three large white plastic numbers denoting the club's name. The red painted walls were covered with photographs and posters featuring various jazz musicians with colourful names like Champion Jack Dupree and Eddie Guitar Burns.

Glen called out to John and pointed towards the billboard, which was mounted on the wall at the side of the stage in order to provide customers with details of the club's forthcoming attractions. "You should do a duet with this guy," He walked over and tapped his finger against the name at the top of the list. It was the well-known jazz singer George Melly. "You could call yourselves Rotten and Smelly!"

"Most amusing," scowled John, folding his arms against his chest. "Can we get some fuckin' drink around here?" he yelled at nobody in particular.

"Can we get some fuckin' help up here?" responded Paul, dryly.

By the time the Sex Pistols went on stage later that evening there weren't many people inside the club, and this only added to the tensions that had been building up between the members of the group. Steve, Glen and Paul clearly looked pissed off, while John was simply pissed. He'd hit the bar with a vengeance as soon as it opened. The majority of the fifty or sixty people at the tables in front of the stage were there to see the other act on the bill, a group with the totally unimaginative name of Plummet Airlines. The only people there to see the Sex Pistols were Simon Barker and his colourful assortment of friends who were now attending every gig that the group played, and even they looked bored.

John was oblivious to either his surroundings or the proceedings as he leapt around on the raised stage screaming out the lyrics to the songs.

Fuck me! Glen thought to himself as he watched John. He's awful tonight! He could see Malcolm and Nils standing near the bar; the looks on their faces said it all. Maybe it's just one of those nights that all groups go through from time to time, he thought. He could see Steve was scowling at John while mouthing something to him but he couldn't quite make out the words above the noise and so made his way across the stage to see what it was that Steve was trying to tell him. "What's up?" he asked, leaning closer to Steve.

"Listen to that cunt!" yelled Steve, angrily.

"Do I have to?" replied Glen, exchanging glances with Paul, who was still pounding away relentlessly on his drums. John interrupted the in-house debate when he lost his balance and stumbled into Glen, who gave him a less than gentle shove back towards the centre of the stage.

Glen could hear John screeching out the chorus to "Pretty Vacant" and, with a quick glance at the set-list that he'd taped on to the side of his amplifier, realised just why John was sounding so terrible. "He's singing the wrong fucking song," he said to himself while staring at John in disbelief. "You're singing the wrong fuckin' song!" he hissed at John.

"What's your fuckin' problem?" asked John, squaring up to Glen.

"My problem is that you're singing the wrong song!" replied Glen, shaking his head at John.

"Do you wanna fight?" said John, forgetting all about the performance. "I'll fight you, you cunt!"

"I'm trying to play my bass thank you very much," replied Glen, turning away from John.

"Come on, then!" shouted John, as he followed Glen across the stage.

"Just fuckin' get on with it, John!" yelled Steve. He was seething at John, who suddenly threw down his microphone and fled from the stage. He pushed his way through the bewildered crowd and headed towards the exit.

Malcolm came rushing over pointing towards the doorway through which John had disappeared.

"He's fucked off in a sulk!" replied Glen, removing his bass guitar.

"What?" gasped Malcolm, as he thrust the glass he was holding into Glen's hand and set off after John. He reached the top of the stairs and spotted John standing at the bus stop further down Oxford Street. "What on earth do you think you're doing, boy?" he asked, resting his hand against the circular metal post.

"I've had enough," shouted John. "Glen's a cunt!"

"Well that may be so," replied Malcolm, jabbing a finger back towards the entrance to the club. "But if you don't get back in there right now you're finished with this group!"

John stared down at the pavement for several seconds, then rushed past Malcolm and disappeared back inside the club. Steve and the others were still standing on the stage with a very bewildered looking Nils when John suddenly reappeared to the applause of the audience, who thought it had all been part of the act. Steve had been so furious with John that he'd yanked on the strings on his guitar until they snapped because he was convinced that the group was over.

"Shall we do 'Substitute'?" asked John, sheepishly. Steve just glared at him before walking off stage with Paul.

Malcolm, who had followed John inside, stepped up onto the stage and grabbed the microphone from where Glen had placed it after picking it up off the floor. "You can see the Sex Pistols this Saturday 3 April, at the Nashville Rooms, at 171 North End Road, West Kensington!" he shouted out to the dwindling audience, grimacing as the microphone shrieked with a sudden burst of feedback. "Everyone welcome!" he added forlornly, before stepping off the stage to find out if there was still a group left to actually play the Nashville gig.

Although the group themselves had considered the gig at the 100 Club a complete disaster, Ron Watts had been suitably impressed to go ahead with his offer of a Tuesday night residency starting on Tuesday 11 May. Malcolm and Nils, working from the flat on Bell Street, were busy organising the distribution of publicity photographs of the Sex Pistols stamped with this address on the back. The pair had also made dozens of telephone calls to possible venues for future Sex Pistols Shows. This was a deliberate attempt to steer the group away from the banal pub rock circuit.

Nils was sat at Helen's kitchen table tucking into a steak sandwich, chuckling to himself as he remembered the time when he and Malcolm had returned home to the flat in Clapham shortly before Malcolm had left Vivienne. They had spent many hours in the tiny kitchen planning out a strategy for the proposed club while Vivienne prepared meals for them and the children. She was a big believer in healthy eating and would take great delight in preparing sunflower seed salads that tasted like the scrapings from the bottom of a rabbit's hutch.

As soon as Vivienne had disappeared back inside the living room to play with the children, he and Malcolm would make some excuse to leave the flat and head towards the nearest restaurant in order to gorge themselves on thick juicy steaks. There was one occasion when Malcolm, finding himself with an evening free from Vivienne and the kids, had invited Nils round to dine with him. Vivienne had naturally prepared one of her drab healthy offerings for them, but she had hardly set foot out of the door before Malcolm consigned the fare to the wastebin and ordered a banquet for two from the local Indian takeaway.

The two were happily tucking into the feast when they heard the front door slamming shut. It was Vivienne. Malcolm and Nils crammed the remaining food into their mouths and threw the incriminating plates into the sud-filled sink as Vivienne came through the door. The curry was quite spicy and still too hot to swallow so they had to sit there unable to speak with their eyes watering while Vivienne stood frowning at them. It was fortunate that she was still suffering from the effects of a head cold, which prevented her from detecting the curry's distinctive aroma. The tears had continued well after Vivienne's departure but these were from the laughter at having escaped her wrath.

Two days before the Sex Pistols were scheduled to play at the Nashville Rooms where they would be supporting the 101ers, Malcolm and Nils set out through the streets of Soho. They were looking for a Maltese gangster by the name of Vincent, who was the owner of a strip club called the El Paradise. They finally managed to track him down at an illegal gambling club on Greek Street. They paused by the club door for several minutes while Malcolm briefed Nils on what he was going to say to Vincent, and then he rang the doorbell. The small porthole set into the heavy black painted door slid open; they could see the sinister face observing them with obvious disdain.

"We have an appointment with Vincent," said Malcolm, smiling to hide the lie. The porthole slammed shut again and they could hear the heavy security bolts being slid back on the opposite side. The same brute that had peered out at them opened the door. He looked like he could go ten rounds with a Sherman tank, and even then would probably only lose on points.

Before Nils had time to react, Malcolm had pushed him through the doorway and run off up the street. After several attempts at trying to explain why he was there, Nils was finally taken through to a small smoke-filled room at the back of the club. There were several circular tables inside the small room but only one was in use, and judging by the faces of those sitting at that table they clearly didn't take kindly to interruptions. The doorman signalled that Nils should wait by the curtained archway as he approached one of the card players and whispered in his ear.

Vincent sat watching Nils while the doorman told him the reason for the intrusion, then quickly dismissed the guy with a casual wave of his hand. He slid back his chair, collected his cards and made his apologies to his colleagues before approaching Nils. "This had better be good, my friend," he said, in his heavily accented English, "for your sake!"

"My friend and I would like to hire your club for the night," said Nils, glancing nervously at the two bullet-headed brutes who had appeared through a side curtain.

"What do you have in mind?" asked Vincent, eyeing Nils suspiciously.

"We're hoping to put a group on and..."

"One hundred pounds!" said Vincent, cutting Nils off in mid-sentence. "In advance!"

"OK, I'll..."

"And no alcohol, comprende?" said Vincent, thrusting a finger in Nils's face.

"Yes, yes, I understand!" replied Nils, backing away towards the door.

Vincent turned away and walked back inside to continue the game of cards, leaving Nils standing facing the two doormen. He fully expected to be helped out of the door and was somewhat relieved to hear it slam shut behind him.

"Well?" asked Malcolm, magically reappearing outside the club.

"It's sorted!" replied Nils, still angry at Malcolm's trickery. "No thanks to you!"

"Well, what's the deal?" asked Malcolm, struggling to keep up with Nils as they crossed the road outside the Regent Palace Hotel facing the statue of Eros in Piccadilly. His outburst upon discovering the gangster's asking price caused passers-by to stop and stare. "It's extortionate. The man's a thief!" He grabbed hold of Nils's arm. "Why didn't you try to knock down the price?"

"Because I..."

"Because you're useless!" exclaimed Malcolm, throwing his arms up in disbelief.

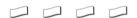

The Sex Pistols' show at the Nashville Rooms passed off without incident and they performed well. The admission price for the evening had been £1, with the group receiving £25 for their troubles. As they shifted their gear from the stage to make way for the main group, the two longhairs who were in charge of the PA system came over to speak with them.

"Good show, tonight!" said the one with the dark wavy hair, as he helped Paul to open up one of his drum cases.

"Thanks," replied Paul, crouching down to pick up his snare drum.

"Have you guys got a manager? Or someone we can talk to?"

"He's over there," replied Paul, pointing over at Malcolm. The two PA guys smiled their thanks and wandered off towards Malcolm.

"Hi, my name's Dave Goodman," said the one who'd spoken with Paul, holding out his hand. "And this is my partner Kim Thraves. We're doing the PA."

"Hello," said Malcolm, warily, "and what can I do for you two gentlemen?"

"We really enjoyed your group," replied Goodman, indicating John and the others. "Would you be interested in making a deal?"

"What kind of deal?"

"We'd be willing to supply you with a PA system whenever you're playing in or around London."

"And we'd do the mix for you guys as well!" added Thraves, brushing a strand of his long curly blond hair away from his face.

"Go on," said Malcolm, still waiting for the catch in the proposed deal.

"What's in this for you?"

"Nothing!" replied Goodman, shaking his head. "We'd like to be involved, and we'll offer you a reduced rate obviously!"

"Obviously," replied Malcolm, smiling at his two new best friends. "Here's my business card."

▭ ▭ ▭ ▭

The next afternoon the group arrived at the El Paradise Strip Club on Brewer Street to set up the equipment for that evening's show.

"Look at the corrie on that one!" yelled Steve, stopping to point at one of the huge gilt-framed photographs of naked girls that adorned the walls of the shabby entrance. He was so engrossed in the décor that he lost his footing on the small flight of steps that lead through to the room they'd be playing in.

"What's that fuckin' smell?" asked Glen, wrinkling his nose in disgust.

"What else do you expect in a shit-hole like this?" said John, dryly, as he covered his nose with his hand. He stepped up onto the tiny stage. "You're gonna struggle gettin' your drums on here!" he shouted over to Paul, idly kicking the row of box lights lying at the front of the stage.

"What's up 'ere, I wonder?" said Steve, standing at the doorway leading to a flight of stairs.

"Dunno!" replied John, jumping from the stage and coming towards him. "Let's find out!"

The two, remembering Nil's description of Vincent's henchmen, crept cautiously up the narrow flight of stairs. Steve paused in front of the heavily scarred door, which was slightly ajar, until he was satisfied that no-one was inside. With a quick glance over John's shoulder to check the stairway Steve opened the door and thought his eyes were deceiving him. The room had been designed to resemble a dungeon. The bare red brick walls were covered with rows of metal hooks from which hung a variety of leather whips, ropes and chains. There were crudely erected shelves filled with a large assortment of dildos, but it was the large wooden chair in the corner of the room that caught their attention. John rushed over and sat down in it, giggling as he toyed with the metal manacles that were fitted to the arms and legs.

"What the fuck?" gasped Steve

"It's like something out of the Spanish Inquisition!" said John, squealing with delight.

"Look at this!" said Steve, giggling as he came towards John holding a dildo the size of a cactus.

"Where the fuck do you put that?" howled John, as they both broke down in tears.

When they eventually came back down the stairs to rejoin the others John was brandishing a steel-tipped leather whip and Steve began chasing Jordon around the room waving an enormous shiny black dildo. She had arrived a few minutes earlier with Michael Collins to prepare the "punch" they were planning to sell to the punters. They would, if questioned, inform the club's owners that it was nothing more than grapefruit juice, but Collins had two bottles of tequila hidden inside his coat, which would be added to the juice just before the club opened its doors. The Sex Pistols were hoping for a decent sized crowd for the show as Malcolm had paid for the leaflets advertising the gig, which had been distributed at the Nashville rooms and the 100 Club.

Jonh Ingham was a journalist with the music magazine *Sounds* and, after reading the *NME*'s review of the Sex Pistols' gig at the Marquee in February, had come along to see for himself what all the fuss was about. If suitably impressed, he hoped to gain an exclusive interview with the group. He was struck by the bizarre dress sense of some of the youngsters coming into the club; he could sense that something out of the ordinary was happening here. He bought a plastic cup of punch from a very striking girl before casually strolling over to join fellow journalist Caroline Coon, who was standing close to the stage.

"What brings you here?" she asked, surprised to see him there.

"Thought I'd check this group out!" replied Ingham, taking a sip from his cup. "I read Neil's review in the *NME* and thought I'd find out more about them."

"So you're here to do a feature on them?"

"Possibly," replied Ingham, shrugging his shoulders noncommittally. "What about you?"

"Oh I've been following them for ages!" replied Caroline, reaching into her bag for her notebook.

"Really?" Caroline ignored the sarcasm in Ingham's voice.

"Yes, really!" She waved over at John, who was standing with Gray. "I've been shopping at SEX for months now!"

Malcolm was enjoying himself immensely. What better way of spending a Sunday night than at a strip club in the heart of Soho watching a group called the Sex Pistols. He waved over at Simon Barker, who had just arrived with his friends who, he thought, wouldn't look out of place on stage themselves. "Who's on the door?" he asked Jordon, helping himself to a cup of the laced punch.

"Leather," replied Jordon, turning away from Malcolm to serve somebody.

"Who?" asked Malcolm, thinking he'd misheard her.

"Leather!" repeated Jordon. "Go and have a look."

Malcolm was still clearly puzzled but he headed towards the club's entrance. He spotted a mysterious figure, wearing a leather hood, standing just inside the doorway trying to entice the people passing along Brewer Street. The leather hood had slits for the eyes and mouth.

"Hello Malcolm," said the figure who was also wearing one of Malcolm and Vivienne's Perv T-shirts. The word perv had been spelt out with the use of small chicken bones.

"Marvellous!" said Malcolm, recognising Jones's high-pitched voice and patting him on the shoulder. The only people that were going to come in here tonight were the young kids that actually wanted to see the group. He started to head back inside before stopping and glancing back at Jones as he hovered towards another unwilling passer-by. "Ahh yes!" he said, nodding slowly. "Leather and bones – Jones."

Nils called out to him as he re-entered the club; he was standing with a rather pathetic looking woman of about thirty-five years old.

"What's the matter?" he asked Nils, glancing from him to the woman.

"This is Nicole!" said Nils, by way of introduction. "She says she was supposed to be working tonight and she wants her money!"

"And how much will that be?" asked Malcolm, looking Nicole up and down.

"Twenty pounds!" said the woman, without waiting for Nils to reply.

"Well you'd better go and see Vincent, hadn't you?" said Malcolm, ignoring the woman's scowl. He started to walk away then stopped suddenly and instructed Nils to pay the woman. The less involvement he had with Vincent, the better. "But she still has to do her act!" he yelled, before disappearing inside. Nils shrugged his shoulders and pulled out a few crumpled notes and handed over four fivers.

Nicole appeared on stage in an outfit that had clearly seen better days and slowly began gyrating to the house music. Steve was sitting in the front row so as to enjoy the full benefit of the unexpected bonus attraction. There were howls of derision from the audience as the poor woman went through her act and when the music finished she hurriedly grabbed up her clothes and fled the stage.

Jonh Ingham had taken up a good position close to the stage and was idly passing the time trying to guess which people in the audience were the two remaining Sex Pistols. He recognised John and Steve from the photograph that had accompanied Neil Spencer's review and had narrowed the possible suspects down to maybe six or seven colourfully dressed individuals. Having grown tired of this game he turned to study John, who was standing a few feet away with Ray Stevenson, who Ingham recognised from the various gigs he'd attended since starting work for *Sounds.*

John was quizzing the photographer about all the various equipment he'd brought with him. He was concerned about the strobe lighting that Stevenson was going to use to enhance the dingy lighting inside the club. John had suffered from meningitis as a child and was still prone to fits, which could be brought on by the effects of strobe lighting, though he had taken the precaution of wearing a pair of dark-lensed "granny glasses" for the evening.

Caroline Coon had also been watching John talking to Stevenson and was biding her time in the hope of catching him before the group went on stage. She seized her moment when John happened to glance in her direction and headed towards him, giving Ingham a look of smug satisfaction as she passed him. Stevenson, sensing that he was surplus to the journalist's requirements, made his excuses and left them to it.

Caroline quickly sensed that John wasn't in the mood to talk about the group and changed tack by asking him instead for his opinions on the race for the leadership of the Labour Party and therefore the prime-ministership of the country.

"I don't know," said John, dryly. "It doesn't really matter who wins. I'd like to think that whoever gets it will make a difference, but I doubt it!"

"So you're saying that the Sex Pistols aren't into politics!" she said, subtly bringing the conversation around to the group.

"I would definitely say we're into personal politics!" replied John. "I can rant on about what's happening to me, but I wouldn't say we're a political group." He pointed over at Steve, who was chatting with two girls near the doorway. "Take Steve for example, for all he cares Foot, Healey and Callaghan could be Arsenal's mid-field. You know what I'm sayin'?" He stared right at Caroline to see if she was listening. "Steve don't give a fuck one way or the other. It has no impact on his life; those cunts in the Houses of Parliament don't give a fuck about the likes of us!"

The Sex Pistols went on at midnight. The tightly packed audience had massed together in front of the stage, cheering and clapping. The row of box-lights which would normally have been raised above the stage were still lying at John's feet and Paul had to squeeze himself past his bass drum to reach his stool where he waited patiently while Glen and Steve tuned their instruments.

"That's my fuckin' shirt!" he shouted loud enough so that the others turned towards him. Paul was pointing at the "You're gonna wake up" T-shirt that Glen had revealed after removing his pullover.

"Yeah, I know," said Steve, looking from Paul towards Glen.

"So how come he's wearin' it, an' it's got your name on it?" asked Paul, pointing a drumstick at the T-shirt.

"Looks good though, dunnit!" said Steve, grinning sheepishly at Paul.

"When you're ready girls!" said John, leaning on his microphone stand.

The group were really in fine form, clearly more relaxed playing to their own kind of people rather than trying to please someone else's audience. Steve, Glen and Paul kept the music tight, allowing John to go wild.

"You'd better like what I'm doing or I'm just wasting my time!" he yelled, above the droning feedback from Steve's guitar as they burst into "Did You No Wrong".

During the song "No Fun", John got so carried away with his performance that he set about smashing the box-lights at the front of the stage, until Vincent and a couple of his heavies suddenly appeared in the doorway.

Malcolm, in a fit of panic, rushed over towards Jordon and Collins who were still selling the tequila laced punch. "Quick girl, get rid of it!"

"Shit!" shouted Jordon, following Malcolm's arm, which was pointing towards the Maltese gangster. "Drink the evidence!"

"What?" gasped Collins, staring at the bucket, which was more than half full.

"Drink it!" repeated Jordon, as she began dipping the plastic cups into the bucket and handing them to people standing close by.

It turned out to be a great night for everybody, with maybe the exception of Vincent, who was left demanding compensation for the smashed lights. He was also missing a leather whip and a couple of dildos.

In response to Jonh Ingham's ravings about the Sex Pistols, the editor of *Sounds* told him to run a story on the group for the following week's edition of the magazine in order to compete with their rivals. Ingham was sure that Caroline Coon would be making similar requests to her editor over at *Melody Maker*. Ingham hadn't been sure how to get hold of the Sex Pistols although he did remember the comment from Caroline Coon that she shopped at SEX on the King's Road. As luck would have it, one of his colleagues overheard the conversation between Ingham and his editor and mentioned that they had received a telephone call from the manager of the Sex Pistols a few days earlier and had kept the number on file.

Ingham called Malcolm and arranged for them to meet at a coffee bar on the King's Road. When he arrived at the appointed place Ingham was slightly disappointed to find that no-one from the group was there. Ingham sat listening while Malcolm gave him his manifesto for the Sex Pistols before consenting to the journalist interviewing the group themselves. Malcolm gave Ingham the address of the rehearsal place on Denmark Street and told him to be there for 7.30 pm.

When he arrived at Denmark Street he found everyone in attendance, except for the charismatic Johnny Rotten.

"He's over the road, in the Cambridge!" said Paul, sensing the journalist's disappointment.

"Is that where we're going?"

"It is, if you're payin'!" replied Steve, grinning. Ingham quickly realised the set-up. No beer meant no interview.

As they made their way to the Cambridge to meet up with John, Ingham chatted with Glen, Steve and Paul about their influences and the state of the British music scene in general. Malcolm was following a few metres behind with Nils, listening in on the conversation but not passing comment himself. "I think we've got one of the converted here," he said to Nils, making sure he was out of the earshot of the journalist.

Once inside the public house, after Ingham had duly paid for the drinks, he was taken over to the table where John was sitting with Tracey O'Keef and Debbie Wilson. They were both members of the Bromley Contingent as everybody now referred to Simon Barker and his friends. The El Paradise show was the first time that Debbie had been to see the Sex Pistols, or to a strip club for that matter, but she was only fifteen.

Malcolm carried on from where he'd left off earlier that day in the coffee bar. Ingham listened politely while scribbling down the more salient points that would be of use for the proposed article. Steve and Paul were a constant distraction as they teased Glen about his new girlfriend. The journalist had been sitting with them for an hour now and had everyone's opinion, except the one that he really wanted.

"OK!" he said, turning to face John. "I've heard it from everyone else. What about you?"

"I hate shit!" said John, suddenly coming to life, his eyes boring into Ingham's. "I hate hippies! I hate long hair!" He paused to stifle a yawn before continuing. "I want to change things, so there are more groups like us!" Then John seemed to lose interest for a moment and glanced around the empty room.

"I want to know..."

"I'm against people who just complain about *Top of the Pops* and don't do anything about it! I want people to see us and then go out and start something, or else I'm just wasting my time!" said John, cutting off Ingham's question.

"The problem with playing in pubs," said Malcolm, interrupting, "is that they're bigger than the groups. The group has to play what the crowd wants, rather than what the group wants to play simply because they can make a living from it!" He paused for maximum effect. "If you want to change things, you simply cannot play those places!"

"That's what really impressed me!" said Ingham, turning to face Glen. "Your songs are what...two to three minutes long?"

"That's right!" said Steve, butting in before Glen got the chance to answer. "I don't bother with guitar solos for two reasons. One, I don't like 'em, and two..."

"He can't play 'em!" said Paul, as everybody laughed.

"An' I can't play 'em," added Steve, tossing a beer mat at his friend.

"Well," said Ingham, getting up from his stool. "I think that I've got enough here." He patted his notebook.

"When will we be in?" asked Steve, idly scratching at his earlobe.

"Hopefully next week," replied Ingham, slipping on his jacket. "But I'll phone you to let you know for definite." He turned towards Malcolm. "Thanks for your time."

"Thanks for the beer!" said Steve, holding up his glass.

"What about the review for the El Paradise gig?" shouted Glen.

"It'll all be in the same feature," said Ingham, walking back towards them.

"I'm hoping I can get a two-page feature out of that and this interview!"

"Yes," said Malcolm, turning to Ingham, "we must get some photos for you from Nils's brother." Ingham nodded thoughtfully then waved his thanks and left.

"Vivienne's really angry with you," said Tracey, leaning forward on her stool and wagging a finger at Malcolm.

"What on earth for?" asked Malcolm, a puzzled expression spreading across his face.

"You didn't get her a birthday card!" said Debbie, laughing with Tracey.

"Good God! I don't even live with the woman anymore and yet I'm still getting grief!"

"He didn't buy me one either!" said John, feigning a hurtful expression.

"Quite true!" said Malcolm, "but I do remember buying you and your friends here – he waved his hand at Steve and the others – several rounds of drinks in the Roebuck!"

"We all got you a card for your thirtieth, didn't we?" said Paul, smirking at Malcolm.

"Yes, dear boy," replied Malcolm, ruefully, "and I can still remember the kind sentiments that you all wrote in it!"

When Ray Stevenson arrived at SEX to show Malcolm and his brother Nils the photographs from the El Paradise, he suggested an outdoor photo session in order to get some pictures of the group away from a stage setting and in a more relaxed atmosphere. He told them that he was free to shoot the session the following weekend unless Malcolm had other arrangements. When Ray arrived at their place on Denmark Street the following Saturday, he found that the group were all there waiting for him. John had suggested to the other three that none of them should wear anything from the shop just to piss Malcolm off. He was wearing a pair of baggy trousers and a natty cardigan that he'd bought at a local Oxfam store. He'd also customised the white shirt that he was wearing by painting the slogans "Antichrist" and "No Future" down the front of the shirt.

The first idea that Ray decided on was to take a photo of all four members of the group squashed together inside the red telephone box outside St. Giles' Church, which was situated just around the corner from Denmark Street. They were on their way towards Soho, when Steve looked round as he heard someone shout out his name.

"All right, Dodge!" shouted Steve, waving an arm at the lad crossing the road and coming towards him. It was an old school friend of his and Paul's. Dave Pierce – known as "Dodgy Dave" both to his friends and the local constabulary.

"Fuckin' hell, boy, what's with the 'shitstoppers'?" said Dodgy, pointing at Steve's straight-leg trousers. "You gotta get with the fashion!" He indicated his own thirty-inch flared Oxford Bags, which covered his shoes hiding them completely.

"I'm in a group!" said Steve, grinning at his friend, "with Cookie!"

"How you doin' Cookie? I ain't seen you two in ages!"

"Not bad, Dodge," replied Paul, smiling. "What've..."

"Fuck me!" gasped Dodgy, cutting Paul off in mid-sentence. "Is the circus in town?" He was pointing over at John, who was standing several metres away with Glen and Ray.

"That's our fuckin' singer!" said Steve, following his friend's stare.

Dodgy stepped closer towards Steve and Paul while casting an occasional glance towards John. "Then this could be your lucky day, boys. Me and a mate of mine bought some hooky musical gear off some Iron that owns a fashion store somewhere up the World's End!" He failed to notice the smirk on Steve and Paul's faces as he said this.

"An 'Iron'?" said Paul, looking puzzled. "What the fuck's an Iron?"

"Iron hoof, poof!" explained Dodgy, grinning. "You boys let me know if you're interested!"

"Will do!" said Steve, still trying to keep a straight face. "Where are you livin' now?"

"Well, I'm back at my mum's place on the Wormholt!" replied Dodgy. "I've, ah, just done a stretch at Her Majesty's pleasure!"

"Oh right!" said Steve, nodding. "Well, we've gotta go. I'll bell you sometime an' we'll have a drink!"

"You do that boy, you do that!" said Dodgy. "Be lucky!"

"Better still, get your arse down to the Nashville next Friday!" shouted Steve as his friend crossed the road.

CHAPTER ELEVEN

On Friday 23 April, Nils once again drove the group over to the Nashville Rooms in West Kensington where they were due to play with the 101ers. Dave Goodman and his partner Kim Thraves were already parked up outside the venue waiting for them and between them they quickly unloaded the two transit vans. Once they had their gear set up on the stage and everybody was satisfied with the soundcheck, they settled themselves at the bar. When the 101ers arrived at the venue they completely ignored the members of the Sex Pistols. They saw them as little more than pretentious upstarts. This was their gig and the Sex Pistols had better remember it.

The Nashville was a well-known venue on the London music scene and the makings of a decent sized crowd were already gathering inside. Many of these people had been present when the two groups played there at the beginning of the month, but some had since cut their hair and changed their appearance. Malcolm was busy chatting to the journalists from the weekly music magazines making sure they were being properly catered for. Another friend of Malcolm's, Ted Carroll, who ran a market stall selling imported records, had offered to act as D.J. for the evening. He was playing a selection of songs from the likes of Roxy Music, The Small Faces and Iggy And The Stooges, which seemed to be going down well with the audience. Simon Barker and his friends were all clowning around on the dance floor enjoying themselves.

The Sex Pistols went on stage around 9.30 p.m. but seemed strangely subdued. John was dressed quite sedately for the occasion wearing a black jacket and trousers, but Steve was wearing another of Malcolm's T-shirts – this latest design depicting a photo of a woman's breasts.

"In case you hadn't guessed," said John, drolly, as he surveyed the crowd, "we're the Sex Pistols."

Steve thrashed out the by now familiar opening chords of "Did You No Wrong". They were playing reasonably well, which was purely down to having a sound engineer who was very much into what the group was trying to achieve. The crowd sitting at the front of the stage, and those gathered at the bar were waiting for something extraordinary to happen. The word on the street was that this group was "different", but tonight it looked like just another Friday night down at the Nashville.

Jonh Ingham was standing over to one side of the stage, keeping one eye on the group, while observing the strange assortment of fans that the Sex Pistols seemed to be attracting. He saw Malcolm and Nils standing together near the mixing desk; a rather sinister looking character with dark spiky hair and wearing a blue lurex jacket was standing beside them. It was John's friend Sid and it was the first time that he'd been to see the Sex Pistols. John had been pleased to hear that his best friend would be attending the gig and had given him a new haircut for the occasion. Sid had accompanied Vivienne, with whom he was now quite friendly after speaking to her at the shop. She smiled at Sid as she passed him on her way back to her seat at the front of the stage.

The group was performing "Pretty Vacant" and John, from his vantage point on stage, was amused as he watched Vivienne giving Malcolm the cold shoulder treatment. He then casually watched her make her way to her seat, which was now occupied by another girl. His eyes widened with glee. There looked like the possibility of a catfight as the girl, who was sitting with her boyfriend refused to budge. The argument became more heated as neither Vivienne nor the girl seemed willing to give in, and then the girl's boyfriend got involved.

The boys on stage lost all interest in their own performance in favour of the developing scene in front of them. Suddenly all hell broke lose as Vivienne slapped the girl across the face and the girl's boyfriend leapt out of his chair, ready to defend her. Then Sid charged over and thumped him. John cackled with delight as his mate began pummelling the unfortunate boyfriend. He almost choked when he saw Malcolm charge across with his arms windmilling. Now it was a free-for-all and nobody in the room was even watching the group on stage. Steve threw off his guitar and dived into the melée closely followed by Glen and John, though the fight was over within a few minutes and the three Sex Pistols climbed back on stage to rejoin their drummer and carry on as if nothing had happened.

After they'd finished their set and dismantled their gear to make way for the 101ers, Malcolm informed them that they were now banned from the Nashville as well as the Marquee.

"What the fuck was all that about anyway?" asked John, still clearly bewildered.

"That girl stole Vivienne's seat!" replied Malcolm, still shaking his head in disbelief at the news that they were banned from another top London venue.

"At this rate we're gonna run out of places to play!" said Glen, sighing.

"Fuckin' women!" snarled Steve, glaring at Vivienne who was dancing away with some of the Bromley Contingent.

The following morning, Malcolm arrived at Denmark Street carrying several copies of *Sounds*, the music paper that Jonh Ingham worked for. The Sex

Pistols were featured on pages ten and eleven. Their double page article included Ingham's review of the gig at El Paradise and the subsequent interview with the group in the Cambridge pub.

"There's nothing like reading about yourselves in the newspapers, eh boys?" said Malcolm, as they feverishly read the article.

"I'll tell you what, John," said Paul, glancing up from his copy of the paper, "Your mate Sid's a bit of a handful."

"Yeah, I know," replied John, smirking. "He told me that he was only sticking up for Vivienne."

"Dunno why," said Steve, angrily. "She's the one who fuckin' started it!"

"It was nice to see her ex-boyfriend sticking up for her as well," said Glen, smirking at Malcolm.

"Yes it was, wasn't it," said John, chuckling.

"Boys," said Malcolm, ignoring John and Glen's comments, "I have some rather interesting news."

"You've found us somewhere to play in London that we're not barred from!" said Glen, sarcastically.

"I've arranged for Chris Spedding to come down here to listen to you rehearsing." He paused for a moment to see if anyone was going to protest. When nobody did he continued. "You may remember seeing him perform on *Top Of The Pops* last year."

"God, who could forget that awful rubbish about motorbikes!" said John, laughing.

"Yes, that was the one," replied Malcolm. "I thought he looked rather good myself!" He smiled at the memory of the inflated prices he and Vivienne had charged Spedding for outfitting him and his backing group in black leather motorcycle outfits. "Anyway," he said, snapping out of his reverie, "Chris has very kindly offered to let you record some tracks at his studios in Clapham."

"So why is he comin' here?" asked John, frowning at Malcolm.

"He wants to choose the songs that he feels will be the best to record," replied Malcolm, spreading his arms out in a gesture of compliance. "And he certainly knows more about this sort of thing than you do!"

John sat bolt upright and narrowed his eyes suspiciously. "And just who's paying for this honour?" he asked.

"I shall," replied Malcolm. "Needless to say, I shall be recouping this expenditure from future shows."

"Ha ha," sneered John, turning to face the others, "How's he gonna do that when no fucker will have us?"

"Yes, I was coming to that," said Malcolm. "I'm looking into the possibility of you playing some shows out of town, maybe up north."

"Oh my God!" moaned John.

"It'll be good experience for you," said Malcolm, hoping to placate John. "In the meantime, I've arranged one closer to home."

"When's that then?" asked Steve, from where he lay sprawled across his bed. He'd given up trying to understand what was written in the featured article on the group, deciding to ask Paul about it later instead.

"The fifth of next month," replied Malcolm.

"Where?" asked Paul.

"It's somewhere on the Finchley Road," said Malcolm, turning to face Paul, "At a place called the Babalu Club. I'm going to contact Capital Radio and get them to advertise the show, so we should get a good crowd down there."

Glen, who'd borrowed his father's car so that he could take Celia out for the day, had agreed to take Malcolm back to his shop in Chelsea for a pre-arranged meeting with a supplier. The other three went downstairs into the rehearsal room. Paul had been meaning to give his drum kit a good cleaning but had kept putting it off. Everything seemed to be covered in beer stains; at least he hoped that's what they were. There were even a few specks of blood from the fight at the Nashville.

Steve was sitting on top of his amplifier strumming the chords that he hoped would fit the set of lyrics that John had brought down a few days before. The new song was to be called "I Wanna Be Me".

"Who was the 'Dread' that I saw you talkin' to last night?" he asked John, who was sprawled in the corner of the room doing the crossword in the copy of *Sounds* that Malcolm had given to him earlier.

"You know him, don't you?" replied John. "His name is Don and he works at Acme Attractions on the King's Road."

"Yeah, I thought it was him," said Paul, polishing one of his cymbals. "I didn't know that you knew him."

"I didn't before last night, not really," replied John, "we just got talkin'. He's all right."

"What was he doin' there last night?" asked Steve, handing John a cigarette.

"He's well clued up is Don," replied John, pausing for a moment. "He's probably heard about us off Krevine, who owns Acme Attractions. An' he said he'd fuck all else to do!"

"What did he say about last night?" asked Paul.

"Oh he enjoyed the fight, and he said we weren't bad either!"

"Really?" said Steve, putting the guitar aside while he finished his cigarette.

"Yeah," said John, "he understands what we're tryin' to do."

"Good!" said Paul, grinning. "Do you think he'd explain it to me?"

"He's gonna take me an' Nils to a reggae club in Dalston called the Four Aces. I can't fuckin' wait!"

"What do you reckon to this Spedding geezer comin' down 'ere?" Steve asked John.

"I think it's a great idea," replied John, exhaling a perfectly formed ring of cigarette smoke. "It'll be a laugh if nothin' else." He turned his attentions back to the unfinished crossword. "The bass player with The Bay City Rollers. Five letters, fourth one's D."

"Dildo!" said Steve, reaching for his guitar.

▢ ▢ ▢ ▢

"Looks all right, don't it?" said John, walking around the Babalu Club. Their equipment was already set up on the small stage in the corner. Dave Goodman and his partner Kim were once again providing the PA for the evening.

"Yeah," replied Kim, nodding at John. "We should get a good sound in here." He stepped aside to allow the owner of the club to come past him with a tray of complimentary drinks.

"You boys gonna fill this place, tonight?" he asked, hopefully, as he set the tray down on a nearby table. "I heard them boys on the radio sayin' you was the new Who." He glanced around waiting for some response. When he didn't get one he went back to reading his paper behind the bar.

The group performed a couple of numbers for the soundcheck while Goodman and Kim twiddled a few knobs and offered their opinions. Kim was right about the acoustics in the small club. All that they had to do now was sit back and wait for the punters to come through the door.

The owner reappeared bringing another round of free drinks. "What time you boys thinkin' of going on?" he asked. "Only I can have these tables and chairs moved out of the way." He swept his arm towards the area in front of the stage.

"We'll let you know," said Paul, helping himself to another drink.

"Any of you boys follow the football?" he asked, sitting down uninvited next to John.

"Yeah," replied John. "I go an' watch Arsenal now an' again."

"Them bloody Scousers have won the league again!" continued the owner, shaking his head. "Bloody ninth time! It says so in the paper."

"Which team do you support?" asked Steve, helping himself to another pint.

"I've followed West Ham since I was a nipper," replied the owner. "I was at the Wembley last year when we beat Fulham. It was a real shame that Bobby had to be playing for the opposition that day." The owner shook his head at the memory of the former Hammers captain and West Ham legend Bobby Moore who had been captaining Fulham against his former club in the FA Cup Final.

"They pissed it," said John, remembering having watched the game with his old man.

"They had George Best and Rodney Marsh playing for them last year, Fulham did!" He stopped talking when John and Paul looked over at Steve and burst out laughing. "Did I say somethin' funny?" he asked them.

"No," said Paul, waving his hand in dismissal. "It's a long story."

"I've seen 'em all, I have," continued the owner undeterred. "Geoff Hurst, Martin Peters, Bobby Moore, all the great players. I was at Wembley in '66 when we beat the Krauts!"

"Wasn't that England?" asked Goodman, smirking at John.

"Same thing back then!" replied the owner, winking at Paul.

"Fat fuckin' chance we'll ever win it again either!" scowled John.

The owner had gone back behind the bar. He'd taken on a couple of young women to help him with the rush, but they had little to do except sit at the end of the bar and chat about last night's television. The owner would glance over occasionally to see what was happening. The group had told him they'd probably go on stage at 9.30 p.m., but with ten minutes to go there were less than twenty people inside the club.

"It's fuckin' dead!" said Glen, glancing over at the entrance.

"Do you think the fight from the Nashville's got anythin' to do with it?" asked Paul.

"Nah," said Steve, shaking his head dismissively. "We've been back there since then, haven't we?"

"Only cos we said it was a private party!" replied Paul.

"Who's gonna want to come and see us when there's a chance they'll get a good kickin'?" said Glen, despondently.

"You're joking!" said John, grinning. "Every fucker likes to see a good scrap! Every time there's a fight on *Match Of The Day* the cameras zoom straight over. That's why most of the people I know go to watch Arsenal in the first place!"

"It's not for the football, is it?" said Glen, grinning at John.

"You sure the doors ain't fuckin' locked?" Steve shouted over towards the bar.

As they were contracted to play, the Sex Pistols waited until almost 10 p.m. before going on stage, but the club was still empty. They were relaxed and played a blinding set for the handful of people that bothered to turn up.

It was a cold bleak Sunday in March and the Sex Pistols were busy rehearsing for the first date of their Tuesday night residency at the 100 Club on Oxford Street. There was, however, another reason for the busy rehearsals. Chris Spedding was coming down to listen to them play in order to decide which of their songs were strong enough to record as demos, with a view to sending them to record companies.

Spedding arrived later that day with Malcolm, but having little interest in musical technicalities, Malcolm made the necessary introductions before making his excuses and leaving them to it.

It's like being on my driving test, thought Glen, as he watched Spedding making notes while they played their set. Spedding had told them to act as if he wasn't there, which was easy for him to say. Glen had seen Spedding quite a few times when he'd worked in Malcolm's shop on Saturdays. "What do you think?" he asked, as Steve and John downed tools for a much-needed cigarette break.

"Good," replied Spedding. "I saw you at the 100 Club the, er...other week." He glanced across towards John, who merely shrugged non-committally. "I went with Chrissie, Chrissie Hynde?"

"Yeah, we know Chrissie," said Glen. "What have you decided on so far?"

"I think 'Pretty Vacant' is a definite," replied Spedding, studying his notepad. "Then 'No Feelings' and the other one is, ah...'Problems'."

"You think they're our best three?" asked John, looking at the others.

"Well in my opinion, yes they are," said Spedding.

"Any idea when we'll be going in to record 'em?" asked Paul, smirking at Steve. None of them had really expected Malcolm to put his hand in his wallet and pay for them to go and fuck about in some recording studio. Even if the demos had been his idea.

"Sure do," said Spedding, flipping the pages of his notebook. "Friday the fourteenth."

"Fourteenth of what?" asked Steve, frowning.

"Of this month."

"What?" gasped Steve, almost coughing up a lung. "This fuckin' month?"

"Why not?" asked Spedding, grinning as Paul began slapping Steve's back in an attempt to try to end the coughing fit.

"Better get fuckin' rehearsin', then," said John, handing Steve his guitar.

Malcolm, as usual, was busy on the telephone when Helen returned from doing the shopping. She could sense it was bad news from the way he sounded. He offered her a casual wave without interrupting his conversation. "No, it's not your fault Roger!" he said, sincerely. "No I understand. What? Yes. Certainly...In the summer? Yes, I'll be in touch...goodbye Roger." He stood up and began pacing around the small living room stopping briefly to examine the bags of shopping that Helen had placed by the kitchen door.

"Did you get hold of the printing set, Helen?" he asked, as she came back into the room. He sighed deeply when she shook her head in the negative. "Really Helen," he said, picking up the telephone, "I ask you to do one small thing... Oh hello Kim," he said into the receiver, disregarding Helen. "Yes it's Malcolm here. I've just had a call from Roger Austin...what? Yes, as in the car...bad news, I'm afraid...Yes, that's right...the show for the seventeenth has had to be cancelled...yes, he'll understand...goodbye." He replaced the receiver in its cradle.

Malcolm paused at the window and peered out into Bell Street and began muttering away to himself. "Why didn't you get hold of the prin..." he began, turning back to face Helen, who was sitting perched over the coffee table. "That's marvellous, abso-bloody-lutely marvellous!" Helen had cut out various letters from a copy of the Evening Standard and laid them out on the table to resemble a ransom note from some would-be kidnapper. Only instead of a demand for money it was an advertisement for the forthcoming Sex Pistols gig at the 100 Club on 11 May.

Malcolm and Nils were on their way to visit John Curd, who was promoting the forthcoming Ramones gig at the Roundhouse on Sunday 4 July. Malcolm was telling Nils all about Helen's ransom note style posters that he'd arranged to distribute to shops and music stores in and around London. "She's at the flat right now, working on some more designs," he said, as Nils parked the car at the kerb in front of Curd's office. "And she's got hold of one of those John Bull printing sets as well," he added before ringing the doorbell.

"Yes, can I help you?" asked the attractive woman, smiling at the two visitors standing before her.

"Oh hello," replied Malcolm, beaming at the woman. "I'd like to speak to John Curd. The name's McLaren. Malcolm McLaren."

"He's not in," replied the woman. The smile disappeared from her face as if she'd been slapped. "I'm his wife."

Not one to be brushed off easily, Malcolm thrust out his hand to prevent Curd's wife from closing the office door. "I'd like to speak to your husband about putting the Sex Pistols on with The Ramones at the Roundhouse!"

"I've told you, he's not here!" said Curd's wife, pushing against the door. "Anyway, he's seen your group and he doesn't like them!"

"It doesn't matter what *he* likes!" shouted Malcolm, beginning to lose his temper. "It's about what the kids want. He can't be an arsehole all his life!" Suddenly the door burst open and John Curd rushed past his wife. He grabbed hold of Malcolm by his jacket and pushed him down the flight of stairs.

"Hold on!" shouted Nils, slowly raising both hands. "We're leaving."

Nils drove the transit van containing Malcolm, the group and their equipment over to Majestic Studios, which was situated just off Clapham High Street near to the common. Malcolm was coming along to see for himself what it was like inside a proper recording studio. Nils' brother Ray had also agreed to come along but he was following behind in his own car. He intended to stick around long enough to snap off a few photos of the group before leaving for another assignment. All four members of the group had spent the previous night at Denmark Street so as to be ready for the appointed time of 10 a.m. Paul had booked the day off work telling his employers that he was off to record their first million seller.

Spedding's sound engineer, Derek, was waiting for them when they arrived. He unlocked the main door before disappearing down a narrow corridor towards the kitchen area, claiming that he couldn't possibly get started without his morning cuppa. While they were waiting for Derek to return, Ray snapped off a couple of shots of the group standing in front of the open doors at the back of the van. The four youths tried their best to look mean and moody for the camera, but it was far too early for such theatricals.

John was wearing his natty pink school blazer, leopard-skin waistcoat and a pair of baggy trousers. He was also wearing the granny glasses that he'd worn at the El Paradise gig. Glen was wearing his Jackson Pollock straight-leg trousers while Steve was wearing a 1950s style drape jacket, giving him the appearance of a teddy boy. Paul was dressed the most casually of the four of them, in his straight-leg jeans, trainers and a grey pullover.

"Come on Malcolm!" said Ray, motioning for Malcolm to stand with the others. "At least take your jacket off. You must be roasting in that get up." He couldn't believe that somebody would be wearing leather trousers and jacket on such a beautiful day.

◻ ◻ ◻ ◻

Malcolm, Nils and the group spent the first hour sitting drinking tea and listening to Derek's stories about the famous musicians who had previously used the studios. They'd been given the grand tour and the gear had been brought inside, although there was no point setting it up until Spedding arrived.

"Ahh, I see you've settled in nicely," he said, stepping into the control room. "Welcome to Majestic Studios!" Spedding tossed his small rucksack down by the side of the mixing desk, smiling at Paul. "This is where I recorded 'Here Come The Warm Jets' with Brian Eno." He remembered the drummer having admitted to being a one-time fan of Roxy Music, the group with which Eno had played keyboards.

"It's fuckin' massive, this place!" said Steve.

"It used to be a cinema," replied Spedding, by way of explanation.

Once he had helped Paul set out his drums correctly so as to avoid unwanted vibrations from the amplifiers he turned his attentions to Steve and Glen. "I think you'll be better using my bass amp," he told Glen, explaining how certain amplifiers can give off a buzzing noise that could spoil the recordings. "I've also got a guitar amp for you Steve."

John remained with Malcolm and Nils while all this was going on, as he wouldn't be required to add the vocals until all the music had been laid down on tape.

"When we're all ready," said Spedding, to get everyone's attention, "we'll run through the songs a couple of times just to get loosened up and then we'll have a go at recording." He stepped into the control room and sat down beside Derek at the mixing desk.

He accepted the pair of headphones from the engineer and slipped them over his ears. "Can everyone hear me?" he asked peering through the glass partition into the room where the group's three musicians were waiting, each wearing an identical headset. They all gave him the thumbs up to indicate everything was ready.

Steve had hardly slept the night before; he was really nervous at being in a studio where Spedding and the engineer would pick up on every mistake. On stage it didn't really matter if he hit the occasional wrong note or played the wrong chord but here it was different. There was also the added pressure of Malcolm constantly reminding them how much money all of this was costing him. He really didn't want to let anyone down and Paul had only made things worse by telling him to watch his timing. He wiped his hands on his trousers and signalled to the others that he was ready to begin, then started playing the opening chords of "Problems".

"So they can play, after all!" said Derek, turning to Spedding as he adjusted the knob controlling the volume on Glen's bass guitar.

"Oh yes," replied Spedding. "These people who are spreading rumours about them not being able to play their instruments haven't even seen them play live!" He tapped his fingers to the beat of Paul's drum sound against the side of the mixing desk.

"That was all right!" he said, speaking into the intercom which linked the two rooms.

"Do you want us to do it again?" asked Steve, rubbing the side of his head to relieve the pressure of the headphones.

"No, try the next one," replied Spedding, consulting his worksheet. "'No Feelings'."

The recording was going well and after they had finished laying down the music for the three songs it was John's turn to put down the vocal track. Once this was done he went to rejoin Glen, Steve and Paul in the control booth.

"Seeing you in the isolation booth reminded me of some crap game show off the telly," said Glen, laughing at John.

"*Mr. and Mrs?*" said Derek.

"That's the one!" said Glen. "My mum and dad never miss it. Bloody awful programme!"

"Right," said Spedding, rising out of his chair, "Me and Derek are gonna take a break now, so I'll just set this up." He reached over and switched on the tape machine positioned next to the mixing desk and waited until the reels began slowly rotating. "Have a listen to what we've done so far and see what you think."

"Sounds fuckin' great to me!" said Steve, turning round to look at the others. John nodded his agreement while hammering out the beat on his knees. He'd been dreading the moment when his vocals would fill the room, but they sounded pretty good.

Malcolm, sitting next to John, had a wry smile on his face as he listened to the recording. He'd told the group that he would be the one fronting the money for the session, but this wasn't true. Chris Spedding, although a recording artist in his own right was also the main session guitarist for RAK Records, which was owned by Mickie Most and it was he, and not Malcolm, that was paying for the demos to be recorded. Most had given the go-ahead for the session with a view to signing the group at a later date.

The music ended and there was silence in the control room apart from the gentle hiss coming from the tape machine as the reels carried on rotating.

"Rewind it," said John, looking over at Paul who was sitting nearest to the tape machine.

"No!" replied Paul, shaking his head.

"Go on, then we can listen to them again!" said John, pointing at the tape machine.

Paul finally relented and leaned across to study the array of buttons and switches on the control panel. He pressed the "stop" button then gingerly pressed the one for "rewind". The two large tape reels slowly began to rewind but then started to speed up faster and faster, giving off a loud whirring noise.

"Get it to stop boy!" yelled Malcolm, pointing towards the machine. Paul stabbed a finger towards the stop button but he was too late and everyone gasped with horror as the tape came loose from the reel and flapped against the other reel.

"What have you done?" gasped Malcolm, glaring at Paul. He feared that he might be held liable for the cost of repairing the machine.

"I didn't do anything!" yelled Paul, feeling embarrassed as the others all pointed and shouted at him. Everyone turned round towards the door as Spedding and Derek came back into the room. They could both tell that something had happened by the guilty expressions on all their faces.

"Cookie's bust your tape machine!" said Steve, pointing accusingly at Paul.

"No, I didn't!" said Paul, although he didn't sound too convinced. His face was as red as a helmet. "Have I?" he asked, sheepishly.

Spedding offered Paul a reassuring smile as he set about reattaching the tape onto the reel. "No, it's my fault. I should have warned you not to touch anything."

"So we don't have to do them all again, then?" asked Glen, looking slightly dejected when Spedding shook his head. "Pity."

"We've still got some guitar overdubs to do," said Spedding, glancing over at Steve. "And maybe some backing vocals."

"Get back in there fatty!" shouted John, giving Steve a dig in the ribs.

"How about a solo for 'Problems', as well?" asked Spedding, looking hopefully at the group's guitarist.

"Huh?" replied Steve, suddenly distracted from his play fight with John. "I don't even do one when we're playin' it live!"

"That's the beauty of a 24 track recording studio," replied Derek. "It allows you to put in the extras that you can't do otherwise."

"I'm only thinking about using a simple pattern that will run along with the basic structure of the song," said Spedding. He could see that Steve wasn't totally convinced. "What key is the song in?"

"Fuck knows!" replied Steve, shrugging his shoulders and looking over at Glen.

"It's in D," said Glen, shaking his head at Steve.

"I don't want these cunts laughin' at me when we do it!" scowled Steve, looking round the room.

"Why not?" asked John, smirking. "You were enjoying yourself laughing at me a short while ago!"

"I'll take care of these three," said Malcolm, rising up off his stool. "We'll go for a stroll and find somewhere to have a drink."

◻   ◻   ◻   ◻

"I think it's time we were heading back to see how they're doing," said Malcolm, raising his glass to his mouth.

"Yeah," said Paul, smirking at John and Glen. "I wonder how Steve's got on?"

"Nils will be back shortly with the van," said Malcolm, glancing at his watch. He'd sent Nils off earlier in the day to pick up some stock for the shop, making full use of the hired vehicle. He'd borrowed it again from the guy that owned the stall on Berwick Street market. As it was a Friday, the owner had demanded an extra five pounds and insisted that the van would have to be back on time for when the market closed.

As the four made their way back along Clapham High Street they talked about the day's activities and how they felt, now that they'd experienced the whole recording process in a fully equipped studio. The three members of the group all admitted to being impressed with Spedding's approach and how he'd handled them as they'd all been shitting themselves when they'd arrived at the studio that morning.

"You should see his girlfriend!" said Glen, remembering seeing the beautiful German girl who had accompanied Spedding on his frequent visits to the King's Road.

"Yes," said Malcolm, nodding his agreement. "But not only is she very attractive, she's also the daughter of a newspaper magnate."

"Lucky sod!" said John, dryly.

When Malcolm and the others arrived back at the studio they found Steve sprawled on a couch in the control room. He was listening to something Spedding was telling him about how the different knobs and dials on the mixing desk worked.

"How did it go?" asked Glen.

"Fuckin' easy!" replied Steve, grinning with self-satisfaction. "Have a listen to the maestro." He reached over and flicked the switch on the controls before sitting back with his hands resting on the back of his head.

Spedding gave them a running commentary on what they had done while they'd been away. The song "Problems" now had a guitar solo running through the middle-eight. "No Feelings" had the opening guitar riff repeated and they had faded in the intro to "Pretty Vacant". He offered to change anything that they weren't happy with, but nobody complained.

"Can we have copies to take with us?" asked Glen, hopefully. He wanted to play the completed songs to his girlfriend Celia. Spedding set up the bank of tape machines in order to run off a few copies for the individual members of the group as they packed away their gear. By the time this was finished Nils had returned with the van. He helped the boys with the loading of the gear and clambered back up into the driver's seat as the group thanked Spedding and Derek for their patience and advice.

"It was my pleasure," Spedding told them while handing several tapes over to Malcolm. "These songs have some of the most expressive guitar lines that I've heard in a long time!" he told Steve as he climbed into the rear of the van.

"That's good, right?" asked Steve, turning round to Glen.

▭ ▭ ▭ ▭

Malcolm was sitting with Michael Collins on the surgical bed in the far corner of the shop. The two men were busy sorting through a pile of swatches of new materials that he and Vivienne were hoping to use in the production of a new range of clothing for SEX. Jordon interrupted their conversation by informing Malcolm that Nils was on the telephone.

"Hello, boy," said Malcolm, resting the receiver in the crook of his shoulder. He had organised a mini-tour of the North of England for the group and, claiming that important business matters had forced him to stay in London, delegated Nils as tour manager. "How's it going up there?"

"They're fucking primitive up here," replied Nils, chuckling. He was calling from Middlesbrough, where the Sex Pistols would be performing that evening.

"Yes, I can believe it," replied Malcolm, remembering his and Bernie's business trips to Scotland, where they had tried to sell off Steve's stolen musical equipment. "What sort of reaction are they getting up there?"

"I don't think the locals are quite ready for the Sex Pistols," replied Nils. "At the first place, in Northallerton..."

"Where?"

"Exactly. It's the arse-end of nowhere!" said Nils, flatly. "Anyway, the boys were standing on stage ready to begin when some old guy wearing his flat cap comes up to the microphone, and I swear this is true..."

"Go on boy, spit it out," interrupted Malcolm, impatiently.

"The old guy says, 'And now, ladies and gentlemen for the very first time up north in cabaret. The Sex Pistols.' You should have seen John's face!"

"God, help us. Mind you, they do say that it's grim up north!" Malcolm paused while Nils inserted more coins into the pay phone at his end. "You are getting paid, aren't you?"

"Oh they're paying us not to play in some of these places!" said Nils.

"What on earth do you mean?"

"Well we were in some Godforsaken place called Whitby and the group had only been on stage ten minutes when someone came in telling them they'd have to stop because they couldn't hear the Bingo downstairs!"

"Where did you say you are now?" asked Malcolm.

"Middlesbrough," replied Nils. "Some place called The Crypt!"

"Ahh yes, isn't that the show they're playing with the Doctors of Madness?"

"Yeah," said Nils, hesitating for a few moments. "There is a slight problem though."

"Really?"

"Yes, really," said Nils. "Apparently we're contracted to play for an hour and a half."

"Yes, go on."

"Well Glen reckons we could stretch it to maybe fifty minutes. At a push!" said Nils.

"Well tell them to play slower!" said Malcolm, chuckling.

"There is one other thing."

"And what's that?"

"This van is fuckin' shit! It won't go uphill," said Nils, sighing. "And this whole fuckin' area is full of hills!"

"Yes, I'm sorry about that," replied Malcolm, sounding anything but sorry. "But it was the best I could do!"

"Lying bastard" thought Nils, staring into the mouthpiece of the receiver. "We should be back in London the day after tomorrow," he said, instead.

"OK," said Malcolm. 'I'll look forward to seeing you then and say hello to the boys for me." He replaced the phone as the pips were sounding down the line warning that the connection was about to be terminated and went back over towards Collins.

The group had hardly had time to unpack their dirty laundry before Malcolm informed them that they would be heading back up the M1 to play a gig in Manchester on 4 June. He reminded them about the two lads that had travelled down from Manchester to watch them play at High Wycombe. It seemed that Pete and Howard had been so impressed by what the Sex Pistols were trying to achieve, they had formed their own group and organised a gig in the hope that they could persuade the group to travel up from London to perform with them.

"Whereabouts in Manchester?" asked John.

"The Lesser Free Trade Hall," replied Malcolm, reading aloud from the letter he'd received from Howard Trafford.

"We'll get paid with mushy peas!" Steve said, grinning.

"Typical of you to think about food!" said John, shaking his head at Steve. "Seriously though, they might take you to visit their treacle mines."

"Fuck off!" said Steve, spotting the wink that John gave Paul.

Glen had some interesting news of his own. He'd been out on the town with his girlfriend Celia when they'd run into Mick Jones. Jones had informed Glen that he was still working with Bernie and that if Glen knew of any drummers he should give him a call. The following day Glen had met up with Mick and a friend of his called Paul, who was the new bass player with Mick's group. They had come across the singer from the 101ers, the group that the Sex Pistols had supported at the Nashville the previous month. Mick, never one to beat around the bush, came straight out and told the guy that although he'd been really impressed by his stage performance at the Nashville he thought the 101ers were shit! The guy, whose name was Joe, readily admitted to Glen that although he'd been "blown away" by the Sex Pistols' performances he was committed to the 101ers. This compliment had pleased Glen immensely and he reminded Mick and Paul about the forthcoming gig with the 101ers at the 100 Club. Only on this occasion the 101ers would be supporting them.

There was definitely a scene growing around the Sex Pistols, especially at the 100 Club on Oxford Street, which they had almost come to regard as their second home. Each week the group seemed to attract more and more new devotees, who would undergo image makeovers in-between shows. It was Simon, Sue Ballion and the rest of the Bromley Contingent who were clearly setting the trends and defining the "Look". John's friend Sid had proclaimed himself to be the Sex Pistols' biggest fan and was ever present at the 100 Club shows. Sid, ever the fashion victim, was desperate to find his own unique style and arrived one evening wearing a small padlock over his crotch like some half-assed chastity belt. He'd also taken to wearing a ladies' garter over his jeans.

The funniest story involving Sid was how he had inadvertently invented a new dance simply because he had jumped up and down in an attempt to see the group on stage. The people standing around him had joined in and now people were calling the new dance the Pogo. The Sex Pistols had grown accustomed to seeing Simon Barker and his friends in the crowd whenever they played in or around London and would often chat with them before and after they went on stage. Simon had invited them to Berlin's parents' house in Bromley, for his Baby Bondage Party.

The four Sex Pistols, Nils and Glen's girlfriend Celia arrived at the house at number eight, Plaistow Grove in Bromley on the Saturday of the Spring Bank holiday weekend. They were just in time to see some of Berlin's transvestite friends arriving by taxi.

"What the fuck!" gasped Steve, although he couldn't resist sneaking a sly look at their arses as they headed up the garden path.

"So this is where Bowie grew up," said John, standing on the pavement outside Berlin's house. He was wearing his familiar baggy striped trousers and a rubber T-shirt from SEX. "Should have brought Sid. He'd have been turning the fuckin' garden over looking for Ziggy souvenirs."

A very striking girl with piercing eyes and short dyed-black hair answered the door. It was Simon's friend Sue Ballion. She was wearing a cheap plastic novelty apron with a cartoon caricature of a nude woman on the front. It was only when Sue turned around that John and the others realised that it was all she was wearing.

John peered through an open doorway into the living room. He recognised most of the people from their shows at the 100 Club amongst other places but he couldn't remember their names. "Where's the drink?" he asked no one in particular. He saw Glen and Celia heading back towards the front door. "Where are you two goin'? he yelled after them. "You've only just fuckin' got here!" He was distracted from hurling further insults at the retreating couple by the sight of Steve, Nils and Paul emerging from the kitchen each clutching several cans of lager. He forgot all about Glen and his stuck-up girlfriend entirely when Simon appeared carrying a large bag of amphetamine sulphate.

Paul came out of an upstairs bedroom, smiling to himself as he zipped up his flies. He'd no idea how long he'd been in there and he wasn't too sure who he'd been in there with, but he could see that it was dark outside.

"Where's Steve?" he asked a small slim girl with a pretty face who was slumped against the wall, half-naked and very much the worse for wear. He remembered having spoken to the girl earlier when they'd first arrived. Paul soon realised that he wasn't going to get much of a response out of her, so he stepped over her outstretched legs and made his way towards the top of the stairs. He was deciding what to do next when he heard a commotion coming from behind the door in front of him. Suddenly the door burst open and there was Steve stripped down to his undies. He stood swaying in the doorway for several moments; he was holding a can of lager in one hand while cupping the ample breast of a young blonde in the other. It seemed to Paul that his friend was struggling to decide which to put in his mouth first.

"Everyone wants to fuck a Sex Pistol!" Steve bellowed at the top of his lungs before stooping forward to suck on the girl's nipple.

John was totally off his head, having gorged himself on a wild cocktail of sulphate and acid. When Paul stumbled across him in one of the other bedrooms he was sitting cross-legged on the floor in front of a small portable record player, accompanying Marilyn Monroe as she sang "I Wanna Be Loved By You". He was trying to place a line of sulphate onto the revolving disc and failed to notice that his friend had even come into the room. Paul was about to leave John to it when he spotted someone's feet sticking out from beneath a pile of coats and jackets. He recognised the winklepicker shoes that were lying by the side of the bed as those belonging to Nils and gingerly began removing the layers of coats until he found Nils himself. Nils had one eye slightly open and a huge shit-eating grin spread across his face while a naked female gamely tugged away on his knob trying to induce an erection. He tried to lift his arm so that he could acknowledge Paul's presence but the arm, like his penis, remained as limp as Larry Grayson's wrist.

Paul threw the coats back on top of the couple and started to leave when he felt John tugging away on the leg of his jeans.

"Look!" whispered John, pulling Paul down towards him. He was pointing towards a child's teddy bear sitting in the corner. "It's coming to get me." He pulled Paul closer towards him. "Don't let it get me!"

"Why don't we leave?" whispered Paul, humouring John.

"I can't!" replied John, rocking to and fro as he continued to stare wide-eyed at the innocuous looking cuddly toy.

"Why not?"

"I can't swim!" John slumped down to the floor and curled up into a foetal position.

Paul decided it was time to leave John to his drug-induced fantasies and went downstairs in search of any remaining cans of lager. The scene that greeted him as he stepped into the lounge was something straight out of a Roman orgy. There were several couples, all in various stages of undress, each oblivious to the couple shagging next to them. It was difficult for Paul to know where he could put his feet without the risk of doing someone a serious injury. He carefully stepped his way over towards the hi-fi and ejected the cassette that was already in there. He reached into his back pocket for his copy of the demo tape from Majestic Studios; he inserted it into the slot and pressed the play button.

Steve was lying on a bed upstairs observing the naked girl, whose name he still couldn't remember, as she sucked his dick. Fuck me, it don't get any better than this, he thought, as the opening chords of "Problems" filled the house.

"Where the fuck am I?" moaned Steve, as he opened his eyes. He was instantly blinded by the glaring sunlight that was flooding in through the open window. He gently raised himself up on one elbow and glanced down at the inanimate female form lying beside him. He contemplated rolling the girl over for a quickie, but knew that he couldn't ignore the mounting pressure in his bladder for much longer. He threw back the covers, ignoring the incoherent protestations from the girl, and climbed out of bed. Steve made his way along the landing although he wasn't sure if he knew where the bathroom actually was. His head was throbbing and he doubted whether he would be able to remain upright for much longer. The pain in his bladder was becoming unbearable and it was then that he spied the large potted plant at the top of the stairs, and without so much as a second thought, proceeded to piss.

With his bladder assuaged, Steve thought about resuming his interest in the girl lying in his bed and was making his way towards the bedroom when he became aware of the commotion downstairs. He could hear somebody screaming at the top of his voice about the state of the house and was pretty sure it had to be the faggot who lived there. The effects of last night's party were evident all over the house. The beer-soaked carpet was littered with empty beer cans, wine bottles and overturned ashtrays.

Steve pushed open the door, which led into the lounge and if he'd thought the upstairs rooms were a mess then he was totally shocked at the state of the one he'd just entered. There were stains of all description on the carpet and furniture. Some of Berlin's mother's prized porcelain figurines had been smashed beyond repair, but it was the gashes in the polystyrene ceiling tiles that would take the most explaining. Sometime during the evening Sue had produced the leather whip that John had stolen from the strip club on Brewer Street and given her friends a demonstration of how to be a successful dominatrix.

Berlin was almost hysterical. He was stamping his bare feet up and down on the Persian rug as he surveyed the carnage. "What am I going to do?" he wailed, burying his mascara-streaked face in his hands.

"We'll help you sort the place out once everyone's gone, won't we Sue?" said Sharon, nudging the girl sitting beside her on the sofa. Sue lifted her head and nodded briefly without bothering to open her eyes. She'd grown tired of Berlin's histrionics long ago.

"Has, ahh, anyone seen my clothes?" asked Steve, from the doorway. He was clutching a hand towel around his waist. "Fuck me John, your eyes look like pissholes in the snow!" he added, glancing across the room to where John was slumped in an armchair. John lifted his head towards the sound of the familiar voice but he still couldn't focus on people's faces properly so he went back to watching the pattern on the wallpaper as it danced around before his eyes.

Nils and Paul were standing in the kitchen nursing mugs of steaming black coffee and chatting to Billy Broad, another of Simon's friends. Billy was asking them if they'd seen the boxing on TV the previous week. Mohammed Ali, the world heavyweight champion had fought Britain's Richard Dunn. The Bradford-born contender may have been the best that Britain had to offer but he was no match for Ali and had been soundly beaten.

"I don't know much about boxing," said Nils, rubbing his temples with the tips of his fingers.

"Neither does Richard Dunn!" replied Paul, chuckling.

"Cookie, where's my fuckin clothes?" asked Steve, whipping Paul with the towel.

"Fuck knows!" Paul retreated to the opposite end of the kitchen and placed his hand over his groin to defend himself against another possible blow from the towel. "Where did you leave 'em?"

"If I knew that I wouldn't be fuckin' askin', would I?" said Steve, relieving Nils of his mug of coffee.

Paul satisfied that the threat of another towel attack was over, rejoined Nils and Billy. "Oy, that's my shirt!" he gasped, pointing over Steve's shoulder towards the girl standing in the doorway. She was wearing Steve's "You're gonna wake up" T-shirt. The girl giggled and darted back towards the stairs. "Come 'ere, you!" shouted Steve, slamming the coffee mug down on the kitchen table. "I'll be back in five minutes...nah, make it ten!"

CHAPTER TWELVE

"Are we there yet?" asked Glen, from his cramped position in the back of the van. "My fuckin' arse has gone numb!"

"Just like your fuckin' head!" retorted Steve, giving Glen a gentle kick on the shin.

"Yes children, we're almost there," said John, from his relatively comfortable position in the front of the van as Nils turned onto Peter Street in Manchester.

"Right," said Malcolm, as soon as Nils parked up in front of the Lesser Free Trade Hall, "you boys get the van unloaded and I'll go and see if Howard's here."

"It's like a fuckin' oven in there!" said Steve, stepping out onto the pavement. He'd lost the feeling in the lower half of his body somewhere near Watford and was pacing up and down, trying to alleviate the pins and needles sensations that were coursing up and down his legs. To the casual observer, he looked like he'd shit his pants.

"I don't see why John gets to sit up front every time!" moaned Glen, helping Paul to carry his amplifier towards the Hall's front entrance.

"Ah leave it out Glen, we're here now!" replied Paul, grimacing at the weight he was lifting.

Malcolm found Howard and his friend Pete standing with the caretaker just inside the main room at the top of the stairs; he had been forced to book the hall as a last minute replacement. He and Pete had originally wanted to put the Sex Pistols on at their college in Bolton but the Student Union at the Institute of Technology had refused permission for the simple reason that they had never heard of the group. Howard guided Malcolm towards the stairway and explained that there was a slight change of plan for the evening.

On their return to Manchester the pair had wasted little time in forming their own group, with Howard nominating himself as singer while Pete chose the less arduous task of playing the guitar. They even had a name for the group – Buzzcocks. Howard had spotted the word whilst reading a review about the TV programme *Rock Follies*, which was quite apt, seeing as the series starring Judy Covington and Rula Lenska, was about a fictional female rock group. Howard had changed his surname to the more adventurous Devoto while Pete was now calling himself Pete Shelley. This apparently had been the name his mother would have chosen had she given birth to a girl.

But just when everything seemed to be taking shape the other two musicians in the fledgling group announced their impending departure after admitting that they were rather less enthusiastic about the musical direction that Howard and Pete were heading in. Despite the bitter disappointment of not being able to perform that evening, Howard had booked a Salford-based group called Solstice to take their place.

"It's a shame," said Malcolm, when they had finished explaining their predicament to him. "But don't give up!"

"Don't worry, we won't," replied Howard, emphatically. "We've already placed an advert in the *NMR* for another drummer and bassist!"

"The NM what?" asked Malcolm.

"The *New Manchester Review*," said Pete. "We've had a reply from someone this afternoon!"

"The guy said that he might even come down tonight," said Howard, nodding thoughtfully.

"Excellent!" replied Malcolm, beaming. Although whether Malcolm's apparent delight was as a result of the pair having located a possible new band member or the fact that it would mean one more paying customer was hard to tell.

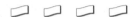

Once the equipment had been set up on the small stage and everyone was reasonably happy with the soundcheck they all set off for a brief tour of the neighbouring pubs. The boys, especially Steve, had almost been reluctant to leave Tommy Ducks, a nearby club, which had scores of ladies' knickers adorning the walls. They arrived back at the Lesser Trade Hall in time to see Pete Shelley install himself in the box office to collect the money. Malcolm, dressed head to foot in black leather, took up position on the street in the hope of enticing the passers-by into the Hall, but without too much success.

"Come on in!" he said, confronting the young couple who were doing their utmost to ignore the strange leather-clad, ginger-haired Londoner. "There's a great group up from London playing tonight." The young guy waved Malcolm away, shaking his head. "They're going to be massive!" he yelled after them before giving up and going back to join Pete inside.

He smiled towards the group of young men that passed him on their way towards the box office. There had been no need for any cajoling as they looked like they were coming in anyway. Malcolm glanced towards the young man standing just inside the doorway. He looked like he was waiting for somebody, as he would occasionally peer inside the entrance. "Are you coming in here tonight, boy?" Malcolm asked, walking over. The guy mumbled something about being there to meet someone. "Are you the new guitarist?" asked Malcolm, eagerly grabbing the lad's arm. "What's your name?" The guy barely had time to reply before Malcolm had herded him inside. "Here's your guitarist, Peter!" he announced triumphantly. "A fellow called Giggle."

"It's Diggle!" said the guy, glaring at Malcolm. "My name is Diggle!"

There were only forty or so people gathered inside the Hall when the Sex Pistols went on stage. Pete and Howard were apologetic for the poor turnout, but Malcolm was far from downhearted. Forty-odd punters are a good turn out for the group's first venture to the city. More importantly, the people who are there are there because they want to see the group.

John stood in front of the microphone, surveying the small crowd before him. He was wearing his favourite baggy stripes, black cap-sleeved T-shirt and a very striking yellow waistcoat from SEX. "Any Southampton fans in here tonight?" he asked, trying to goad the audience into a reaction. The jibe was aimed at any possible "Reds" in the audience and was in reference to the FA Cup Final, which had taken place a few weeks earlier, when Manchester United had been defeated 1-0 by the unfashionable second division team from Hampshire. John received a few jeers but also cheers from the Manchester City supporters amongst the crowd.

The atmosphere within the Hall was very relaxed; it almost seemed as though there was a sense of kindred spirit between group and audience. When some quick-witted individual shouted out for Eddie And The Hot Rods just as the Sex Pistols were about to begin playing the song "New York" everyone laughed – including the group.

"This one's a pop song," announced John, clearly enjoying the banter with the audience.

"Aren't they all?" someone shouted out, to generous applause.

After the performance the members of the Sex Pistols mingled with the audience, chatting with several people who had definite ideas on forming their own groups. When they finally set off home to London in the early hours of the next morning they left, not only with the promise of a return date, but also the possibility of an appearance on the TV programme *So It Goes*. Tony Wilson, the *Granada Reports* presenter, who had been in the audience that night also hosted the late-night half-hour music programme, which was in its first series. The programme was made by Granada TV and went out on air at 10.30 p.m. on Sunday evenings throughout the northwest of England. Granada, however, was closely linked to London Weekend Television, which meant the show was also broadcast in the London area and Malcolm would have been foolish to refuse Wilson's invitation.

On Tuesday 15 June the Sex Pistols were back at the 100 Club with the 101ers acting as support for the evening. This would be the 101ers last performance with singer Joe Strummer. Joe had received the nickname because of his simple approach to playing the guitar, which was hit six strings or none at all. Joe, having seen the writing on the wall, had announced his departure from the 101ers in order to team up with Mick Jones for his, as yet, unnamed group.

Nils had driven the group and their equipment the short journey from

Denmark Street where he was now living, having taken over from Glen as Steve's new roommate. Glen had tired of the hardships of trying to get by on what money he was earning in the group and had moved back to his parents' house in Greenford. They arrived to find Malcolm was already waiting for them inside the club and was engaged in an intense conversation with Ron Watts at the end of the bar. Watts had been more than happy with the Sex Pistols' Tuesday night residency. The traditionally quiet mid-week night was now making the club a tidy amount of money and that was the reason why Malcolm had wanted to speak with him. If Watts wanted the Sex Pistols to continue playing the Tuesday night residency then he would have to increase the group's fee. Although the promoter felt that he'd been slightly manipulated he couldn't deny Malcolm's business logic, but before he even had the chance to argue the point, Malcolm suddenly waved his hand at Bernie Rhodes and wandered off towards his old friend.

"Bernie, what a surprise!" he said, guiding Rhodes away from the bar and out of Watt's earshot. "What brings you down here?"

"I'm here to see the singer for my new group!" replied Bernie, eagerly. He was about to continue when Malcolm interrupted him.

"So this must be young Michael," Malcolm said, turning towards Mick. "I didn't recognise you without all that hair!"

"Got it cut, didn't I?" replied Mick, grinning.

"And this must be Paul, I presume." Malcolm nodded towards Mick's new bass player. "I hear that you boys have shanghaied the singer from the 101ers."

"That's right," replied Mick, grinning.

"I came down tonight to see if you would be interested in putting something together with the Sex Pistols and my new group," said Bernie, lamely. He looked clearly chagrined at having had his thunder stolen.

"Of course, Bernie," replied Malcolm, barely hiding the condescension in his voice. "Your boys can *support* us anytime." He put extra emphasis on the word "support", just to let Bernie know where he stood.

The Sex Pistols were on top form that evening and introduced their latest song "I Wanna Be Me". The song was a vitriolic attack on the music journalists who had been sniping at the group for some time now by hinting that the group couldn't play their instruments. This was despite the fact that a letter had been circulated to all the music papers in which Chris Spedding categorically denied any involvement in playing with them when they recorded their demos at Majestic Studios in May. Spedding was in the audience that night and had brought along Nora, his German girlfriend. Steve had steamed straight in there and arranged a date with Nora while Spedding was busy talking to Malcolm about RAK's reactions to the Sex Pistols' demo tape. Another unexpected bonus from the evening was the invitation to replace the now defunct 101ers at the Mid-Summer Music Festival, which would take place at the Assembly Hall in

Walthamstow.

The Sex Pistols returned to the 100 Club on 29 June. The support group for the evening was Seventh Heaven, and they were subjected to a torrent of abuse from the strongly partisan crowd with John's friend Sid being one of the main culprits. Sid was thoroughly enjoying his newfound celebrity status as the Pistols' number one fan and was constantly surrounded by a small coterie of eager-to-please kids.

Nick Kent, the journalist and one time member of the Sex Pistols – in his eyes at least – was there to review the gig for the *NME*. He was standing at the bar scanning the wonderful array of fans standing around him, hoping for a burst of poetic inspiration for the opening lines of his article, when he spotted Malcolm standing with John a few metres away and was slightly unnerved by the way they seemed to be studying him. A few seconds later he noticed that the pair had been joined by Rotten's rather oddball friend, who everyone was now calling Sid. Sid was glaring in his direction and seemed to be taking some sort of instructions from the other two. Kent acted as if he hadn't noticed the three of them watching him and continued surveying the crowd, but when he glanced in their direction several minutes later to find them still watching him he knew that they were plotting something.

The other three Sex Pistols were already on stage awaiting the arrival of their singer. Kent sensed that John was aware that he was holding up the proceedings but was somehow reluctant to leave his friends until he was sure that Sid understood whatever it was that he and Malcolm were saying to him. John finally took his position in front of the microphone and stood silently watching the young kids, eager with excitement and anticipation, pushing and jostling each other for a better viewpoint. Sid would normally have been in amongst the thick of it, leaping around, showing everyone how to do the Pogo, but tonight he was standing at the back of the room. He was still watching what was happening on stage, but was also keeping a watchful eye on Nick Kent, who was standing less than two metres away.

Kent was aware that he was being observed, but tried to ignore Sid's presence while he concentrated on watching the Sex Pistols performing for their adoring fans. The group, free of all inhibition, seems to be enjoying the performance as much as their audience; they fed on the crowd's energy, which in turn produced an even greater frenzied spectacle on the tiny stage.

"This one's for the journalists that have been saying we can't play!" bellowed John, above Steve's grinding guitar. "It's called 'I Wanna Be Me'!"

This was the signal that Sid had been waiting for and he swaggered towards Kent and purposely caught the journalist on the shin as he passed. Kent grimaced at the sharp burst of pain that exploded up his right leg, but other than purse his lips, he failed to react. This seemed to confuse Sid, who had expected Kent to at least hurl abuse at him which would then have given him the excuse he was looking for. Sid circled around a pillar and kicked Kent again as he passed him before walking away.

Kent looked all around him to see if there was anyone watching who might intervene on his behalf, but all eyes were on the Sex Pistols. He could see Sid coming back towards him and this time he wasn't alone; a very disturbing looking individual with short-cropped bleached-blond hair had joined him. Kent, his eyes glued to the stage, stepped back, giving the pair more than enough room to pass. This time however, Sid didn't walk past. He simply stopped and stood with his back towards Kent, purposely obstructing the journalist's view of the stage.

Kent first tried moving to his left and then to the right, but no matter which way he turned Sid appeared to block his view of the stage. Kent was well aware that those standing around him were happily monitoring the situation and although he was anxious to avoid confrontation, he was equally reluctant to lose face. He cleared his throat before tapping Sid on the shoulder to inform his tormentor that he couldn't see the stage. Sid wheeled around and was about to swing for Kent with a bicycle chain, when his peroxide-haired accomplice suddenly produced a small knife and held it up towards Kent's face.

The journalist was in real danger of losing more than his credibility and automatically raised his hands towards his face in self-defence, which allowed Sid to casually brush his accomplice aside and attack Kent with the chain. Kent collapsed to the floor in a heap as blood poured from the wound in his head. Sid waded into the crumpled figure lying at his feet and struck the journalist twice more with the chain before calmly walking away. The barman rushed from behind the counter and helped Kent back up onto his feet. The severely shaken journalist had no intention of hanging around to see if Sid was going to come back to give him a second helping and fled towards the doorway leading out of the club.

On Sunday 4 July the Sex Pistols, along with Bernie's new group The Clash acting as support, travelled up to Sheffield to play at a pub called The Black Swan, more familiarly known to the locals as The Dirty Duck. The real reason for the outing to South Yorkshire was to get the Sex Pistols out of the capital in an attempt to avoid all the media hype surrounding The Ramones gig at the Roundhouse. Malcolm's plan backfired because the gig was a complete shambles. The Clash's debut performance was ruined as all four members were clearly suffering from a case of first night jitters. Even Joe seemed unable to steer the group through the storm and it didn't help matters that Mick, much to the amusement of the audience, had to tune Paul's bass guitar for him at the end of every song.

The Sex Pistols were also guilty of having an off night and their lacklustre performance failed to ignite the largely apathetic Sheffield audience, although there were a handful of people who seemed to appreciate what the group was trying to achieve. At the end of the show John derided the small crowd by announcing that they should feel humble in the presence of such a great band. The reason that the Sex Pistols were great was because they hailed from

London and any band that operated from within the capital had to be great. The howls of derision that greeted John's outburst left him and the other members of the group with little doubt as to whether they would be offered a second invitation.

Two days later the Sex Pistols were back on familiar ground and playing to familiar faces at the 100 Club. This time they were supported by The Damned who were being managed by Andy Czezowski, yet another one of Malcolm's associates. The Damned had been together for less than two months and before that evening had played just four gigs over consecutive Saturdays at a gay bar in Lisson Grove. The 100 Club on Oxford Street was now the epicentre of a movement that nobody could quite explain. When the Sex Pistols had first played there at the end of March there had been only a mere handful of people there to witness the performance. In less than three months a scene had developed, which had its own culture, language and the self-importance that naturally accompanies any musical rebellion. The Bromley Contingent was at the forefront of the movement but they were in danger of becoming overshadowed by Sid who, thanks to the incident with Nick Kent was now rejoicing in his new moniker of Sid Vicious.

Tensions were running high within the cramped confines of the rehearsal room behind Denmark Street, with Steve in particular coming under attack for his apparent lack of input on the new tunes. Steve, having grown tired of being the scapegoat for the group's lack of inspiration, decided to vent his anger upon Glen for not having any ideas. "You must have somethin', Glen!" he yelled, flicking his cigarette butt towards the bassist.

"Why is it always down to me?" demanded Glen. "You're the one that's fucking living here!"

"What's that supposed to mean, you cunt?" said Steve, edging closer towards Glen.

"Well you've got nothing else to do with your time, have you?" replied Glen, standing his ground.

"Let's knock it on the head for tonight, eh?" offered Paul, hoping to diffuse the situation. "We can come back again tomorrow night."

"You said that last night!" said John, shaking his head.

"And the night before," said Glen, removing his bass guitar. He walked across the room towards Steve holding out his hand for Steve to give him his guitar. "I still can't get used to how small the neck is on one of these things," he said, crouching down and balancing the Gibson across his knee.

Glen slowly began strumming the open strings and altered the tuning until he was satisfied with the sound. He already knew the basics of the guitar, having once owned an acoustic version when he was still at school. John and the others watched in silence as Glen began to play various chord patterns in the hope of picking out a decent tune. He would play one pattern for a few bars while pondering its merits before moving on to another. John was almost at the point of screaming and running for the hills when Glen finally hit upon a rather catchy pattern by strumming the G high up on the twelfth fret before sliding down to strum an F then an Em a D and a C. He then slid his fingers back up the fretboard and strummed the F and Em chords in quick succession to give the tune an easy flowing rhythm.

"That's fuckin' excellent!" said Steve, staring open mouthed at Glen. "Show me what you're playin'."

"Keep playing the pattern while I work something out on this," said Glen, retrieving his own instrument.

John had forgotten all about fleeing and had retreated to his customary position in the corner of the room where he sat scribbling away on his notepad. Paul, relieved that they were finally doing something constructive, pounded out a steady drumbeat for Steve and Glen to follow while they chopped and changed the tune's pattern until it started to sound like a proper arrangement.

John, thanks to the lengthy discussions with Malcolm and Bernie, already had the basic idea for a new song based on the pair's steadfast convictions that Britain was heading for both political and social chaos. Malcolm believed that it was only a matter of time before the have nots, as he liked to call the growing number of unemployed, would one day rise up to overthrow the government as their Russian counterparts had under Lenin in 1917. Malcolm's political beliefs were shared by Jamie Reid, an old friend from his college days. Reid, on Malcolm's invitation, had been drafted in to help with the visual propaganda of the Sex Pistols and was currently designing a series of flyers for the group's forthcoming shows.

John intended to call the new song "Anarchy In The UK", which was not only clear, precise and to the point, but also had a nice tuneful ring to it. All he had to do now was make the necessary alterations until the verses and chorus fitted in with what the other three were doing. The idea had come to him whilst listening to a conversation between Reid and Malcolm when the two men had repeatedly used the phrase whilst describing, what was in their eyes at least, the imminent collapse of social order in Britain.

"Have you got something already?" gasped Glen, as John stood up and approached the microphone.

"Yeah sort of," replied John, holding up the pad in his hand. "Can we run through it a few times though, cos I'm still not sure about some of it."

They were buzzing again, as was usually the case when they had the bit between their teeth. The earlier squabbles quickly forgotten, Glen inadvertently took control as he always did when it came to arranging an idea into a structured song; he seemed to have a natural talent for it, although the others would have rather died than actually admit this to him. Paul and Steve stood watching and waiting, somewhat impatiently, while Glen worked out a pattern for the middle-eight and added a bridge. John had once again retreated to the corner to make further adjustments to the lyrics. He had studied English Literature at school and was therefore a firm believer in the maxim: "why use two words to convey your message when one will suffice?" It was especially relevant in lyric writing.

When Glen was satisfied that Steve was familiar with the alterations to the chord structure for the tune, they played the opening intro together with a verse and chorus before ending after the improvised middle eight.

"What's that bit at the beginning?" Glen asked, pointing towards the two lines that John had hastily scribbled at the top of the page.

"I am an antichrist," said John, eyeing Glen.

"We know that!" said Steve, pausing to light his cigarette, "but tell us what you're singin'!"

"Oh what wonderful repartee," said John, derisively.

"Is that really what you're singing?" asked Glen, getting back to his earlier question.

"Yes," replied John, flatly. "I am an antichrist; I am an anarchist!"

"It's a bit cheesy, ain't it?"

"You got anything else that rhymes with antichrist?" asked John, scowling at Glen.

Glen shrugged his shoulders and returned to his amplifier. He could see that Steve and Paul didn't have a problem with the lyric so he wouldn't gather any support there. "I like the rest of it," he said, cautiously. "I just don't like that first bit."

"Well I don't like you!" snapped John, dismissing Glen by turning his back to him.

"So I don't get any say in what we do?" shouted Glen, beginning to lose his temper.

"Drop dead!" said John, glaring at Glen. "You stick to writing the tunes!"

"Oh is that what I do?"

"Yes!" snapped John. "I can't think of any other reason why you're here, can you?" Glen gritted his teeth and slowly counted to ten. He thought about taking the matter further but quickly decided against it. He'd learned that there wasn't much point trying to reason with John when he was in one of his moods.

"Fuck it!" he said to himself, running his fingers through an E scale to drown out any further discussion. "If he wants to make a prick of himself, then let him."

Malcolm was standing in the middle of Steve's room, which also served as the group's official headquarters, shielding his eyes against the sun's glare on yet another scorching Sunday afternoon. The boys down at the Met office were predicting that this summer would be the hottest on record, which was all well and good for "Johnny ice-cream van", but had left Malcolm with a shop full of unsold rubberwear. "Well, what do you think?" he asked, returning his gaze towards John and the others. He had come up with the idea of the group recording a new series of demos and wanted Dave Goodman, who was standing nervously beside him, to serve as both producer and engineer for the proposed sessions. If Steve and the others seemed less than enthusiastic about their manager's suggestion then it was more to do with the hectic weekend they'd just endured, rather than any opposition to the idea of recording another set of demos.

On the Friday they had played at an all-nighter at the Lyceum Ballroom. They hadn't gone on stage until the early hours of Saturday morning so they had procured a large supply of amphetamine sulphate to help keep them awake. During the performance John had stunned the Afghan clad crowd, and his fellow Sex Pistols alike, by stubbing out cigarettes on his forearms. After the show he had offered no explanation for the masochistic display and nobody had dared to ask.

On the Saturday night they had played at a pub on Charing Cross Road called The Sundown and were contracted to play two sets. The first set didn't begin until ten o'clock, so they were forced to take even more speed and were totally wired by the time they took to the stage. As a result the group's erratic performance was too much for the pub's clientele and they were politely informed that a second set wouldn't be required.

Now they had been awake for over forty-eight hours and the effects of the sulphate had begun to wear off. They were all too fucked to even care what day it was and yet here was their manager – the guy who had booked them to play the Lyceum in the first place – trying to spur them into making arrangements to record more demos.

John seemed to be suffering more than the others, but then again he and Sid had been permanent fixtures in the ballroom's toilets, snorting the speed through a tightly rolled five pound note like it was going out of fashion. He was curled up on the floor with his head resting on one of the pillows from Nils' bed and gazing at the ceiling. Glen was sitting in the chair opposite, while Steve and Paul were both sprawled across Steve's bed with their hands resting over their eyes. Malcolm was oblivious to their suffering and continued unabated.

"If I'm going to go out there," he said, jabbing a finger towards the window, "then I think I should be able to offer these record companies something that's worth listening to!"

"All right, whatever!" groaned Steve, covering his face with a pillow. "Just shut the fuck up!"

Goodman had told Malcolm that he wanted to capture the energy the Sex Pistols created when they were on stage, but also wanted the boys to feel relaxed while recording the new demos. Steve, in the hope of avoiding any unnecessary travel, had jokingly suggested using the rehearsal room downstairs and was totally surprised when everyone else agreed. Malcolm, who would be spared the expenses of hiring a recording studio, had happily seconded the motion. The timing of the proposed recordings couldn't have been better as far as Paul was concerned because he was on his two-week summer holidays away from the brewery, which at least saved him from taking more time off at a later date. John also seemed content that the group would be recording the demos on their own turf, but Glen was slightly less receptive to the proposed demo sessions.

He was dubious of Goodman's boast that he could get better results on his portable 4-Track mixer than Chris Spedding, who'd had a fully equipped professional studio at his disposal. Malcolm had been hoping to get things up and running that very afternoon, but on further inspection of his charges he arranged for Goodman to bring his equipment down on the Tuesday, which would hopefully give the boys time to recover.

Goodman and his partner Kim arrived shortly before lunchtime on the following Tuesday morning and once the group had helped with the unloading of the equipment, they set about rearranging their own equipment in order to suit the engineer's wishes. Glen's doubts were growing by the minute, especially when Goodman informed them that he was hoping to recreate a "live on stage" situation, which to Glen's mind defeated the whole purpose, but he kept his views to himself.

While the boys moved the amplifiers around Goodman gave them a brief run-down on what he proposed to do during the time available. It had already been decided that the group would record seven songs, two of which – "Pretty Vacant" and "No Feelings" – had been previously recorded at Majestic Studios with Spedding. The other five songs were "Seventeen", "Submission", "Satellite" and the group's two latest offerings "Anarchy In The UK" and "I Wanna Be Me". Goodman intended to record the songs on his 4-Track in Denmark Street before transferring them onto 8-Track at Riverside Studios in Chiswick, where they would also record John's vocals and some guitar overdubs. The completed songs would then be taken over to Decibel Studios in North London for the final mixing.

Glen couldn't believe that Goodman was intending to use a portable 4-Track mixing desk, which had been set up on Steve's bed upstairs, to record the sessions. He knew that two of the four tracks would have to be held in reserve for John's vocals and Steve's guitar overdubs, which left just two remaining tracks to record the group as a whole. This would mean the group would not only have to play the songs as they would in a live situation, but would also mean having to complete each song in just one take. They wouldn't have the luxury of a proper studio where different recordings could be spliced to get the best results. There were, Glen begrudgingly admitted, several pluses to them using their own rehearsal room. There was no cash layout, except for the reels of tape, and as there were no deadlines to meet they could take as many breaks as they liked.

As a result of the group recording in such familiar surroundings the atmosphere was far more relaxed and they managed to record the songs without too much effort. They were also open to new ideas and willing to experiment with their material. At Riverside Studios they recorded John's vocals using a Neumann microphone through a compressor, while at Decibel Studios they added the overdubs, which included Steve doing his Roy Castle impersonation by blowing through the spout of a kettle for the song "Submission".

On Tuesday 20 July the Sex Pistols took a welcome break from the recording and mixing of the new demos. They returned to the Lesser Free Trade Hall in Manchester to play with The Buzzcocks – Howard and Pete finally having found suitable replacements for the group. Paul wasn't too impressed at having to spend his twentieth birthday wedged inbetween two amplifiers in the back of a transit van, but he planned to make up for it later.

Howard and Pete had certainly done their best to promote the gig and there were far more people inside the Hall than on the group's previous visit, although the majority of the audience were denim or leather clad with hair half-way down their arses. They had even enlisted the services of another local group that was operating under the marvellous name of Slaughter & The Dogs. The Wythenshawe-based group were far from overawed at the prospect of playing on the same bill as the Sex Pistols and had accordingly designed a poster for the gig, which placed themselves as top billing.

The Buzzcocks, aware of their obvious shortcomings, were first on stage and gave a spirited if somewhat nervous performance. Howard and Pete seemed far more concerned that they had the right image on stage rather than how they sounded. Howard was wearing straight-leg Levis while Pete was far more adventurous with his skin-tight salmon pink trousers that had been altered on a friend's sewing machine. The Sex Pistols were very impressed by the Buzzcocks' style and attitude and offered words of encouragement as the group left the stage to generous applause. Malcolm was also suitably impressed and promised to return the favour by inviting The Buzzcocks to play a gig with the Sex Pistols in London in the very near future.

Next on stage were Slaughter & The Dogs. The group was made up of sixteen and seventeen-year-old scallys who seemed totally unfazed at playing to an older audience. They had built up a steady following of young kids from their run-down neighbourhood and these kids were in the audience wearing homemade badges with the group's logo on them. Their thirty-odd minute set comprised songs which sounded more as if they belonged on the terraces of the local football grounds than at such a prestigious venue as the Lesser Free Trade Hall.

The Sex Pistols took to the stage to wild applause from the people gathered at the front of the hall. John stood motionless, surveying the crowd, as if searching for a familiar face. He casually ran his fingers through his ginger spiked hair as Paul counted the group in to their opening number. Steve powered into the opening chords of "I Wanna Be Me", which acted as a catalyst to spur the audience into a unified frenzied mass. Unfortunately the set was marred by problems with the sound because Goodman had inadvertently used faulty amplifiers when rigging up the PA system, but neither the group on stage nor the excited audience seem to care. This was the first opportunity the Sex Pistols had to play "Anarchy In The UK" in front of a live audience and the anthemic chorus produced an enthusiastic response from those leaping around at the front. There were occasional flare-ups between the local youths and the fans who had travelled down from London to watch the group, but nothing too serious.

Once again the Sex Pistols mingled with the kids who stayed behind. John was the centre of attention yet again, especially with the girls, but he acted naturally and seemed to have grown accustomed to his newfound fame. A group of local lads excitedly said that they had formed their own group after witnessing the Sex Pistols' performance several weeks earlier. John laughed at their black humour when they told him that the name for their group was the Stiff Kittens.

Tony Wilson was also there again, apologising to Malcolm; it seemed that the TV show *So It Goes* was currently off the air, although a second series was due to start in the near future. Malcolm, although disheartened at the news, was astute enough to realise the importance of getting the group some television exposure and agreed to return to Manchester in a couple of week's time.

Malcolm was spending an afternoon with Ben and Joe at the flat on Nightingale Lane; it had been several months since his break-up with their mother yet neither boy seemed to have been unduly traumatised by recent events. He still had most of his clothes stored at the flat and was taking the opportunity to sort through an assortment of clothes lying in a dishevelled heap at the bottom of a wardrobe. He was about to turn his attention to the shirts hanging from the rail when he came across a crumpled garment, which he had at first mistaken for scrap material. Upon closer inspection he realised that it was a striped shirt, which someone had firstly dyed a dirty grey colour before adding crude vertical stripes of crimson and black paint.

Malcolm disentangled the shirt from the pile and spread the garment out on the floor in front of him. Whoever had been responsible for the creation had also added several rectangular patches of dyed cloth to the shirt, each with a hand painted slogan scrawled upon them. He lifted the shirt from off the floor. "Prenez Vos Desirs Por La Realite," he read aloud, pausing briefly to translate the message. Another slogan read, "A Bas Le Coca Cola".

"What's this?" he asked, stepping into the tiny kitchen where Vivienne was preparing the children's lunch.

"Oh that," replied Vivienne, laughing nervously as she wiped her hands on a towel. "It was just an idea that I started working on." She shrugged her shoulders as if to dismiss the unfinished garment.

"I like it!" said Malcolm, spreading the shirt out on the kitchen table, moving the plates and cutlery out of his way. "It reminds me of the uniforms the Jews were forced to wear in the death camps during the war. It still needs a lot of work though."

Together they spent the next couple of hours tossing ideas into the air, finally deciding upon a series of features that would give the person wearing the shirt a sense of non-political awareness. By the time the shirt went on sale at SEX, Vivienne had added a small linen patch depicting Karl Marx, the man credited with being the father of communism, which would give the appearance that the person wearing the garment held left-wing political views. She had then customised the shirt by adding SS badges and other Nazi regalia such as a swastika armband, which would appear to support right-wing fascism. Malcolm had provided the finishing touches by stencilling the slogan "Only Anarchists Are Pretty" down the front of the shirt.

The heat wave was now well into its third month and the government had been forced to take the unprecedented steps of asking the British public to save their bath water for use in the garden or to clean the car. The relentless heat certainly gave vent to a more relaxed atmosphere in the capital. It was fun to go down to Hyde Park and sunbathe, watch the girls in their skimpy bikinis, eat ice cream or perhaps drag the television out into the garden and watch the latest events at the Olympic games taking place in Montreal. It certainly wasn't fun, however, to be baking in the back of a transit van that was travelling up the M1 to Manchester.

Tony Wilson had kept the promise made to Malcolm and booked the Sex Pistols to appear on *So It Goes*, but not even the prospect of being on the telly was easing Glen's awful feelings of claustrophobia. Steve and Paul were also huddled together in the back of the dilapidated van, but they seemed oblivious to the stifling heat and they amused themselves with bouts of play fighting and telling each other stupid jokes.

"Here, I've got one for you," said Paul, tugging hold of Steve's shirt. "What's small, pink and highly inflammable?"

"Dunno."

"Nikki Lauder's ear!" said Paul, giggling at his own joke. This was a sick reference to the horrific accident at the German Grand Prix, where the Austrian racing driver had been badly burned and was fortunate to escape with his life.

Once the laughter had died down, John called everyone's attention to an article in the newspaper that he was reading. "Listen to this!" he said, before reading out the account of John Stonehouse, the disgraced Labour MP who had been regarded by many politicians from both sides of the House of Commons as a future prime minister. Stonehouse had been sentenced to seven years' imprisonment after being found guilty on nineteen counts including forgery and theft. He had even faked his own death by leaving his clothes on a Miami beach, before resurfacing in Australia under an assumed name and carrying a false passport in his attempt to avoid capture.

"I went to a party at Linda's once," said John, pausing to accept a cigarette from Nils, "and this guy was there!" He stabbed a finger at the photo of Stonehouse which accompanied the front-page story. "The cunt was standing in the corner of the room with one arm around some tart, a joint in the other and asking where the coke was!" John turned around to accept a light from Nils as he slowed down in the traffic. "And he didn't even share the fuckin' spliff!"

Since John's conversation with Don Letts at the Nashville in April both he and Nils had accompanied the Rasta to several reggae clubs in and around London. As Letts would always prepare a "Jamaican cone" for the car journey to the clubs, the pair now considered themselves to be experts on the smoking of cannabis. The girl, Linda, whose party John was referring to, was called Linda Ashby. She was a dominatrix who worked out of a flat in St. James' Hotel, which faced the Houses of Parliament.

Linda bought all her fetish clothing from SEX and had since become friendly with Malcolm, Vivienne, the group and most of the Bromley Contingent, who she had met at Louise's, a reclusive club on Poland Street in Soho. The private club was owned by an aging Polish lesbian and was the secluded haunt of Soho's prostitutes, who would spend the early hours relaxing after a night on their backs. Simon Barker and his friends were frequent visitors to the club. Their bizarre dress sense often left them open to ridicule or confrontation in most pubs and clubs but Louise's was somewhere they could relax and be themselves. It had been through Simon, Sue Ballion and the other members of the so-called Bromley Contingent that the Sex Pistols began frequenting the club, which had come about after John had learned that this was the place where they always headed after attending one of their gigs.

As soon as the Sex Pistols had arrived at Granada TV Studios and unloaded their gear, they were taken on a tour of the building. Steve and Glen had changed clothes in the back of the van and were now wearing the new Anarchy shirt, as Malcolm and Vivienne were calling their latest creation, but both had removed the swastika armband. Jordon, who had travelled up to Manchester by train with Malcolm, was also wearing one of the new shirts – including the offending swastika armband – and this was causing some consternation amongst the production crew.

Tony Wilson, who was also accompanying the visitors on the tour of the studio, was providing Malcolm with a brief outline on the proposed format for that evening's show which would be broadcast live. Wilson had somehow cajoled his superiors at Granada into allowing him to invite the Sex Pistols onto the show, which would be dedicated to giving unsigned groups their first television exposure. The other groups scheduled to appear on the show were The Bowles Brothers and Gentlemen. The latter were standing on the studio stage dressed in suits made from blue satin and were regarding the members of the Sex Pistols with obvious distaste. Jordon had been making her way back from the ladies' toilets when she'd overheard them slagging off the Sex Pistols and had clambered up onto the stage in order to defend her friends.

Wilson was rushing around the studio making sure that everyone was aware of the importance of adhering to the strict timetable. He'd already given each group their allotted time slot of three to three and a half minutes and it was vital for the show's schedule that the groups limited their song to within that timeframe. As the show was broadcast in front of a small studio audience, which mostly consisted of students from the university, the show's producers had employed a relatively unknown Australian comedian called Clive James to act as a warm-up. James was there simply to provide entertainment for the audience before the show went on air and during the commercial break. The Australian had tried to raise a laugh from the studio crew by commenting on the clothes worn by the Sex Pistols and their entourage, but soon clamped up when Jordon called him a "Baldy Old Sheila".

The Sex Pistols had decided to perform "Anarchy In The UK" for the show. To Malcolm it was the obvious choice. What better way to introduce the group's manifesto into the minds of Britain's disenchanted youth than with John's opening battle cry of: "I am an antichrist, I am an anarchist". This was the reason Malcolm had wanted Steve and Glen to wear the Anarchy shirts so that the connection would be instantly recognisable.

John looked magnificent in his customised pink blazer, striped baggy trousers and torn white shirt. His hair was a tangled mass of ginger spikes that framed his pale angular face and a safety pin dangled from his right earlobe. Each group had been given the opportunity to perform one of their songs as a way of warming up before the show went on air. Glen had suggested "Problems", which they all enjoyed playing, but they were only halfway into the song when he snapped one of his guitar strings. Wilson made full use of the enforced break by joining the group on set while Nils rushed off to fetch the replacement strings that he had inadvertently left in the van.

"So, John," he said, clutching his script board to his chest. "You didn't want to come on your own?" He had originally wanted to interview John on the show but when Malcolm refused, he relented and agreed to allow the group to perform live. "What is this, safety in numbers?"

"Nah!" said Glen, accepting the pack of replacement strings of Nils, "it's cos you're a cunt, Tony!" Wilson stood transfixed, a fixed grin on his face. He looked away from the group who were all grinning at Glen's comment. Once the broken string had been replaced and tuned, the group resumed playing the song before returning to the hospitality room for more liquid refreshments.

The comedian Peter Cook, who was also appearing on the show, was sitting in the hospitality room helping himself to the free booze. It was obvious that Cook had perhaps already had more than his fair share, but none of the studio crew seemed willing to risk becoming the target for the comedian's legendary rapier wit. Cook had accepted Wilson's invitation to come on the show and give an interview so that he could promote his new Derek and Clive album, which he'd recorded with long-time comedy partner Dudley Moore.

John and the others returned to the hospitality room just in time to witness a very uncomfortable looking Clive James trying to match Cook in a bout of verbal jousting. The Australian was boxing well above his weight and in need of a mercy killing. John grabbed a can of lager from the refrigerator before heading over to talk to Cook. James was clearly relieved by the distraction and saw it as his opportunity to steer the drunken comedian away from abusing him and the entire population of Australia by commenting on John's appearance.

"It would appear," said Cook, in between mouthfuls of vodka and orange, "that I'm surrounded by the Antichrist and the Antipode." He turned towards John and saluted him with his glass before downing the contents. "And I know who I'd rather have a drink with!"

"I ahh...I only...," stammered James, growing red in the face.

"I'm sorry," said Cook, looking the Australian up and down. "I thought you just farted!"

"Bye bye Bruce," said John, waving at James as he scurried out of the room.

Once everyone was in their allotted place the studio director gave Wilson his cue to introduce the Sex Pistols, but before he had a chance to speak Steve and Glen, accompanied by Paul's crashing cymbals, produced a wailing feedback from the stage which drowned him out.

"You can probably hear them warming up right now!" yelled Wilson, grimacing at the cacophony of noise. "Take it away fellas!"

John's face appeared on the studio monitors as he grabbed the microphone stand. "Bay...beee!" he wailed, leaning towards the nearest camera. "Woodstock come in for me." He paused long enough for Steve, Glen and Paul to come crashing in with the intro to the song before completing his impromptu adlib. "Get off your arse!"

The cameramen, who were under the assumption that they would be working to the prearranged script, soon found themselves struggling to keep any of the three mobile Sex Pistols in shot. John would look into the camera for a few seconds then suddenly duck out of sight leaving the viewers at home with nothing but the studio walls to look at. Steve and Glen were bouncing around the stage in an attempt to create as much confusion as possible. Then Steve realised that his monitor wasn't working and kicked the microphone stand away in disgust, which triggered Malcolm into ordering Nils to throw a plastic chair onto the stage.

One of the cameramen zoomed in towards John, who at last seems to be co-operating by staying in shot. His maniacal stare was beamed directly into thousands of living rooms across the northwest and John, unable to resist his chance to ingratiate himself upon the viewing public, raised his arm and gave them the finger.

The cameraman turned sharply towards Jordon who had joined the group on stage. She was still wearing the swastika armband, but the studio bosses had forced her to cover up the offending insignia with sticky tape. Steve decided that he wasn't sharing the stage with anybody other than the band and sent the poor girl, who had only been following Malcolm's instructions, sprawling with the sole of his boot.

Wilson swivelled around in his chair and watched the show's producer storming across the studio towards him. It was obvious from the pained expression that his patience with the group's antics was growing thinner with each passing second. The scheduled three and a half minutes had long since passed, but John and the boys were thoroughly enjoying themselves and were not willing to relinquish the stage. They eventually ended the tune in a frenzied burst of feedback after clocking up over seven minutes of the thirty-minute show, leaving studio bosses and studio audience alike sitting in stunned silence, unable to quite comprehend what they'd just witnessed.

John, Steve and Paul fled the stage and followed Malcolm, Nils and Jordon back towards the hospitality room while Glen remained behind to pack his gear away. The production crew had also abandoned their posts and he could see the shell-shocked students gradually making their way towards the exits. He wheeled around at the sound of a door opening behind him and saw an old guy standing in the doorway clutching a broom.

"Are you with the group?" he asked, pointing the broom towards Glen.

"Yeah," replied Glen, expecting a lecture about how the music was too loud and how he'd fought in the war for the likes of him. "What of it?"

"I thought you were bloody marvellous!" said the old guy, sniggering into his hand. "It's about time someone showed these cunts!" And with that he turned away and started to sweep the floor, leaving Glen utterly bewildered on the empty stage.

CHAPTER THIRTEEN

Saturday 21 August was the day that the Sex Pistols were scheduled to perform at the first European Punk Rock Festival. This was the name that had been given to the growing movement by journalist Caroline Coon. The term "punk" was the derogatory name given to the male inmates, who were used for sexual favours in America's penitentiaries and had later become a byword to describe the low life and criminal elements on the streets of America. The term "punk" had since been used to describe the style of music being performed by the groups playing in New York's CBGB's and Max's Kansas City. Yet again, the Sex Pistols' reputation as troublemakers served to work against them when the members of Eddie & The Hot Rods, who were also booked to perform at the festival, protested about being on the same bill as the Sex Pistols. They still hadn't forgiven the Sex Pistols for their antics when the two groups played together at the Marquee Club in February. This together with the group's ban from playing at the Nashville worried some of the French promoters and they were thrown off the bill.

The Clash, in a show of solidarity, announced that they would not perform at the festival unless the Sex Pistols were reinstated, but the other major London group The Damned felt no such compulsion and happily travelled to France in order to play at Mont De Marsan. The Sex Pistols had to content themselves with an appearance at The Boat Club in Nottingham.

Malcolm, knowing how disappointed John and the others had been at being denied the opportunity to play abroad, organised a trip to Paris where the Sex Pistols would perform on the opening night of a new nightclub in September. He had also renewed contacts with Roger Austin, the manager of a cinema in Islington called the Screen On The Green. He planned to hold an all-nighter, which would begin at midnight once the cinema had closed.

Malcolm instructed Jamie Reid to design the posters and handbills for the event, which would take place on Sunday 29 August. For the handbills Reid used a silhouette image of John and Steve's faces taken from an earlier gig framed together with contact sheets from their shows at the 100 Club under the title "Midnight Special". He also invited the members of each group appearing at the show to add their own designs to the promotional posters, which Austin had agreed to display inside the cinema.

There would be three groups performing on the night. The Buzzcocks had readily accepted Malcolm's invitation and travelled down from Manchester. The

Clash, as a thank you gesture for their refusal to perform at Mont De Marsan, had also accepted the invitation while the Sex Pistols would naturally be headlining the event. In between groups, the cinema would screen two Kenneth Anger movies: *Kustom Kar Kommandos* and Malcolm's favourite film *Scorpio Rising*, and John Gray had agreed to act as resident DJ for the evening.

It seemed that Malcolm was still holding some sort of personal grudge against his old friend Bernie and stunned everybody by announcing that he would only allow The Clash to perform on the proviso that they not only provided a stage, but that they would have to build it as well. To add insult to injury he also insisted that the members of The Clash would also have to go out onto the London streets and fly-post Reid's handbills.

Malcolm was hoping that the event would attract the attentions of the major record companies. He'd already sent out dozens of tapes of the Denmark Street recordings produced by Dave Goodman along with press packs put together by Reid and Helen. So far, the reactions from the record companies to the Sex Pistols had been negative for various reasons. There was the unprovoked attack on Nick Kent, for although Sid wasn't actually a member of the group, he was considered close enough to the Sex Pistols' camp for the group to be guilty by association. Howard Thompson who was an A&R representative for Island Records had also witnessed Sid's attack on Kent.

There were also the accusations from the Doctors of Madness, the group which the Sex Pistols had supported at the Crypt in Middlesbrough earlier in the year. The group claimed that Steve had sneaked into the dressing room while they were out on stage in order to relieve them of their valuables. Simon Draper at Virgin Records and Dave Dee at Warner Brothers had also declined Malcolm's overtures, while Mickie Most, head of RAK Records and the man responsible for funding the Sex Pistols' recording session at Majestic Studios had made it plain that he wanted nothing more to do with the group.

The Midnight Special at the Screen On The Green was being viewed as a special event both by the groups performing and fans alike. The members of the Bromley Contingent were all there dressed to impress. Sue Ballion or Candy Sue as she was now calling herself looked especially striking in her SEX fetish clothing. She was wearing fishnet stockings with little gold tassels attached, black imitation leather knickers and matching suspender belt. A pair of imitation leather boots, one of which was of normal size while the other was laced up to her thigh and a matching imitation leather glove that stretched all the way to her shoulder. Sue completed her ensemble by wearing a peep-hole bra, which exposed her pert breasts. Another girl, also called Sue, had spent hours patiently applying her make-up and styling her hair in order to give herself a feline appearance and was known to her friends as Sue Catwoman.

By the time The Buzzcocks took to the stage the cinema was filled with a colourful array of fans, journalists, photographers and the A&R representatives from record companies that the Sex Pistols had managed not to offend. The Buzzcocks performed badly, which could have been due to nervousness at playing their first gig in the capital, although the poor sound coming from Goodman's PA didn't do them any favours. The Clash didn't fair much better. They failed to ignite the crowd with their two to three minute blasts of guitar-fuelled frenzy, and they too experienced problems with the PA system. There was however no sign of any such problems when the Sex Pistols took to the stage, which promptly caused Bernie to accuse Malcolm of purposely sabotaging his own group's chances of stealing the Pistols' thunder.

Steve's guitar was a chugging powerhouse of chords and wailing feedback, while Glen's bass sounded like a runaway express train as it thundered along in perfect conjunction with Paul's drums. Whether they were trying to impress the journalists and the A&R men gathered at the bar or just simply enjoying the occasion was hard to tell, but either way they performed brilliantly. John was simply unbelievable that evening, screeching out the lyrics like some demented beast from the bowels of hell. What was unknown to the others until after the show was the fact that John had accidentally rammed the head of the microphone into his mouth during "Pretty Vacant". The microphone had knocked out a capped tooth and was causing him excruciating agony every time he drew an intake of breath.

After the show everyone commented on John's electrifying performance without realising just how much pain he'd been forced to endure in the name of entertainment. John was also forced to suffer the anguish of having to watch Steve leaving the cinema with Spedding's ex-girlfriend Nora. John had worked up the courage to approach Nora before going on stage and had thoroughly enjoyed their conversation. He'd been intrigued by her intellect and knowledge on current affairs and her guttural German accent had only served to increase his attraction to her.

Two days later on Tuesday 31 August a riot broke out at the Notting Hill Carnival. This was the third and final day of the annual event, which celebrated the Afro-Caribbean culture in London and indeed the rest of Britain. During the riot, shops were looted, cars were overturned and set on fire – thirty-five of which belonged to the police. Over one hundred and fifty people were injured and another sixty were arrested. Around three hundred and fifty police officers were injured, some of whom received stab wounds.

The fighting had erupted when a police officer tried to arrest a black youth suspected of being a pickpocket. The young officer had been pelted with bricks and when colleagues went to help, the scuffle quickly developed into running skirmishes up and down Portobello Road. The angry mob then marched on the Notting Hill police station where they were driven back by officers armed with dustbin lids for protection.

That same evening the Sex Pistols were in action once again at the 100 Club with The Clash acting as support. Mick Jones together with Joe and Paul had attended the carnival and happily regaled everyone with their accounts of the riots, which became increasingly exaggerated with each pint of lager. Singer Joe and bass player Paul claimed to have been present when the first bricks had been thrown and had been very fortunate to escape being caught up in the carnage.

The Clash performance was a lot better that evening, maybe as a result of their experiences earlier in the day. The songs were still rough around the edges and in need of a little fine-tuning but the group was willing to learn from its mistakes and everyone admitted that Mick, Joe and Paul were exhilarating to watch on stage. The Sex Pistols also put in yet another good solid display. They performed another new song entitled "Liar", which John had written as a scathing attack on the apparent double standards of MPs and other prominent figures in British society. He was incensed by the hypocrisy of those entrusted to serve in high office who claimed to be upstanding pillars of the community, yet regularly attended sex and drug orgies held at Linda Ashby's flat in the St. James' Hotel.

On the morning of Friday 3 September the Sex Pistols and their small entourage gathered in Steve's room on Denmark Street in readiness for the trip to Paris. The previous night the group had played at the Nag's Head in High Wycombe with the Suburban Studs from Birmingham acting as support for the evening. They had witnessed the Sex Pistols' performance at Barbarella's the month before. The High Wycombe gig had been hastily arranged by Malcolm as a warm-up for the Paris shows where the Sex Pistols were due to perform at the opening night of a new nightclub called the Club De Chalet Du Lac.

Everyone sat waiting for Malcolm who was making last minute phone calls from the telephone box around the corner. Vivienne arrived with Jordon shortly after Malcolm had returned and immediately began chastising him for not helping make the necessary arrangements for the care of the children whilst they were away. Dave Goodman and his partner Kim Thraves would also be travelling to Paris with the party and were both downstairs in the group's rehearsal room making last-minute checks on the equipment to make sure nothing would be left behind.

The travelling party arrived at Heathrow Airport with plenty of time to spare only to find that Malcolm had forgotten to bring his passport with him. To make matters worse, he seemed to have overlooked the small matter of obtaining a carnet, the invaluable document which waived the excise duty on any exported goods that the traveller planned to bring back into their native country. After several frantic phone calls and a fair amount of grovelling the carnet problem was resolved. The missing passport, however, was not so easy to sort out and as a result the party missed their 10 a.m. flight to Paris.

The airport authorities finally relented and allowed Malcolm to travel without his passport, but the unforeseen error meant having to travel on a later flight and all his careful planning had been for nothing. John and the others took great delight in teasing him while they waited in the departure lounge but Malcolm did have his revenge by tricking the boys into searching under their seats for the emergency parachutes.

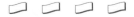

"Excuse me!" said Glen, waving his hand to catch the attention of the pretty blonde stewardess making her way down the central aisle. "It's my mate's birthday," he jerked his thumb towards Steve sitting next to him, "and we were wondering if you could explain the Mile-High Club to us."

"Certainly sir," replied the girl, returning Glen's smile. "This is a term given to when the aircraft reaches a certain altitude, resulting in a subtle change in cabin pressure which sometimes causes certain people to talk and behave like small children."

"That's funny," said Steve, who'd spent the last minute peeking through the gap between the buttons on the stewardess's blouse. "I always thought it was about shaggin'!" The stewardess walked off laughing in spite of herself and returned several minutes later with a glass of champagne for Steve.

Ray Stevenson was sitting next to Malcolm; they were discussing the reactions of their fellow passengers to the bondage shirt that John was wearing. He had literally brought Heathrow's departure lounge to a standstill because his fellow travellers had no reference point for the strange looking garment, except maybe for the straight jackets worn by the patients of mental institutions. The garment featured straps, which ran across the front of the shirt and up through the arms to restrict the wearer's movements. The shirt also featured several straps, which could be fastened onto buckles sewn into the trousers. There was also a strap connecting the trousers at the knees. The whole ensemble was finished off with the addition of a "bumflap" made from a towelling material.

The bondage suit, as the whole outfit was named, had all the usual fetish trappings associated with clothing from SEX. When Malcolm had asked John why he wasn't wearing the trousers, John had told him that this was his first experience of flying and couldn't be sure of how many times he might need to use the toilet.

Once the party had cleared French Customs the others stood back while Malcolm, using his limited knowledge of the language did his best to order two taxis. When the party arrived at the Hotel Parc Royal he ordered Nils to remain in one of the cars and head over to the nightclub while he organised everything at the hotel. The nightclub, which was situated on the Bois De Boulogne, was behind schedule and when the Sex Pistols entered the club they found workmen were still busy laying the stage flooring and painting the tables and chairs.

By the time Goodman and Kim arrived with the group's equipment and the PA system, the stage had been finished although Glen and Steve were dubious about the actual strength of the structure, which resembled a zebra crossing. Thick black strips ran across the glass floor, which would hopefully be illuminated from underneath when in use. The group set their equipment up on the brand-new stage and ran through a couple of songs while Goodman and Kim worked the controls of the sound system. The workmen remaining inside the club stood watching the bizarrely dressed Englishman, not really sure what they were witnessing. When the group were satisfied with the arrangements they headed back to their hotel for a chance to relax. Steve, however, had no intention of relaxing; he had far more pressing matters on his agenda.

"I'll see you later," he said, smirking at Paul.

"Where are those two going?" asked Glen, watching Steve and Malcolm walking out of the door.

"Malcolm's gettin' Steve his birthday present," replied Paul, grinning.

It had been three years since Malcolm's last visit to the French capital. This was during his time managing the New York Dolls so he was all too familiar with the city's red light district.

"What about down here?" asked Steve, pointing towards the secluded entrance of an alleyway just off the main thoroughfare.

"Yes, you'll definitely find what you're looking for down there boy," replied Malcolm. He had promised Steve that he would pay for him to visit a prostitute as a birthday present. Steve stepped up to the first door they came to and rang the bell. A huge man wearing a black suit opened the door and silently ushered them inside. He had a jagged scar stretching from the corner of his mouth up towards his left ear, which gave him a permanent sneer.

The room was quite small but expensively decorated. Several narrow tables and comfortable looking sofas were set out facing the well-stocked bar. A plump middle-aged woman appeared through a side curtain and came towards them.

"I ain't fuckin' that!" whispered Steve, pulling a face.

"Quiet!" hissed Malcolm, nudging Steve in the ribs. He smiled at the woman who gestured for them to sit down before turning back towards the curtain and clapped her hands sharply. Within seconds, several gorgeous, scantily clad young girls appeared from behind the curtain and lined up in front of the bar. They pouted and smiled towards the two visitors before being instructed to sit up on the high stools lined up in front of the bar. The woman, who was obviously the brothel's madam, indicated that Steve and Malcolm should make their choice from the girls.

"How many can I have?" asked Steve.

"One, for God's sake!" replied Malcolm, shaking his head.

"How much?" Steve shouted over towards the girls.

"No boy," said Malcolm, exasperated. "One has to deal with the madam."

"How much?" Steve shouted over towards the madam.

"You're not dealing with some scrubber in Soho now!" cried Malcolm,

----

wishing he'd sent Paul with Steve. "These are French ladies. One has to act accordingly."

"Well come on then you closet!" said Steve. "What do I have to do to get my knob sucked?"

"C'est combien," replied Malcolm, shaking his head as Steve leapt up out of his chair and headed over to the slim olive-skinned girl sitting closest to him.

"Combien darlin'?" asked Steve, feeling pleased with himself. "Combien?"

"No no!" cried Malcolm, holding his head in his hands. "I didn't mean say Combien! To ask how much in French one has to say "C'est combien!'"

"Yeah whatever," replied Steve, grabbing hold of the girl's hand and disappearing through the curtain.

The madam gestured for Malcolm to choose from one of the girls for himself. Malcolm smiled politely as he shook his head to decline the offer. The madam then offered herself to him.

"Non merci, madame," said Malcolm, beginning to feel very uncomfortable. The madam accepted the rejection and smiled politely before clapping her hands again and the remaining girls disappeared back through the curtain only to be replaced by several young Arab boys. "Madame!" yelled Malcolm, indignantly. The woman shrugged her shoulders and sent the boys away before helping herself to a drink from the bar.

Steve reappeared thirty minutes later grinning from ear to ear. "One more?" he asked, hopefully, sitting down next to Malcolm.

"You need to save your energy for tonight, boy!" replied Malcolm, signalling to the woman behind the bar. "How much?" he gasped, clutching the slip of paper in his hand.

"Now now," said Steve, wagging a finger at Malcolm. "C'est combien?"

Simon Barker, Steven Bailey, Sue Ballion and Billy Broad had made the journey to Paris in Billy's yellow postal van and after a quick change of clothing they set off towards the nightclub. Sue was wearing the same outfit that she'd worn at the cinema in Islington, complete with cupless bra and swastika armband. A group of young men who had also been making their way towards the club spotted Sue and her friends and quickly surrounded the group and started to maul Sue while her three companions tried their best to restrain the men's amorous advances. Sue, tired of being groped, reacted angrily and punched one of the men in the face in a bid to escape, but two of his friends suddenly produced knives and began making menacing threats towards Sue and the others. Fortunately a police car appeared at the end of the road, which gave Simon and his two friends enough time to drag Sue inside the club.

In keeping with local tradition there was no entrance fee for the club's opening night and as it wasn't often that Parisians got anything for free, the club was packed to capacity. Although they were safely inside the club there was no respite for Simon, Steven or Billy as they struggled to shield Sue from further attacks. The Parisians were deeply offended by Sue's foolish and insensitive decision to wear a swastika armband. The club's promoter sent a couple of his security people over to escort the English people to another room, though this was purely out of his desire for a successful evening than any concern for the foolish girl's safety.

Glen stood surveying the audience seated at the tables in front of the stage. He spotted Nils' brother Ray, who was jostling with several local photographers who were all trying to obtain a good position. Glen had overheard Malcolm telling John that Caroline Coon and Jonh Ingham had also travelled over from London in order to review the gig for their respective papers, but if they were there then he couldn't see them.

Steve was standing on the other side of the stage making minor adjustments to his guitar's tuning. He'd earlier regaled Glen and the others with his account of Malcolm's birthday treat. It was also Glen's girlfriend Celia's birthday and he was wondering if she'd received the twenty-one carnations that he'd ordered before leaving for Paris. He'd tried to phone her earlier but the lines were constantly engaged.

"This fuckin' stage is gonna kill my eyes!" scowled John. He was dressed resplendently in full bondage suit, which he'd customised with safety pins and crucifixes. Steve and Glen were both wearing brand new Anarchy shirts for the evening. Steve seemingly satisfied with his guitar sound nodded towards Paul before blasting out the opening chords of "Anarchy In The UK", which the group now regarded as their anthem.

The Parisian audience was very appreciative of the Sex Pistols' lively performance and even applauded the group back for an encore. The club's management had allowed Simon and Billy back into the main room to watch the show while Steven stayed behind in the group's dressing room to look after Sue, even lending her his jacket to cover her modesty.

"I don't wear this armband because I'm some sort of Fascist!" she said, feeling miserable at having missed the group's performance.

"You don't have to explain yourself to me, girl," said Malcolm, placing a hand on her shoulder. "But you must remember that we are in a former Nazi occupied country."

"Especially on a day like today," added Jonh Ingham, who had joined the group backstage.

"What's so special about today?" asked Paul, smirking at Steve's crestfallen expression.

"Today's the third of September," replied Ingham. "The day the Second World War started."

"Fuckin ace!" said Steve, beaming with self-satisfaction.

Malcolm introduced everyone to his old friend Charles Le Duc de Castlebarjec, who had come along to witness Malcolm's latest venture into music management. Castlebarjec invited them all on a tour of Paris nightclubs including Le Dome, Le Coupole and the rather less French sounding Harry's Bar. The French aristocrat was very impressed by the bondage suits and the Anarchy shirts that the group were wearing. He kept touching the garments while constantly praising Malcolm and Vivienne for their brilliant vision and their bold use of colours and materials.

"Who is this Castlebollock cunt?" Steve asked Glen, as soon as they were out of earshot. He'd thought the Frenchman had been trying to touch him up.

"He's one of Malcolm's friends from way back," explained Glen.

"Apparently he's fuckin' loaded and lives in a hotel!"

"So how come we ain't stayin' there with him instead of that shit-hole?" snarled Steve, glancing over at Castlebarjec.

"Because all Malcolm's friends suffer from the same affliction he does," said John, dryly. "Short fuckin' arms an' deep pockets!"

Malcolm glared over at John to show that he'd overheard the sarcastic comment but Castlebarjec seemed unconcerned and politely asked if everyone would like more drinks.

As the group had been booked to perform a matinée show at the Club De Chalet Du Lac on the Saturday afternoon, Caroline Coon suggested that everyone should meet up at Les Deux Magots for lunch. This was the café where the French writer Jean-Paul Sartre used to hang out with his friends and she knew this would appeal to Malcolm's sense of theatre. She and Ingham were the first ones to arrive, closely followed by Nils and Ray Stevenson. Jordon and Vivienne arrived in a taxi clutching their shopping bags and sat down next to the two journalists. For a moment the sight of the travelling party entrenched outside the café had almost made her believe that she was back in London.

Malcolm joined them soon after, bringing Castlebarjec and two other Frenchmen along with him. One of them was Michel Esteban, the owner of the French music magazine *Rock News*. The latest edition of the magazine contained a feature on SEX and the article was hailing Malcolm and Vivienne as "Couturiers Situationnistes".

Esteban signalled to a passing waiter to bring a bottle of red wine before continuing his conversation with Malcolm and Castlebarjec. "It was very foolish," he said, in his heavily accented English, "to ban the Sex Pistols from playing at Mont De Marsan."

"Well you're right there, Michel," replied Malcolm, nodding his agreement. "All this nonsense about violence at our shows has been totally exaggerated by the music press in England. But we do have friends championing our cause." He smiled over towards Caroline and Ingham sitting at the next table.

"The Punk Rock Festival could have been a real success," said Castlebarjec, pouring himself another glass of wine. "But without the Sex Pistols?"

"Quite!" said Malcolm, allowing his friend to refill his own glass. "How can you have a punk rock festival without any punk rock groups?"

"The Damned played the festival," said Ingham, interrupting Malcolm.

"My point exactly," replied Malcolm, dismissing Ingham's comment. "I myself am hoping to stage a similar event in London, which will give the kids a chance to get involved in," he hesitated for a moment, "oh, I really dislike using the term punk rock. I prefer to think of it as a new wave of street fighting young kids, who are ready to throw out the old order."

"When are you thinking of staging the festival?" asked Caroline, hastily reaching into her bag for her notebook. This was certainly news to her and Ingham.

"The sooner the better," replied Malcolm, slapping the table with the palm of his hand. 'It will be at the 100 Club, as everyone looks upon it as the home of the London punk scene and..." He was interrupted by the sudden scraping of chairs as the local photographers sitting nearby rushed past them. "What on earth..?" gasped Malcolm, turning to see what was causing such a commotion. It was John. He had arrived at the cafe wearing his tatty red sweater, which was ripped up the seams. A crucifix was dangling from a safety pin fastened to his breast and he was also wearing his dark granny glasses and a recently purchased black beret. The local shopkeepers and pedestrians alike stood open-mouthed as he preened for the cameras. Castlebarjec turned towards Malcolm nodding his approval.

The Sex Pistols returned to the nightclub later that afternoon to play their scheduled matinée show. They played in front of a depleted audience, as the club was less than a third full. The promoter explained to Malcolm that although the previous evening had been an undoubted success, there had been no entrance fee. Today however, anyone wishing to see the group would have to pay. He tried to assure Malcolm that this was no reflection on the Sex Pistols themselves and he would welcome them back anytime they wished.

CHAPTER FOURTEEN

"Did you see that group on telly last night?" asked Alan, passing Mick the teaspoon. The two seventeen-year old apprentice painter and decorators were on their Monday morning tea break. Their boss George was sitting across from them reading his newspaper.

"You mean the one on *So It Goes*?" replied Mick, nodding as he stirred his cup of tea. "What were they called...Sex Pistols?"

"Sex Pistols!" blurted out George, glancing up from the page-three dolly bird. "What sort o' bloody name is that for a pop group?"

"That's nowt, George," said Alan, once he and Mick had stopped laughing. "They've got a singer called Johnny Rotten."

"Get out of it," gasped Mick, spitting the mouthful of tea back into his cup before he choked.

"Honest!" said Alan, tearing the wrapper from his Twix. "Our David's really into music and he gets the *NME* delivered every week. There was an article about the group the other week."

"That's how our Tracy come along," said George, wistfully staring at the floor.

"What?" asked Mick, chuckling at George's strange comment.

"A bloody rotten 'johnny'!" George yelled, indignantly. "Bloody thing snapped, didn't it?"

"Lucky for Tracy," said Alan, smiling.

"Yeah, she's all right your Tracy," added Mick, nodding thoughtfully. "I wouldn't say no."

"You won't say no to this either!" shouted George, standing over Mick with his arm raised. Then he realised they were winding him up again. "Bloody cheek!" he said, sitting back down.

"It sounded like they were singing 'I am an antichrist'," said Mick, getting back to their earlier subject.

"Yeah they did," said Alan, thoughtfully. "But the song's called 'I Wanna Be Anarchy'!"

"I wanna be anarchy," said Mick, repeating the song's title over and over. "What's anarchy, George?"

"What's anarchy? I'll tell you what bloody anarchy is!" replied George, getting to his feet, which usually signalled the end of tea break. "Havin' two cheeky buggers like you workin' for me. That's anarchy!"

▭ ▭ ▭ ▭

"He's not doin' enough!" snapped John, gazing at the poster advertising a Sex Pistols gig in West Runton, near Cromer in Norfolk that was stuck on the wall of Steve's bedroom. Nils was sprawled on the mattress beneath the window that served as his bed. Steve and Paul were both lying on Steve's bed and Glen was sitting in a nearby chair. All eyes were on John as he paced the room. John glanced back towards the poster in disgust. He'd thought the days of playing shit-holes like the West Runton Village Inn were well and truly behind them, but now he wasn't so sure.

"Come on John, be fair," said Glen, as much to end the awkward silence as anything else, "Malcolm got us the gigs in Paris."

"My point exactly!" yelled John, resting his arm on the clothes rail by the wall. "Yes we have played in Paris. But what a coincidence! The gigs just happen to coincide with Paris Fashion Week." He glared at Steve's Anarchy shirt hanging on the rail. "We were nothing more than showroom dummies making a noise!"

"We're playin' loads of gigs," said Steve, beginning to tire of John's ranting.

"I know!" replied John, becoming more and more frustrated with his fellow band members. "I know we've played loads of gigs," he yelled across at Steve. "And all right, the Paris gigs were free, but what about the fuckin' rest?"

"What are you goin' on about?" asked Glen, frowning.

"Tell 'em, Nils!" said John.

"Tell 'em what?" asked Nils, wishing to be left out of it.

"Tell them about the strip club on Brewer Street for a start!" snapped John.

"When we played the El Paradise," said Nils, beginning to feel like he was under interrogation, "after I'd paid the owner his hundred pounds, I handed the rest of the money over to Malcolm."

"How much was that?" asked Glen, suddenly taking an interest.

"A hundred and fifty," replied Nils, avoiding eye contact with Glen.

"So where's the money now?" asked Steve, jumping up from his bed.

"Where is it now?" said John. 'I'll tell you where it is now. It's payin' the fuckin' rent at 430 King's Road, that's where!" He snatched up the packet of cigarettes lying on the table. "I remember having to get the tube home that night with half the fuckin' audience!" He paused to light his cigarette. "And you're thinkin' of packin' your job in for this?" he yelled at Paul, who didn't bother to reply.

"All right then," said Glen, when John had calmed down enough to listen. "It's time we got him down here and got him to sort out some sort of contract, so we know where we are!"

"Finally!" said John, clasping his hands together in mock prayer. "That's what I've been sayin' all along." He walked over and joined Nils on the mattress. "And make sure it's fuckin' legal!"

John snatched up the sheet of paper that Nils had shown them on his return from a meeting with Malcolm at the shop. It contained a list of proposed gigs which Malcolm had arranged in the North of England. This was what had caused the argument in the first place. "So boys and girls," he said, reading from the list, "after sampling the delights of gay Paree, we now bring you Whitby, Leeds, Chester, Ribchester...Ribchester? Where the fuck is Ribchester?"

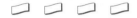

While Nils drove the Sex Pistols around the North of England, Malcolm remained in London to finalise the details for the planned Punk Rock Festival which would take place on Monday 20th and Tuesday 21st of September at the 100 Club on Oxford Street. The festival was less than two weeks away and Malcolm still hadn't enough groups to fill both nights. He'd called an impromptu meeting one evening at Louise's on Poland Street. Those in attendance with him were Bernie Rhodes, Ron Watts, Helen, Jamie Reid and a friend of his called Sophie Richmond, who had worked with Reid at the Suburban Press after leaving Warwick University in 1972. She had recently returned to London from Aberdeen to take up Malcolm's offer to help out as his secretary. Also at the table was Jake Riviera, owner of the independent record company, Stiff Records. He had recently taken over as manager of The Damned who were now signed to his label.

The second night of the Festival had already been sorted out. The Vibrators, who had supported the Sex Pistols when they played at the 100 Club the previous month, would play two sets, one of which would be with Chris Spedding making a guest appearance. The Damned would headline, with The Buzzcocks from Manchester completing the line-up. Malcolm wanted the Monday night to be the festival's main night. The Sex Pistols would naturally be headlining with Bernie's group, The Clash, and the recently formed Subway Sect to act as support. Michel Esteban had suggested inviting a French group called Stinky Toys to play at the festival. Malcolm had agreed and pencilled the group in with a view to ending the night's entertainment but he still needed one more group. He was so desperate to complete the billing that he'd provided Subway Sect with enough money to pay for a week's rehearsal at Mano's Restaurant in Chelsea.

Sue Ballion, Steven Bailey and Sue Catwoman were sitting at a nearby table listening in on Malcolm's conversation.

"We've got a group," said Sue, ignoring the looks of disbelief on her friends' faces. She couldn't really believe that she'd said it herself.

"What?" gasped Malcolm, frowning at her. "You, girl...since when?"

"Oh we've only just started," replied Sue, eagerly. "There's me, Steve and..." Sue Catwoman vigorously shook her head refusing to become involved. "And Billy, Billy Idol," she shouted over towards the blond-haired youth talking to Sid on the other side of the room.

"Don't I know you, boy?" asked Malcolm, stroking his chin while he tried to place Billy.

"Yeah!" replied Billy, grinning. "It's me, Billy Broad! I was in Paris with you and the Pistols."

"Sex Pistols!" said Malcolm, correcting him. "You've dyed your hair!"

"Umm," said Billy, glancing anxiously at the people sitting at Malcolm's table and wondering what was going on.

"And what was it she called you?" asked Malcolm, wondering if this was some kind of elaborate joke.

"Billy Idol," replied Billy, grinning at Sid. 'That's what the teachers at school used to call me."

"And you're playing in a group with these two, are you?" asked Bernie, not even bothering to mask the scepticism in his voice.

"And Sid's on drums!" said Sue, quickly grabbing hold of Sid's sleeve to divert Malcolm's attention away from Billy who still looked totally confused.

"Am I?" asked Sid, cramming a handful of sweets into his mouth. "Oh that's right, yeah I am." He nodded enthusiastically although he also had no idea what Sue was talking about.

"Do you have a drum kit, Sid?" asked Bernie, grinning in spite of himself.

"Er, no," replied Sid, shrugging his shoulders. "Have you?"

"Do any of you have any equipment at all?" asked Malcolm, growing impatient.

"I've got a guitar!" said Billy.

"Well it's a start, I suppose!" replied Malcolm. "But that's all right, you can always borrow whatever else you need from The Clash!" He didn't even look at Bernie who felt obliged to agree to Malcolm's proposal or risk falling foul of one of his moods at a later date.

Bernie also offered Sue and her friends the use of The Clash's rehearsal room in Chalk Farm. By the time of their first group rehearsal together Billy had had a change of heart and had gone off to form a group with his friend Tony James. Billy's replacement in the fledgling group was Marco Pirroni; he was a friend of Sue Catwoman's and also a frequent visitor to SEX. The so-called rehearsal was a non-event in terms of writing any songs. Marco was the only musician out of the four people in the group, but nevertheless the group was included on Monday night's bill. They had chosen the name Siouxsie And The Banshees, which had come about after watching an old Hammer Horror film starring Vincent Price called The Cry Of The Banshee.

Malcolm knew that he could rely on Caroline Coon and Jonh Ingham to provide full and exclusive coverage of the event for their respective music papers. He had sent out dozens of invitations to various record companies throughout London in the hope that the festival would generate sufficient interest in the Sex Pistols and finally land the group a recording contract. Jamie Reid had designed the festival posters using the photo taken by Ray Stevenson in which all four Sex Pistols were crammed together inside the telephone box outside St. Giles' Church.

◻ ◻ ◻ ◻

Mick stood waiting nervously on the Lodestar car park while Alan paid the taxi driver. He could see the two burly doormen standing outside the entrance of the club. They were both under eighteen, the legal age required for admission, but Alan had told him that the owners were less strict during the week. They were there to see the Sex Pistols, neither of them having forgotten the experience of seeing the group on television. It had been Alan's brother that had informed them about the Lodestar gig, which he'd spotted in the gig guide in the *NME*.

Mick had been so captivated by the group that he'd visited every local record store that he could think of in the hope of buying a record by the Sex Pistols, but nobody in any of the shops had even heard of the group let alone stocked their records. The last shop he'd tried was Marshall's Records on Whalley Road in Accrington. The shop also served as a café and this was where Mick would while away his Saturday afternoons, unless he was watching his favourite football team Burnley F.C. The atmosphere inside Marshall's Café was so relaxed; all you had to do was buy something to eat or drink and you could spend all day in there listening to the records of your choice being played in the next room.

Once again, Mick was out of luck. The girl working behind the counter had checked the shop's new releases for the previous three months but there was no mention of any records by the Sex Pistols. He had wanted the record principally so that he could learn the words to at least one of the group's songs before the impending Lodestar gig.

With his fruitless search seemingly at an end, Mick had decided to remain in the café and took a seat by the window. He was absentmindedly stirring his coffee while watching some guy in a battered leather jacket distributing leaflets to the people sitting at each table. When the guy approached Mick's table he had begrudgingly accepted a leaflet but tossed it into the ashtray without bothering to read its contents. He drained his cup and was about to leave when he heard one of the girls sitting at the next table mention the name Sex Pistols. She was holding one of the leaflets that had been handed out a few minutes earlier. Mick went back and fished the leaflet from out of the ashtray. It was a flyer advertising the forthcoming Sex Pistols gig at the Lodestar, with the added attraction of a reduced price entry to the club. The afternoon hadn't been entirely fruitless after all.

Alan had suggested going out for a couple of drinks in Blackburn before travelling to the Lodestar. He had assured Mick that he knew the pubs where the landlords weren't too fussy about the legal age limit. They were both excited at the prospect of seeing the Sex Pistols and had talked of nothing else all that week. They were making their way towards the town centre when they bumped into several of Alan's old school friends who were on their way to watch Blackburn Rovers. Mick, being a Burnley supporter, was well aware of the bitter rivalry which existed between the two sets of supporters and was silently praying that his friend wouldn't accidentally drop him in the shit.

Mick needn't have worried about being denied admission to the club. The bouncers hardly gave them a second glance as they inspected the flyers before ushering them towards the cash register. Once inside, the pair headed towards the bar, but Mick was still conscious about his age and seeing that Alan was at least capable of growing a beard he handed over the money to buy a round of drinks. While Alan was patiently waiting his turn at the bar, Mick wandered across the room in order to get a closer look at the guy wearing a battered leather jacket standing on the raised stage. It was the same guy that had handed him the flyer in Marshall's Café. Mick was almost tempted to mention this fact but quickly decided against the idea, as the guy seemed far too preoccupied with making last minute checks to the equipment.

Mick stood leaning against a pillar by the side of the dancefloor and pretended to examine his cuticles whilst occasionally glancing towards the open doorway at the rear of the stage. He could see several people milling around inside what he believed to be the Sex Pistols' dressing room, but didn't spot anyone that he recognised.

"That's the guitar they used when they were on the telly," he said excitedly, pointing towards the stage when Alan rejoined him. Mick accepted one of the pint glasses that Alan was holding and waited until the guy in the leather jacket had returned to the dressing room before casually strolling over towards the stage. Mick crouched down in order to make a closer examination of Steve's Gibson Les Paul guitar and, satisfied that he wasn't being observed, gently ran his fingers over the strings.

"What do you think you're doin'?" a voice shouted out, causing Mick and Alan to spill their beer in their haste to stand up. When Mick turned around he fully expected to find himself being confronted by one of the bouncers who would surely question his age before throwing him out on his arse. To Mick's relief, it wasn't the bouncers or anyone else working at the club. It was Paul Young, the lad who lived a few houses away from his girlfriend, Sue.

"What the fuck are you doin' here?" gasped Mick, shocked to see somebody else there from Accrington.

"I scrounged a lift off my cousin Tommy," Paul replied pointing over to the lad standing over near the bar. "Tommy Crookston. Do you know him?"

"Yeah, sort of," Mick said nodding. "I think he was the year above me at school."

"Did you see the Pistols on So It Goes?" asked Alan, as Paul turned back towards him. Paul was about to reply when Mick realised that he was being ignorant and made the necessary introductions.

"Yeah," replied Paul, matter-of-factly. "Our Tommy's been playing the drums for years now, so he's really into music and always let's me know when there's something worth watching on the telly."

"Well I never knew that," said Mick, glancing back towards Tommy, who was still struggling to get served.

"What, that Tommy plays the drums?"

"No," quipped Alan, leaping in, "that you can afford a television." He grinned as Mick added a "boom-boom" for good measure.

"Sorry, Paul," Alan said feigning sincerity, "just a bit of painting humour."

"It never fails to add colour," Mick said smirking at Paul's baffled expression.

"I'm playing bass in Tommy's group," Paul, said to return the conversation to somewhere close to normal. "We practise in my granddad's garage on Emma Street."

"Ahh," said Mick, nodding thoughtfully. 'I wondered who it was that was making that awful racket!"

"Are we that bad?"

"Worse!" replied Mick, grinning. "We can hear you from Sue's house."

"How far away's that?" asked Alan.

"About two hundred metres?" replied Mick, looking at Paul for verification. "You know where they're building the new sports centre close to where I live?"

"Yeah, think so," Alan replied, nodding.

"Well Emma Street is facing the bit where they're going to put the all-weather pitch."

"Have you met Sue?" Paul asked Alan, who shook his head indicating that he hadn't. "She's all right, for a twelve year old."

"Get fucked!" Mick said grinning.

"Oh, right, she's not twelve," said Paul, smirking at Alan's expression. "But she can't be more than fourteen!"

"Old enough to bleed," said Alan, winking at Mick, "old enough to butcher."

"And who are you goin' out with?" Mick asked Paul. "Or are you still seeing Pam?"

"Pam? I don't know anyone called Pam!" replied Paul, frowning as he tried to figure out who Mick was on about. "Pam who?"

"Pam of your fuckin' hand!" said Mick, joining his thumb and forefinger together and moving his wrist up and down.

"You're being a bit generous there, aren't you?" said Alan, nodding towards Mick's hand.

"Don't you start as well!" sighed Paul.

"Sorry," said Alan, patting Paul on the shoulder. "I couldn't resist!"

"What did you think of the Sex Pistols," asked Paul, changing the subject, "on *So It Goes?*"

"We thought they were fuckin' brilliant, didn't we?" said Mick, glancing at Alan as he said this. "Did you know that their singer's called Johnny Rotten!"

"Yeah, I knew that," replied Paul. "But did you know that he's standing behind you!" Mick whirled round to find himself face to face with John, who was trying to get past him.

"Hiya," Mick mumbled, moving aside to allow John and the other three Sex Pistols to get past him. "Do you think he heard me?" he asked, sheepishly. Alan and Paul were too busy chuckling into their beer to offer a reply.

When Mick, Alan and Paul returned to the bar to buy some more drinks before the Sex Pistols came on stage, they were forced to wait until the woman standing behind the bar had issued instructions to one of the bouncers. It seemed that a group of lads from Preston were inside the club and she didn't want any trouble between them and the locals from Blackburn. Once Alan had obtained the drinks, the three lads positioned themselves near to the right-hand side of the stage just as the Sex Pistols came through the dressing room door.

"Isn't that the jacket he was wearing on telly?" asked Paul, above the feedback from Steve's guitar.

"Has to be," replied Alan. "I doubt if the cunt's got two of 'em in his wardrobe."

John stood chewing on his fingernails while he waited for Steve to make some last minute alterations to the settings on his amplifier. "Er, in case you were wondering," he said, when Steve seemed satisfied, "we're the Sex Pistols." He gripped the microphone stand with both hands as Steve launched into the intro for "Anarchy In The UK". Despite the wild energy emanating from the group on stage the dance floor remained empty, but Mick could see that the lads from Preston were obviously well into the group. Several other youths also ventured to within spitting distance of the stage but the majority of the Wednesday night crowd remained in the bar area, watching with mild curiosity.

There was a short interruption during the song "Problems" when Steve broke one of his strings. John took advantage of the unscheduled break to indulge in a spot of audience baiting. He eyed the group of lads standing at the edge of the dancefloor but had no intention of offending the converted. Instead he looked over towards the other side of the dimly lit room in search of his first victim. He surveyed the entire room before returning to the young couple who were sitting at a table close to the fire exit and decided that the guy's ridiculous perm could not go unpunished. "You wanna sue the fucker that did that to your head?" he said, hoping the guy would take the bait.

"Get off, you're shite!" an unseen voice shouted out from the semi-darkness, much to the delight of those standing near the bar.

"Fuckin' hell, I don't fancy yours much!" retorted John, indicating the guy's girlfriend. "How long did you spend thinkin' that one up?"

"Yeah fuck off back to your mushy peas!" shouted Steve, drowning out the heckler's response with the opening chords to "New York".

The Sex Pistols completed their forty-minute set without any further complications. The lads from Preston thoroughly enjoyed the performance and even ventured onto the dancefloor during "Pretty Vacant". Mick and his two friends, encouraged by the lads from Preston and fuelled with Dutch courage, also stepped out onto the dancefloor and were soon jumping around and punching the air in time to the music. The group was clearly inspired at this show of support and responded accordingly. They even came back on to give the audience an encore of "Liar", which John dedicated to the former Prime minister, Harold Wilson.

Once Mick was convinced that the group wouldn't be coming back on stage again he rushed off to the Gents as he was in urgent need of a piss. He'd almost been dancing cross-legged towards the end of the last song but had been reluctant to leave the dancefloor for fear of missing something. By the look of things he hadn't been the only one in need of the toilets and he had to stand in line behind the lads from Preston, but at least he could pass the time talking about the group's performance while waiting his turn.

Mick hated having to use the Gents in a public place, as he was terribly "piss proud". All it needed was for someone to come and stand at the side of him and that would be it, nothing would come out, but as soon as he got back outside he'd be bursting to go again. He stood before the urinal and closed his eyes so that he could focus on the job in hand by imagining that he was in the comfort of his own bathroom. Thankfully the two lads that had been standing on either side of him had departed and he sighed with contentment as the pressure in his bladder ebbed away.

He zipped up his trousers and had walked across the room to wash his hands at the sink when he heard the door opening behind him. He turned around and smiled politely towards the guy and started to look away before realising that it was the drummer from the Sex Pistols. "Great show tonight," he said, stepping into the built-in cubicle to tear off some toilet roll to wipe his hands.

"Thanks," replied Paul, nodding his appreciation.

"I saw you on *So It Goes* the other week," continued Mick, holding the door open for Paul.

"What did you think?"

"Fuckin' brilliant!" replied Mick, as the two walked over towards the bar area. He spotted John and the other two Sex Pistols standing at the bar. Steve was signalling to Paul that his drink was waiting.

"This lad saw us on *So It Goes*," said Paul, indicating Mick, who had been about to rejoin his own friends. "Sorry mate, what's your name?"

"Mick."

"Well I'm Paul, this is Glen and that's Steve." He paused to accept a pint from Steve. "Nils is our road manager and that's John." Mick could see that John was studying him and wondered if he remembered their earlier encounter.

Mick glanced over towards his two friends who were standing several metres away with bemused expressions on their faces. Alan raised one of the glasses that he was holding to indicate that it was Mick's, but Mick had no intention of leaving, especially now that he'd been introduced to the members of the group and waved them over to join him.

"I've got a mate called Paul Young," said John, shaking Paul's hand. "Any relation?"

"Don't think so," replied Paul, shaking his head, earnestly. "I don't even know anyone in London."

Mick was thoroughly enjoying himself chatting with the group but he couldn't help feeling slightly uncomfortable by the way John seemed to examine his clothing whenever he spoke to him. Mick was wearing his brand-new Levi denim jacket and a pair of "patch-pocket" trousers, which were the height of fashion at the time, but standing next to John he felt ridiculous. There was also the fact that he had shoulder length wavy hair and hadn't set foot in a barber's shop for over two years.

"I like your shirt," he said, pointing towards the shirt that Steve was wearing. "You wore it on the telly, didn't you?" Mick moved closer so he could read the stencilled slogan on the front of the shirt. "Only anarchists are pretty." He smiled at Steve, but it was obvious to everyone that he hadn't understood what it meant.

"It's an 'Anarchy' shirt," said Steve, glancing down towards the garment. "We've got a song called 'Anarchy In The UK'."

"The one we played on *So It Goes*," said Glen, by way of explanation.

"Oh right," said Mick, glancing towards Alan, "no wonder I couldn't find it." He quickly told them about his fruitless search for the record.

"You can't buy it!" scowled John, "because we ain't got a record deal yet!"

"Oh," replied Alan, sensing that this was somehow a sore subject with John.

"Where can I get one of these?" Mick asked Steve, pointing at his shirt again.

"At SEX," replied Steve, casually.

"Where did you say?" gasped Paul, not really sure that he'd heard right.

"It's the name of the shop that our supposed manager owns!" said John, sneering.

"Whereabouts is that then?" asked Paul.

"Er, London," replied John, smiling at Paul's pained expression. "The place where you don't know anyone."

Nils dug into his jacket pocket and produced a business card, which he handed to Mick who was standing the closest to him.

"Are you playin' anywhere else round here?" asked Mick, handing the SEX business card over to Alan.

"No," replied Glen, shaking his head. "Our next gig is on Friday, but you won't be allowed in."

"Why not?" asked Paul.

"Because it's at Chelmsford Prison!" said Steve, grinning.

"And they might not let us back out again," added John, laughing

"Straight up," said Paul, grinning at the three blank faces in front of him, "we're playin at the prison."

"Nils, get these boys a drink," said Steve, gratefully accepting another pint from the bar. 'It's still free beer for the group, ain't it?"

"We're playing for the prisoners because they've been good little boys," said John, smirking, "unlike their comrades in Hull!"

This was in reference to the riot at Hull Prison at the beginning of the month, which had lasted sixty-five hours and resulted in over a million pounds worth of damage inside the prison.

"We do like playing to a captive audience," said Glen, grinning at Paul.

"We're playin' the punk festival at the 100 Club, as well," said Steve, turning towards Nils who was still busy handing out the drinks. "Have you got any more of them flyers?"

"Yeah," replied Nils, fishing into another of his jacket pockets. "It's next Monday, if you're interested."

"Where's that?" asked Paul, reaching for the flyer.

"The 100 Club on Oxford Street," said Glen.

"In London," said Mick, sighing.

"How did you know that?" asked Paul.

"Because everything's in fuckin' London," said John, turning to face Paul, "except of course, anyone you know."

"I used to play Monopoly when I was a kid," said Mick, grinning at John's remark. "There's no chance that George will give us time off!" he added, glancing at Alan.

"No, but I'm skint anyway," said Alan, despondently.

"We're definitely gonna come and see you again though," said Paul, glancing at Mick and Alan who both nodded their agreement.

"Well you've got the number of the shop," said Nils, indicating the SEX business card in Alan's hand. "Just ask for Malcolm and if he's not there then somebody will be able to tell you where we're playing."

"You got a pen on you?" Steve asked Nils, reaching for the flyer that Paul was holding. He placed his drink on the bar before scribbling something down on the back of the flyer. "Here's my address," he said, handing the flyer back to Paul.

"What does that say?" asked Mick, trying to decipher Steve's handwriting.

"Denmark Street," replied Steve, frowning. "I live in Tin Pan Alley."

Mick and the others didn't wish to outstay their welcome so with promises to contact the shop for information about the group's future gigs they headed off to join Tommy Crookston who was trying out his best chat-up patter on the pretty brunette behind the bar. Mick had to admire Tommy's taste for the barmaid bore more than a passing resemblance to the American actress Jacqueline Smyth from the TV series *Charlie's Angels*, but it was painfully obvious to everyone watching that Tommy's amorous advances were destined to remain unrequited and that the girl's sole interest in her would-be admirer was for him to relinquish his grip on the empty glass he was waving around. Tommy, it seemed, had been under the misguided impression that him being the drummer in a group would have been sufficient to impress Miss Smyth and Mick almost choked on the last of his lager when he heard Tommy announce, in his broad "Eee-Bye-Gum" accent, that not only did he hail from London, but that he was in fact Johnny Rotten's cousin, Tommy Vomit.

With Miss Smyth having departed without so much as a glance in his direction, Tommy finally accepted that his two hopes, Bob and None, had left the building and offered to give Mick a lift back to Accrington and drop Alan off in Blackburn as it was on the way. As the lads were making their way across the club car park towards Tommy's Ford Cortina Alan spotted John and Nils standing near the rear entrance. John shouted something that Mick and the others couldn't quite understand.

"Is everythin' all right?" asked Alan, as they approached John.

"Oh yeah, everything's fine!" replied John, sarcastically. "We're all fuckin' knackered and I'd like to see my bed sometime this side of Christmas. Only we can't load the gear until Steve's finished with the van!"

"What do you...oh, I see what you mean," said Mick, looking over towards the van, which was parked several metres away. It was rocking from side to side.

"He's pulled a tart!" said Nils grinning, before disappearing back inside the club.

◻ ◻ ◻ ◻

Dave Goodman turned the transit van onto Springfield Road in Chelmsford and pulled up outside the entrance of the maximum-security prison. The group had been instructed to be there for 3 p.m. sharp but Paul would be meeting the rest of the group later, after he'd finally quit his apprenticeship at the brewery. He reckoned it was better to jump before he was pushed because of his mounting absenteeism from work due to the demands of touring. After his shift, he was going for a farewell drink with his mates from work.

At 3 p.m. precisely the main gates were slid open and Goodman was waved through by one of the guards. Much to everyone's surprise, they were not searched. A second guard appeared and escorted them through the prison's exercise yard and up into the officers' canteen, where they were treated to sandwiches and tea while they awaited the arrival of their drummer. As soon as Paul arrived, looking slightly worse for wear, they were escorted down into the hall where they would be performing. They played three songs during the soundcheck while the inmates waited patiently outside. One of the warm up numbers was a cover of the Sweet hit "Wam Bam Thank You Mam", although there were no plans to actually perform the song during the show.

"Fuckin' hell," moaned Steve, peering through the curtain from behind the small stage where they had been asked to wait while the inmates were escorted in, "there won't be any birds!"

"Don't worry Steve," said Nils, grinning. "I'm sure you'll still be able to play." The Sex Pistols walked onto the stage one by one through a gap in the backdrop, upon which an artistically minded lag has painted large billboard advertisements such as Coke, Cinzano, Pot and LSD. John received plenty of wolf whistles from the seated prisoners as he removed his jacket to reveal his customised white shirt. He gave the audience a twirl to show them his own handiwork and they were equally appreciative of John's crudely painted slogans "Anarchy" and "No Future".

"Greetings from Her Majesty," he yelled out, to be greeted with more cheers and whistles. Steve and Glen launched the group into "Anarchy In The UK", followed by "I Wanna Be Me", and John goaded the inmates by announcing that dancing was permitted.

Steve and Glen had to improvise during the song "Seventeen", when Paul drunkenly tumbled from his drum stool. He stood up, grinning sheepishly, and bowed in response to the thunderous cheers before resuming playing. The enthusiasm of the inmates rubbed off on the group and they returned to play two encores. As they finally left the stage, one of the guards standing at the side raised an arm to halt John's progress. "Go on," he said, indicating the prisoners, "do another one."

"No, replied John, shaking his head. "I can't be bothered. I'm so lazy."

At the end of the show the inmates were filed out to be escorted back to their cells with the exception of the three or four who had been assigned to stack the chairs and help with the loading up of the group's equipment.

"Fancy comin' with us?" Steve asked the one helping him load his amplifier into the van.

"No thanks," replied the inmate, smirking. "I'm out of here in a month anyway."

"And he'll be back in his cell before Christmas," said one of the guards, winking at Steve. "Seriously though, thanks for coming."

"No problem," replied Glen, leaning out of the passenger window. "They were a good bunch."

"Oh there's no good uns in here, lad," replied the guard, shaking his head. "If they were any good they wouldn't have got themselves caught!"

The following Monday afternoon anybody who was even remotely connected with the Punk Rock Festival gathered inside the 100 Club on Oxford Street. The Sex Pistols had already been down and set up their gear, done their soundcheck and headed off back to Denmark Street, leaving the other groups on the bill to sort themselves out. The four members of Subway Sect were currently on stage doing their soundcheck. The group was – as they openly admitted – heavily influenced by the Sex Pistols' attitude and the more observant members of the small gathering inside the club could also point out the similar way that their singer Vic Goddard composed himself in front of the microphone.

The newly christened Siouxsie Sioux Ballion was sitting with her Banshees, patiently waiting to go on stage for their own soundcheck.

"Are you nervous, Sid?" asked his friend Viv Albertine, who was sitting beside him.

"No, not really," replied Sid, casually. "I'm just gonna go crash, bang, wallop 'til someone stops me." As he said this he suddenly leapt up out of his seat, ran across the room and vaulted over one of The Clash's highly distinctive pink monitors. Bernie had ordered Mick and the others to paint their equipment fluorescent pink in order to stop one of the other groups "accidentally" mistaking it for their own.

Joe Strummer, who was sitting at a nearby table chatting to journalist Jonh Ingham, was on hand should the Banshees require help with setting up The Clash's equipment on stage. Joe was complimenting Ingham on the shirt that he was wearing. The journalist had stencilled the slogan "No Elvis, Beatles or the Rolling Stones", which featured in the chorus of The Clash song "1977", down the front of the garment.

"Who did it for you, man?" asked Joe, turning back to face the journalist once he was certain that Sid was behaving himself.

"I made it myself, actually" replied Ingham, trying to sound nonchalant. "I wore it in Paris when I was over there with the Pistols."

"You're kiddin'!" cried Joe, gleefully. He was about to hail Bernie in order to show him the shirt, but was distracted by the sudden commotion coming from the stage.

Joe and Ingham rushed across to find Bernie had somehow become involved in an argument with Sid.

"You're a mean fuckin' Jew!" yelled Sid, stabbing a finger towards the bespectacled Bernie who'd taken offence at the swastikas that Siouxsie and Sid were both wearing and had rescinded his offer of allowing the Banshees to use The Clash's equipment.

"Oh Sid, calm down!" said Paul Simonon, jumping up onto the stage. "What the fuck's goin' on?"

"He's objecting to this!" cried Sid, pointing to the crude swastika that he'd drawn on his vest with a black felt-tip pen.

"I've tried explaining to him that we're not havin' a go at Jews!" protested Siouxsie, glancing down towards her own swastika armband.

"I don't care," yelled Bernie, dismissing her claims. "You're not using our equipment and that's final!" But just when it looked as if Siouxsie and her Banshees would be spectators rather than participants at the festival Malcolm came to their rescue by offering them the use of the Sex Pistols' equipment.

Ron Watts had spent the last few days telling anyone willing to listen that not only would the festival be a total success but that hundreds of kids would be queuing up to see the groups. "I was right," he said, strolling past Jonh Ingham and Caroline Coon on his way towards the door at the side of the bar. "But you didn't believe me."

"Believe you about what?" asked Caroline, frowning at Ingham.

"About the hundreds of people that are coming here tonight!" said Ingham, sarcastically.

"That's right," replied Watts, a smug look spreading across his face. "They're queuing around the block as we speak."

"Yeah sure," replied Ingham, shaking his head. He'd been a regular visitor to the club over the last four or five months and knew what sort of crowds the Sex Pistols were capable of attracting.

"Go and see for yourself," said Watts, reappearing behind the bar.

"Come on," said Caroline, not really sure if they were being taken for a ride. She and a very reluctant Ingham made their way up the flight of stairs and stepped out on to Oxford Street to find a queue of kids stretching to the end of the block. Caroline shook her head in disbelief then pulled out her pocket camera and snapped off a couple of photos, which she thought might just merit featuring in her article.

"They won't all get in!" said Ingham, as they made their way back down the steps but quickly changed his mind when he saw the pound signs in Watts'

----

eyes.

The reason for the Sex Pistols' absence from the 100 Club that afternoon was because Nils had arrived unexpectedly to escort them to a meeting with Malcolm and his solicitor Stephen Fisher at the solicitor's offices in Dryden Chambers. In reaction to John's criticisms, Malcolm had set up his own management company, which he named Glitterbest, having bought the name "off the shelf" for a hundred pounds. He had also instructed Fisher to draw up a contract between himself and the group for an initial three-year period with options for a further two years.

The contract that Fisher had drawn up was biased in favour of the management because the solicitor had been careful to reserve several rights, which were hidden inside legal clauses and put every aspect of the Sex Pistols' career in Malcolm's control. Clause 14 stated that the name Sex Pistols belonged to and was owned by the management. In return for all managerial services, Malcolm, through Glitterbest, would receive twenty five per cent of all group earnings. Glitterbest would receive all moneys from record companies, out of which Malcolm would also take twenty five per cent, plus taking a further massive fifty per cent from all Sex Pistols merchandising. Glitterbest would take care of all business involving the Sex Pistols and provide bi-yearly accounts.

Upon arrival at Fisher's office, the four members of the group were each given a photocopy of the managerial contract. Glen tried to make sense out of the document, but it was worded in such a way that only a qualified solicitor would have been able to fully understand it, which is exactly what Malcolm had intended. Glen quickly gave up and handed the contract back to Fisher.

"Can we get somebody to have a look at it for us?" he asked.

"Somebody like who?" asked Malcolm, glancing nervously towards Fisher.

"A solicitor," replied Glen. "Someone who can explain it to us."

"Oh there's no time for that, boy," said Malcolm, avoiding eye contact with Glen. "It's got to be signed here and now!"

"Why?" asked Glen, wondering if he was the only member of the group that was concerned about what was happening.

"So I can strike a deal with the record companies!" replied Malcolm, pointing towards the office door behind him. "They'll be banging that door down tomorrow, desperate to sign you boys."

Steve was the first to react by picking up the pen that Fisher had strategically placed beside the original draught of the contract on the table. He grabbed up the contract and scribbled his signature by the side of his name then casually handed the pen to Paul.

"I hope you've read this!" scowled John, glaring at Glen as he snatched the pen from Paul's hand. "Cos I'm gonna sign it and if it's wrong, it's your fault!"

Glen sat there totally dumbfounded. After all the arguments about getting a legal document drawn up, which would give them some sort of protection against Malcolm, here they were with a document that they hadn't even bothered to touch, other than to sign their names. He glanced up from the table towards Malcolm and Fisher, who were both standing behind the solicitor's desk. He was convinced that they were being shafted and the evidence was right there before his eyes in black and white, but there didn't seem much point in arguing any further so he reluctantly picked up the pen and signed next to his name.

Malcolm came from around the desk rubbing his hands together. "Come on, boy," he said, gesturing towards Nils. "We need you to witness it."

Nils stepped forward and picked up the contract. He wasn't going to even pretend that he understood what was written on the pages that he was holding but was anxious to know if Malcolm had kept his promise from when he'd offered Nils a partnership. "Is there anything in here for me?" he asked. Nils could see from Malcolm's reluctance to even look him in the eye that there wasn't going to be any partnership. He glanced over towards John, who had told him several months ago that he would leave the group if Malcolm reneged on his promise, but John was staring at the wall as if Nils wasn't even in the room. He quickly scribbled his name on the contract before handing it to Fisher. The solicitor quickly scanned the page containing the five signatures before placing it in his office safe.

"We're the er...Subway Sect," singer, Vic Goddard, nervously informed the sea of faces in front of him. Standing next to him was the group's guitarist, Rob Miller, who had only been playing the instrument for three months. He slowly started to strum the opening chords of their first song "No Love". Although the Sect claimed to be influenced by the Sex Pistols, their style of music was completely different. The tunes were constructed from high-pitched, jagged guitar riffs over which Vic sang his lyrics in a rigorous monotone. The group's image was a reflection of the way they felt about the drabness of everyday life. Their world was bland and grey and so they dyed their clothes to match their feelings. The audience seemed cautious about how to react to the group on stage. Sporadic applause greeted each new song of which they only had five. "Everyone's a prostitute," Vic shouted out as he surveyed the crowd. "And everyone's a prison!"

Caroline Coon watched Vic and the other members of the group leaving the stage to generous, if somewhat stilted, applause. "What did you think of them?" she asked Michelle and Bruno, who were wearing identical leopard-skin jackets. She had struck up a conversation with the two sixteen year-olds earlier, having recognised them from the front of the queue when she had taken her photographs.

"I think they're great!" replied Michelle, looking at Bruno for confirmation of the statement.

"Somebody just told me that it was Subway Sect's first time on stage," said

Bruno, glancing over towards Vic Goddard who was gratefully accepting a pint from someone at the bar.

"Yes, it was," replied Caroline, "although you wouldn't have guessed."

"I haven't been this excited in ages," said Bruno, applauding Siouxsie as she stepped up onto the stage.

Siouxsie was really playing to the audience, with her dark hair streaked with flashes of crimson red for the evening, although she was moderately dressed compared to her appearance at recent Sex Pistols shows. She was wearing a pair of black fitted trousers and matching jacket, with a tiny pair of scissors hung from a chain around her neck. Steve Bailey or Steve Spunker as he was now calling himself for the first, and rumour had it the only, Banshees performance was wearing a white shirt with a small Union Jack sewn onto the right breast. He had also bleached his hair at the temples, resembling a younger version of Grandpa from the American TV show The Munsters. Marco, the only musician in the group's line-up, was wearing black trousers and one of Malcolm and Vivienne's Anarchy shirts. Sid, clearly enjoying himself on Paul's drum kit, was living up to his earlier promise to Viv Albertine by hitting any drum or cymbal with total disregard for timing.

The Banshees had let it be known prior to the festival that they would be performing their own version of "Goldfinger", from the James Bond film of the same name, but had changed their minds at the last minute. The vast majority of the audience stood in stunned silence while watching Siouxsie recite lines fro The Lord's Prayer against a cacophonous wailing feedback and snatches of the Beatles' "Twist And Shout", Dylan's "Knocking On Heaven's Door" and "Deutschland Uber Alles". Steven's face was devoid of any expression as he plucked each note, more out of hope than design. He was clearly nervous but that was hardly surprising, as he had no previous knowledge of the musical instrument in his hands.

The group had been playing for over twenty minutes when Sid, who had been merrily pounding away with his eyes closed, finally looked up and saw Marco signalling that he was ready to stop. Sid threw his drumsticks to the floor and casually walked off stage, followed by the rest of the group.

Simon Barker rushed forward and hugged Sue. "How was it?" he asked.

"Well, the ending was a mistake," replied Sue, grinning. "I thought we'd carry on until someone pulled us off." She stopped talking while she and her friends listened to the announcement from Ron Watts who was standing on stage. The promoter thanked Siouxsie and the Banshees for their efforts and announced that The Clash would be next on stage, after a short delay due to unforeseen circumstances. Watts looked directly at Sid as he said this, in reference to his earlier dispute with Bernie, but Sid was too wrapped up in his newfound fame to notice.

Caroline and Jonh Ingham were standing at the bar surrounded by various A&R representatives from the record companies whom Malcolm had invited.

"What did you think of the Banshees?" she asked Howard Thompson who was there on behalf of Island records.

"You really want to know?" asked Thompson, grimacing. "I thought they were bloody awful!"

"You're kidding!" said Nils, who had been listening in on the conversation. "They were fucking fantastic!"

The Clash took to the stage and were greeted with wild applause from the audience, though it was only the fourth gig that they'd played together and the nerves were still showing. The group had been reduced to a four-piece since their last gig at the 100 Club when they'd supported the Sex Pistols after the unexpected departure of guitarist Keith Levine, but there was a sense of expectancy from those crowded at the front of the stage because The Clash was one of the main attractions of the Punk Rock Festival.

The four remaining members of the group were definitely looking the part in their paint-splattered trousers and shirts. Bass player Paul was wearing a leopard-skin print shirt and matching brothel creepers. He'd adopted the stance of a gunslinger for his stage act, his guitar dangling down by his knees. His musical ability though, like the majority of the groups playing the festival, was rudimentary. He still had tiny stickers, to help him identify the notes, strategically positioned along the neck of his guitar and was still relying on Mick to tune the instrument for him. He had first tried out as the singer in another of Mick's groups calling themselves London SS, but had only really agreed to help out as he was Mick's mate. Bernie, however, had spotted something special in Paul and persuaded him to learn an instrument.

On the signal from Joe, they powered into their first song "White Riot", written as a direct result of Joe and Paul's experiences during the violent clashes between the police and the West Indian youths at the Notting Hill Carnival the previous month. In fact, it was Paul who had suggested adopting the name "Clash" for the group after remarking on how often the word was used in the daily newspapers whenever they were describing a conflict.

Drummer, Terry Chimes, barely had time to draw breath before the group launched into their second song "London's Burning". This was a new composition written by Mick and Joe in homage to the night-time view of London from the high-rise block of flats where Mick was now living with his grandma.

The Clash's sound came at you like a speed-fuelled locomotive in danger of coming off the rails. As soon as one song ended it was quickly followed by the next. During their set Mick broke a string on his guitar and seeing that the members of the group didn't even have enough money for food, let alone the luxury of spare strings, everyone took full advantage in the unexpected interruption to catch their breath.

Joe quickly ran out of witticisms to amuse the massed throng of sweaty bodies in front of him and so he pulled out his pocket-sized transistor radio, in the hope of perhaps finding a tune for the audience to listen to. By chance he stumbled upon a political debate on the current troubles in Northern Ireland and held the radio up to the microphone. Dave Goodman quickly latched on to what Joe was doing and added an echo delay effect from the PA system. There was total silence within the 100 Club as everyone listened to unseen voices talking about unseen places in the troubled province. Then Mick signalled the end of the political broadcast by hitting a power chord and Joe acknowledged him by tossing the radio onto his jacket, which was lying on the floor, as Mick powered into "Protex Blue", the group's tribute to the Durex industry. The Clash ended their eleven-song set with "1977". "Danger stranger," Joe bellowed out above the staccato guitars. "Better paint your face...No Elvis, Beatles or the Rolling Stones in 1977!" The audience was left wondering if this was a portent for the future.

Caroline made a beeline for Paul Simonon as soon as he stepped from the stage. She had more than just a professional interest in The Clash's bass player. "How are you feeling?" she asked him.

"Great," replied Paul, pausing for breath, "but I've gotta get better!" His face was dripping with sweat and his clothes were clinging to his wiry frame. "I'm never gonna be content because I know I can do a lot more with the bass, yeah?" He paused to wipe his brow with his shirtsleeve in an attempt to stop the sweat from stinging his eyes. "Most of 'em just stand there, don't they? John Entwhistle an' Bill Wyman?" He was clearly excited as more and more people crowded round to congratulate him on the group's performance. "I wanna give the audience a good time, an' give myself a good time as well."

Paul glanced round when he heard Joe shout his name and readily accepted the pint of lager from the singer before heading towards the stairs. Caroline was almost tempted to follow him but remembered that she also had a job to do. "What's it like playing with someone like Paul?" she asked Joe. "Someone who's still learning as he goes along, compared to your time with the 101ers?"

"It's really great," replied Joe, nodding enthusiastically. "When a musician knows all the notes and chords it can get really boring. It ain't exciting for them anymore and they're just playin' for playin's sake. All the emotion's gone, you know?" He paused to take a drink before continuing. "That's what makes it really exciting playing with someone like Paul because there ain't no rules." He pointed over towards Mick Jones, who was standing a few metres away talking to Sid. "My style of playin' is really rudimentary and Mick's is great, so we make an interesting combination."

A massive cheer erupted around the club bringing Caroline's interview with Joe to a premature end. They both looked over towards the stage and discovered that the reason for the uproar was that Paul Cook had taken his seat behind the drums. The audience once again surged towards the front, even those who, up until now, had been content to stand over by the bar pressed forward to get a better view of the stage. The atmosphere inside the club reached fever pitch. It was the moment everyone had been waiting for. There was an even louder cheer when John stepped up onto the stage to join the rest of the group. He was wearing the full bondage suit, which he had customised by adding safety pins, badges and crucifixes; there was even a metal bottle-opener dangling from one of the D rings on his jacket.

The Sex Pistols were definitely the group everyone was there to see. The group of the here and now. The months of hard graft and constant gigging were now finally beginning to pay off for the group. Not only had they grown in stature, but they'd also become supremely confident in their musicianship. For a group that had only been playing together for a little over twelve months they had matured both as a working unit and as individuals; which could only have come from having an unshakable conviction about what they were doing. The Sex Pistols adopted an attitude of complete indifference towards the music industry as a whole and music journalists – with the exception of Coon and Ingham – in particular. They made no apologies and offered no quarter to those who stood in their way.

The atmosphere inside the small club was thick with spine-tingling anticipation as the audience waited for the chaos to commence. Steve raised his Gibson until the neck was pointing towards the lighting before leaping into the air and thrashing out the by now familiar opening chords of "Anarchy In The UK". John grasped the microphone stand with both hands and thrust it into the air, which acted as the catalyst for the audience to come alive.

Simon Barker stood at the side of the stage and watched as the audience surged towards the stage in unison with the music. He was happy that the group was finally receiving the attention that they deserved although he couldn't help feeling a sense of sadness at the same time. He looked over towards the photographers, who were jostling each other to get the best shots of the group. Where were they six months ago? he thought to himself, remembering the freezing winter nights that he and the rest of the Bromley Contingent had spent travelling around London in order to watch the Sex Pistols' early gigs. He felt that he had the right to be there, not like some of this lot who were there simply because they'd read about the group in the music papers. He couldn't help feeling that the party was over in terms of the group being their own little secret.

John seemed strangely subdued; he seldom communicated with the audience and rarely ventured away from the microphone stand. It could be that he was becoming disillusioned with the Sex Pistols' association with Malcolm's so-called Punk Rock festival, which to his mind was nothing more than one man's desire to act out his fantasy of becoming the next Brian Epstein. Or perhaps he was contemplating his rash decision to sign Malcolm's contract without first seeking proper legal advice.

Steve, on the other hand, was relishing every moment in the spotlight and manoeuvred about the compact stage as if he'd received the encyclopaedia of "rock 'n' roll stances" for his birthday earlier in the month. He had unwittingly developed his own unique guitar style and the crudely painted slogan on his amplifier was no longer the cause for the ridicule that it perhaps once was.

Paul, aided and abetted by Glen's pulsating bass, ground out a solid rhythmic backbeat, which ensured that the Sex Pistols' three-minute rants on Britain's social and economic decline were delivered at a melodic yet dynamic tempo. The two seemed to have developed an almost telepathic understanding and effortlessly propelled the group along towards a chaotic yet orchestrated crescendo.

The Sex Pistols had barely left the stage before the club rapidly began to empty, despite the fact that there was still one more group left to play on the bill. The Stinky Toys, who had travelled hundreds of miles in order to play at the festival, refused to perform in front of the handful of people remaining and Malcolm and Ron Watts tried to pacify Ellie, the groups' singer, with assurances that her group would be granted top billing on the following night. She was furious at the blatant lack of respect towards her group and proceeded to berate them in her native tongue. She finally pushed the two men aside and bolted up the stairs and out on to Oxford Street where, without the quick thinking of a passer-by, she would surely have been killed by an oncoming double-decker bus

The Sex Pistols weren't at the 100 Club for the second night of the festival as they were performing at the Top Rank in Cardiff. It meant that the younger element of the previous night's audience was replaced by denim and leather clad twenty-somethings. The first group on stage was the French group Stinky Toys and although the audience was mildly curious, they offered no response to the group's first three songs. Ellie, a very striking girl with long blonde hair that swirled around her face as she swayed to the music and the other three musicians in the group seemed less than comfortable playing to the passive London crowd and they disappeared as soon as their short set was completed. The group would have been better off fulfilling their original commitment and performing on the Monday night, because the handful of people who had remained then were actually willing to listen to them.

The Damned were the main attraction from all the groups on Tuesday night's bill. They were regarded as the new movement's third most prominent group, behind the Sex Pistols and The Clash, and there was already a feeling of excitement about them. Their lead singer, Dave Vanian, modelled himself on Bela Lugosi, the movie actor most famous for portraying Count Dracula in the horror films of the 1940s and 50s. He dressed entirely in black and wore white face paint with black circles around his eyes. His jet-black hair was swept back away from his forehead giving him an eastern European aristocratic appearance. All that was lacking were a pair of incisors and a sweeping cloak.

Bass player Ray Burns, recently re-christened Captain Sensible, was strutting around the stage in a pair of black wrap-around shades and his favourite Marc Bolan T-shirt. Bryan James, the group's guitarist and main songwriter had recently returned from living in Belgium where he played in a group called

Bastard. The group's fourth and undoubtedly most colourful character, their drummer Chris Miller, had also chosen to adopt an alter ego and was now operating under the moniker Rat Scabies.

The Damned opened their set with "Neat Neat Neat", a sulphate-induced three-minute explosion of guitars. The next song was "New Rose" and Dave gleefully informed the audience that it would be the group's first single for Jake Riviera's Stiff Records. They were barely into the song's opening verse, though, when Dave's microphone began crackling and cutting out altogether, but the group carried on regardless, until during a rendition of the Beatles' classic "Help", which the group had recorded for the B-side of the forthcoming single, guitarist Bryan was forced to bring an untimely halt to the proceedings when he broke a string. Unfortunately for The Damned, their singer hadn't brought along his transistor radio.

"Who's 'ere to listen to the music?" yelled Rat, as he leapt out from behind the drums. He prowled around the stage, encouraging the audience to throw things at him, but soon tired of this and began to beat out a staccato drum pattern on Sensible's guitar.

Sid and his fellow Banshees, Sioux and Steve, were watching The Damned from the bar area as the group resumed its set with a cover of Iggy & The Stooges' "Feel Alright". Sid and the others had resorted to their more familiar roles as fans of the new music and were dressed accordingly, though they were still basking in their newly acquired fame and were even considering the possibility of doing some more gigs, mainly at the behest of Nils Stevenson, who was still sounding sincere in his enthusiasm for the Banshees' debut performance. Nils had hoped to get Malcolm involved, but the Sex Pistols' manager, although impressed with the Banshee's courage and attitude, was somewhat less diplomatic and suggested that Nils' time would be better spent on helping Subway Sect.

"The Damned are shit!" shouted Sid, turning away from the stage, having grown tired of the group's pantomime theatrics. His two friends were in total agreement, but before they had a chance to respond Sid suddenly drained his beer glass and hurled it towards the group on stage. Fortunately, the projectile failed to reach its intended target; it did however strike a supporting pillar and the flying glass cut several people, including Dave Vanian's girlfriend.

The Damned's frontman leapt from the stage and charged into the audience in a desperate attempt to find the culprit, though he quickly abandoned the search and rushed over to check on the seriousness of the injury to his girlfriend before returning to the microphone. Vanian was seething with anger and although he and the rest of the group continued playing, the fun had clearly gone out of the performance.

As a result of Sid's foolish behaviour three people suffered severe cuts and were in urgent need of medical attention. Rumours soon spread through the excitable crowd that Vanian's girlfriend had a piece of glass stuck in her eye. This was the sort of thing one might have expected down at Stamford Bridge or Millwall on a Saturday afternoon, but not in the sedate surroundings of a

London jazz club and Mr Hunter, the Club's owner, joined The Damned on stage and warned the audience that he would be forced to terminate the festival if any more glasses were thrown. He also informed the subdued crowd that Ron Watts, apart from calling for an ambulance, had also alerted the police.

The entertainment resumed with the first of two sets from the Vibrators, who openly admitted that they didn't consider themselves to be a part of the punk scene, although the group had undergone a remarkable image transition since supporting the Sex Pistols. They began their set with "I Saw You Standing There", followed by a cover of the Rolling Stones' classic "Jumpin' Jack Flash".

By this time the police had arrived at the club and uniformed officers stood guard at the exit while plain-clothed detectives mingled with the audience in order to ask questions and take statements. At first nobody seemed to know for sure just exactly who had been responsible for throwing the glass, as most people had been watching the stage when the incident occurred. Eventually though, the detectives whittled down the list of potential suspects after several people came forward and pointed towards Sid, who was nonchalantly drinking at the bar.

The audience retreated from the stage, leaving a large empty space on the dancefloor where the two senior detectives stood conferring with several uniformed colleagues, together with Watts and Hunter. The Vibrators continued unabated while the officers, oblivious to what was going on behind them, consulted their notebooks. Satisfied that they had located their man, they signalled to the two officers standing at the bottom of the stairway before converging on the bar area. Sid, fully aware that he had been singled out, had little chance to react as he was dragged from his stool and bundled towards the exit.

Caroline Coon had been monitoring the situation and tried to intervene on Sid's behalf. She chose not to heed the police warning and followed them outside still protesting Sid's innocence. She was still arguing with the officers when the Black Maria pulled up outside the club and she threatened to use her journalistic connections to expose police brutality as Sid was thrown into the back of the van. Finally, one of the detectives lost patience and ordered Caroline's arrest as well.

Back inside the 100 Club, Chris Spedding joined The Vibrators on stage. Dressed in black leather jeans and matching jacket, he performed his former chart hit "Motorbikin'". The Damned's Captain Sensible also decided to join in the fun and leapt up on stage to help out with the choruses. For the grand finale The Vibrators played a pumped-up version of Jerry Lee Lewis' "Great Balls Of Fire", before ending their second set with Chubby Checkers' "Let's Twist Again".

The next and last group to come on stage was The Buzzcocks from Manchester. They had improved greatly since their previous performance in London when they supported the Sex Pistols at the Screen On The Green in Islington. Singer Howard, who had dyed his hair bright orange for the show, announced to the audience that he was only in the group temporarily and didn't even enjoy being on stage, but The Buzzcocks put in a creditable performance;

guitarist Pete Shelley and bass player Steve Diggle combined with drummer John Mayer to provide the melodic thrust for Devoto's lyrics, which were cleverly thought-out observations on normal everyday life.

The songs, delivered in Devoto's tongue-in-cheek style, were short even by Punk standards, lasting no more than two or three minutes and with titles such as "Breakdown", "Orgasm Addict" and "Oh Shit". The group's final song and indeed the last song of the two-day festival was entitled "Boredom". Howard hunched at the front of the stage and held the microphone close to his face as he drove his message home. "Now I'm living in a movie, but it doesn't move me!" His eyes searched through the crowd as if he was hoping to find someone who could truly empathise with his feelings. His impassioned monologue was accompanied by Shelley's innovative two-note guitar solo. "You know me...I'm acting dumb!" Devoto paused for effect, allowing the atmosphere inside the club to slowly build as the music increased in tempo. "You know the scene...very humdrum!" He nodded his head in conjunction with the beat as if he was sharing some vital secret with those gathered at the front. "Boredom, boredom, boredom!" The last word was delivered as a statement on life rather than a lyric. He replaced the microphone and casually stepped from the stage. The show was over. Shelley removed his guitar and leant it against his amplifier, allowing the droning feedback to fill the room.

Sid and Caroline were taken to nearby Bow Street Police Station. The journalist was released without charge. Sid, however, was not so fortunate. Besides receiving a severe beating at the hands of the arresting officers he was sentenced to serve a custodial sentence at Ashford Remand Centre, where several years earlier Sex Pistol Steve Jones had served out a sentence.

Steve even accompanied Nils to visit Sid later, joking that he'd only done so in order to show Nils the way. Sid, although happy to see familiar faces, was suffering from depression at being incarcerated and was also having trouble sleeping. His moment of stupidity had not only landed him in Ashford but also resulted in all punk rock groups being banned from the 100 Club – including the Sex Pistols, despite the fact that they were performing in Cardiff at the time of the incident. The Sex Pistols were now banned from the Marquee, the Nashville Rooms, Dingwalls and the Rock Garden, as well as the 100 Club. It seemed that the whole of London was closing its doors to them.

CHAPTER
FIFTEEN

Nick Mobbs was sitting in his office at EMI's headquarters in Manchester Square in northwest London. A copy of the previous Friday's *Evening Standard* was lying on the cluttered desk before him. He was absentmindedly toying with a C90 cassette while contemplating what to do about the Sex Pistols.

He had been cajoled by Mike Thorne, a fellow employee at the company, into attending the Sex Pistols' showcase gig at the Screen On The Green Cinema at the end of August. Thorne had witnessed one of the group's early appearances at the 100 Club and had been championing them ever since. The night before Mobbs had travelled up to Doncaster in order to witness the group's performance at the Outlook Club, which was situated close to the town's railway station. This had been the third time that he had ventured out to watch the group playing live and while being appreciative of what the Sex Pistols were trying to achieve, he was still unsure as to the long-term prospects of signing the group to a company as prestigious as EMI.

Mobbs absentmindedly leafed through the pages of the *Evening Standard*, stopping when he reached the two-page feature on the 100 Club Punk Festival. He had attended the event and had to admit to being impressed by what he had seen, in terms of the enthusiasm and raw energy generated by both groups and fans alike. But he was still unconvinced that this raw energy, so easily created on stage, could be readily transferred onto vinyl. He'd already been in contact with Terry Slater over at EMI Publishing, who he knew was making overtures towards signing the Sex Pistols for a ten thousand pound advance against publishing rights. This did not, however, mean that EMI was prepared to offer the group a recording contract. For although they were branches of the same company, EMI Publishing and EMI's Record Division were two entirely independent entities and were housed in separate buildings.

Mobbs smiled wistfully as he tried to imagine his stiff-collared superiors at EMI working hand-in-hand with someone like Johnny Rotten. EMI saw itself as a traditional company with traditional values and Mobbs himself knew that he was viewed by some of his bosses as nothing more than a token gesture to represent the company's interests in the current pop trends. They were willing to make concessions by allowing Mobbs to wear denim jeans in the office and grow his hair beyond the length they considered to be acceptable, but Mobbs knew EMI could easily carry on regardless of what was happening in the current record market as the company was earning millions of pounds each year on the Beatles' back catalogue alone. His bosses were reluctant to invest thousands of pounds developing new acts, which might never be recouped, when they had such an easy means of revenue at their disposal. This head-in-the-sand philosophy seemed set to continue despite the fact that the group Queen, fronted by the flamboyant Freddie Mercury, had scored a massive hit with "Bohemian Rhapsody" at the beginning of the year. The song, despite being over five minutes in duration, had topped the British singles charts for seven weeks.

Mobbs removed his spectacles and gently rubbed his temples, then cleaned the lenses with his handkerchief before replacing them. He leaned forward and pressed the button releasing the intercom. "Show Mr. McLaren in would you please, Janet." He stood up and came out from behind his desk as the door opened. He had already been introduced to the Sex Pistols' colourful, if somewhat erratic, manager at the Screen On The Green and had been impressed with McLaren's style. "Good to see you again, Malcolm," he said, shaking hands. "Please, take a seat."

"Thank you," replied Malcolm, smiling politely as he settled himself into the chair placed on the opposite side of the desk. He was dressed in black leather jacket and trousers, a pair of black suede ankle boots and a very expensive looking polo neck sweater. Malcolm, whilst under the pretext of standing up in order to adjust his trousers, had strategically positioned one of the group's press packs, put together by Sophie Richmond and Jamie Reid, on Mobb's desk.

Mobbs returned to his own chair and sat observing the man sitting opposite and purposely ignored the press pack while he decided how best to handle the situation. "I've listened to the tape that you sent me," he said, gesturing towards the cassette on the desk, "but I'm not convinced that the Sex Pistols will work on vinyl."

"But surely that is just your own personal taste," replied Malcolm, sitting bolt upright in his chair. "I'm not asking you to like the group. What I am asking, is that you give the young kids who are into the Sex Pistols music the chance to go out and buy a record of their favourite group!" He slapped his hand down on top of the press pack in a subtle attempt to bring Mobbs" attention to the object. "If you're not prepared to do something for the kids, then the music industry is finished. It's all washed up. Over!" He leaned back in his chair awaiting Mobbs' reply.

"Oh I think the industry will survive," replied Mobbs, purposely keeping the condescension from his tone. Yet again he'd been impressed with Malcolm's spiel. But then, one would expect the manager of an up-and-coming pop group to try his best to promote his own act.

Malcolm threw his arms up in despair. "If you can't sign something that's new and right in front of your eyes, then you're living in the past!" Mobbs was about to object but Malcolm wasn't finished. "You might as well shut up shop and go home!" Malcolm's face was now almost as red as his hair. He sat back breathing heavily, then casually turned his attention towards some unseen blemish on his trousers. He dabbed a finger against his tongue and proceeded to rub at the imaginary spot, careful to avoid making eye contact with Mobbs.

Mobbs sat in silence for a few moments with his hands resting behind his head while he studied Malcolm who was still attending to his trousers. He knew deep down that what Malcolm was saying was true and that neither his nor the personal tastes of anyone else within EMI should be allowed to affect the way the company operated. If the company wanted to be recognised as a major force in modern music then it should be willing to take occasional risks. If EMI didn't sign the Sex Pistols then it was surely only a matter of time before one of their competitors did. He could still remember laughing at the news that someone had approached EMI and various other record companies peddling a tape hoping to secure a recording contact for a bunch of young tartan-clad Scottish misfits. The smile however had soon been wiped from his and many other faces when the Bay City Rollers, as the group was called, had gone on to sell millions of records worldwide.

"I'll still need to talk to my boss Bob Mercer," said Mobbs. "It won't be easy, but I promise you I'll do my best."

Malcolm walked out of the building's main doors and cast a curious eye towards the darkening skies before hailing a passing taxi. He now had two major labels interested in signing the Sex Pistols. Chris Parry, the head of Polydor Records, was very keen to get the group to put pen to paper and had even paid for the Sex Pistols to record some new demos at the company's own De Lea Studios later in the month. Malcolm glanced back towards Manchester Square as he clambered into the taxi. Now that EMI were finally showing interest there would be no contest. As far as he was concerned EMI was the only record company he wanted for the Sex Pistols, but he was still interested to see just how far Polydor would be willing to go in order to sign the group.

Photographer Bob Gruen was spending a couple of days in London before returning to his native New York after completing an assignment in Paris. He'd decided to delay his return to the Big Apple to catch up with friends and acquaintances living in the British capital. Gruen had met Malcolm during the Englishman's ill-fated previous venture into music management with The New York Dolls. In fact it had been The Dolls' former lead singer, David Johansen, who had given Gruen a magazine featuring an article on both SEX and the Sex Pistols, and the American had reacquainted himself with Malcolm before flying out to the French capital.

Malcolm had taken his friend to Louise's in Soho where they had whiled away the hours bringing each other up to speed on mutual friends living in the two cities. Gruen had also been introduced to Steve, Glen and Paul but any hopes the American had of getting some group photos of the Sex Pistols were sadly dashed because John had stayed at home nursing a sore throat.

The American had been taken aback upon first entering Malcolm's shop as he'd simply been unable to comprehend that anyone would actually want to be seen wearing the clothing on offer – let alone pay for it. A closer inspection during his subsequent visit had caused him to alter his opinion, although he strongly doubted that he'd be able to make use of the small gift that Malcolm had presented to him as a memento of his visit. Gruen had tried to picture himself walking through Times Square wearing a T-shirt bearing the image of a naked prepubescent boy smoking a cigarette and wondered how long he would last before he was either attacked or arrested.

Malcolm had invited his old friend to accompany him to a second evening's helping of relaxation within the sedate surroundings of the club on Poland Street. Gruen glanced around the dimly lit room. A row of large mirrors secured against the wall directly above the fitted seats gave the impression that the room was much bigger than it actually was. He spotted a few people that he'd met on his previous visit to the club and although he had forgotten most of the names he definitely remembered their haircuts. He smiled at Sue Catwoman as she strolled past him on her way to rejoin her friend who was sitting at a nearby table. There was also another Sue, but he remembered the girl telling him that she was now the singer in a group and was known as Siouxsie, using the same spelling as in the North American tribe of the same name. Gruen had thought that an afternoon in SEX had prepared him for anything, but he was still shocked to see that the girl was brazenly wearing a Nazi armband.

Malcolm ordered a round of drinks before guiding the American towards the corner table where Steve and John were sitting with Helen and another girl who introduced herself as Jo. The table was littered with near-empty glasses and discarded cigarette packets while the group's combined beer fund consisting of several one-pound notes lay on top of a soiled serviette. Steve was sitting in between the two girls wearing a brand-new T-shirt, which featured one of Malcolm's latest designs. Although Gruen himself felt slightly uncomfortable at having to look at the life-size print of a perfectly shaped pair of women's breasts, he couldn't help but be impressed by the way both girls seemed at ease with a garment that would set the feminist movement back a hundred years.

Gruen sat down in the chair directly facing John, who chose not to bother introducing himself and seemed far more interested in scrutinising the American's every move. It was almost as if he was studying a creature that he had heard and read about but was actually seeing for the first time. John was wearing his natty pink blazer and his beloved striped trousers. The black beret stylishly angled towards one side of his head was purchased during the group's trip to Paris.

"How's the throat?" asked Gruen, pointing towards the woolly scarf wrapped around John's throat.

"Fine," replied John, still eyeing the photographer intently.

"Malcolm thinks it would be a good idea for us to meet up for a photo shoot," he added, realising that John wasn't going to expand on his condition.

"When?" asked Steve, dumping his empty glass on the table.

"How about tomorrow?" asked Gruen, flitting glances between the two.

"You might as well come down and watch us rehearse," said Steve, offering the American one of his cigarettes.

"Sure, that's a great idea," replied Gruen, declining Steve's offer. "Malcolm says that I'll need to take a cab to someplace called Tin Pan Alley. Is there such a place?"

"Course there is," replied Steve, grinning at Gruen's bemused expression, "everyone's heard of it."

"So just how will I find you guys?" asked Gruen, leaning forward on his stool.

"Just tell the driver to stop when he hears a bloody tuneless racket!" said John, sneaking a quick glance at Steve.

"Can you sing, John?" asked Gruen, pointing towards the scarf again.

"Nah," replied Steve, cutting in before John had the opportunity to reply

"Oh right," said Gruen, nodding in understanding, "because of the throat."

"No," said Steve, feigning a look of concern.

"What then?"

"Because he just can't," yelled Steve, placing his arms around their two female companions.

Gruen hadn't needed to take John at his word in order to find the group's rehearsal room, but he did have to enquire at several different shops before finally securing directions.

"Do you wanna cup of tea?" Steve asked his guest reaching for the pan lying on top of the broken television set.

"Sure," replied Gruen, gazing around the tiny upstairs room that Steve called home.

"We ain't got any milk," said Steve, shrugging apologetically.

"Don't worry about it," replied Gruen, scanning the room for somewhere to sit.

"Just chuck that shit on the floor," said Steve, nodding towards the pile of dirty clothes on his bed.

Gruen gingerly picked up the clothes and placed them on a nearby chair that was already overloaded with dirty laundry.

"Won't take long," said Steve, crouching down in front of the stack of battered albums that were propped up by the side of a portable record player. "You know this lot, don't you?" he asked, holding up a copy of the New York Dolls" first album.

"Yeah," replied Gruen, nodding, "they're a great bunch of guys."

"Do you still see Thunders?"

"Sure, from time to time," replied Gruen, reaching over to pick up the album sleeve. "Actually I was with John the other day. We went for a drink in the village with Jerry Nolan and his girlfriend Nancy." The photographer had spent a lot of time with the outrageous Glam-rock outfit, taking hundreds of photographs of them both on and off stage. He'd had some great times with them and had been offered lots of different things – most of them illegal. Yet here he was with one of the Sex Pistols, the group that Malcolm had told him were similar in attitude and outlandish behaviour to The Dolls and all he'd been offered since his arrival had been a cup of tea.

They both turned towards the doorway as Paul and Glen came in to the room.

"All right," said Paul, nodding towards Gruen. "I see you've found us all right?"

"Yes, eventually," replied Gruen, smiling ruefully as he remembered his encounter with the Greek proprietor of Zeno's Books on Denmark Street. The American had spent a very exasperating ten minutes trying to make himself understood.

Once Paul and Glen had settled themselves down on the mattress beneath the window they helped Steve provide Gruen with a brief history of how the group had originally come together.

"So it's not just me that finds John difficult?" asked Gruen, after hearing Glen's account of when John had fled the stage during the gig at the 100 Club in March.

"How do you mean?" asked Glen.

"Last night at Louise's," replied Gruen, "the way he kept staring at me made me feel uncomfortable."

"He can be a right wanker at times," replied Steve.

"Excuse me?" said Gruen, frowning.

"He's a tosser," said Steve, grinning at the American's bewildered expression.

"A twat," said Paul, joining in the fun.

"He's a cunt!" said Steve.

"I think I understand what you guys are getting at," said Gruen, smiling. "English humour."

Gruen stood up and wandered over towards the far wall so that he could examine the posters advertising the group's gigs in West Runton and the more recent 100 Club Punk Festival.

"Are you guys playing any more shows?" he asked.

"Not for a couple of weeks," replied Glen, shaking his head. "We were supposed to be playing some gigs down in Devon and Cornwall, but they had to be cancelled because of John's throat."

"It's a pity you aren't playing while I'm in town," said Gruen, sitting back down on the bed almost knocking over the as yet untouched cup of tea. "I would have liked to have seen you guys playing in front of your own fans."

"You'll get your chance," replied Paul, "when we get to America."

"Are you guys coming to the States?" asked Gruen. "Malcolm never said anything about it."

"Well there's nothing planned," said Steve, grinning. "But we wouldn't mind playin' to all you cowboys."

Gruen picked up the copy of Sounds lying at the foot of Steve's bed and began leafing through the pages until he found Jonh Ingham's two-page feature on the 100 Club Punk Festival. "Malcolm did tell me that he was close to getting the group a record deal."

"Yeah," replied Glen. "It looks like we'll be signing to Polydor."

"Are they any good?"

"They're not bad," said Paul, nodding thoughtfully. "We're s'posed to be going into their studios to record some new demos."

The conversation was brought to a sudden halt as John entered the room.

"Fuckin' hell, it's freezin' out there!" he scowled, rubbing his hands together. He was wearing a dark blue suit that looked like it had just lost an argument with a lawnmower. There were rips and tears on both the jacket and trousers, which John had safety-pinned back together again. The jacket had also received John's usual treatment and was festooned with small chains, crucifixes and badges. There was even one featuring the club crest of his beloved Arsenal FC on the lapel.

"Maybe we could get some pictures now that you're all here," said Gruen, reaching down to retrieve the camera from his travel bag.

"Fuckin' hell!" shouted John, turning away from the portable hotplate that Malcolm had provided for Steve and Nils' cooking needs. "I've only just got here!"

When John was eventually coaxed into relinquishing his monopoly on the hotplate, Gruen had the group pose at the bottom of the stairway leading into their rehearsal room before going out onto Denmark Street for some outdoor shots.

"Come on, Bob!" yelled Steve, blowing into his cupped hands. "I'm freezin' my Max Walls off." He was shivering uncontrollably despite having purposely worn his thick woolly jumper, but the other three were suffering far worse from the effects of the arctic wind gusting down the street as they all were wearing nothing more substantial than their jackets.

"Just a couple more? OK guys?" replied Gruen, stepping forward to get a close-up of John. He had spent countless hours photographing some of the world's most famous rock stars, yet had rarely seen anyone quite so photogenic as the Sex Pistols' frontman.

Once Gruen was satisfied with the street shots he suggested taking some action shots of the group rehearsing. It was just as cold inside as it had been outside, but at least they were now protected from the freezing wind. The photographer used up his last roll of film taking shots of the group while they ran through several of their own compositions before ending with "Substitute", which they knew to be one of the American's favourite songs. It was only when Gruen put his camera away that he noticed that Glen's Fender Precision bass guitar had only the D and G strings remaining. This was pretty amazing considering the rumours that he'd heard about the group not being able to play their instruments. Most of the musicians he'd worked with would have struggled to name the notes on the bottom two strings let alone have to rely on them to actually play a full song.

Malcolm arrived unexpectedly in an agitated state and it was obvious that something was weighing on his mind. "Come on!" he said, clapping his hands together, "there's no time to lose!"

"Why?" asked Glen, placing his bass guitar on its stand. "Are we going somewhere?"

"Nils is outside in the car," replied Malcolm, pointing towards the doorway. "We're going to sign the contract."

"What?" gasped Steve, staring at Malcolm in disbelief. "We're goin' to Polydor now?"

"No boy, we're not," replied Malcolm, a furtive smile spreading across his face. "We're going to Manchester Square – the home of EMI Records!"

Malcolm, Nils, the four members of the group and a rather bemused Bob Gruen arrived at EMI's head offices where they were ushered up to the spacious offices of Nick Mobbs' immediate superior Bob Mercer. Malcolm's solicitor and Glitterbest co-director was already waiting for them. Mobbs, aided and abetted by Mike Thorne, had berated Mercer until he'd agreed to arrange a meeting with EMI's chairman, Sir John Reid, in order to put forward their reasons why the company should sign the Sex Pistols.

Despite having strong reservations of his own Hall finally relented and gave Mobbs permission to have a provisional contract drawn up which was then delivered to Fisher's office for the solicitor's perusal. Fisher made several changes to the document before returning it to Manchester Square. The contract was for an initial two-year period with two further one-year options, which could only be taken up by the company. In return, the Sex Pistols would receive a forty thousand pound, non-returnable advance against future royalties, which under clause 17 was to be paid directly to Glitterbest. Twenty thousand pounds would be paid on completion of the signing and the remaining twenty thousand would be paid in twelve months time on 8 October 1977. EMI also agreed to pay reasonable recording costs, which would be deductible against future royalties. The Sex Pistols and Glitterbest would have the final approval on all record sleeve designs.

Mercer gave a somewhat stilted and unconvincing welcoming speech, which was hardly surprising seeing that he planned to have as little to do with the group as possible. One of the girls from the secretarial pool came in with a tray of glasses and proceeded to hand them out while Mercer begrudgingly opened the champagne. Malcolm had invited Gruen along so that the American could take the official signing photograph and he hurriedly ushered everyone over towards Mercer's desk. "Come on, boy!" he shouted, gesturing for Nils to join them. "Get in the picture."

Nils shook his head and walked out of the room. He'd realised that Malcolm wasn't going to fulfil his promise of giving him an equal partnership in managing the Sex Pistols. He couldn't believe that Malcolm would expect him to continue with the mundane day-to-day stuff while leaving himself to bask in the group's reflected glory. The final straw had been when Malcolm had invited Fisher, a solicitor with no previous knowledge of the music business or any interest in the Sex Pistols other than financial gain. Malcolm, as usual, had gone where the money was and fuck everyone else.

After dropping Malcolm and the others off at Denmark Street, Nils drove over to Bromley to ask Sue Ballion and Steve Bailey if they required any help with their group.

The Sex Pistols moved into Lansdown Studios in Holland Park in order to record their first single for EMI. The record company had originally wanted "Pretty Vacant" to be the group's first release, but had relented when the group insisted that the first single must be "Anarchy In The UK". Although Lansdown Studios was somewhat smaller and less well equipped than Majestic Studios where they had recorded their first demos with Chris Spedding, it was a vast improvement on their own cramped rehearsal room behind Denmark Street. EMI had also bowed to the group's wishes that Dave Goodman be allowed to produce the single even though they had been highly critical of his previous attempt at recording the group.

Malcolm arrived later that morning with Jamie Reid and the two men seemed as excited as the group themselves at having reached the stage where they would be actually making a record that would be available for people to buy in the shops. Malcolm peered through the glass partition that separated the control room from the musicians; he was puzzled as to why Steve was wandering around the studio in his bare feet as if he was about to go paddling rather than attending to the serious business of recording a record. He also noticed that Steve was wearing yet another new T-shirt from his shop, this one featured the artwork used for the posters promoting the Sex Pistols shows in Paris. Malcolm had superimposed the image of the naked youth smoking a cigarette onto a solid imprint of the body of Glen's bass guitar. "You know, it's amazing just how many of my T-shirts that boy has," he said, stabbing a finger towards Steve, "and I've yet to see him pay for one!"

He signalled for Goodman to call a halt to the proceedings and took a seat next to Reid as John and the others stepped into the control room. "I've had a call from Chris Parry over at Polydor," he announced as soon as they were seated. "I've given him the bad news."

"How did he take it?" asked Glen.

"Well, let's just say he wasn't very happy," replied Malcolm, grinning. "He was actually calling me to find out when we could sign the contract."

"How much was he offering anyway?" asked Paul.

"Does it matter?" asked Malcolm.

"Yeah," said Glen, leaning forward on his stool, "go on, tell us!"

"Twenty thousand."

"Is that all?" said Steve, shaking his head. "Bollocks to that!"

"Send The Clash round," said John, mischievously.

"How's it going in there?" asked Malcolm, changing the subject.

"Not bad," replied Goodman, pausing briefly to consult his notes, "but I still don't think I've found the sound I'm looking for."

"It sounded all right to me," said Glen, glancing towards the engineer. He was fed up with playing the same song over and over just because Goodman was hoping to capture the "live sound" that he'd experienced at various Sex Pistols gigs up and down the country. Goodman had suggested that Glen, Paul and Steve play the tune at different tempos, firstly by slowing it down and then speeding it up, which, as everyone agreed, had sounded terrible. Malcolm had tried to inspire the group by spraying "Anarchy" onto the glass partition with a can of shaving foam, but this had only resulted in a shaving foam fight between himself, Jamie Reid and John.

As with all recording sessions, the musicians had to record the tune's basic pattern before the singer could even begin to start recording his vocals. John had been standing around all day with nothing to do except watch and wait, while the others grew increasingly frustrated at their failure to record the track. The group spent an unprecedented four days holed up inside Lansdown Studios, unable to record a three and a half-minute pop song. Bob Mercer and the rest of the powers-that-be over at EMI headquarters were beginning to wonder whether they had made a big mistake in allowing Mobbs to sign the Sex Pistols.

▭ ▭ ▭ ▭

"Let's have a look," said Mick, making a grab for Alan's copy of *Sounds*, which was lying open at pages twenty-two and twenty-three. "Welcome to the Rock Special", announced Jonh Ingham's banner headline, which ran across the top of both pages. It seemed that the journalist also had reservations about calling the new music Punk.

"How the fuck do you pronounce that?" asked Alan, moving aside to allow Mick the chance to read Ingham's account of the 100 Club Punk Festival from the previous month.

"It's probably Suzi," replied Mick, studying the word "Siouxsie", which lay directly above Alan's paint-smeared fingernail. "You know, as in Suzi Quatro?"

"And how do you know that?" asked Alan, giving Mick a strange look.

"Because the Sioux were a tribe of North American Indians," replied Mick. "They defeated General Custer at the Battle of the Little Big Horn." He had loved to re-enact the famous battle with his collection of Timpo plastic toy soldiers when he was younger.

"Oh yeah, I remember now," said Alan, sarcastically. "It was one-nil weren't it?"

"Two-one," replied Mick, smirking. "Crazy Horse got the winner in extra-time."

"Listen to this!" said Alan, turning his attention back to the article. "There's someone here calling himself 'Sid Vicious'."

"Fuck off," said Mick, scanning the page to see where Alan was looking.

"Look, it's there," said Alan, pointing towards a blurred photograph of Siouxsie and The Banshees. "It says here that he's their drummer."

"Siouxsie And The Banshees is a great name for a group," said Mick, as he continued reading the article.

"It mentions SEX," said Alan, "the shop they were telling us about."

"Have you still got that business card?" asked Mick.

"Yeah," replied Alan, nodding, "why?"

"Because I wouldn't mind going down to London to have a look," said Mick, "and I know that Paul's up for it."

"How is Paul anyway?" asked Alan. "I haven't seen him since the Lodestar."

"Oh, he's all right," replied Mick. "He's trying to get me to join his group."

"And will you?"

"Might do," said Mick, thoughtfully.

Mick continued reading the article while Alan nipped out to the local shop. The two were working at St John & Augustine's primary school in Accrington while the pupils were on their mid-term break. "It says here that you can buy trousers with zips in them at SEX," he said, turning around as Alan returned with his dinner.

"Mine have already got a zip in," said Alan, frowning, "so I can have a piss."

"Yeah, but it doesn't go right round the arse, does it?" replied Mick, grinning. "It also says they sell bondage suits, whatever they are when they're at home."

"I'll ring the shop on Saturday morning," said Alan, taking a bite out of his sandwich, "to see if I can find out when the Sex Pistols are next playing in London, then we can make a weekend of it."

"I'm definitely getting one of them Anarchy shirts," said Mick, unpacking his home-made lunch. "It says in there that they're hand-painted."

"No need to waste good money on a shirt that's hand-painted," said Alan, casually.

"Why not?" asked Mick, his sandwich poised in front of his mouth.

"Just bring one of your shirts with you tomorrow and I'll happily slap some emulsion on it for you," replied Alan, smirking.

"Did you read that bit about the Bromley Contingent or whatever they're called?" asked Mick, ignoring Alan's last comment.

"Yeah," replied Alan, enviously. "It sounds like they follow the Sex Pistols everywhere."

"So does that make us punk rockers?" asked Mick, grinning.

Their conversation was brought to an abrupt halt as their boss George appeared in the doorway looking as if he was chewing a piss-soaked thistle.

"All right, George," said Mick, apprehensively, as George strode towards them.

"Don't bloody all right me!" shouted George, pointing back towards the doorway. "Come with me."

"What's up?" asked Alan, glancing towards Mick.

"What's up?" shouted George, his face growing an angry shade of purple. "What the fuck's that up there?"

"Oh shit," said Mick, pursing his lips.

The school had once served as a church and still had the original latticed wooden beams running the length of the ceiling. Mick had spent the morning on the erected scaffold applying a thick coat of white emulsion undercoat to the ceiling to cover the myriad cracks. He had soon grown bored with the task and it was during one of his unscheduled breaks that he'd noticed that there were seven latticed squares running across the width of the ceiling – the same number of letters that made up the word Anarchy. In an attempt to make the job more enjoyable Mick had spelt out the Sex Pistols' song title across the whole of the ceiling then proudly displayed his very own Michelangelo creation to Alan who'd been working in another part of the building.

Unbeknown to Mick, the pale blue eggshell paint that he'd applied as the final coat wasn't thick enough to hide the brush strokes from his earlier masterpiece. What couldn't be seen from the top of the scaffolding was all too evident to someone standing at ground level.

"This used to be my bloody church!" yelled George, almost foaming at the mouth. "I were a bloody altar boy here!"

"I'll do it again," said Mick, purposely avoiding eye contact with Alan, who was standing behind George, grinning like a loon.

"Too bloody right you'll do it again!" shouted George, looking from one apprentice to the other. "And in your own time too!" He turned away towards the door before looking back at the two lads. "Jesus Christ, I don't know what's happened to you two since you saw that bloody group on telly. I really don't!"

On Tuesday 12 October the Sex Pistols took a much-needed break from recording their first single in order to play at Dundee Technical College. This was the group's first gig north of the border and nobody was willing to travel all the way up to Scotland in the back of a market trader's dilapidated transit van. Steve had volunteered to travel up to Scotland with Dave Goodman and his partner Kim with all the equipment. Now that he'd had a taste of life in a recording studio he was interested to know all about the recording process and spent the entire journey pumping the two engineers for information.

John, Paul and Glen took the more comfortable option of travelling by train. It was the first time that any of them had seen the English countryside and they were thoroughly enjoying themselves. The boys even had the luxury of a whole compartment to themselves, for none of their fellow passengers seemed willing to sit with John.

"Now I know what it's like to be a fuckin' goldfish!" he said, nodding towards the two young children with their faces pressed to the glass window.

"Have either of you two heard the news about Malcolm?" asked Glen, turning away from window.

"He's dead," said John, flatly.

"No," replied Glen, giving John a funny look, "he's back with Vivienne."

"So I was right the first time," said John, turning to face Paul. "He is dead."

"Do you wanna hear this or not?" asked Glen, growing impatient with John's antics.

"If we must!" replied John, scowling.

"It's not definite," said Glen, nodding furtively. "It's just a feeling."

"Then see a doctor," added John, before returning his gaze to the seemingly endless stretch of rolling fields outside their window.

"What makes you so sure?" asked Paul, frowning at Glen.

"Well," said Glen, leaning forward in his seat, "I went round to the flat on Bell Street to see him and Helen went real quiet like and said he wasn't there."

"Well done, Sherlock!" scoffed John. "In case you've forgotten, Malcolm's got a fuckin' office in Dryden Chambers."

"I tried there first, didn't I?" retorted Glen. "But Sophie was acting very mysterious and she told me that she hadn't seen him for days!"

"That still don't prove anythin'," said Paul, remembering how he had been the first one to break the news of Malcolm's split with Vivienne.

"Ahh," replied Glen, wagging a finger in front of the others. "Your mate Sid works in the shop now, doesn't he?"

"So?" asked John, shaking his head. "What's that got to do with anything?"

"Well, I was talking to him the other day and he let it slip that he has to wait outside the shop until they come and open up in the morning." He glanced at Paul and John. "Don't you see? Sid said 'they'. *They* open the shop!"

"So they open up together," said Paul, chuckling. "It is their shop!"

"But why should they arrive together when she's still at the flat in Clapham and Malcolm's supposedly living with Helen on Bell Street?" asked Glen, leaning back in his seat. "The two flats are miles apart."

"Fuck me!" exclaimed John. "They're a fuckin' odd pair, those two."

"It makes sense though, when you think about it," said Paul. "She did come to Paris with us an' Helen didn't, and they have got a kiddie."

When John returned from paying a visit to the toilets situated at the end of the carriage, he noticed that someone had been to the buffet car as there were three plastic cups of tea on the small tray positioned under the window.

"Ughh, this tastes fuckin' awful!" he grimaced, placing the cup back down. "Has one of you pissed in this?"

"It'd be an improvement, wouldn't it?" replied Glen, shaking his head in disgust.

"We were just sayin," said Paul. "Your mate Sid's calmed down a bit lately."

"Yeah," agreed John, nodding. "His little holiday in Ashford Remand Centre seems to have given him a fresh outlook on life."

"He's enjoying working in the shop," added Glen.

"And he's got his little group together," said John, contemplating a second assault on his cup of tea.

"What, he's still with the Banshees?" asked Paul.

"Oh no," replied John, shaking his head. "He's playing with his new girlfriend, Viv." He grinned at his unintended double entendre. "You know what

I mean?"

"What're they called?" asked Paul.

"I've christened them the Flowers Of Romance," replied John, chuckling to himself. "I have no intention of ever playing the song again, so they can have it."

"It's a good name for a group," agreed Glen. "What are they like?"

"Fuckin' awful!" said John, grimacing. "It's all 'one-two-three-four, let's go' nonsense, but my best mate's the singer so I'll do what I can to help."

The following weekend the Sex Pistols, along with Dave Goodman, moved into Wessex Studios in Highbury, North London. They had been asked to leave Lansdown Studios on account of the graffiti that had mysteriously appeared on the walls during their time there. Any thoughts that the change in surroundings would also bring about a change in fortunes were quickly dispelled as Goodman wasted reel upon reel of expensive tape trying to capture the group's live energy.

To relieve the monotony, they recorded several other songs such as "No Fun" and "Substitute". The engineer even suggested an impromptu jamming session in an attempt to alleviate the growing tensions.

"What?" gasped John, from the seclusion of the sound booth.

"They want to do 'Johnny B. Goode'," repeated Goodman, through the intercom.

"God," sneered John, in disbelief. "I don't know it!" Suddenly the opening bars of the Chuck Berry classic came blasting through into his headphones. He began ad-libbing by throwing in the odd lines that he did know before giving up altogether. "Hey Steve, I know. Let's do 'Roadrunner'!" he shouted out during a lull in the music but the others ignored the request and carried on playing the tune. "Stop it!" yelled John, angrily. "It's fuckin' awful. Torture!" Steve finally relented and began playing the chugging chords to the Jonathon Richmond song. "I don't know the words," said John, chuckling to hide his embarrassment. "Someone shout out how it starts."

"One, two, three, four, five, six, seven, eight," Paul shouted out in time to the beat. "'Roadrunner, rock on.'"

"I can't hear you, Paul," said John, trying to adjust his headphones while the others meandered their way through the tune. "Do we know any...?" He waited until the others had finally stopped playing. "Do we know any other people's songs that we could do?"

Various people called in at the studios to see how things were going and to offer their opinions, but nobody seemed to be able to say: "that's it, that's the one". Glen was convinced that they were playing the tune correctly and that the problem lay in the inexperience of their engineer. The only one who didn't seem fazed by the whole saga was Steve; he was thoroughly enjoying himself trying out all the different guitars that belonged to the studio.

Glen removed his bass and headed over towards the Bechstein grand piano on the other side of the room; he had studied piano as a child and could still pick out a tune. At first Steve was annoyed at the interruption but after a while he became more and more interested in the tune that Glen was experimenting with.

"What's that you're playin'?" he asked, walking over to the piano.

"Dunno," replied Glen, shrugging. "It sounds all right though, doesn't it?"

"Can you show me the chords on this?" asked Steve, picking up the Gibson Flying V guitar he'd been playing earlier.

"Yeah, no problem," replied Glen, getting up from the piano. He slipped the guitar over his head and started to pick out the chords to the tune. "Right, I've got it now," he said looking up at Steve. "It starts off with an A Flat then slide up one fret to A Diminished..."

"Don't gimme all that bollocks!" snapped Steve, impatiently. "Just show me how it goes."

"Philistine," said Glen, shaking his head. He should have known that it was a waste of time trying to show Steve anything different. He only really liked to play the basic chords, which gave him a much heavier sound. Steve strummed the chords until he had familiarised himself with the basic pattern while Glen went to retrieve his own guitar from its stand. He was about to start accompanying Steve when John came rushing over. He was clutching a pencil and a sheet of paper.

"I can't believe it!" he yelled, sitting down on the piano stool.

"What can't you believe?" asked Glen, frowning.

"I wrote this song ages ago, well it's more of a poem really," replied John, excitedly, "but it fits in with what you're playin'." He held up the sheet of paper upon which he'd scribbled a few lines of a song. "It fuckin fits!" he said leaping up.

"Well, let's hear it," said Steve, as he began strumming the chords to the new tune.

"It's called 'No Future'," said John, pointing to his scribbled lyrics. "Keep playin' and I'll come in when I'm ready." Paul joined them and sat down on the recently vacated stool.

"'God Save the Queen, the fascist regime. It made you a moron, potential H-bomb'." John nodded his head in time to an imaginary beat that Paul would have otherwise provided. "'God save the Queen, she ain't no human bein'. There is no...'" He realised that the others had stopped playing. "Why have you stopped?" he asked.

"Let's have a look at those lyrics," said Glen, holding out his hand. "Fuck me, John!" he gasped, looking from John then back to the set of scribbled lyrics he was holding. "They're a bit strong."

"They're meant to be!" replied John, angrily. He had come up with the idea for the lyrics several months earlier while eating his dinner at his parents' council flat in Finsbury Park. His father had been watching a television programme about the planned celebrations for Queen Elizabeth II's Silver Jubilee, which would take place in June 1977. With the opening line of the

British national anthem running through his head, he pushed aside his empty dinner plate and set about writing his own tribute to the reigning monarch's twenty five years as sovereign. He had then stored away his poem believing that he would never have the chance to use it with the group, as there was no set pattern or a recognisable chorus.

Glen looked towards Steve and Paul but quickly saw that he wasn't going to get any help from them and he really didn't want another argument with John. He wasn't the only one to have noticed how John seemed to be going out of his way in order to pick a fight with him, because Malcolm had mentioned it on several occasions, and had also told him what John had been saying behind his back. He shrugged his shoulders and handed the lyrics to Steve.

"Where's the chorus?" asked Steve.

"There isn't one," replied John, shaking his head. "I told you, I wrote it down in one go. It only took me about twenty minutes."

You do surprise me, thought Glen, resisting the temptation to voice his opinions.

"It needs a chorus, don't it Glen?" asked Steve.

"No, not really," replied Glen. He could feel John's eyes burning into the back of his head, but didn't bother to turn round.

The new song was the only productive thing to come out of their stay at Wessex Studios as Goodman had failed yet again to deliver the finished version of "Anarchy In The UK". Bob Mercer over at EMI was by now extremely concerned that the group had spent ten days trying to record three minutes of music, which certainly didn't bode well for the future. When one of EMI's staff, sent down to Wessex by Mercer, reported that he'd been attacked with buckets of water and refused admittance, he'd ordered Nick Mobbs to get down to the studio to find out what was happening.

The Christmas deadline was fast approaching and so far EMI had nothing to show for their troubles, not to mention the vast amounts of money being eaten up in wasted studio time. Mobbs sent Mike Thorne down to the studio so that he could listen to whatever rough mixes Goodman had to offer. After consulting with Glen, the EMI engineer remixed the tune and cut an acetate disc, which he then took back to Manchester Square. The record company rejected the Goodman acetate out of hand and insisted that the group would have to go back into the studio at the earliest opportunity, but this time with an engineer of their choice.

On the same day that the Sex Pistols returned to Wessex Studios to continue working on their first single, The Damned's debut single "New Rose" was released on Stiff Records. The producer EMI chose to replace Goodman at Wessex was Chris Thomas, who had worked with such notable acts as The Beatles and Pink Floyd. It had been Paul's suggestion to approach Thomas because of his work on several of Roxy Music's albums, although Thomas himself was somewhat less than enthusiastic about the proposal when Mike Thorne visited the producer's home to offer him the job.

The reason for Thomas's reluctance was that having witnessed the Sex Pistols' midnight performance at the Screen On The Green Cinema in August, he had been left far from impressed. But he had not counted on Thorne's persistence and finally relented and consented to the EMI man arranging a meeting between himself and the group to discuss the possibility of them working together.

The hastily arranged meeting took place at Thomas's home, where the producer first listened to the Goodman acetate version of "Anarchy In The UK" before being asked for his opinions on how to improve the track. Thomas, to the relief of all concerned, agreed to help the group, but time was running out for the Sex Pistols because EMI had scheduled Friday 26 November as the day of the single's release.

The first morning was spent setting up the group's equipment and the group's three musicians were amazed at how much time Thomas, with the help of Wessex's resident engineer Bill Price, spent on making sure that everything was just right. There was an attention to detail that had previously been missing, such as the placing of a metal flight case against Steve's amplifier, which, Price explained, would give a much harder edge to the guitar's sound. The engineer also placed a couple of ambient microphones in strategic positions to record all the peripheral sounds in the room, which Thomas intended to later mix together with the finished version to give it a fuller sound.

After lunch Steve, Glen and Paul took up what were by now their all too familiar positions inside the studio's recording room. John hadn't bothered to come down with the rest of the group because he had no intention of spending any more time sitting around with nothing to do. Thomas instructed the three to play the basic rhythm track five times from start to finish while he and Price manned the controls. They had barely started their third run through when Thomas signalled for them to stop.

"Now what?" asked Steve, removing his guitar.

"That should do it," replied Thomas, smirking at the "I Hate Pink Floyd" T-shirt that Steve was wearing. He wondered what his old friend Dave Gilmour, Pink Floyd's lead singer, would say if he knew that he was working with such people. "Come in and have a listen."

The three Sex Pistols filed into the control room and sat staring at one another in disbelief; they couldn't believe that someone was telling them the track was finished in ten minutes after previously spending ten whole days without success.

"You really think you've got it?" asked Glen, still not convinced by what Thomas was telling them.

"Sure," replied Thomas, smiling at Glen's startled expression. "I'm going to take the first half from the second take and splice it together with that last one you just did."

"Will that work?" asked Paul, looking slightly doubtful.

"It should do," replied Price, as he set about putting what he was saying into practice.

It took the experienced engineer less than five minutes to splice the two takes together and once this was done he returned to his seat at the mixing desk beside Thomas. At the end of the recording both men turned triumphantly towards the group.

"Well?" Thomas asked.

"The timing's out," said Paul, hesitantly, "on my snare drum." He noticed the look that passed between Thomas and Price and fully expected them to dismiss his claim, but surprisingly they remained silent and replayed the tape.

"You're right, Paul," said Thomas, giving the drummer an appreciative nod. "But not to worry. We can rig up a tape delay to double the snare pattern."

Price asked for total silence from everybody while they replayed the tape. "The timing is still slightly out at the beginning of the third verse," he said, stroking his chin, "but that's where we spliced the two takes together."

By the time John arrived later that afternoon the others were sitting on the couch drinking beer. "I s'pose you still ain't done it yet!" he scowled, removing his jacket and tossing it at Glen.

"Oh yes we have," replied Glen, batting the garment away from him. "We've finished. It's your turn now."

"You've finished?"

"We're ready to lay down the vocals, John," said Thomas from behind the mixing desk.

"Good job I came then," replied John, before following Bill Price through into the studio's sound booth. Thomas wanted to record John's vocals onto one track in order to save the remaining tracks for Steve's guitar overdubs. John's throat was still suffering from the effects of the lousy PA at the group's recent gig at Bogarts in Birmingham, where, yet again, he'd been forced to shout in order to make himself heard over the noise on stage. Thomas and Price spent half an hour or so coaching John on how to use tone rather than volume to get the best out of his lyrics before recording his vocals onto three separate tracks, which they then edited down onto a single track. By the time it came to actually mixing the finished version, Steve, Paul and Glen were all sound asleep upstairs leaving John, Bill Price and Chris Thomas down in the control room.

"That's it," beamed John, listening to the final mix. "That's our anthem!"

CHAPTER SIXTEEN

With the arrival of the cheque for ten thousand pounds for signing the group with EMI Publishing on 12 October, Malcolm had thirty thousand pounds of the record company's money and felt that he was now in a much stronger position to defend his corner. He had already won the first battle in regards to "Anarchy" being the group's first single and he and Reid had just returned from a meeting with Nick Mobbs at the company's head office in Manchester Square, where they had discussed the proposed artwork for the single. Malcolm, from his position as a director of Glitterbest had vetoed all the record company's ideas for sleeve design, as was his right as part of the contractual agreement.

Both he and Reid were vehemently opposed to the idea of the record company using a photograph of the Sex Pistols to promote the single. Not only did they consider the idea clichéd but they also wanted the group's identity to remain a mystery to the record buying public. Malcolm had come up with the idea of issuing the single in a plain black sleeve accompanied by a poster featuring Reid's design of a torn Union Jack held together with safety pins and paper clips.

It had been during the discussions with Mobbs that Malcolm had inadvertently learned that EMI was planning to release the Sex Pistols' debut single on their progressive rock label "Harvest", but Malcolm was having none of it and he told Mobbs straight. The Sex Pistols had signed a recording contract with EMI and it would say EMI on the label.

There had also been another reason for Malcolm's unannounced visit, which was to collect the completed registration forms to be sent to the Performing Rights Society. He had already made the boys aware that failure to do so could jeopardise any future royalty entitlements. Malcolm gave each form a cursory glance to make sure they had been filled in properly. He couldn't resist a wry smile on seeing the word "Rotten" scrawled in the pseudonym section on John's form. He was also impressed with the fact that Steve had managed to complete his own form because he knew that Steve had left school barely able to write his own name. But once Steve had started to see his name appearing in the music papers, he'd begun to make a genuine effort and with help from the others was making steady progress.

Satisfied that all the forms were in order Malcolm then proceeded to provide the group with an up-to-date detailed account of his efforts to try to organise a full scale UK tour to promote their debut single. Reid's friend Sophie Richmond, now acting as Malcolm's PA, had been given the responsibility of organising the tour itinerary, which included hotel bookings, coach and driver, tickets and promotional posters etc. She in turn had enlisted the help of Simon Barker who was also working in SEX.

Malcolm, meanwhile, had his own itinerary to attend to and was hoping to bring both The Ramones and Talking Heads over from New York while The Vibrators – together with Chris Spedding – would complete the tour billing. The Vibrators had recently signed to RAK Records, which was owned by Mickie Most, the man who had paid for the Sex Pistols' first recording session at Majestic Studios. So far, neither The Ramones nor Talking Heads had confirmed they would play on the tour, as there were disputes about who would actually headline the bill.

The stressful combination of trying to run a successful business, and manage a pop group while butting heads with a corporate giant such as EMI was beginning to have an effect on Malcolm. He had called in at the group's rehearsal room to inform them about the latest developments with the tour and had been hoping that his visit would be a brief one as there was a mountain of paperwork waiting for him on his return to 430 King's Road.

"Are you listening to me?" he snapped, glaring over towards John who was showing Paul an article that he'd spotted in the newspaper he'd been reading.

"Yeah, I'm listening," replied John, glaring defiantly at Malcolm. "I was just saying to Paul that maybe we should get Jimmy Carter to open up the shows for us."

"What are you talking about, boy?" gasped Malcolm, looking totally bewildered.

"Well he is a comedian, isn't he?" said John, chuckling to himself. He was referring to the US presidential election victory by the Democrat's candidate Jimmy Carter over the Republican candidate and current president Gerald Ford.

"The Republicans didn't have a chance after the Watergate scandal," said Glen, shaking his head.

"You're right there," said Reid, leaning across John so he could read the article. "Those fools actually pardoned Nixon, which is rather like admitting you're an accessory after the fact!"

"God only knows how Callaghan is going to work with a goddamned peanut farmer," said Malcolm, allowing himself to be drawn into the discussion. "As if we haven't got enough troubles."

"I know," replied John, turning the pages of the newspaper. "Have you seen this about the IMF as well?"

"Not more fuckin' bombings!" scowled Steve.

"They aren't terrorists, you oaf!" said John, sniggering at Steve's comment. "It's the International Monetary Fund. It would seem that not so 'Great' Britain has had to go cap in hand and apply for billions of dollars to try and keep the fuckin' country afloat." He tried his best to simplify his explanation but quickly realised that Steve only wanted the newspaper so that he could have another peek at the page-three girl. He was only interested in two things, the group and girls and not necessarily in that order.

"I do have a rather interesting piece of news myself," said Malcolm, pausing until he had everyone's attention. "I was going to wait until I had received confirmation but you may as well know now."

"Well spit it out then, you closet!" said Steve, hurling a pillow towards Malcolm.

"It seems that EMI are in negotiations with the BBC, as they are extremely keen to have the group appear on *Nationwide*."

"What?" said Glen, excitedly. "You mean playing in the studio?"

"Yes," replied Malcolm, nodding. "If all goes according to plan Mobbs says they're hoping to film you performing your new single on Thursday 11 November, which they will then broadcast the following evening."

"What's *Nationwide*?" asked Steve.

"*Nationwide*, Stephen!" explained Malcolm, "is the BBC's flagship programme on current affairs. It's broadcast five nights a week after the six o'clock news, even you must have heard of it!"

"I don't watch telly," scowled Steve.

"Only because it's fucked!" said John, glancing towards the decrepit television set standing against the wall.

"They're doing a feature on punk rock," continued Malcolm, grimacing at his use of the word punk. And naturally they want you on the show as the media regard the Sex Pistols as being the leaders of the so-called movement."

"Oh right," said Steve, jumping up from his bed after Paul had kindly explained which TV programme Malcolm had been referring to. "I'm gonna shag Sue Lawley!"

"You most certainly will not!" cried Malcolm, his face frozen in horror.

Mick, Paul and Alan were travelling down to London on the overnight National Express coach after hearing about the Sex Pistols show at the Notre Dame Hall in Leicester Square on Monday 15 November. Alan had learned about the gig after contacting SEX to see if there was any possibility of purchasing the clothes by mail order. The three youths were far too excited to sleep and were passing the time discussing the Sex Pistols' TV performance on *Nationwide* the previous Friday.

All three of them had undergone a serious transformation of their appearance since attending the Sex Pistols' Lodestar gig. Alan and Paul had both paid a visit to the barbers to get themselves a punk rock haircut, while Mick had gone one step further and hacked off his long curly brown locks with his mother's home-care cutting comb. They had spent the previous Saturday afternoon rummaging through the piles of second-hand clothing in the local Oxfam shop on Warner Street in Accrington. Each of them bought an outfit comprising an old-fashioned jacket, straight-leg trousers and various granddad shirts, which they then set about tearing up and pinning back together with safety pins. Mick was also wearing a pair of original 1950s brothel creepers, which had been given to him by his Uncle Vincent, who had been a teddy boy in his youth.

"Did you see John's face when that woman asked him if he was happy with being called a punk?" asked Mick, chuckling.

"I thought she had said 'pump rock', at first," said Paul.

"I'll give you pump rock!" replied Alan, as he lifted himself up out of his seat and farted.

The coach journey, which seemed to have lasted forever due to the number of scheduled stops the coach had made in order to pick up more passengers, was almost at an end. The only highlight had been when the coach had pulled in for a twenty-minute break at the Blue Boar Services at Watford Gap. When the lads from Lancashire had entered the building they could see that the place was utterly deserted apart from the odd long-distance lorry driver and a handful of their fellow passengers. Mick and Alan had gone straight to the restaurant while Paul stopped off to pay a much-needed visit to the Gents. The two were sitting at a table near the windows nursing cups of coffee watching Paul as he came shuffling through the doors. This was the 'graveyard shift', the time when the cleaning staff took advantage of the respite in trade to mop the restaurant floor. One of the cleaners had positioned several plastic chairs across the floor forming a walkway to the self-service counter should anyone require refreshments while she got on with her task. Paul, in his zombied state, was oblivious to all of this and casually pushed the chairs to one side before heading straight towards his friends. It was only when the poor woman screamed at the trail of dirty footprints on her nice clean tiles that he realised anything was wrong. Needless to say the three of them beat a hasty retreat back to the coach with the cleaner's thick Irish brogue still ringing in their ears.

With their journey almost at an end there was little point in trying to get some sleep and there was nothing of interest to see on the deserted London roads on the other side of the window.

"I went to see *One Flew Over The Cuckoo's Nest*, last week," said Mick, wiping a hand over his eyes to try to stay awake.

"What did you think of it?" asked Alan, chuckling at the memory of when he'd seen the film a couple of weeks earlier.

"Oh, it's brilliant," replied Mick. "I nearly pissed myself when they were playing basketball."

"What was the loony called?" asked Paul, leaning forward to join in with the conversation.

"They were all loonies," said Alan, grinning. "It's set in a fuckin' lunatic asylum!"

"Would you mind keeping your language down!" said the woman sitting opposite, looking at Alan as if he was something her cat had regurgitated.

"That's some bad hat, Harry," said Paul, glancing up at her felt trimmed bonnet.

"What?" gasped Mick, giggling at the woman's blank expression.

"What's that off?" asked Paul, leaning back in his seat dismissing the woman completely. "You wanna talk films? Tell me what film that line's from."

"I've no idea," replied Mick, still chuckling at the woman's obvious discomfort. "Give us a clue."

Paul began slowly humming the theme tune to the film in question, which brought even more bemused glances from those sitting around them.

"*Jaws!*" said Mick, nodding. "Classic film."

"Are you serious?" asked Alan, frowning at his two companions. "It's about a rubber fish!"

"They used a real shark when Hooper's in the cage!" said Paul, defiantly.

"You go in the cage," said Mick, imitating Robert Shaw's portrayal of Quint from the film, "cage goes in the water."

"You go in the water," said Paul, joining in the re-enactment, "shark's in the water – our shark." He was so engrossed in talking about his favourite film that he even began singing the next line from the script. "Farewell an' a do to you fair Spanish ladies..."

"Farewell an' a do to you ladies of Spain..." added Mick, helping out with the harmony. They both stopped abruptly, realising that they had attracted the attention of every passenger on the coach.

"I reckon you two would be right at home in that lunatic asylum you mentioned earlier," said the bald-headed man sitting in the row behind.

The coach finally pulled into London's Victoria Station at just after 6 a.m. It was still dark outside and the surrounding shops and cafés had yet to open their doors, so the three lads headed for the station's waiting room to seek refuge from the cold. They remained there for an hour or so before finally venturing out onto the capital's streets and within twenty minutes were merrily tucking into a hearty breakfast in a burger bar. After breakfast they set off looking for the nearest tube station with Mick acting as their unofficial tour guide – the reason being that he was the only one of them to have previously visited the city, although this had been several years ago and with his parents so it really was a case of the blind leading the blind.

Their intended destination was the shop on the King's Road but Mick was unable to locate a station of that name on the map and spent several minutes wandering around until he procured the assistance of a station guard. They walked out of the Sloane Square tube station, which was situated across the road from the opening to the legendary thoroughfare. They had sought further assistance from the guard who had collected their tickets but he had been unable to help as the only 'sex' shops he knew about were in Soho.

The road seemed to stretch for miles and it was pretty obvious that they weren't going to find number 430 any time soon. They spent the next hour making their way along the road, stopping occasionally to study the imaginative window displays.

"You can fuck this for a game of soldiers," said Alan, planting himself down on a wooden bench. "My feet are killing!"

"I think you're right," agreed Mick, as he and Paul sat down on either side of him. "Let's get a taxi."

They stood waiting by the side of the road, waving at any black cab that came past, but they all seemed to be occupied.

"Here's one," shouted Paul, flagging down the vehicle. "How much to SEX?" he asked the driver.

"It's a shop," added Mick, quickly noticing the driver's wary look. "Number 430."

"Two quid," replied the driver, flatly.

"Two quid!" cried Alan, shaking his head in disbelief. "I could buy a bloody taxi back home for that."

"Look at that!" yelled Paul, excitedly pointing towards the large pink letters denoting the name of Malcolm's shop.

"Some right wierdos go in there," said the taxi driver, accepting his fare. "You'll be right at home, mate!"

"You go first," said Mick, giving Paul a gentle shove towards the shop door.

There were several young people inside the shop; some were casually examining the clothing on the rails while others stood around listening to the tune blasting out from the jukebox in the corner.

"I've never seen anything like this," gasped Mick, gazing at the sheets of pink and black rubber that were draped down from the ceiling.

"I've never seen anything like her, either," whispered Alan, staring open-mouthed at Jordon. She was standing in front of the surgical bed wearing a black rubber dress, fishnet stockings and a pair of black spider boots. "I wouldn't mind gettin' her on that bed, would you?" He quickly lowered his voice as Jordon headed towards them.

Normally Jordon would leave the prospective customers alone, but she decided the three new arrivals looked slightly overwhelmed by their surroundings. "Do you need any help, boys?" she asked, smiling cheerfully.

"I want one of them!" said Mick, pointing towards the Anarchy shirt that Simon Barker was wearing. "How much are they?"

"Twenty-five pounds," replied Jordon, chuckling at Mick's shocked expression. "Where are you boys from then?"

"Lancashire," replied Alan. "Are you the girl I spoke to on the telephone?"

"Probably," replied Jordon, nodding. "I remember speaking to someone with your accent."

"How much did she say the shirts were?" Alan asked Mick, watching Jordon's arse as she wandered off to attend to another customer.

"Twenty-five pounds!" hissed Mick, shaking his head. "Two week's fuckin' wages!"

"You've got to get one though, haven't you?" replied Alan, shrugging. "We're here now."

"I'll only have a tenner left if I do!" said Mick, pulling out his money. "I'll just have to be careful, won't I.' He counted out the required amount and headed back towards Jordon. "Have you got a medium?"

"They're all the same size," replied Jordon, guiding Mick towards the rail containing the shirts.

Paul and Alan were busy examining the wide range of T-shirts that was on display inside the shop.

"Fuckin' hell!" gasped Alan, pulling out a sleeveless white shirt with two small zips sewn into the chest area. "Can you imagine your mum's face if she pulled this out of the washing machine?"

"'I groaned with pain as he eased the pressure in'..." said Paul, as he began reading the slogan. "She'd throw me out!" He was trying desperately to stifle a fit of giggles, but lost all control when Alan showed him the "cowboy dudes" T-shirt that he'd found.

Alan was still rifling through the T-shirts when Mick rejoined him. "Let's have a look," he said, resting his hands on the rail while Mick took the shirt from the carrier bag.

"I couldn't decide which one to get," said Mick, shrugging. "They have some that say "Dangerously Close To Love" down the front, but I've bought one like Steve's instead."

"'Only anarchists are pretty'," said Alan, reading out the slogan. "Do you know what it means?"

"No," replied Mick, grinning, "but it sounds good."

"Wait 'til you see what Paul's buying," said Alan, nodding over towards their friend who was standing at the counter with Simon Barker. He showed Mick a T-shirt similar to the one Paul was buying.

"He'll get arrested if he wears that in Accy!" exclaimed Mick, staring at the image of the two cowboys.

"Tell your friend to keep that T-shirt in the bag," said Vivienne, who was eavesdropping on their conversation, "or he'll get arrested!"

"Will do," replied Alan, studying the woman's clothes.

"I'm Vivienne," she said strolling over towards Mick and Alan. "I own the shop. Jordon tells me you've come all the way from Lancashire to see the Sex Pistols?"

"Yeah, that's right" replied Mick. "Are you going?"

"Oh yes," replied Vivienne, nodding, "we'll be going, won't we Sid?"

"Sid Vicious!" gasped Mick, staring at the dark-haired lad standing near the wall. "From Siouxsie and The Banshees?"

"Ooh Sid, you're famous in Lancashire," said Vivienne, motioning for Sid to join them. "But he's not with that group anymore. He's a romantic flower, aren't you, Sid?"

"It's Flowers of Romance," mumbled Sid, scowling at Vivienne. "Have you seen The Pistols before?" he asked, looking past Vivienne towards Mick and

Alan.

"Yeah, at the Lodestar in Ribchester," said Alan. "What about you?"

"What, you kiddin'?" sneered Sid. "I've seen 'em loads of times."

"Look what I've got!" said Paul, inadvertently interrupting the conversation as he proudly revealed his purchase.

"You gonna wear that?" asked Sid, eyeing Paul up and down.

"Course I am!" replied Paul, returning Sid's gaze. "What do you think I'm gonna do with it, eat it?"

"Er, this is Sid Vicious," said Mick, hoping to avoid seeing if Sid lived up to his name.

"Oh hello," said Paul, his innocent smile defusing the possibility of Sid taking offence, "pleased to meet you."

Mick and Paul stood chatting to Simon and Sid while Alan continued searching through the clothes, unable to decide what to spend his money on. He'd wanted to buy a cowboy dudes T-shirt but Paul had beaten him to it.

"What do you think of this?" he shouted over to his two friends, holding up a black shirt with thick straps running across the chest to form an "X".

"Yeah, it's smart," replied Mick, wandering over towards Alan. "Try it on."

"Have you seen this?" asked Paul, handing Alan the flyer that advertised the Sex Pistols' show at Notre Dame Hall. The flyer contained a black and white photo of John and Steve and all the relevant information.

"On stage at last, Sex Pistols," said Alan, reading aloud, "London's outrage."

"It finishes at eleven," said Mick, pointing to the flyer, "so we should make it back to Victoria Station to catch the coach."

"An excellent choice if I may say so," said Malcolm, who was standing behind them. "The shirt I mean."

"Yeah, I'm gonna buy it," replied Alan, giving the newcomer a curious glance.

"These lads have come down from Lancashire, Malcolm," said Vivienne, walking towards them, "just to watch the group playing at the Notre Dame."

"Splendid!" beamed Malcolm. "Are you friends of Howard's?"

"Who's Howard?" asked Paul.

"Howard's the singer in a group called Buzzcocks," replied Malcolm, seizing the opportunity to sound knowledgeable. "They're awfully good!"

"Oh that Howard," said Mick, pretending to recognise the name. "No, don't know him."

"Well never mind," said Malcolm, dismissing the subject. "Perhaps I'll see you boys tonight." He gave them another beaming smile before heading off towards the stairs with Ray Stevenson.

"Who the fuck was that?" asked Mick as he held the door open for his two friends.

▱ ▱ ▱ ▱

Malcolm and Ray had just returned from Dryden Chambers where the two men had spent the entire morning sifting through the large collection of photographs that Ray had taken of the Sex Pistols since witnessing one of their shows at St. Albans in February. The photographer had captured some great stage shots from various gigs in and around London, but there were also some very good candid photos of the group that Stevenson had taken during an afternoon wandering through the streets of Soho. Malcolm was intending to use these photos, together with another collection that the photographer had taken of Simon Barker and the rest of the Bromley Contingent at Linda Ashby's flat for the *Anarchy In The UK* fanzine. He was hoping to have the fanzine ready in time for the forthcoming UK tour.

Malcolm had got the idea for the fanzine from an ex-bank clerk called Mark Perry, who had started his own fanzine entitled *Sniffin' Glue* simply because he was fed up with the established music magazines such as *Sounds* and *NME*. Perry, who had subsequently shortened his name to Mark P. in order to throw off any prying minds from the local dole office, had released his first issue the previous August. The homemade fanzine had featured articles on Perry's favourite bands such as Blue Oyster Cult, The Flamin' Groovies and The Ramones – the group which had first alerted him to a raw and exciting form of music from America called Punk. But it wasn't until Perry had accompanied Caroline Coon down to the 100 Club to watch the Sex Pistols that he began to dedicate the fanzine solely to the new genre.

Mick, Paul and Alan stood on the corner of Denmark Street watching the flow of traffic making its way along Charing Cross Road. They'd been hoping to locate the Sex Pistols' rehearsal room but Alan had somehow lost the 100 Club flyer bearing Steve's address.

"Let's try in there," said Mick pointing towards the sign above Zeno's Bookstore. "At least it'll be warm," he added, sensing his two companions" reluctance.

"Excuse me," said Alan, drumming his fingers on the counter until the owner looked up at him.

"What you want, my friend?"

"We're looking for someone called Jones," explained Alan.

"*Jaws?*" replied the old man, frowning. "It's a movie."

"You just can't get away from it," said Mick, chuckling with Paul at Alan's pained expression.

"Have you got Robert Shaw's autobiography?" asked Paul, in the hope of finding a book on the Westhoughton-born British actor who had played the part of Quint in *Jaws*.

"Show?" repeated the owner, stroking his chin slowly. "I have very good book on Chelsea Flower Show.

"That'll be his mum," said Alan, trying not to laugh.

"Can I borrow your pen?" asked Mick, pointing towards the biro lying by the side of the cash register. He wrote Steve's name down on a scrap of paper before showing it to the old man.

"This is you?" asked the old man, taking hold of the paper.

"No!" gasped Mick, becoming increasingly frustrated, "he lives somewhere round here."

"He plays guitar?" said Alan, mimicking the actions.

"Ahh, young boys," replied the Greek, nodding. "Dress very funny, like you."

"That's them!" said Mick, nodding excitedly.

"Why you not say so before?" cried the old man, coming out from behind the counter. "Instead waste my time!" He guided them out of the bookstore and pointed to the archway leading to the Sex Pistols' rehearsal room. "Through there," he said, cupping his hands over his ears to show what he thought of the group's musical abilities. "Drive me crazy!"

After several fruitless minutes of hammering away on the door the three finally admitted defeat and headed back towards Tottenham Court Road tube station.

They had little trouble finding their way to Leicester Square, but needed the help of a policeman to locate Notre Dame Hall as the building was hidden away down a side street.

"What's a sprung maple floor, when it's at home?" asked Mick, pointing towards the sign above the venue's doorway.

"Fuck knows," replied Alan, cupping his hands to his face while he peered through the glass-fronted doors.

"It's not open yet!" shouted the lad they'd noticed skulking in the doorway opposite the hall.

"Yeah, it's only half five," said Mick, identifying the broad Yorkshire accent. "We were hoping the group might be here."

"You've missed 'em," replied the lad, pointing towards the street exit. "They fucked off about twenty minutes ago!"

"Where are you from?" asked Paul, walking towards the doorway.

"Donny."

"As in Osmond?" asked Mick, grinning.

"As in Doncaster, you cunt!" the lad retorted angrily. "What about thee?"

"Accrington," replied Paul. "Oh, and Blackburn," he added for Alan's benefit. "What's your name?"

"Brian, Brian Jackson."

Paul made the necessary introductions and the four lads strolled back towards Leicester Square in search of somewhere to shelter against the freezing wind.

"Have you seen the Sex Pistols before, Brian?" asked Alan.

"Aye, at the Outlook Club in Donny." He paused to see if Mick was going to say anything before continuing. "And I saw them in Birmingham as well."

"You get about a bit, don't you?" said Paul, nodding appreciatively.

"Where did you get that?" asked Brian, watching as Mick removed his jacket and slipped his brand-new Anarchy shirt over his head.

"SEX," said Paul, showing Brian the cowboy dudes T-shirt.

"Where is that fucking shop?" asked Brian, shaking his head. "I spent all bastard day looking for it, but I couldn't find it!"

"It's right down the other end of the King's Road," explained Mick, "at the World's End."

"And it fuckin' seemed like it, an all," added Alan, much to the amusement of his friends.

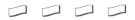

At just after seven o'clock the four lads paid the one pound entrance fee and made their way down the winding flight of stairs leading into the circular-shaped basement auditorium.

"Is that a television crew?" asked Mick, pointing towards the cluster of people gathered around a woman with long auburn hair and thick glasses who was interviewing various members of the audience.

"Looks like it," replied Alan, nodding excitedly as Paul and Brian returned with the drinks. "Come on."

The woman in question was Janet Street-Porter and she was the presenter of a current affairs programme for London Weekend Television. Janet was a fan of the Sex Pistols and had persuaded her bosses to allow her to dedicate that week's edition of the programme to the rebellious new youth culture. Mick and Alan listened to Janet as she interviewed a guy that resembled Rolf from the Muppets Show. Rolf was obviously very pissed and kept ranting on about the British rock giants Led Zeppelin and how, in his opinion, groups like Zeppelin were finished. Mick nodded his agreement although he himself had been listening to the group less than six months ago.

For lack of anything more interesting to pass the time they followed the film crew around the hall watching as Janet purposely singled out the more imaginatively dressed individuals to ask them a few questions. She spoke to two teenage girls who were dressed in plastic bin-liners, fishnet stockings and a heavy-duty dog chain, which linked the two together. Then a lad with short bleached-blond hair with musical notes dyed in black, who was wearing a homemade prison shirt with his inmate's number stencilled on the back.

Paul pointed towards Simon Barker, who had just arrived with a slim attractive girl with short dark hair. Mick had a strange feeling that he'd seen her somewhere before but couldn't place her.

"This is Siouxsie," said Simon, introducing his friend, "from the Banshees."

"Right," said Mick, smiling. "We saw your picture in..." He stopped suddenly, feeling his cheeks burning as he remembered that the photograph in *Sounds* had shown her exposed breasts.

"Well at least I'm famous for something," replied Siouxsie, enjoying Mick's obvious embarrassment.

"She's fuckin' gorgeous!" said Brian, after Siouxsie and Simon had excused themselves in order to join their friends gathered at the front of the stage.

"Yeah," agreed Alan, studying Siouxsie's arse as she walked away. "Why hasn't she got her tits out tonight?"

"Cos it's fuckin' freezin' out there," said Mick, smirking. "They'd be stickin' out like chapel hat pegs!"

"Umm, but it'd be somewhere to hang this," replied Alan, holding up his carrier bag.

▢   ▢   ▢   ▢

A cheer rose up from the crowd as the Sex Pistols appeared on stage for what would be the group's first appearance in London since being banned from the 100 Club as a result of the glass-throwing incident involving Sid. Mick had already spotted John's friend standing with Vivienne at the right-hand side of the stage. He was looking very sinister in his studded black leather jacket and dark glasses.

"Look!" shouted Alan, excitedly as he pointed towards Steve. "He's wearing the same shirt that I've bought."

"And Glen's wearing the same as me," said Mick, indicating the Anarchy shirt he was wearing. "But what the fuck has John got on?"

"Dunno!" replied Paul, shaking his head at the sight of John's bondage trousers. "Am I seeing things or are his legs tied together?"

John stood with his hands resting on the microphone stand while he surveyed the colourful array of kids gathered in front of the stage. "Hello," he announced in a drawling voice as Steve blasted into "Anarchy In The UK".

"What the fuck are they doing?" asked Alan, pointing over towards a small section of the crowd who were jumping up and down on the spot.

"Dancing, I think!" replied Mick, chuckling at the bizarre sight, which left him and his friends in two minds about whether to watch the group on stage or the kids in the audience.

"That's the woman we were talking to in the shop," said Paul, pointing towards Vivienne who had suddenly decided to join the group on stage. She seemed oblivious to the insults and beer that were being hurled at her from certain sections of the audience.

"Who is she?" asked Brian.

"She's called Vivienne."

"She owns SEX, doesn't she?" Brian asked, furious with himself for not having located the shop, "with Malcolm McLaren, the Pistols' manager?"

"Ahh, that's who it was," said Paul, remembering their earlier encounter with the guy asking about Howard and his Buzzcocks. "We've met him as well."

"She's fucked in't head," said Brian, shaking his head and pointing over towards Vivienne. "They're fuckin' spittin' at her, the dirty cunts!"

The four lads pushed their way through the crowd to get a better view of the stage as the Sex Pistols returned for a well-deserved encore. There had been a slight delay in the proceedings due to Glen's impromptu decision to destroy his bass speaker so that Malcolm would be forced into buying him a new set-up from his twenty thousand pound EMI advance; and Steve had mischievously encouraged Glen's frenzied assault knowing that the group would be called back on stage for an encore. Though if the audience were aware that Glen's instrument had suddenly been rendered impotent for the encore, they were far from caring.

"We'd better get going!" said Mick, glancing anxiously at his watch as the group left the stage, "or we'll miss the coach." They said their goodbyes to Brian, who had decided to spend a second night sleeping in his car so that he could pay a visit to SEX, and left with their ears ringing.

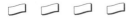

On the same weekend that the group went into EMI's eight-track studio in Manchester Square, the *NME* ran a story announcing that both The Ramones and Talking Heads had pulled out of the forthcoming Sex Pistols UK tour. Malcolm had wasted little time in putting together a new line-up by replacing the two American groups with The Clash and The Damned, while Chris Spedding and The Vibrators were carried over from the original billing. He was also making arrangements to bring Steve's hero, Johnny Thunders' new group The Heartbreakers over from New York.

The Sex Pistols had been booked into EMI's basement studios by resident engineer Mike Thorne who was hoping to record several songs with a view to selecting the group's second single. The four songs recorded were "Liar", "Problems", "No Feelings" and the new song "No Future", which they had written during their ill-fated stay at Wessex studios. Thorne recognised the fact that the song had potential, but with a running time of over five minutes was in need of some serious pruning. The group had given the song its first public airing during their performance at Hendon Polytechnic on the Friday night, where John had sung the lyrics reading from a sheet of paper.

On Friday 26 November the Sex Pistols debut single was released on EMI Records in a plain black sleeve accompanied by the fold-out poster designed by Jamie Reid. The group had originally intended to record "No Fun" for the single's B-side but had later changed their minds and used "I Wanna Be Me" from the recordings made by Dave Goodman at Denmark Street in July. EMI however, made the mistake of crediting both songs to producer Chris Thomas and Goodman was threatening to serve an injunction on the record company unless he was credited as being the producer for the B-side. The credits were duly altered but from then on the single would be issued in the normal red/orange company sleeve – and without the bonus poster. Caroline Coon at *Melody Maker* and Jonh Ingham at *Sounds* naturally both chose the record as their single of the week. Ingham headed his review by saying: "This ain't no revolution, it's the same old rock 'n' roll but younger".

On another page in the same magazine was a press release by The Vibrators announcing that they had also decided to pull out of the Sex Pistols' December UK tour.

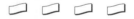

The four Sex Pistols, along with Nils and John's friend Gray were gathered in the upstairs room in Denmark Street to watch the LWT Punk Special hosted by Janet Street-Porter. The journalist had also paid a visit to Denmark Street in order to interview them for the programme.

"Shut up, it's startin'!" yelled Steve, backing away from the recently repaired television set and taking his place on the bed next to Paul. He cheered wildly when the screen suddenly filled with live footage of the group performing on stage at the Notre Dame. He grabbed hold of the ladies' costume wig that he'd found and been hiding behind his back and placed it over Glen's eyes, obscuring his view of the television.

Next on screen was Janet herself, introducing the itinerary for the programme as the screen flicked between images of Mark P.'s fanzine *Sniffin' Glue* and its American counterpart *Punk* by a guy called Legs McNeil, before switching to footage of Janet interviewing the group's fans inside Notre Dame.

"Where did all those stickers come from?" asked Paul, as the camera zoomed in for a close-up of John standing on stage. He was referring to the "I survived the Texas Chainsaw Massacre" stickers promoting the movie of the same name that John and various members of the audience seemed to be covered in.

"Don't know," replied Glen, glancing around the room, remembering the day when Janet and her film crew had arrived to record the interview. They had all been really excited about being interviewed for the telly but he, Steve and Paul had quickly realised that Janet's sole interest was in John.

He glanced back towards the screen to watch the black and white footage of The Who performing "My Generation". Next up on screen was Ron Watts, the promoter, standing in the doorway of the 100 Club, telling Janet about his own experiences of seeing the Sex Pistols performing at High Wycombe on the night when John smashed the microphone belonging to Screaming Lord Sutch.

"If we were so good, how come you fuckin' banned us from your club, you cunt?" Steve yelled angrily as he flung his empty can at the screen.

The programme's host reappeared on screen showing footage of her interviews with Siouxsie Sioux, Steve Bailey, Simon Barker and Jo Faul in a café. Siouxsie is telling Janet all about the Banshees' debut performance at the 100 Club Punk Festival two months earlier.

"Look at me!" shouted Steve, proudly, as the screen filled with a shot of him from Notre Dame. The camera zoomed in on Steve as he took a drink from a fan's beer bottle while still playing. "Didn't spill a fuckin' drop, mate."

"It's not bad, is it?" said John, laughing at the footage showing the moment when someone in the audience hurled his beer at Vivienne while she was dancing on stage.

"Not for you, it isn't," replied Glen, as the programme was temporarily halted for the commercial break. "What was it like for you, John? I love you John. Can I suck your dick for you John?" he said, mimicking Janet Street-Porter from the interview.

"People loved me," mimicked Paul, joining in the fun.

"Fuck off!" snarled John, grabbing up the discarded wig and throwing it at Paul. "You're jealous because she was only interested in talking to the 'star'."

Everyone quietened down as the programme resumed, showing Janet sitting in the studio talking about the emergence of new groups that had been inspired by the Sex Pistols. There was a series of groans from around the room as Joe, Mick and Paul from The Clash appeared on screen dressed in their paint-splattered shirts.

"We went down Camden," Janet informed the viewers, "to ask The Clash: 'How did Punk start?'"

"What the fuck are you askin' him for?" yelled Steve, angrily. "Fuck off back to the 101ers!"

"Oh look, there's Glen's boyfriend," said John, pointing at Mick Jones.

"You're hilarious, John," replied Glen. "You should be on the stage."

"Ha ha, quite right, dear boy," sneered John. "But not with you!"

"First time we saw that cunt he had hair half-way down his arse!" yelled Steve, tossing a second empty can at the television set.

"None on his head," said Paul, grinning, "just halfway down his arse!"

Ron Watts reappeared, telling Janet that he agreed with the 100 Club's decision to ban all punk groups from the venue, because of the lunatic fringe that caused trouble wherever the Sex Pistols played.

"It ain't no lunatic fringe," said Gray, laughing, "it's just Sid!"

"He may not have a fringe," said John, chuckling, "but he sure is a lunatic!"

"Watch this bit!" said Paul, sitting upright and pointing towards the television set as Steve's bedroom appeared on screen. It was the footage taken when Janet and her crew arrived to interview the group. It showed Janet talking to John, who was sitting on Steve's bed, when suddenly Steve leaped up from under the covers wearing a cowboy dudes T-shirt and a pair of tight-fitting leopard-skin print underpants.

"She don't even look at you, mate," said Paul, patting Steve on the head.

There was another burst of derision as Janet was heard pondering whether John could be regarded as the new David Bowie and whether the inevitable success of the group would see him become part of the establishment. She then asked John how he would react if the record were to become successful and how would this make him any different from a group like The Rolling Stones.

John responded by telling Street-Porter that he didn't need a house in the country or a Rolls Royce and that he had no intention of living in the South of France because he was happy where he was. It was at that point that Paul had decided to interject by adding that John was living in Finsbury Park with his mum.

"I'd forgot about that," said Glen, laughing. "Nice one, Paul."

"Cunt!" said John, glancing over to where Paul was sitting on the bed. "You don't say much do you? But when you do!"

"Look at my moves!" said Steve, bringing everyone's attention back to the footage from Notre Dame showing the group performing "No Fun". "Guitar hero, or what?"

"Most definitely 'what', dear boy," replied John, suddenly howling at the sight of a semi-naked female dancing at the back of the hall. The girl, unaware that the camera is focused on her, is gyrating to the music.

"Ugh!" cried Glen, cringing at the sight of the girl's flabby white arse. "That shouldn't be on the telly."

"Nah," replied Steve, leering, "it should be sat on my face!"

On Monday 29 November the Sex Pistols, together with The Clash acting as support for the evening, travelled up to Coventry to play at the city's Lanchester Polytechnic. The show was reasonably well attended and both groups received generous applause from the small, yet enthusiastic audience. The polytechnic's student union, however, was rather less pleased and refused to pay either group on the grounds that they were Fascists. The student union claimed that the lyrical content of The Clash's "White Riot" and the Sex Pistols' "No Future" had caused offence to several of their members.

Malcolm already had more than enough on his plate trying to organise the Sex Pistols' forthcoming UK tour and decided to leave the matter in the hands of Stephen Fisher. He felt that EMI were not doing enough to promote the group's single, despite receiving numerous assurances to the contrary from the record company's managing director Leslie Hill. Hill claimed that the Sex Pistols' single was receiving the same amount of funding as any other record released by EMI. Malcolm remained unconvinced but he did, however, manage to cajole Hill into providing extra funding for the tour, which was scheduled to begin at Norwich University on Friday 3 December.

The Sex Pistols along with The Clash and The Damned were busy rehearsing at the Roxy Theatre on Craven Park Road in Harlesden, while Johnny Thunders and the rest of the Heartbreakers were due to arrive at Heathrow Airport later that day. The idea behind the rehearsals was to record the amount of time that it would take for each group to set up and remove their own equipment at the end of their set. The members of The Clash and Damned were sitting with various friends in the front two rows of cinema seats watching the Sex Pistols running through their set. The tour was yet to actually get underway and there were already tensions mounting in the rival camps.

Malcolm had made it quite clear that although The Damned had been given second billing on the posters, they would in fact be opening the proceedings. This was down to the simple fact that Malcolm didn't like their manager, Jake Riviera, and this was his way of putting him in his place. As The Damned were signed to Riviera's Stiff Records, the company would be paying for their group's expenses, while Glitterbest would be picking up the tab for The Clash and The Heartbreakers.

John was standing motionless in front of the microphone, wearing a baggy striped mohair jumper to help him keep warm inside the cold empty theatre.

"Hey, John," shouted Glen, above the feedback from Steve's guitar, "shall we do 'Anarchy'?" John was about to reply but was distracted by the sight of Nils bounding down the centre aisle towards the stage.

"There's a Daimler outside," said Nils, jerking a thumb over his shoulder towards the exit. "You're going on the *Today Show*."

"No we're fuckin' not!" shouted Steve, angrily. "We've loads of stuff to get sorted out." He turned his back on Nils and resumed playing.

"The tour starts in two days," said Glen, nodding his agreement at Steve's outburst. This was the first time that any of them had heard about this and as flattering as appearing on television was, they really did have plenty of hard graft ahead of them.

"Malcolm told me to tell you," replied Nils, calmly, "that if you don't come along, you won't be getting any wages."

"Fuck!" yelled Steve, kicking his amplifier.

"Looks like we're goin' back on the telly again then, don't it!" said John, replacing the microphone back in its cradle and jumping down from the stage.

Earlier that day Eric Hall, who was employed as a "plugger" in the EMI press office, had found himself with a slight dilemma. The rock group Queen had been forced to cancel their appearance on the local evening magazine programme the *Today Show* because the group's singer, Freddie Mercury, had a severe toothache. Hall, although no great fan of the Sex Pistols' music, suggested using the group to fill in as a replacement. At first Malcolm had been unsure. He knew that the boys were busy rehearsing down in Harlesden and wouldn't take kindly to having their routine disrupted. But when EMI offered him the services of a company limousine to collect The Heartbreakers from the airport, he readily agreed and contacted Nils at the theatre and gave him the necessary instructions to get the boys ready to leave. Then he contacted Simon Barker at the shop, telling him to round up some of his friends and get over to the Thames Television Studios on Marylebone Road.

When the Sex Pistols arrived at the studio they found Malcolm waiting for them in the reception. They were then escorted up to the hospitality room on the fourth floor where they found Simon Barker, Siouxsie Sioux, Steve Bailey and another friend of theirs called Simone. Malcolm was pleased to see that they were all wearing various items of clothing from his shop.

"There's gotta be somethin' better than this!" yelled Steve, dismissing the small cans of Heineken lager on the table. "Ha ha, this is more like it," he chortled, upon finding two bottles of Blue Nun white wine.

Bill Grundy, the *Today Show*'s regular presenter, was sitting over by the television set watching the antics of the group and their friends. He'd only just been informed about the change to that night's show after having returned to the studio from his daily trip to the local pub for a liquid lunch with some of his colleagues.

"So, what do we know about this lot?" he asked one of the researchers. "At least the tarts are worth fucking, I suppose." He listened to the scant information that the researcher had managed to collect on the Sex Pistols and pursed his lips upon hearing about the group's recently released debut single. They were going to be sorely disappointed if they were expecting some free publicity for their record on his show.

"Make-up in five minutes, Mr. Grundy," said a pretty brunette, standing inside the doorway.

"How long have I got them for?" Grundy asked the researcher, waving a hand towards the girl to acknowledge that he'd heard her.

"Oh about three minutes, if that," replied the researcher. "All you have to do is make some sort of an introduction and then we'll run a clip of the group playing their new single."

"Where on earth have you got that from?" asked Grundy, as he made his way towards the door.

"We've borrowed it from their record company," replied the researcher, stopping to check his notes. "Apparently it's from their recent appearance on *Nationwide*."

"Oh well!" replied Grundy, sarcastically, "If Auntie has had them round for tea, then I suppose we have to be seen doing something similar."

"They start a nationwide tour on Friday," said the researcher, ignoring Grundy's remark. "Just ask them a couple of questions about that."

Grundy muttered something under his breath before glancing over at the group one last time as the door closed behind him. He had been the first man to interview The Beatles on television but if he remembered rightly, he hadn't thought much about them either.

"Have you seen that lot, in there?" he said to Tony Bulley, the *Today Show* director and Michael Housego, the studio producer, as they came towards him in the corridor. "I told Jeremy that I didn't think that I should have to interview the likes of them!" He walked off before the two men had a chance to reply.

Malcolm had purposely brought along a copy of that week's edition of the *NME* in the hope of getting a reaction from John and the others regarding the scathing remarks made about the Sex Pistols in the paper's interview with a group called The Stranglers. The Guildford-based outfit had been just another struggling group on the London Pub Rock circuit before climbing aboard the punk bandwagon.

"We used to go down the Hope & Anchor just to laugh at them!" scowled John, jabbing a finger at the photograph which accompanied the interview. "Fuckin' arseholes."

"How can they claim to be a part of the new punk movement," said Glen, shaking his head. "Their drummer must be at least fifty!"

The discussion was brought to an end when the pretty brunette came over to tell them that they would be required for the opening sequence of the show. They followed the girl presuming that they were being taken into a large studio, but instead found themselves in a tiny room full of lighting and camera crews. Michael Housego, the studio producer, signalled for the four members of the group to be positioned in front of camera one.

"Would you let your daughter go out with one of these?" said an unseen voice. "They are the Sex Pistols and we'll be meeting them later in tonight's programme."

"Bloody cheek!" exclaimed Glen, as they were led back towards the hospitality room.

When the time came for the four Sex Pistols to go on set and do the interview, they were ushered through the cramped studio to where four black leather swivel chairs had been lined up next to Grundy; Siouxsie and their other friends were manoeuvred into position behind the group. Steve, having downed the majority of the two bottles of wine that he'd found earlier, was extremely pissed. He removed his woolly jumper to reveal the tits T-shirt that he was wearing, which would be good for a laugh seeing as the programme was going out live. They sat watching as one of the production crew counted down using the fingers of one hand to give Grundy his cue.

"Chains around the neck," said Grundy, smirking towards the camera, "and that's just it fellas, yeah, innit?" He swivelled round in his chair to keep in shot as the camera moved into position. "They are punk rockers, the new craze." He paused to glance briefly at the group. "They tell me they're heroes, not the nice clean Rolling Stones." He jerked a thumb towards them, but kept his eyes on the moving camera. "You see, they're as drunk as I am. They are clean by comparison. They are a group called the Sex Pistols." He was momentarily distracted by Steve's loud cheer at hearing the group's name mentioned. "And I'm surrounded by all of them. Let's see them in action!" He turned around the moment that he was off camera and glared at Steve, who had been reading out from Grundy's autocue that appeared on the monitors in front of them.

Malcolm stood watching from off-set. Everything was going according to plan. The group were live on television, their fans behind them were all wearing clothing from his shop which meant plenty of free publicity and the clip was being played showing the group performing their new single.

"Plug the record," he silently pleaded with Grundy. "Plug the damn record!"

Grundy glanced up from his monitor as the clip finished and turned to face the group, but purposely avoided any mention of the fact that the single was currently available in the shops. "I'm told," he said, slapping his notes against his thigh, "that this group has received forty thousand pounds from a record company." He paused for a moment to watch Glen smirking and waving into the cameras. "Doesn't that seem...er...to be slightly opposed to their anti-materialistic view of life?"

"No!" replied Glen, grinning at Grundy. "The more the merrier."

"Really!" exclaimed Grundy momentarily surprised at this blatant lack of denial.

"Oh yeah," replied Glen, waiting for Grundy to continue.

"Well tell me more then."

"We've fuckin' spent it, ain't we!" yelled Steve, placing his empty plastic cup on the studio table.

"I don't know," said Grundy, resting his chin in his hand. "Have you?"

"Yeah," said Glen, chuckling at Steve's outburst. "It's all gone."

"Really?"

"Down the boozer," continued Glen, nodding.

"Really," repeated Grundy, risking a quick glance over towards Michael Housego who was standing off camera, "Good Lord. Now I want to know one thing?"

"What?" asked Glen, trying to keep a straight face.

"Are you serious or are you just making me...," Grundy paused for a moment while he corrected himself, "trying to make me laugh?"

"No," replied Glen, smirking, "it's gone, all gone."

"Really?"

"Yeah!" replied Glen, enjoying the attention.

"No!" said Grundy, fidgeting in his chair, "I mean, about what you're doing?"

"Oh yeah!" replied Glen, glancing towards the monitors again. He hoped that Celia was watching all of this.

"You are serious?" said Grundy, placing his hand under his chin again, trying to compose himself. "Beethoven, Mozart, Bach and Brahms have all died..."

"They're all heroes of ours, ain't they?" said Glen.

"Really?" exclaimed Grundy. "What are you saying, sir?"

"They're wonderful people!" said John, speaking for the first time since the interview started.

"Are they?" asked Grundy, turning his attention towards the weirdo sitting on the end.

"Oh yes!" said John, leaning forward in his chair. "They really turn us on!"

"Well, suppose they turn other people on?" said Grundy, hoping to keep the weirdo talking.

"That's just their tough shit," replied John, mumbling the last words.

"It's what?" asked Grundy, realising what John had said.

"Nothing!" replied John, quickly looking into the camera. "A rude word. Next question?"

"No no," said Grundy, deciding he would show this scruffy bunch who was in charge. "What was the rude word?"

"Shit!" said John, feeling his cheeks flush as he said it.

"Was it really?" replied Grundy, feigning shock. "Good heavens, you frighten me to death!"

"Oh, all right Siegfried," said John, smiling.

Grundy ignored John's reply and turned his attention to the fans standing behind the group. "What about you girls behind?" he asked, winking suggestively at Siouxsie.

"He's like your dad isn't he, this geezer," said Glen, turning towards Steve and John. "Or your granddad."

"Are you worried?" Grundy asked Siouxsie, "or are you just enjoying yourself?"

"Enjoying myself," replied Siouxsie, feeling slightly silly.

"Are you?"

"Yeah," replied Siouxsie, still surprised that Grundy was talking to her instead of the group.

"Ahh, that's what I thought you were doing," said Grundy, a smug grin spreading across his face.

"I've always wanted to meet you," said Siouxsie, wincing at how cheesy it sounded.

"Well we'll meet afterwards, shall we?" asked Grundy, winking again.

"You dirty sod!" said Steve, thoroughly bored with the proceedings. "You dirty old man!"

"Well keep going, chief," replied Grundy, hoping to provoke Steve into a reaction. "Keep going. Go on, you've got another five seconds. Say something outrageous!"

"You dirty bastard!"

"Go on, again!" urged Grundy, looking directly at Steve.

"You dirty fucker!" said Steve, glancing over towards the camera.

"What a clever boy!" said Grundy, placing a hand over his mouth to mask his smile.

"What a fuckin' rotter!" said Steve, exhaling cigarette smoke.

Grundy looked on bemused while Glen and Paul struggled to keep from pissing themselves. "Well that's all for tonight," he said, turning back to face the cameras. "The other rocker, Eamonn – I'm saying nothing else about him – will be back tomorrow. I'll be seeing you soon." He turned back towards the group. "I hope I'm not seeing you again. From me though, good night."

The show's theme tune filled the studio as the credits rolled up on the monitors. Grundy sat totally bemused as he watched Steve leap up out of his seat and begin gyrating in front of the camera.

Malcolm was waiting for them in the hallway when they burst through the studio doors. "You boys have just made history!" he said, nervously glancing towards the lift doors as if he expected them to be arrested at any moment.

"The cunt deserved it!" yelled Steve, as he and the others rushed past him on their way to the exit.

The next morning, the Sex Pistols would wake up to find themselves spread across the front pages of every newspaper in the country. The media backlash that would plague the group for the rest of their short-lived career had begun.

THE END

Epilogue

As a result of their infamous appearance on the *Today Show*, the Sex Pistols went from being London's best-kept secret to public enemy number one. The Anarchy Tour of December 1976 lay in ruins as venue after venue cancelled the shows. The Sex Pistols and the other groups on the bill would play only three out of the original nineteen dates, which amounted to estimated losses of around ten thousand pounds. The group also suffered a setback with their debut single as staff at EMI's processing plant refused to have anything to do with the Sex Pistols.

◻ ◻ ◻ ◻

On Thursday 6 January 1977 while the group was on a mini-tour of Holland, EMI issued a statement announcing that the record company and the Sex Pistols had mutually agreed to terminate the group's recording contract. Malcolm, however, was not quite willing to be so diplomatic and later claimed that the Sex Pistols had been sacked. On 9 March 1977 the group would sign with A&M Records for a hundred and fifty thousand pounds over two years and record their second single "God Save The Queen"/"No Feelings" AMS7284. The record company would terminate the contract one week later after reconsidering the implications of having a group like the Sex Pistols on its roster. The single was never officially released although a few copies did make it onto the black market where they currently fetch prices in the region of two thousand pounds.

On 13 May 1977 the Sex Pistols signed to Richard Branson's Virgin Records for fifteen thousand pounds, and the group would release three singles for the label while Johnny Rotten was still a member of the group. These were "God Save The Queen"/"Did You No Wrong" (VS181) on 26 May 1977. "Pretty Vacant"/"No Fun" (VS184) 01 July 1977 and "Holidays In The Sun"/"Satellite" (VS191) October 1977. The album "Never Mind The Bollocks Here's the Sex Pistols" VS2086 was released to critical acclaim in October 1977.

◻ ◻ ◻ ◻

On Thursday 24 February 1977 bassist Glen Matlock announced that he was leaving the Sex Pistols, citing personal differences between himself and singer Johnny Rotten as the reason for his departure. Malcolm and the three remaining members of the group would later claim that Glen had been sacked because of his apparent liking for The Beatles. Glen quickly formed the Rich Kids with Steve New – who had auditioned for the Sex Pistols as a potential second guitarist in September 1975 and ex-Slik frontman Midge Ure. During the 1990s he toured as part of Iggy Pop's backing group.

◻ ◻ ◻ ◻

    Glen Matlock's replacement as bass player in the Sex Pistols was Sid Vicious, born John Simon Richie on 10 May 1957. Sid's previous musical experiences prior to joining the group consisted of a brief stint as the drummer for Siouxsie And The Banshees and as the vocalist in the squat group Flowers Of Romance. Shortly after joining the group Sid met up with an American groupie and heroin addict Nancy Laura Spungen, who in turn introduced Sid to heroin to which he soon developed a chronic dependence. The Sex Pistols would fumble their way through the rest of 1977 playing only a handful of UK gigs as a result of being blacklisted by local councils. They would play their last ever UK show with Sid at Ivanhoes in Huddersfield on Christmas Day 1977, which had been organised for the families of the town's striking firemen.

    On Tuesday 3 January 1978 the Sex Pistols flew out to America for a seven-date US tour. The original tour had been for nineteen dates but was subsequently shortened due to problems over the issuing of visas as a result of all four members of the group having criminal records. After the final show on Saturday 14 January at Winterland in San Francisco, Johnny Rotten offered Steve Jones and Paul Cook an ultimatum; it was either him or Malcolm, who John had accused of trying to ruin the Sex Pistols. Steve and Paul chose to follow Malcolm to Rio de Janeiro in Brazil in order to record a single with the Great Train Robber Ronnie Biggs. The Sex Pistols were finished.

◻ ◻ ◻ ◻

    On Tuesday 15 August 1978 Sid played a farewell gig at the Electric Ballroom in Camden Town, North London. His backing group consisted of fellow ex-Sex Pistols bass player Glen Matlock, Glen's fellow Rich Kid Steve New and former Damned tub-thumper Rat Scabies. The following day Sid and his girlfriend Nancy moved to New York City in an attempt to launch Sid's solo career in the USA. The American public, however, although amused at the antics of the British punk rock group, had rather less enthusiasm for a former Sex Pistol strung out on heroin. On Friday 11 October 1978 the police were summoned to room 100 at the Chelsea Hotel on West 23rd Street. Upon entering the apartment, they found Sid lying comatose on the bed, while Nancy's body lay slumped beneath the sink in the bathroom with a recently purchased hunting knife protruding from her abdomen. Malcolm together with Sid's mother, Ann Beverley, flew out to New York to arrange the fifty thousand dollar bail for Sid, who had formally been charged with Nancy's murder.

    On Friday 2 February 1979, Sid was released from the city's Rikers Island Prison. At a party to celebrate his release from prison at the apartment of his new girlfriend Michelle Robinson, Sid took a lethal dose of almost pure heroin. He was twenty-one years old.

With the demise of the Sex Pistols, Johnny Rotten reverted to his real name of John Lydon and formed Public Image Ltd (PIL) with his friend "Jah Wobble" also know as John Wardle and ex-Clash guitarist Keith Levine. The group would go through many personnel changes during its lengthy career and despite having several successful singles in the British pop charts, John would never achieve the recognition that he'd enjoyed with the Sex Pistols. In 1994 he released his autobiography: "No Dogs, No Blacks, No Irish", in which he speaks honestly about his time in the Sex Pistols. In 1997 John released his first solo album: "Psycho's Path". John is currently living in Los Angeles with his wife Nora.

Steve Jones and Paul Cook continued working with Malcolm on the film *The Great Rock 'N' Roll Swindle*. This is the film in which Malcolm gives his own Faginistic account of how he created the Sex Pistols in order to destroy rock 'n' roll from the inside, while making a million pounds on the way. Apart from taking acting parts in the movie the pair were actively involved with the accompanying soundtrack. The double album spawned several Sex Pistols singles including "No One Is Innocent" featuring the vocal talents of exiled Great Train Robber Ronnie Biggs and "Silly Thing", with Steve providing the vocals. In 1979 they formed The Professionals, recording two albums and several singles but split two years later without ever achieving any notable success.

Steve soon tired of dragging around the "ex Pistol" tag and relocated to Los Angeles where he not only continued to play guitar, but also developed an addiction to heroin. Paul Cook remained in London where he would briefly become the manager of the highly successful female group Bananarama. In the mid-eighties he joined up with another of Malcolm's former charges ex-Adam And The Ants and Bow Wow Wow bass player Mathew Ashman in The Chiefs Of Relief. He has also enjoyed a successful career working as a session drummer most notably with ex-Orange Juice frontman Edwyn Collins.

On completion of the film *The Great Rock 'N' Roll Swindle*, Malcolm returned to music management with the group Bow Wow Wow, whose fourteen-year-old female singer was discovered singing in the local launderette. He would later move to New York City where he became involved with rap artists such as the Rock Steady Crew before having solo success with Duck Rock. In 1986 Malcolm was re-united with his former charges when John Lydon had his petition to have the Sex Pistols dissolved heard in the High Court. He also made sure that Malcolm would no longer have any legal claim to any aspect of the Sex Pistols.

Steve Jones and Paul Cook had originally sided with Malcolm against Lydon but later changed their minds upon finally hearing the evidence. Lydon won the case, which ensured that all future moneys earned by the Sex Pistols would be evenly distributed between the surviving former group members. Sid's mother, Ann Beverley, would receive the moneys owed to her late son through her right as the legal executor of his estate.

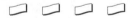

On Tuesday 18 March 1996 the four original members of the Sex Pistols, Steve Jones, Paul Cook, Glen Matlock and Johnny Rotten held a press conference at their old stomping ground, the 100 Club on London's Oxford Street to announce plans for the "Filthy Lucre" re-union world tour. On Sunday 23 June 1996 the Sex Pistols played in front of more than thirty thousand people in Finsbury Park, North London and Mick, Alan, Paul, Tommy and Brian were all there to see them.

About the author

Mick O'Shea is 42 years old. He lives with his wife Jakki, in his home town of Accrington, Lancashire, and works in the New Business Department at Compass Finance PLC. The 'semi-fictional' *Only Anarchists Are Pretty* was Mick's first attempt at novel writing (the manuscript's first draft was completed in spring 2000), but it was a fantasy-adventure featuring his two cats, Oscar and 'Big' Sid, that produced his first published novel *The Zootopia Tree* (2002). He still enjoys listening to the Sex Pistols and honestly rates *Never Mind The Bollocks* as the best album of all time. His other musical tastes are pretty much 'old school' as well, in that his other favourite bands are The Clash, Stiff Little Fingers, The Ramones, & Guns 'N' Roses.

Mick's other passion is military history, especially the Battle of the Little Bighorn of 1876, and he has recently completed a manuscript based on the legendary battle and the life of its most celebrated participant General George A. Custer.

Other Titles available from Helter Skelter

Coming Soon

Everybody Dance
Chic and the Politics of Disco
By Daryl Easlea
Everybody Dance puts the rise and fall of Bernard Edwards and Nile Rodgers, the emblematic disco duo behind era-defining records "Le Freak', "Good Times" and "Lost In Music", at the heart of a changing landscape, taking in socio-political and cultural events such as the Civil Rights struggle, the Black Panthers and the US oil crisis. There are drugs, bankruptcy, up-tight artists, fights, and Muppets but, most importantly an in-depth appraisal of a group whose legacy remains hugely underrated.
ISBN 1-900924-56-0   256pp   £14.00

Currently Available from Helter Skelter

This Is a Modern Life
by Enamel Verguren
Lavishly illustrated guide to the mod revival that was sparked by the 1979 release of *Quadrophenia*. *This Is a Modern Life* concentrates on the 1980s, but takes in 20 years of a Mod life in London and throughout the world, from 1979 to 1999, with interviews of people directly involved, loads of flyers and posters and a considerable amount of great photos
Paperback   ISBN 1900924773   224pp   264mm X 180mm, photos throughout
UK £14.99   US $19.95

Smashing Pumpkins
by Amy Hanson
Initially contemporaries of Nirvana, Billy Corgan's Smashing Pumpkins outgrew and outlived the grunge scene and with hugely acclaimed commercial triumphs like *Siamese Dream* and *Mellon Collie and The Infinite Sadness*. Though drugs and other problems led to the band's final demise, Corgan's recent return with Zwan is a reminder of how awesome the Pumpkins were in their prime. Seattle-based Hanson has followed the band for years and this is the first in-depth biography of their rise and fall.
Paperback   ISBN 1900924684   256pp   156mm X 234mm, 8pp b/w photos
UK £12.99   US $18.95

Be Glad: An Incredible String Band Compendium
Edited by Adrian Whittaker
The ISB pioneered "world music" on '60s albums like *The Hangman's Beautiful Daughter* – Paul McCartney's favourite album of 1967! – experimented with theatre, film and lifestyle and inspired Led Zeppelin. "Be Glad" features interviews with all the ISB key players, as well as a wealth of background information, reminiscence, critical evaluations and arcane trivia, this is a book that will delight any reader with more than a passing interest in the ISB.
ISBN 1-900924-64-1   288pp   £14.99

Waiting for the Man: The Story of Drugs and Popular Music
Harry Shapiro

From Marijuana and Jazz, through acid-rock and speed-fuelled punk, to crack-driven rap and Ecstasy and the Dance Generation, this is the definitive history of drugs and pop. It also features in-depth portraits of music's most famous drug addicts: from Charlie Parker to Sid Vicious and from Jim Morrison to Kurt Cobain. Chosen by the BBC as one of the Top Twenty Music Books of All Time. "Wise and witty." *The Guardian*
ISBN 1-900924-58-7   320pp   £12.99

The Clash: Return of the Last Gang in Town
Marcus Gray

Exhaustively researched definitive biography of the last great rock band that traces their progress from pubs and punk clubs to US stadiums and the Top Ten. This edition is further updated to cover the band's induction into the Rock 'n' Roll Hall of Fame and the tragic death of iconic frontman Joe Strummer.
"A must-have for Clash fans [and] a valuable document for anyone interested in the punk era." *Billboard*
"It's important you read this book." *Record Collector*
ISBN 1-900924-62-5   448pp   £14.99

Steve Marriott: All Too Beautiful
by Paolo Hewitt and John Hellier £20.00

Marriott was the prime mover behind 60s chart-toppers The Small Faces. Longing to be treated as a serious musician he formed Humble Pie with Peter Frampton, where his blistering rock 'n' blues guitar playing soon saw him take centre stage in the US live favourites. After years in seclusion, Marriott's plans for a comeback in 1991 were tragically cut short when he died in a housefire. He continues to be a key influence for generations of musicians from Paul Weller to Oasis and Blur.

Love: Behind The Scenes
By Michael Stuart-Ware

LOVE were one of the legendary bands of the late 60s US West Coast scene. Their masterpiece Forever Changes still regularly appears in critics' polls of top albums, while a new-line up of the band has recently toured to mass acclaim. Michael Stuart-Ware was LOVE's drummer during their heyday and shares his inside perspective on the band's recording and performing career and tells how drugs and egos thwarted the potential of one of the great groups of the burgeoning psychedelic era.
ISBN 1-900924-59-5   256pp   £14.00

A Secret Liverpool: In Search of the La's
by MW Macefield

With timeless single "There She Goes", Lee Mavers' La's overtook The Stone Roses and paved the way for Britpop. However, since 1991, The La's have been silent, while rumours of studio-perfectionism, madness and drug addiction have abounded. The author sets out to discover the truth behind Mavers' lost decade and eventually gains a revelatory audience with Mavers himself.
ISBN 1-900924-63-3   192pp   £11.00

The Fall: A User's Guide
Dave Thompson

Amelodic, cacophonic and magnificent, The Fall remain the most enduring and prolific of the late-'70s punk and post-punk iconoclasts. *A User's Guide* chronicles the historical and musical

background to more than 70 different LPs (plus reissues) and as many singles. The band's history is also documented year-by-year, filling in the gaps between the record releases.
ISBN 1-900924-57-9   256pp   £12.99

Pink Floyd: A Saucerful of Secrets
by Nicholas Schaffner £14.99
Long overdue reissue of the authoritative and detailed account of one of the most important and popular bands in rock history. From the psychedelic explorations of the Syd Barrett-era to 70s superstardom with *Dark Side of the Moon*, and on to triumph of *The Wall*, before internecine strife tore the group apart. Schaffner's definitive history also covers the improbable return of Pink Floyd without Roger Waters, and the hugely successful *Momentary Lapse of Reason* album and tour.

The Big Wheel
by Bruce Thomas £10.99
Thomas was bassist with Elvis Costello at the height of his success. Though names are never named, *The Big Wheel* paints a vivid and hilarious picture of life touring with Costello and co, sharing your life 24-7 with a moody egotistical singer, a crazed drummer and a host of hangers-on. Costello sacked Thomas on its initial publication.
"A top notch anecdotalist who can time a twist to make you laugh out loud." *Q*

Hit Men: Powerbrokers and Fast Money Inside The Music Business
By Fredric Dannen £14.99
Hit Men exposes the seamy and sleazy dealings of America's glitziest record companies: payola, corruption, drugs, Mafia involvement, and excess.
"So heavily awash with cocaine, corruption and unethical behaviour that it makes the occasional examples of chart-rigging and playlist tampering in Britain during the same period seem charmingly inept." *The Guardian*.

I'm With The Band: Confessions of A Groupie
By Pamela Des Barres £14.99
Frank and engaging memoir of affairs with Keith Moon, Noel Redding and Jim Morrison, travels with Led Zeppelin as Jimmy Page's girlfriend, and friendships with Robert Plant, Gram Parsons, and Frank Zappa.
"Miss Pamela, the most beautiful and famous of the groupies. Her memoir of her life with rock stars is funny, bittersweet, and tender-hearted." Stephen Davis, author of *Hammer of the Gods*

Psychedelic Furs: Beautiful Chaos
by Dave Thompson £12.99
Psychedelic Furs were the ultimate post-punk band – combining the chaos and vocal rasp of the Sex Pistols with a Bowie-esque glamour. The Furs hit the big time when John Hughes wrote a movie based on their early single "Pretty in Pink". Poised to join U2 and Simple Minds in the premier league, they withdrew behind their shades, remaining a cult act, but one with a hugely devoted following.

Bob Dylan: Like The Night (Revisited)
by CP Lee £9.99
Fully revised and updated B-format edition of the hugely acclaimed document of Dylan's pivotal 1966 show at the Manchester Free Trade Hall where fans called him Judas for turning his back on folk music in favour of rock 'n' roll.

Marillion: Separated Out
by Jon Collins £14.99

From the chart hit days of Fish and "Kayleigh" to the Steve Hogarth incarnation, Marillion have continued to make groundbreaking rock music. Collins tells the full story, drawing on interviews with band members, associates, and the experiences of some of the band's most dedicated fans.

Rainbow Rising
by Roy Davies £14.99

The full story of guitar legend Ritchie Blackmore's post-Purple progress with one of the great 70s rock bands. After quitting Deep Purple at the height of their success, Blackmore combined with Ronnie James Dio to make epic rock albums like *Rising* and *Long Live Rock 'n' Roll* before streamlining the sound and enjoying hit singles like "Since You've Been Gone" and "All Night Long." Rainbow were less celebrated than Deep Purple, but they feature much of Blackmore's finest writing and playing, and were one of the best live acts of the era. They are much missed.

Back to the Beach: A Brian Wilson and the Beach Boys Reader REVISED EDITION
Ed Kingsley Abbott £14.00

Revised and expanded edition of the Beach Boys compendium *Mojo* magazine deemed an "essential purchase." This collection includes all of the best articles, interviews and reviews from the Beach Boys' four decades of music, including definitive pieces by Timothy White, Nick Kent and David Leaf. New material reflects on the tragic death of Carl Wilson and documents the rejuvenated Brian's return to the boards. "Rivetting!" **** *Q* "An essential purchase." *Mojo*

Harmony in My Head
The Original Buzzcock Steve Diggle's Rock 'n' Roll Odyssey
by Steve Diggle and Terry Rawlings £14.99

First-hand account of the punk wars from guitarist and one half of the songwriting duo that gave the world three chord punk-pop classics like "Ever Fallen In Love" and "Promises". Diggle dishes the dirt on punk contemporaries like the Sex Pistols, The Clash and The Jam, as well as sharing poignant memories of his friendship with Kurt Cobain, on whose last ever tour, The Buzzcocks were support act.

Serge Gainsbourg: A Fistful of Gitanes
by Sylvie Simmons £9.99

Rock press legend Simmons" hugely acclaimed biography of the French genius.

"I would recommend *A Fistful of Gitanes* [as summer reading] which is a highly entertaining biography of the French singer-songwriter and all-round scallywag" – JG Ballard

"A wonderful introduction to one of the most overlooked songwriters of the 20th century" (Number 3, top music books of 2001) *The Times*

"The most intriguing music-biz biography of the year" *The Independent*

"Wonderful. Serge would have been so happy" – Jane Birkin

Blues: The British Connection
by Bob Brunning £14.99

Former Fleetwood Mac member Bob Brunning's classic account of the impact of Blues in Britain, from its beginnings as the underground music of 50s teenagers like Mick Jagger, Keith Richards and Eric Clapton, to the explosion in the 60s, right through to the vibrant scene of the present day.

"An invaluable reference book and an engaging personal memoir" – Charles Shaar Murray

On The Road With Bob Dylan
by Larry Sloman £12.99

In 1975, as Bob Dylan emerged from 8 years of seclusion, he dreamed of putting together a travelling music show that would trek across the country like a psychedelic carnival. The dream became a reality, and *On The Road With Bob Dylan* is the ultimate behind-the-scenes look at what happened. When Dylan and the Rolling Thunder Revue took to the streets of America, Larry "Ratso" Sloman was with them every step of the way.

"The *War and Peace* of Rock and Roll." – Bob Dylan

Gram Parsons: God's Own Singer
By Jason Walker £12.99

Brand new biography of the man who pushed The Byrds into country-rock territory on *Sweethearts of The Rodeo*, and quit to form the Flying Burrito Brothers. Gram lived hard, drank hard, took every drug going and somehow invented country rock, paving the way for Crosby, Stills & Nash, The Eagles and Neil Young. Parsons' second solo LP, *Grievous Angel*, is a haunting masterpiece of country soul. By the time it was released, he had been dead for 4 months. He was 26 years old.

"Walker has done an admirable job in taking us as close to the heart and soul of Gram Parsons as any author could." **** *Uncut* book of the month

Ashley Hutchings: The Guvnor and the Rise of Folk Rock – Fairport Convention, Steeleye Span and the Albion Band
by Geoff Wall and Brian Hinton £14.99

As founder of Fairport Convention and Steeleye Span, Ashley Hutchings is the pivotal figure in the history of folk rock. This book draws on hundreds of hours of interviews with Hutchings and other folk-rock artists and paints a vivid picture of the scene that also produced Sandy Denny, Richard Thompson, Nick Drake, John Martyn and Al Stewart.

The Beach Boys' Pet Sounds: The Greatest Album of the Twentieth Century
by Kingsley Abbott £11.95

Pet Sounds is the 1966 album that saw The Beach Boys graduate from lightweight pop like "Surfin' USA", et al, into a vehicle for the mature compositional genius of Brian Wilson. The album was hugely influential, not least on The Beatles. This the full story of the album's background, its composition and recording, its contemporary reception and its enduring legacy.

King Crimson: In The Court of King Crimson
by Sid Smith £14.99

King Crimson's 1969 masterpiece *In The Court Of The Crimson King*, was a huge U.S. chart hit. The band followed it with 40 further albums of consistently challenging, distinctive and innovative music. Drawing on hours of new interviews, and encouraged by Crimson supremo Robert Fripp, the author traces the band's turbulent history year by year, track by track.

A Journey Through America with the Rolling Stones
by Robert Greenfield UK Price £9.99
Featuring a new foreword by Ian Rankin

This is the definitive account of their legendary '72 tour.

"Filled with finely-rendered detail ... a fascinating tale of times we shall never see again" *Mojo*

The Sharper Word: A Mod Reader
Ed Paolo Hewitt
Hewitt's hugely readable collection documents the clothes, the music, the clubs, the drugs and the faces behind one of the most misunderstood and enduring cultural movements and includes hard to find pieces by Tom Wolfe, bestselling novelist Tony Parsons, poet laureate Andrew Motion, disgraced Tory grandee Jonathan Aitken, Nik Cohn, Colin MacInnes, Mary Quant, and Irish Jack.
"An unparalleled view of the world-conquering British youth cult." *The Guardian*
"An excellent account of the sharpest-dressed subculture." *Loaded*, Book of the Month
ISBN 1-900924-34-X   192pp   £9.99

Backlist

The Nice: Hang On To A Dream by Martyn Hanson
1900924439   256pp   £13.99
Al Stewart: Adventures of a Folk Troubadour by Neville Judd
1900924366   320pp   £25.00
Marc Bolan and T Rex: A Chronology by Cliff McLenahan
1900924420   256pp   £13.99
ISIS: A Bob Dylan Anthology Ed Derek Barker
1900924293   256pp   £14.99
Razor Edge: Bob Dylan and The Never-ending Tour by Andrew Muir
1900924137   256pp   £12.99
Calling Out Around the World: A Motown Reader Edited by Kingsley Abbott
1900924145   256pp   £13.99
I've Been Everywhere: A Johnny Cash Chronicle by Peter Lewry
1900924226   256pp   £14.99
Sandy Denny: No More Sad Refrains by Clinton Heylin
1900924358   288pp   £13.99
Animal Tracks: The Story of The Animals by Sean Egan
1900924188   256pp   £12.99
Like a Bullet of Light: The Films of Bob Dylan by CP Lee
1900924064   224pp   £12.99
Rock's Wild Things: The Troggs Files by Alan Clayson and J Ryan
1900924196   224pp   £12.99
Dylan's Daemon Lover by Clinton Heylin
1900924153   192pp   £12.00
Get Back: The Beatles' Let It Be Disaster by Sulpy & Schweighardt
1900924129   320pp   £12.99
XTC: Song Stories by XTC and Neville Farmer
190092403X   352pp   £12.99
Born in the USA: Bruce Springsteen by Jim Cullen
1900924056   320pp   £9.99
Bob Dylan by Anthony Scaduto
1900924234   320pp   £10.99

Firefly Publishing: An Association between Helter Skelter and SAF

The Nirvana Recording Sessions
by Rob Jovanovic £20.00

Drawing on years of research, and interviews with many who worked with the band, the author has documented details of every Nirvana recording, from early rehearsals, to the *In Utero* sessions. A fascinating account of the creative process of one of the great bands.

The Music of George Harrison: While My Guitar Gently Weeps
by Simon Leng £20.00

Often in Lennon and McCartney's shadow, Harrison's music can stand on its own merits. Santana biographer Leng takes a studied, track by track, look at both Harrison's contribution to The Beatles, and the solo work that started with the release in 1970 of his epic masterpiece *All Things Must Pass*. "Here Comes The Sun", "Something" – which Sinatra covered and saw as the perfect love song – "All Things Must Pass" and "While My Guitar Gently Weeps" are just a few of Harrison's classic songs.

Originally planned as a celebration of Harrison's music, this is now sadly a commemoration.

The Pretty Things: Growing Old Disgracefully
by Alan Lakey £20

First biography of one of rock's most influential and enduring combos. Trashed hotel rooms, infighting, rip-offs, sex, drugs and some of the most remarkable rock 'n' roll, including landmark albums like the first rock opera, *SF Sorrow*, and *Rolling Stone*'s album of the year, 1970's *Parachute*.

"They invented everything, and were credited with nothing." Arthur Brown, "God of Hellfire"

The Sensational Alex Harvey
By John Neil Murno £20

Part rock band, part vaudeville, 100% commitment, the SAHB were one of the greatest live bands of the era. But behind his showman exterior, Harvey was increasingly beset by alcoholism and tragedy. He succumbed to a heart attack on the way home from a gig in 1982, but he is fondly remembered as a unique entertainer by friends, musicians and legions of fans.

U2: The Complete Encyclopedia by Mark Chatterton £14.99
Poison Heart: Surviving The Ramones by Dee Dee Ramone and Veronica Kofman £9.99
Minstrels In The Gallery: A History Of Jethro Tull by David Rees £12.99
DANCEMUSICSEXROMANCE: Prince – The First Decade by Per Nilsen £12.99
To Hell and Back with Catatonia by Brian Wright £12.99
Soul Sacrifice: The Santana Story by Simon Leng UK Price £12.99
Opening The Musical Box: A Genesis Chronicle by Alan Hewitt UK Price £12.99
Blowin' Free: Thirty Years Of Wishbone Ash by Gary Carter and Mark Chatterton UK Price £12.99

www.helterskelterbooks.com

All Helter Skelter, Firefly and SAF titles are available by mail order from
www.helterskelterbooks.com
Or from our office:
Helter Skelter Publishing Limited
South Bank House
Black Prince Road
London SE1 7SJ

Telephone: +44 (0) 20 7463 2204 or Fax: +44 (0)20 7463 2295
Mail order office hours: Mon-Fri 10:00am – 1:30pm,
By post, enclose a cheque [must be drawn on a British bank], International Money Order, or
credit card number and expiry date.

Postage prices per book worldwide are as follows:

UK & Channel Islands	£1.50
Europe & Eire (air)	£2.95
USA, Canada (air)	£7.50
Australasia, Far East (air)	£9.00

Email: info@helterskelterbooks.com